# Common Ground

By Naomi Ishiguro

*Escape Routes*
*Common Ground*

# Common Ground

## NAOMI ISHIGURO

TINDER
PRESS

First published in Great Britain in 2021 by Tinder Press
An imprint of HEADLINE PUBLISHING GROUP

2

Cataloguing in Publication Data is available from the British Library

Hardback ISBN 978 1 4722 7329 1
Trade Paperback ISBN 978 1 4722 7332 1

Designed and typeset by EM&EN
Printed and bound in Great Britain by Clays Ltd, Elcograf S.p.A.

Headline's policy is to use papers that are natural, renewable and recyclable
products and made from wood grown in well-managed forests and other
controlled sources. The logging and manufacturing processes are expected
to conform to the environmental regulations of the country of origin.

HEADLINE PUBLISHING GROUP
An Hachette UK Company
Carmelite House
50 Victoria Embankment
London EC4Y 0DZ

www.tinderpress.co.uk
www.headline.co.uk
www.hachette.co.uk

*For Ben Noble, for my parents,*
*and – especially considering this is*
*a book about friendship – for*
*all my wonderful friends.*

# PART ONE

# 2003

# 1

Goshawk Common, Newford, Surrey. Not the most remarkable expanse of open country, scrubby grass and tumbling hillside in the south of England, just as Newford probably wasn't the most remarkable town. Still, the common had its charm, especially on those early autumn afternoons when the heathland came to life with crispness and with colour, and when rabbits dodged through tufts of grass while thrushes, robins and blackbirds sang in the trees beyond.

It was on an afternoon like this that thirteen-year-old Stanley Gower rode his bike down Aldershot Road and along Goshawk Road, before turning off the tarmac and on to the grass of the common. He was pedalling fast, now. Maybe faster even than he'd ever pedalled before. Onwards he careered, a dart veering straight into the heart of the quiet, rustling peace of the heath, the wheels of his Falcon Stealth thundering over the terrain in such a way that even if he'd been cycling with his eyes closed – like in that Roald Dahl story, for instance, about the man who could see without his eyes – he'd have been able to tell that his wheels were rattling over grass and stones now, that he was away from the town completely.

He was free here. A free man. Or a free bird, even, because really why should he have to be a man – a boy – a *human* at all? He'd much rather be a bird, then he could fly around all day. And how weird and cool the world must look from above. Although probably the birds were used to it and wouldn't think of it as weird or cool at all. Probably they'd think the way we see things from down here as we walk and run and cycle around is weird and cool. But his eyes were watering again a little now, tears escaping in spite of himself, making his broken, sticky-tape-mended glasses slip down his nose. Probably it was the cold air doing it, or because he was moving so fast. Probably that was definitely it. He blinked the tears away, anyway, trying not to think about it all too much because that was all done for the day, wasn't it? That was all over till tomorrow, now that he'd arrived finally in this place where there were huge skies, and woods, and already fallen autumn leaves – now that he was here on the common, where no one cared that his school uniform was second-hand and didn't fit properly, where he could finally be left alone. And look! There was even a rabbit, there, hopping up ahead, along the path in front of the Falcon Stealth's thick wheels. Be careful, little rabbit! This world is harsh and merciless and it'll give you no warning at all, that's for certain, and you won't last long in it if you keep jumping out into the paths of zooming bikes.

On gentle, sloping ground now, Stanley coasted forward on his own momentum, steering round the rabbit – good luck, little guy! May you do a better job of looking after yourself than I have! – and then he was pedalling again, faster, switching back up the gears to give himself some resistance, something tangible to push against. And he was flying onward again now, over the grass and into the sunset-streaked sky up ahead, all the colours melting a bit since his eyes were running properly now in spite of his blinking, sending his glasses slipping down his nose again, the glasses he'd thought Mum would be so angry to see broken but which she hadn't mentioned at all when she'd picked him up from school earlier – a not mentioning which somehow, instead of making things easier, had only made everything feel even worse.

And then there came an unhealthy clicking sound from the Falcon Stealth, and the feeling of something slipping out from under his feet, and suddenly the free-soaring falcon was faltering – his bike chain was slipping off, and his pedals were spinning and he was just a thirteen-year-old human boy again, wobbling on a stupid second-hand bike that couldn't seem to make it more than ten minutes down the road without the stupid chain messing up.

Stanley braked, climbed off, laid the Falcon on its side in the grass and tried his best to force the chain back into place. Except bloody hell it was stiff and not going on like it usually would. He'd told Mum he'd sit quietly at home and read and eat the Hula Hoops she'd given him while she napped, and now there was bike oil all over his fingers and over his jeans where he'd wiped his stupid hands without thinking and now he would arrive back home in a mess with a broken bike – which she'd assume he'd broken today, seeing as he hadn't told her the chain had been all messed up from the beginning. He wasn't quite sure why he hadn't told her. Just that the Falcon had been a birthday present from her, and some instinct had told him not to ruin everything by mentioning it at the time.

And of course he'd be late back, too, no doubt. She only ever slept for half an hour, forty minutes maximum if she was very tired, and she was working the night shift tonight, wasn't she? So most likely she'd be awake in ten minutes from now at the latest, and home was more than ten minutes' walk away, meaning that he'd have no time to get there and clean up and hide the stupid bike before she saw it. He'd have to turn up all covered in oil, having ruined his jeans probably, and now his fingers hurt too from trying and failing to fix it as well as the rest of him from all that in the playground earlier, and it really wasn't his day, he wished he lived in Narnia, in Hogwarts, in anywhere but Newford – and then to top it all off here was another rabbit now, stopped still and staring at him. What is it you want, little guy? I'm kneeling, just kneeling here, in the grass. Is that allowed? Or is this your particular favourite patch of grass I'm kneeling on? Would you rather I moved?

But the rabbit's head twitched, its eyes flicked to something behind Stanley, and then it turned on its tail and bounded away, just as he became aware of the sound of another bike coming up behind him, a less rusty bike from the sounds of it, a much smoother ride – how could it be that his bike was simultaneously so oily and so rusty? And then Stanley turned to the sound of brakes and there was an older boy there, wearing a motorcycle jacket with all these patches and things. And he had sunglasses on too, this older boy, and greased-back hair and earphones in that Stanley could hear were blasting loud, tinny music, and Stanley couldn't even identify what type of bike he had at all because it had been spray-painted black and green – probably by this older boy himself, judging by the messiness of the paintwork. But how much older was this boy really? He seemed eighteen, seventeen maybe . . . except that then he raised his sunglasses, pushing them back on the top of his head, and Stanley started to think he was maybe a little younger than that. The boy tugged out his earphones, reached into his jacket pocket, pulled out a shiny Discman, and paused his music.

'You alright, mate?' he said, stowing the Discman and earphones carefully away again and frowning at Stanley like he was some strange curiosity found lying by the side of the road – which in a way, he was. 'You always talk to rabbits? What happened to your glasses?'

Of course – of course this older boy would laugh at him. That same old nasty prickling feeling started up behind Stanley's eyes again, and as he opened his mouth to say something, he found he'd lost all ability to summon and to order words. It was all just like at school, and yet a feeling that was so alien to being out here on Goshawk Common, where he was used to being free, permitted to come and go unharmed, unpicked on.

'Chill out, mate,' said the older boy, jumping off his bike now, setting it down in the grass next to Stanley's. 'I was just asking.'

His accent wasn't quite like other people's round here, Stanley noticed then. There was something else in it that conjured somewhere different, far away, outside and far beyond the little world of Newford. Somewhere, maybe, that reminded him a little of *Coronation Street*.

'I'm Charlie, by the way,' said this older boy. 'D'you need a hand?'

Charlie talked as he messed with the chain. 'It's no bother at all,' he was saying. 'I just got off work and actually I wasn't really sure what to do with myself. I mean, it's a weird old place, Newford. Before I came down here I thought there'd be loads going on. My brother told me there was, anyway, but my theory is that was just a ploy to get me to come back. I was away for a bit, you see – but fucksake you've a bastard of a chain here, mate, you know that?'

At first Stanley felt a bit affronted, embarrassed at how obvious it clearly was that he wasn't able to fix his bike himself, and annoyed at having the feeling of peace he'd almost found a moment ago so completely disrupted. A large part of him wanted to tell this Charlie to back off and leave him alone, as who did he think he was, after all? Muscling in like this and getting involved without even being asked, drawing attention to Stanley's bike's crappiness, not to mention to his general uselessness? Then again though, it wasn't like Charlie was laughing at him, or anything. He didn't seem to be at all, actually. And, really, when Stanley thought about it properly, it was probably kind of good of him to help. Good of him, in fact, that seemingly without thinking about it at all he'd got right off his own bike, stopped going wherever he was going and got down in the damp grass, without seeming to mind that his hands were covered in oil now, too.

And more than that, he also found himself strangely grateful for the fact that this Charlie was a talker. Stanley wasn't a talker. He tended to stay quiet and stare at people – which made them feel uncomfortable, Mum said. He didn't mean to do it. It was just that no matter how much he wanted to say stuff, it somehow never happened right. He never found it easy, and then whenever he forced himself to speak he would only end up saying something weird that no one outside his own head could ever understand.

Like on the first day at school, the first day of St Reginald's, which felt like ages ago now – like he'd been there forever already, and not in a good way – though it could only have been a few weeks. They'd gone round the class saying what they wanted to be when they were older, and everyone had said stuff that made everyone else nod and ask questions and the teacher write whatever they'd said on the board – policeman, interior designer, singer, actor, dancer, all the usual stuff, he couldn't say really what they'd said now, but anyway – he'd gone and said that when he was older he'd like to be either Merry or Pippin from *The Lord of the Rings*. He'd meant it to be funny, he supposed, but then Miss Kennedy had asked him *why* with this look on her face like he'd been deadly serious, and what he'd said had concerned her, and then everyone else in the class had stared at him too, of course. Stared at the new scholarship kid. The kid in the stupid, ill-fitting second-hand uniform, who was always tripping over his feet in shoes that had been bought 'for growth'. Stanley had found himself paralysed, unable to talk, to conjure even a few words to explain even in the most basic terms what he'd meant, unable even to locate his vocal cords and say any simple set-piece phrase like *it was a joke*. He'd remained in that state for the rest of the lesson, sitting in silence while everyone else despised him and thought he was weird. Long story short, then, it was a nice change, the way this Charlie talked with ease, as if he didn't even notice the difficulty Stanley was having in thinking of anything rea-sonable to say in reply.

'I just moved here, see, from my dad's,' Charlie was saying. 'Or, I wasn't living with my dad, not really, only stay-ing for a bit, but then the rest of my family were somewhere else before, and I was only a kid anyway last time we were here. So what I mean really is I haven't met too many people round here yet – apart from my family of course, and then all the guys at work . . .'

Charlie finally managed to slide the chain back into place. He wasn't just older. Though at first glance he looked a bit scrawny in that giant leather jacket, he was obviously much stronger, too. One of those wiry guys who could lift stuff and climb stuff and punch stuff harder than Stanley could ever dream of doing. Charlie sat back on his heels and wiped the oil off his hands and on to his jeans – without thinking twice about the mess, it seemed.

'And the thing is,' he continued, looking over the grass towards the trees, 'even if I'm only somewhere for a few months or whatever it is, I still like to get to know it. You know, the history of the place. What it all means, why it's there. All the people who lived their lives in it, and built things and had kids and died in it before we were even born, you know?' Charlie stared out at the trees a little longer, then nodded down to the Falcon.

'Fixed your bike,' he said.

Stanley opened his mouth, panicked a little in spite of himself, coughed, and managed to choke out a, 'Thanks.'

'What was your name again?'

'Stanley. Stan.'

'Which is it?'

'Stan. If you like.'

Charlie stood up and made to head over to his own bike again. 'Nice meeting you, Stan,' he said.

'Wait,' Stan said, too quickly, surprising himself, as surely he'd be waiting for Charlie to leave, so he could relax again, just be on his own without having to worry about accidentally making anything go wrong?

But Charlie had stopped, and was watching him now, hands in pockets. Waiting, no doubt, for him to spit out whatever it might be that he had to say for himself, so he could get on his way.

'So you're from Manchester, then?' Stan asked him, mainly just for something to say.

'Nah,' Charlie said. 'Or my dad's from there. I stayed with him almost a year, nearly. Or for the spring and summer, more like, I suppose. But I'm from round here, really,' Charlie said. 'Not Newford though. All over.'

'Where d'you go to school?' Stan asked Charlie.

'Don't go to school, do I?'

'But . . . how? Don't you have to? Don't your parents make you go?'

'Naw,' Charlie sank his hands deeper into his pockets. 'Not any more.' He studied Stanley. 'You're a bit of an odd one, mate, aren't you?'

And that should have hurt. Stanley knew it should have done. And yet somehow, he completely surprised himself by laughing. 'What about you?' he found himself replying, and the words sounded weird as he said them, as if someone else was in control of his vocal cords now, and he was listening to his own voice resonating out somewhere else, somewhere far away and separate from himself. 'You're not so normal yourself.'

Charlie laughed. 'Good,' he said. 'That's the way I like it. See, I can't help but think if people think you're normal in a town like this then surely that just means you're boring. No offence meant, like, if you grew up here. Did you grow up here?'

Stanley nodded.

'Suppose someone had to,' said Charlie. 'Mind you, it's not all bad. I always like a good common. D'you know the history of this place, Stan?'

Stan shook his head.

'Neither do I, being honest, not really. But the thing is, right, the thing with commons is that it means they were common land, you know? That they still are, to some extent at least. So this place belongs to us, just as much as it belongs to anyone. We have just as much right to be here as anyone else.'

'I never knew that,' said Stan.

'Right, well, now you do. Come and find me any other time you fancy a history lesson.' Charlie picked up his bike and climbed on. 'Anyway, I'd best be off. Got stuff to do and all. I'm sure I'll see you round.'

'Whereabouts d'you live?' said Stan.

'I work at the boxing gym. Just over the way,' Charlie nodded his head, back down the path. 'It's a bit of a slog but you get to use the gym for free on Sundays, so it could be worse.'

And then he was off, cycling away down the path, leaving Stanley blinking at what had just happened, at the strangeness of having just had a full conversation with someone like Charlie, someone older and obviously so much cooler, with all the usual social rules and hierarchies that underpinned the days at school having somehow melted away.

And then of course the moment passed, and he was aware again of his mum back home, who'd be up by now and wondering where he'd got to. Aware of the oil on his jeans, and the tape on his glasses and the bruises on his ribs and the scrapes on his elbows hiding under the long sleeves of his sweater. He watched Charlie disappearing, just a retreating figure in the distance now, indistinct in his oversized jacket, hunched over the handlebars. And after only a moment's hesitation—

'Thanks for fixing my bike,' Stan yelled down the path, after him.

He wasn't even sure Charlie would hear him, whether his voice would be loud enough to carry over the distance between them. He was just about to turn around to go home when Charlie stuck out a hand, and waved.

# 2

Later, sitting opposite Helen, his mum, in the low, buzzing light of the kitchen, Stanley shovelled forkfuls of macaroni cheese into his mouth and wondered about what Charlie had said, out on the common.

*I work at the boxing gym. Just over the way.*

And thinking about it too, Charlie had seemed exactly the kind of person he had always imagined might be into boxing. Not to say he'd looked thuggish, or anything. Not at all. Just . . . unafraid. Authoritative. Capable.

Stanley was distracted from his thoughts then though by the sound of Helen sighing, as she turned over a page in the magazine she had open on the table in front of her. He watched as she rubbed her eyes. Strands of her light brown hair were falling from her ponytail into her face, but she didn't seem to notice. She was having her breakfast now, kind of. The meal she always had before going in to work the night shift. A cheese sandwich and a mug of coffee, with the coffee smelling so good Stanley would often nag her to let him have a mug of his own. Of course she never let him, saying he'd only be hyper and wouldn't sleep – which he didn't quite believe, seeing as she drank so much of it and still managed to be sleepy all the time. Anyway though, sometimes, if she was in a good mood, she'd let him try just a sip, and even though the bitter taste was inevitably a disappointment it would still always feel a bit like a special treat, a little victory, to have convinced her, even just for a moment, to have let him in on this particular aspect of adult life.

Looking up properly now from the sticky mass of food on his plate, he watched her across the table as she chewed a corner of her sandwich, slowly, and then as she rubbed her eyes again, still staring down at the magazine which was all pictures of some beach resort now. He decided he wouldn't ask for any coffee tonight. It didn't feel like that kind of evening.

'Mum,' he found himself saying instead. 'You know the boxing club? Up past the common?'

A slight frown creased the skin between her eyebrows, and he knew this probably wasn't right either, that he should just stop talking, keep quiet, let her have some peace before going into work, but still the words seemed somehow to cascade out of him, before he could stop them.

'Dad used to box, didn't he? Like when he was around my age?'

Helen put her sandwich down, and chewed her lip. 'He was a bit older,' she said. 'Why was that in your head, Stanley?' she asked.

But of course, he'd probably messed things up now. She always said she was happy to talk about Dad whenever he wanted, but it never went well when he tried, he knew that. He shrugged, ducked down to his plate, muffled the guilty feeling spreading through him now with another mouthful of pasta.

Before Helen had packed away most of the old photos that had been up around the house, taking them all to the attic, there had been this picture of Dad at the back of the cluster they'd always kept on the mantelpiece. It was strange to think now, but when Dad had still been here Stanley had never really asked him about it properly, had taken the photo completely for granted as just another familiar object he'd find out the full story behind later, all in good time. There were so many things like this, he was finding. Sometimes it seemed he came across a new one, a new thing he'd never get to ask Dad about, every day. In this picture anyway, Dad had been wearing boxing gloves, he'd had a medal around his neck, and he'd been smiling. More than anything though, he'd just looked so young, not much more than a boy himself and so lit up with life that, thinking about that photo now, it seemed almost unbelievable to Stanley that it really could have existed, and that the human being it captured could really be the same person he'd said goodbye to, in those last awful weeks at the hospital.

'Wasn't he once the best in Newford, or something?' he asked Helen.

She brushed her hair out of her face and smiled, though it didn't make her look any happier. 'Third in Newford, love,' she said. 'Though that was all a long time ago now.'

And then the alarm clock went off in the hall, telling them both it was time for her to go to work. Stanley followed as she went to take her things from the pegs by the door. She always had to leave. She always had to be at work.

'Sorry,' he told her, hovering in the door frame as she shoved pen and notepad in her bag.

Helen only shrugged, and turned away, fastening the buttons on her coat. 'You miss him,' she said. 'No need to be sorry for that.' Then suddenly sounding bright and business-like, speaking to him now in the blandly friendly, brisk tone

Stanley suspected she might use while talking to patients at work, she asked him – 'So what'll you do with yourself this evening then? Anything nice on the telly?'

'I think I'll just carry on with my book. I'm reading that one about Greek and Roman myths. It's really good.'

And she smiled at that, properly smiled. Even came over and tried to give him a hug, and though of course he wriggled away from her he found he was also kind of glad.

'How ever did you get to be so clever?' she said.

'Mum,' he groaned. 'Stop it.'

She'd been prone to moments like this ever since Gran had put him in for the thirteen-plus scholarship exam for St Reginald's, and he'd actually passed. Every time school or homework or even just books were mentioned these days, she'd only go and get all weepy and weird and embarrassing. He was just backing away again, thinking she might try and grab him for another hug, when her smile slipped a bit, and she looked so sad, suddenly.

'I'm so proud of you, Stanley,' she said. 'You do know that, don't you?'

Stanley nodded, and didn't know what to say.

Then pulling the folds of her coat tight around her, Helen opened the door and waved goodbye, heading out into the chill of the autumn night to the hospital.

*

He tried to read, he really did. And a lot of him actually wanted to as well. It hadn't been a lie he'd told when he'd said he was enjoying his book. Of course he was. He was in the middle of the story about the Minotaur, and the Minotaur was awesome. So why, then, when he'd cleared up the plates and washed the pots and wiped the table, had he gone up to his room and picked up his book and sat on the bed and drawn the covers right up to his chin and pushed his glasses up to his nose again – why was it that in this setting, which should be so peaceful and so welcome and so cosy after all the trials of the day, that he just couldn't seem to sit still?

There was simply no position he could twist himself into that seemed at all natural. It was like his limbs had suddenly got longer or more awkward, just unwieldy, and he didn't know how to fold them or to organise them any more so that they fitted in the small space allotted to them. And then when he tried to read, his mind somehow seemed unable to focus on the words, getting caught up again in the day at school just passed, and the week before that, and then too in thoughts of the days ahead, the weeks ahead, the weeks stretching to months stretching to years, none of which seemed to offer any opportunity for escape. And of course it didn't help take his mind off things that every five seconds he had to readjust his broken glasses.

He read the same paragraph three times, getting to the end of the page only to find he hadn't paid attention to a single thing that had happened, and that what he was read-ing made no sense. And now he was too hot under the duvet too, and he found himself hating the way it made him feel like he'd been tucked in like a child when it wasn't even eight o'clock yet, when it was hardly even dark.

He threw the duvet off and went downstairs. He paced up and down for a while in the kitchen but found that it was too small, somehow; he felt as if he was always almost bumping into things and having to be careful where he stepped. He thought about making himself sit down, calm down and just turn on the telly. He wasn't even sure what would be on. *Neighbours* or *Top of the Pops*, probably. Stuff the other kids were always on about at school. He picked up the remote and stared at it a moment. Then he put it back down, picked up his bike, and went out.

Where to, Stan? Where to? It felt weird being out like this on his own, after tea, in the twilight, under his own steam. Like he was breaking some kind of rule, though he wasn't, not really. Mum had never said he couldn't go out, he just never did, that was all. But where was he going, clicking round the quiet streets on his newly mended bike? Where would someone like that Charlie from the common go, for instance, if he were out and about like this of an evening? Surely this was the kind of thing someone like Charlie would do all the time, easy, not even thinking about it? Stan clicked his way down Woodside Lane. All the hedges and the matching houses – wheelie bins and mesh garden fencing, red brick and polished white doors and window frames.

*If people think you're normal in a town like this then surely that just means you're boring*, Charlie had said, hadn't he? Could that be right? Looking around himself now it didn't seem impossible. Everything Stan passed, after all, looked kind of the same to him as everything else. Well kept, net-curtained and neat. The same flowers in all the front gardens, and no one had so much as painted their door a different colour, or even decorated their wheelie bin. Come to think of it, neither had he and Mum – what did that mean? Did it mean anything?

Clicking on down Woodside Lane now, the houses fell away on his right, leaving the road open to the actual woods, or to a neatly clipped hedge, anyway, behind which there were woods . . . Oh but it was alright, Newford. What did Charlie know? Could Manchester really be all that much better than this? Stan turned down Foxburrows Road. What a good name for a street, *Foxburrows Road*. He bet there wasn't a Foxburrows Road in Manchester. And where had Charlie lived before that? Where had he grown up? He hadn't really said, had he? *All over*, had been about the extent of it.

The matching roofs of the houses lining the way either side of Stan stood solid and quiet against still-glowing sky, the trees from the woods just visible in silhouette behind them, and suddenly, Stan found himself thinking of Monopoly houses, wondering if this is how it'd feel to be shrunk down to the size of an ant, and creeping around the board.

He turned off and picked up the pace, cycling faster through the sleepy silent streets, cutting through the estate and up on to Spelman Road – and he'd be lying to himself now if he said he was just meandering, that he didn't know exactly where he was going, that he hadn't, in fact, had a plan from the second he'd locked the front door behind him, even from the moment he'd shut his Greek myths book and got back out of bed. The boxing club, that was where he was headed. That was where Charlie would go.

He pedalled hard then free-wheeled round the long curve of tarmac until the rows of houses stopped suddenly, space opening out, and then there it was, up ahead, lights in the windows glimmering at him across the expanse of an empty car park – a sprawling almost-bungalow, every wall a differ-ent shade of grey. He coasted up to it and braked.

He could hear voices coming from inside. Male voices, shouting and laughing. Cracking jokes, it sounded like. He couldn't make out any words from here but he recognised the rhythm of the sounds. There were lulls, dips dominated by singular, more prominent voices, then sudden explosions back into noise, everyone talking over each other again. Was Charlie among them? Stan listened harder, trying to pick him out. Tall shadows moved in the windows, behind the blinds, then the lights in the far corner of the building began to click off, and then more lights followed, darkness spreading inwards, taking over – before the front door swung open and two tallish boys strode out across the car park, big bags over their shoulders, sweat in their hair, tracksuit tops zipped up against the now quite chilly night air. Stan could see their breath in the air as they talked.

'It's not about that though,' one of them was saying. 'If he keeps up with all that then it's over, he's fucked, I promise you . . .'

They were older than Stan was, obviously. And bigger, too. But he still couldn't help but be a little surprised that they were still so young. Surprised and disappointed, even. He'd expected men, coming out bruised and black-eyed and bleeding. Not boys like this – just like anyone, like people from school, who were probably off home for their tea now, and then maths homework, and the school bus in the morning.

Stan stood up on his pedals and began riding around in a slow circle, turning to face back the way he'd come, still keeping an eye on the boxing club door but with a kind of *I shouldn't be here* feeling creeping up on him now. *This place isn't for me.* And then another group of boys stepped out, one of whom he recognised. It was Charlie, of course, and Stan felt such a rush of triumph then to find he'd been so dead right in guessing where Charlie might go, and at having actually managed to find him again like this so easily when part of him had been wondering if he'd ever see Charlie again, if that conversation on the common hadn't been some weird kind of fluke.

Charlie looked so at home here though, amongst these people. He had a bag over his shoulder and tracksuit on like the rest of them, and was rolling a cigarette, licking the paper like it was automatic for him, that action, like he'd done it a million times before – which he probably had, come to think of it – and he was laughing a little at something someone was saying.

It was a terrible mistake to have come here. Stan understood that now. He couldn't let Charlie see him like this, hovering like some pathetic kind of stalker, waiting outside where he'd known Charlie worked. Why had he come here? What a weird thing to do – what a fucking *creepy* thing to do, even. He hadn't meant it like that at all, though. He'd been curious, that's all. And also maybe – maybe even hopeful? Hopeful that he might have stumbled upon a place which, though it was only round the corner from all the usual familiar haunts and streets, might have offered him a way to step outside the endless maze that life felt like these days, an alternative to both the unspoken sadness of home and the daily battle of school. A place he could go to learn how to feel like he had for those ten minutes on the common with Charlie – as if he were a person just like anyone else, with a solid right to be there, and to take up the space he was occupying.

Who had he been kidding, though? This place was just like anywhere else – worse, even, as it was boxing, and Mum hated boxing – or at least was weird about it, in that way that she was weird about anything these days that reminded her of Dad. What was he doing? He had no business looking for another world here when he knew how it would upset her. Really he had no business looking for other worlds at all. This was Newford, not Narnia. Things like other worlds simply didn't happen here. He should get himself home now, before any of them clocked him. He should go back to bed to read so that he wouldn't have lied to Mum at all when he'd told her earlier he would read his book, making her look so proud and also . . . what had that look been? Just as she'd been leaving the house?

He pushed down on the pedals and was setting off into the night just as he heard a voice ring out behind him – loud, confident, a little bit northern.

'Oi, Stan, is that you?'

And then more voices . . . But he was off now on his way and couldn't hear what they were saying.

# 3

It started again on the school bus the next day. You'd think they would let him wake up a bit first, have a minute to digest his breakfast, give him half a chance. Did they not need to wake up, too? Were they not human? Or did they open their eyes each day in a fury, the name of Stanley Gower burned on the inside of their lids? Or maybe the whole world was actually one big lie, like that film Mum loved so much, what was it? The one with Jim Carrey in. *The Truman Show*. Yeah maybe it was actually like that and he was Truman, and this whole thing an experiment to see how much crap he was capable of taking. Maybe Huxley Edwards and his two lackeys weren't even real people at all, but robots, programmed with the sole instruction of making him as miserable as possible.

Ah but that was probably delusional. That at least would have the bonus of meaning he was a little bit important. These boys probably never even thought about him when he was out of sight. And how he wished he could say the same of himself about them. How he wished he could ban them from his brain for every second they weren't physically in front of him. How he wished he could stop them affecting the way he behaved and thought all the time, not only in school but always, when probably they'd never even notice if he just stopped coming in one day, and it was only when they clapped eyes on him that they were suddenly reminded of how repulsive he was, and were compelled to do something about it. That would be why it always started on the school bus, with no morning respite – they saw him, were reminded, had to act. And he'd sat off to the side today and everything, trying to keep a low profile. He'd even worn a hat. Perhaps the hat had been an error.

The three of them muscled over and sat in the seats around him, other kids moving out of the way to give them room, Eddie Franks's face getting redder and more furious by the second, Huxley Edwards's by contrast getting paler, his eyes brighter.

'Nice hat,' Huxley said.

Definitely the hat had been a mistake.

'Where d'you get it?'

'I found it,' Stan muttered, dipping the brim down, over his eyes.

'What was that, Stanley? Did they not teach you at peasant school that it's rude to mumble?'

Stan shrugged, aware that in spite of himself and all his resolutions to stand his ground and not let these three get to him, he was still edging back now, pressing himself into the small gap between the bus seat and the window.

'So this hat, anyway, Stanley. Am I to understand it isn't yours? That you stole it? Is that what they teach in peasant school? Stealing?'

'It's my dad's,' Stan lied, pointlessly – and he didn't know why he'd said that, exactly. The words had just come out.

'What was that? I told you to speak up, didn't I?'

'It's my dad's,' Stan said again. This time the words came out far louder than he'd meant them to, and from the expression on Huxley's face he could tell he'd gone and done it now. Stan cast a quick look up the two rows of seats stretching to the front of the bus. All the other kids were sitting so quiet and so good in their uniforms, pretending this whole situation didn't exist.

'Ah,' said Huxley, glancing around at his mates, nodding as if they'd arrived at something important here. 'If there's anything I can't stand, it's a liar. You don't have to lie to *us*, Stanley. Who is it, exactly, you're trying to impress? We all know you've got no dad.'

'I do though,' Stan said, talking back to Huxley in spite of himself, though he knew it was a stupid idea, that it would definitely be more sensible to keep his mouth shut and his head down until Huxley and the others got bored and went away. The fact was though that he did have a dad, of course he did. Just because his dad wasn't around any more didn't mean he'd never existed. It wasn't the same thing at all. And that felt important to assert, somehow, in spite of everything.

Stan hadn't exactly told anyone at school what had happened, with the cancer. It hadn't been a deliberate policy, more that no one had really seemed trustworthy enough. It had been difficult to avoid the subject of fathers entirely though, especially given the amount of time everyone here seemed to spend talking about what their dads did for work, and so Stan had found himself constantly dodging the question – something which Huxley, of course, had been quick enough to pick up on.

Huxley was laughing now, setting off his friends, all three of them cackling away in Stan's face at what he'd said about Dad. And though Stan knew he couldn't really have expected anything better it still stung, still felt horrible, having them laugh like that at the most awful thing he'd ever known to happen, at the biggest loss he'd ever had to face.

'Really, Stanley?' Huxley continued, catching his breath amid all the supposed hilarity. 'And is he the one who picks out your clothes?'

Which set them all off again, of course. And not for the first time Stan found himself wondering why Neil or Eddie never did the talking. It would have provided some basic variation at least to have one of them baiting him for a change. They were bigger lads than Huxley, so why did it seem he had the run of them? They were like a chorus there, like a Greek chorus, like the one in his book, just making sounds and backing Huxley up on everything. But Huxley was reaching forward now, for the brim of Stan's hat – just some baseball cap he'd found in the bottom of his mum's cupboard, with a fish or a dolphin or something embroidered on the front. Huxley tweaked it off Stan's head, and spun it round in his fingers, to assess the front.

'Save the whales,' Huxley said.

'What?' said Stan.

'Is your dad some tree-hugging hippy or what?'

'Sorry?'

'Save the whales, is what I said,' said Huxley. 'Hang on – don't tell me you've been walking around with something written across the top of your head and you hadn't even had the presence of mind to check and see what was there? Not very intelligent are you, in spite of all the books? Not very smart.' He passed the hat to Eddie, and Stan started to give up all hope of ever getting it back. 'In fact, Stanley,' Huxley continued, 'can you tell me what you do have going for you? Because when you first showed up at this school I was sure there had to be something. Even though you didn't exactly look promising, I told myself you couldn't be a total waste of space, otherwise they'd never have let you in. Now though, I do have to admit that I'm really starting to wonder.'

No words, no retort would come to Stan's mind, and he only felt more exposed now without the comfort of the peak of his cap.

'Look at his face,' said Neil then. 'What a fucking loser.'

Stan felt something inside him crumble, and, in spite of himself, his eyes began to spark.

'Although I have to say,' Huxley continued then, 'your mum's alright though. I mean she'd almost be decent-looking, if she took better care of herself. Bit young to have a kid your age, though. Is she your actual mum? Or what was it, teenage pregnancy?'

That set them all off properly cackling, Huxley and Eddie and Neil, and Stan could see some of the others further up the bus starting to laugh too, kids who hadn't seemed to be taking sides either way until now. And then Huxley reached forward again, towards Stan's face. Stan flinched. Huxley grinned. And then with an action so easy, so calm, so entitled it was almost gentle, he lifted off Stan's glasses.

'I'll just hold on to these for bit,' he said, beginning to unwind the masking tape from around the fractured frame.

And Stan knew he couldn't just let this happen. That he had to say something, do something. That apart from anything else glasses were valuable, and much more important than just some stupid baseball cap. What would someone like his dad have done, faced with a situation like this? What would someone like that Charlie do, even, from the boxing club, and out on the common?

It seemed like everyone was laughing at him now though. All the kids in the seats around them. Huxley finished peeling the masking tape off his glasses just as the bus turned off Church Street, pulling up in front of the school. He caught the two pieces and slipped them into his blazer pocket, neat as you like, dropping the tape on the floor.

'I'll see you at break,' he said, standing up, giving the cue it seemed for his friends to follow. 'Cheer up, loser. If I'm feeling generous, I might even give you them back.'

And Huxley leaned over then, as if to clap Stan on the shoulder – but before Stan could flinch away or even knew what was happening, he was being shoved hard, right into the seatback in front of him. Ducking his head out of pure reflex, he took the blow solidly on one of his temples, and pain flashed through his skull and behind his eyes as he tried to pull himself together, blinking, head spinning, all blurry-eyed anyway now without his glasses.

He straightened up just in time to see the three of them finally walking away, thank God, heading down the aisle, first off the bus as usual. And even though without his glasses Stan couldn't make out anything so precise as the particular facial expressions of the others on the bus around him, he could still tell enough to know that everyone was avoiding looking at him, reaching for bags and jackets and staring off in different directions so they wouldn't accidentally catch his eye.

Without his glasses he could hardly even see out the window. Anything further than a few feet away was really quite blurry and furred round the edges. He'd have to explain to Mum what had happened to her cap too, when he got home. Although, would she even notice it was missing? She was always too tired when she worked nights. She was always too tired these days full stop. He shuffled down in his seat and waited as everyone else pushed past, jostling in the aisle and down the steps, on to the pavement and through the gates. The driver nodded to him as he passed, anyway. All the drivers knew Stan. He was always the last one off.

# 4

Huxley didn't give him back his glasses. The pieces were still in his blazer pocket, as far as Stan could tell. Probably he wouldn't see them again now. Or Huxley would do something awful to them before he gave them back. Just because Huxley's dad was some big shot in London, that was all. Just because Huxley's dad wore a dry-cleaned suit and had three different cars or something to choose between depending on his mood, and a stupid box in Twickenham Stadium so Huxley and all his stupid mates could go and watch the rugby with champagne and oysters or whatever it was they had up there. Probably that box was the only reason Huxley had any friends at all, as it could hardly be because of his warm and generous personality now could it?

Stan glowered out the window next to Helen in the car. At least the fact that she was so often late meant Huxley and the others didn't tease him as much as they could have done, about being picked up from school by his mum like a six-year-old. And seeing her now he could see what Huxley meant – *if she took better care of herself*. Her hair was an unkempt tangle, shoved back in the same ponytail she wore it in every day, and she was still dressed in the same old grey skirt and battered shoes she always wore to work, and the bags under her eyes were bad enough to make it almost look like she'd walked into something. He couldn't remember the last time he'd seen her wear anything nice, or put on make-up . . . oh but that was such a horrible thing to think. What was he doing now, letting Huxley get under his skin like this? His mum worked hard, that was all. And that was something to be proud of – helping people and looking after people at the hospital and then managing all by herself now at home as everyone always said, though she wasn't all by herself really, as he was there with her, wasn't he? But he was proud of her, of course he was. Everyone always said he should be. He just got tired of it all sometimes. He got tired of everything and couldn't help but wish sometimes that things in his world were the same as however they were in everybody else's.

And if he couldn't have that, then maybe at least she could say something about the fact his glasses were missing? Because he could tell she'd noticed. The second she'd clocked him at the gate he'd seen it in her face – the disappointment, the resignation. He wasn't going to mention it because how could he explain it? How could he tell her what had happened? It was impossible. Especially after all those mean things they'd said about her, and about Dad. But still he'd need some new glasses, wouldn't he? He couldn't carry on like this, unable to read people's faces properly if they were more than five feet away, and with the board at school so blurry he'd got in trouble about it twice today already . . . although at least that meant he would probably start doing worse, getting worse marks, which might give Huxley less reason to notice him, the new kid in the second-hand clothes who'd been stupid enough to reveal himself as a swot who actually cared about learning – somehow apparently the least cool thing you could do in school.

He could hardly ask her though for a new pair of glasses, straight out, just like that, could he? Not when she hadn't mentioned it deliberately. It would seem weird, almost embarrassing. And then there was the fact he felt kind of guilty these days asking her for anything, as she always seemed so overstretched, so pushed for time, so tired. She worked so hard and now he couldn't even hold on to one measly pair of glasses. A part of her must have been thinking that at least.

They turned on to the Eastern Road and pulled up outside the house. Helen got out without saying anything and slammed the door behind her. Yeah, that was definitely what she was thinking. And she was right to, wasn't she, really? Why hadn't he stood up to Huxley? Or stopped him nicking the glasses, at least?

It was only up in his room, changing out of his school clothes for the afternoon – feeling the weight of them lifting as he unbuttoned his collar and peeled off the scratchy grey socks – that he saw what had been written on the back of his shirt the whole day. There'd been a scuffle in the playground at break, with them all grabbing at him and shoving him and messing with that stupid cap – Huxley or Neil or Eddie or one of them anyway had kept that too, which was fine, good riddance, he hated that stupid cap – but how had he not noticed there was something written on his back? *Blowhole*, it said, in ragged, blotchy blue fountain pen ink. Well fuck you, too. *You've been walking around with something written across the top of your head and you hadn't even had the presence of mind to check and see what was there,* Huxley had said that morning on the bus. There was a kind of justice to it. A certain kind of symmetry. At least Mum hadn't noticed the writing either. Or had she been deliberately ignoring that, too? Surely not. What would he do now, though, about washing it? The thought of trying to get the ink out without her noticing made him feel wearier still.

He stashed the shirt under his mattress, pulled on his jeans and a jumper, ran downstairs, picked up his bike and was out the front door again without saying a word to Helen. He couldn't face it. Couldn't face the idea of the two of them sitting there in the kitchen with their cups of tea, made to feel ashamed of each other because of some prick like Huxley when really that was the opposite of what they should be feeling – or the opposite of what he should be feeling about her, anyway.

He pedalled away and turned into Aldershot Road, Goshawk Road – the Monopoly houses and silver hatchbacks a blur to him now with his stupid useless eyes and inability to stop other people nicking his glasses . . . but that was okay, a blur was quite nice in fact, it softened the edges, made everything that little bit less real. He pedalled faster and faster and faster until he was on the common with the grass and trees and woods and sky and no one around to tell him he had no right, that he wasn't good enough to be there.

\*

The hazy, late afternoon sun was dipping below the crest of the hill, meaning Stan must have been sprawled in the grass for nearly an hour now, at once exhausted and restless. He was jerked from his doze by the sound of bike wheels on the path behind him.

He sat up, blew a rogue bit of grass off his face – and then he put a hand out to steady himself and accidentally slammed it down on the pedal of his own bike which he'd forgotten was next to him, putting far too much weight on it and yelping with the pain. He was studying the damage to his palm when Charlie braked next to him.

'Ay up,' he said. 'You alright?'

'Yeah fine, I'd just – I'd drifted off I think and then I shoved my hand down here like this and then, well. I'm fine, it doesn't matter.'

'I wondered if you fell,' said Charlie.

'Naw,' said Stan. 'I'm not quite as crappy on a bike as that. Even if I've got no glasses.'

'Right, yeah. I thought you looked different,' said Charlie. 'You lose them or what?'

'Something like that,' said Stan. He rubbed his eyes as if to try and make everything a little clearer. The funny thing was, though, that it was actually a little easier to talk to people, maybe, when everything was a little fuzzy, a little at a remove.

'Did I see you last night?' said Charlie. 'Going past the boxing club? Up on Spelman Road?'

Stan stared for a minute, tried to think of some clever excuse before giving up and just saying, 'Yeah', because it was true.

'I called after you,' said Charlie. 'Did you not hear me?'

'I did,' said Stan.

'Didn't think to say hi?'

'Not really,' said Stan.

'Not even after I fixed your bike?'

Stan shrugged.

'Oh. Cheers,' said Charlie.

'Anytime,' said Stan.

Charlie laughed. And then, to Stan's complete and staggering surprise, Charlie climbed off his bike, put it down next to Stan's by the path, and came and sat down right next to him in the grass. Stan didn't know what to say. He pulled himself up to sit a little straighter, noticing as he did that the autumn afternoon suddenly felt a little warmer around him, the last rays of sun a little brighter. Charlie unpacked an array of packets and pouches from his pockets and began rolling a cigarette.

'Smoke?' he said.

'Nah,' said Stan. 'My mum's a nurse. She says it kills people.'

'Ah,' said Charlie. 'Something's got to.'

'It's a horrible death, my mum says.'

'Something else'll get me first.'

'Like what?'

'I dunno. If I knew I'd plan for it, wouldn't I? Motorbike crash? Fight gone awry?'

'You've got a motorbike?'

Charlie shook his head. 'Not yet I don't, but that doesn't mean I haven't got plans.' He tapped the side of his nose.

'To die in a motorbike crash?'

'Obviously not, but it happens, doesn't it? Things like that happen constantly, all the time.'

'Do they?'

Charlie shrugged. 'They can do, yeah.' He shook his head, as if dismissing an unwelcome thought, then licked the Rizla, smoothed it down. 'I only mean, you never can tell what'll happen to you next. It could be fucking *anything*.' He stuck his cigarette behind his ear, and grinned.

'I suppose,' said Stan.

'It's true,' said Charlie, then jumped to his feet. 'What happened to your glasses?' he said.

'Got pinched,' said Stan.

'Serious?' said Charlie. 'Someone walked right up to you' – he experimentally mimed going up to Stan and seizing phantom glasses – 'and grabbed them right off your face? What for? Doesn't everyone need different glasses anyway?'

Stan shook his head, not laughing or anything, though he knew Charlie was joking and at least a smile would be polite. 'It's not like that,' he said.

'Right,' said Charlie.

'It's this guy in my year,' said Stan, throat tightening, mouth drying, not even sure why he was still talking. 'He just likes messing with me. He doesn't even need glasses. He's got perfect eyesight, I think.'

'Fucking people with their fucking perfect eyesight,' said Charlie.

'Don't you have perfect eyesight?' said Stan.

'Yeah, but I don't expect it to last.' Charlie jumped to his feet, picked up his bike and angled it out towards the path again. 'You shouldn't have let him,' he said. 'Cunts like that, you let them think they're fine to wipe their feet all over you, they'll wipe their feet all over you.' He climbed on to his bike.

'Yeah well, maybe next time,' said Stan.

'Good man,' Charlie said, and then he held his fist up in the air. The gesture stirred something in Stan, some memory. Curled up on the sofa, watching telly and eating custard creams with Helen over the summer, still weeks before he'd started at St Reginald's and everything had got so complicated. All the documentaries she'd made them watch because she'd said they might come in useful once he got to school, for History and that, back when they'd still thought fitting in at St Reginald's would involve being smart, and caring about learning things. That documentary about the Spanish Civil War. Stan mirrored Charlie's fist automatically, and felt suddenly better for it.

'Nae pasaran,' said Charlie.

'What?' said Stan.

'Means "they shall not pass". It's like an anti-fascist thing in general, but this one's Scottish. Heard about it from a mate, from up near Glasgow.'

'It's Scottish?' said Stan. 'It sounds more – I don't know. Spanish.'

Charlie nodded. 'Yeah, it was Spanish originally. The "nae" kind of makes it Scottish though, see? It's because back in the seventies there were these factory workers, up in East Kilbride, I think it was. They refused to repair the engines of some fighter jets they were meant to be fixing after they found out they were being used by Pinochet, for the military coup in Chile. And that's what they said, in solidarity. "Nae pasaran."' He said it this time in a surprisingly convincing Glaswegian accent.

'Who's Pinochet?'

'Nasty military dictator. Not been paying attention in history, Stan?'

'Never learned about Pinochet. Or East Kilbride. Just about Tudors and things like that.'

'Tudors?'

'You know, like Henry the Eighth.'

'Oh right,' Charlie squinted at Stan like he'd said something particularly puzzling. 'Each to their own I suppose.'

'How – how d'you get to know so many weird things? You don't go to school.'

'Weird things?' Charlie laughed.

'But you do know about weird things. Those factory workers in Glasgow, or – or East Kilbride. Nae pasaran. Pinochet. That thing about commons. Common land.'

Charlie shrugged. 'No idea, just find stuff interesting I suppose.' He grinned, and then pushed off along the path, giving Stan a wave as he did so.

\*

Stan got home as it was getting dark and Helen was washing up her plate and mug, hair tied back, ready for work.

'There's bread in the cupboard and beans in the pot,' she said. 'Ice cream too, if you want it.'

'Thanks,' said Stan, still hovering in the kitchen doorway.

'You okay?' said Helen. And then when he didn't reply, 'I didn't know where you'd gone, Stanley, I was worried.'

'I was only on the common,' he said. 'For some air. I didn't go far.'

'You were gone for ages,' she said.

'Yeah,' said Stan. 'I was reading.' And he didn't know why he said that. Why he sort of lied to her, and didn't mention Charlie. Something about the smoking, maybe? Or the stuff about motorbikes?

'There's nothing you want to talk about, is there, Stanley?' said Helen.

And he couldn't help but think she looked a little bit hopeless there, with her wet hands still held out over the sink, dripping away. All worries and work and no . . . what was it? No *nae pasaran*. That was it. He couldn't quite see her expression properly without his glasses on but he knew only too well what it would look like – that combination of concern and weariness, that look of hers that just said *tell me everything's okay, even if it isn't, so that I don't have to worry about you any more*. And maybe things were okay. Kind of. Huxley Edwards wasn't everything, after all.

He waited until Helen had left for work to help himself to dinner, and as he ate he read his Greek myths book, finally finishing the story of Theseus and the Minotaur. And then as he fell asleep that night he imagined himself as Theseus, the Minotaur bearing down on him. *Nae pasaran!* he would cry, before ramming his bike straight into the vulnerable folds of its stomach.

# 5

As September faded into October it became a bit of a pattern. School ticked over, Stan doing his best to avoid Huxley and Neil and Eddie and the rest, with varying success, and then almost every evening afterwards Stan would ride his bike to the common, to meet Charlie.

And they would sit on the grass while Charlie rolled cigarettes or smoked and Stan watched the beginnings of the sunset or the trees with their tops all swaying in the wind, and Charlie would talk about things Stan had never heard of or thought about before. Like the gigs he'd been to with his dad up in Manchester, or stuff to do with boxing, or with motorbikes – mainly about how good his dad was at fixing them. He'd talk about the stuff he'd done with various girls in the different places he'd lived, and then he'd talk too about all the odd things he knew, about stuff that had happened or about people that had lived in the past who Stan had never even heard of – often having something to do with Newford. Stan found those the most interesting bits, really. Not because he wasn't interested in music or motorbikes or boxing or girls, but because the things Charlie told him showed Newford in a new light, making this small home-town of his seem suddenly peppered with interesting sparks of history.

It was, too, simply Charlie's sheer open curiosity about places and their pasts that had Stan interested. At school, in spite of everything Stan had been told before he'd got there about how clever everyone at St Reginald's would be, intellectual apathy was rapidly becoming the most reliable index of coolness. Anyone who worked hard and gave a shit about reading or thinking or learning anything was a loser, inherently – Stan the biggest loser of them all with his nose always in a book. Charlie wasn't uncool though, wasn't a nerd or a geek – Charlie didn't even go to school – and yet he was so curious, always finding this stuff out and thinking about it, what it meant, why it was interesting.

One afternoon, for instance, Charlie made Stan bike with him all the way across town past the station to an empty shopfront on Giles Street.

'Used to be a pub, this,' Charlie said, frowning at it. It had been painted white but in reality now looked a similar shade of grey to the sky. To Stan it seemed completely unre-markable. 'Blown up by the IRA in the seventies.'

'IRA, that's Irish Republican Army, isn't it?'

'Yep,' said Charlie.

'I've heard my mum talk about them sometimes. They do bad things, don't they?'

Charlie didn't reply immediately, just stared at Stan with an amused, puzzled look on his face. 'They really don't teach you anything in that school of yours, do they?' he said, eventually.

Stan shrugged.

'Can't rely on them, mate,' Charlie said. 'Never just rely on what people tell you. You've got to go out and investi-gate. Ask questions. Go to the library. Read books.' Charlie clapped Stan on the shoulder. 'Now, I'm going to the chippy. You coming?'

'I should go home,' Stan said. 'My mum hates takeaways. They drain your bank account and clog your arteries, she says.'

'But it's your money, right? From the paper round?'

Stan nodded.

'And it's your arteries, I'm assuming? Unless you've got some morbid deal on, to donate your veins to a five-hundred-year-old uncle when you come of age, or something?'

'What?' said Stan.

'Well exactly,' said Charlie. 'Come on.'

They jumped on the bikes and left Giles Street behind, zooming up Leapdale Avenue to the chip shop by the Odeon. The sky had darkened fast, the nights setting in early these days and anyway rain on the way, and the lit-up sign beckoned them from the line-up of shops, radiating promise and the scent of burning chip fat.

Food obtained, they walked with their newspaper-wrapped parcels along the pavements under the street lights, cold rain misting their hair and their faces, ink and grease bleeding out over their hands. Stan noticed how Charlie ate chips the way he did everything else, like he was *hungry* in all senses of the word. No table manners, all speed and relish. Stan found himself reminded of the baby birds in the nests you'd see in the trees by the common in spring, mouths stretched wide, reaching up towards their mothers with no shame or reticence about wanting whatever she'd brought for them for themselves, no deference or apology or embarrassment.

'Would you look at this?' said Charlie, through a mouthful of food. He was stabbing a grease-covered finger at the newspaper wrapped around his chips. Stan had to lean close and squint to see it properly, still not having any glasses.

*Mount Street Cemetery Gatepost Reduced to Splinters – After Bin Lorry Crashes Into It*

'Local news,' said Charlie. 'I love it. What does yours say?'

'Um, hang on. *Sinkhole Investigation Must Continue Unimpeded, Woking Vicar Says.*'

Charlie laughed so hard he choked on his chips, and Stan had to reach up and whack him on the back.

'Why have you moved around so much?' asked Stan, in the calm after the hilarity subsided. 'Like Manchester, and everything. You've lived in so many different places.'

Charlie shrugged, chewing chips. 'Manchester was just to see my dad, for a bit. We'd never had much of a chance just to spend time, you know? Like even when he lived with us he always seemed busy, always off on some new plan or adventure he'd dreamed up, and it was my mum and my nan and my uncle who were around, for the most part. And then when he left, I thought – I don't know. I don't know what I thought. I'm not even sure I'll go back again, now, to Manchester.'

'I thought you liked it there?'

'Yeah, I suppose.' Charlie shrugged, then paused a moment in the process of wolfing his food to look up and out at the rain. 'I talk a lot about my dad,' he said, 'I know I do. But he's not . . . he has a different side, too. And it's not always great with him, all the time. He's just got his own things going on really, you know?'

Stan nodded as if he understood, though he wasn't sure he did, really.

Charlie sighed, and went back to his chips. 'Speaking honestly, mate, even six months seemed too much. Don't get me wrong, he made an effort and all, but when it came to it he didn't need me around. He has his own life, up there. Besides, it wasn't like I didn't have things to get back here for, too. It just makes sense, like this. With us separate.'

'My dad's not about any more, either,' Stan found himself telling Charlie then.

'Really? How come? D'you still get to see him sometimes though?'

Stan shook his head, then took a deep breath. 'He died. Nearly a year ago now,' he said. He found he couldn't even look up at Charlie. Just stared at his damp trainers on the slick grey of the wet pavement.

'Jesus. Stan, mate. I had no idea. You should have said.'

Stan shrugged. 'S'okay,' he said. 'Or, well. You know. I miss him.'

'Yeah. You would. I mean, of course you would. He's your dad.'

And Stan felt something untwist inside him then, felt some knot in his stomach he hadn't even quite realised was there unclench just a little at finally having been able to mention his dad like this, without all the confusion and guilt that haunted his attempts to bring him up with Helen, or the awfulness of the other kids at school. He'd been avoiding the subject with Charlie almost automatically, since that was just what he did with everyone else. It was surprising, though, what a relief it was to have finally said something, and told him about it.

They stopped walking when they reached the street corner before the overpass, and stood in the drizzle, wolfing the last of their food with cars shooting by alongside and overhead, the wheels louder and lights brighter on the rain-soaked road surface.

'Where did you like living the most?' Stan asked then. 'Out of all the places?'

Charlie frowned. 'Maybe Farnham,' he said. 'I had a proper girlfriend there, for a bit. Zoe Church. A real good-girl type, but not boring or anything. She was kind. Probably still is, for all I know. And you should have seen her, Stan. Honestly. Rack on her like you wouldn't believe.'

Stan felt himself freeze. He tried to make his face non-chalant, but embarrassment seemed to have frozen his jaw, somehow, and stopped him from chewing. He tried to swallow, and choked.

Charlie paused in the process of hoovering his food to laugh and whack him on the back.

'Bloody hell,' he said. 'Look at you. We're going to have to introduce you to some girls.'

'I'm thirteen,' said Stan, eyes on his shoes, the pavement, the road, a passing car – looking at anything but Charlie.

'Exactly,' said Charlie. 'I mean, you are – you do like girls, don't you, Stan?'

'Yes,' Stan yelped. 'Or like – y'know. What are you saying?'

'Don't worry,' Charlie grinned, pushing another handful of chips into his jaws. 'Don't freak out. I wasn't asking if you fancied me.'

And then Charlie was cackling at the appalled look on Stan's face – and Stan couldn't think of anything at all clever to say so he just chucked a chip at him instead, which Charlie caught in his ink-stained hands and summarily devoured.

'Now that's exactly what you've got to learn, Stan,' he said. 'Don't panic like that and give your enemies something they want.'

'It was just a chip.'

'But an indicative chip.' Charlie scrunched his newspaper up and hurled it into the road. Stan watched it get run over, crushed under the wheels of successive cars and vans as he folded up his own greasy newspaper, and slipped it neatly into his jeans pocket, to throw away properly later.

\*

'Hungry?' called Helen from the main room when Stan got home, wheeling his bike through the front door, propping it up against the hallway wall in exactly the same place it always rested, a smudge on the paint where the handlebars touched it. He leaned on the door frame, and looked in at her there with her feet up on the coffee table and her hair in the towel and the mug in her hands – probably long empty, from the way she was holding it, as if there was no chance of it spilling. The TV wasn't on. How long had she been there? Simply staring into space?

'Nah,' he said. 'Got chips on the way home.' He swung himself round the door and headed towards the stairs, heading up to his room.

'School friends?' called Helen, and he hated the strange note of hope he could hear there in her voice.

'Just on my own,' he called back, halfway up the stairs already.

Again, there he was, lying to her about Charlie. A few months ago he would never have dreamed of lying to his mum like this, and now he was doing it automatically, almost without thinking at all. Why was that? Was it the shame he'd feel at the relief she'd surely show at him finally having a friend? That was part of it, surely. He couldn't face that. But then there was Charlie's loudness. The way he filled more space than was allotted to him. His cigarettes and talk of girls and his recklessness and messiness. He was the opposite of Stanley, in many ways. The opposite, that is, of anything that Helen ever praised or valued these days.

'Oh, sweetheart,' she said, as if on cue. 'What did you do that for? It's a waste, and it's bad for you. You know that.'

'Dunno,' he shrugged, and continued up the stairs.

'Stanley,' she called after him, and he thought about stopping, going back downstairs and explaining more, maybe even telling her about Charlie, because part of him wanted to, of course. But then she just didn't sound like she meant it enough, calling after him like that. As usual, she sounded too weary for anything new, for anything disruptive, active, spontaneous – even simply within the context of a conversation. There would be no point in trying to explain to her. She'd only try to quiet him down, picking faults in whatever it was he told her in that way she always seemed to do, now. He stayed quiet and carried on up to his room, and as he'd guessed, she was too tired to call him back again.

# 6

'C'mon, the Rolling Stones played here. *Mick Jagger*, Stan. Think about it. It's a little piece of the legend, right here in Newford, of all places.' Charlie thumped him on the back, probably intending to knock some vim and vigour into him but instead only making Stan flinch.

'You never know,' said Charlie. 'Maybe some of it'll rub off on you. Ten minutes inside and you'll meet some girls, stop apologising for yourself, go off somewhere and get some new clothes . . .'

'What's wrong with my clothes?' asked Stan.

Charlie rolled his eyes, and shoved him through the pub doors.

Stan had known this was a terrible idea. From the first he'd had an instinct about it. But it took him a moment to realise quite how terrible because the world still blurry with his lack of glasses. Because wasn't that Huxley Edwards's voice that Stan could hear now, echoing loud in the beer-smelling air around him? He squinted, studying the groupings of people around tables – and yep, of course. Typical. Huxley Edwards out of context, out of uniform, sitting at a table of lads by the stairs with a drink at one elbow and his older brother at the other.

And Stan had said, hadn't he? He'd said they shouldn't go like this into town, that there was no point, that they'd be better off staying round the common and the boxing club, places where Huxley would never think to go, despite them only being a simple fifteen-minute bike ride away – not even that. And now something was bound to happen and it would be awful, and Charlie would finally see, too, just how much of a loser he really was, how hated he was by literally everyone else in this stupid town. They had to go. They had to get out of here now, before Huxley saw them.

'He's looking at you a bit funny,' said Charlie, stepping up behind Stan. 'You know him?'

Too late, clearly. Too fucking late. Now what? Now take a step back, and another. Back away, just like that, towards the door. But there was Charlie suddenly gripping his arm.

'What you doing?' Charlie hissed. 'You look like an absolute muppet, sidling backwards like an HGV or something, like you should be making that vehicle reversing noise, y'know?' Charlie made the noise surprisingly convincingly, a particular beeping sound that did absolutely sound like a lorry backing out of a drive. 'What's with you, Stan? He the cunt who stole your glasses?'

The pub had people in it, of course it did, it was 5 p.m. on a Thursday, and this was a pub with a bit of rock 'n' roll history not too far from the centre of town. But it wasn't *busy* per se. And Charlie never lowered his voice. Huxley was staring over at Charlie now. Then he leaned over and said something to his brother. His brother three years above at school, large as life here with his combed-back hair, a jawline so cartoonishly sharp it looked as though you could slice paper off it, and dressed, like Huxley, in a branded polo shirt Stan wouldn't know how to decode the subtler social signals of – beyond, that is, the obvious expense he'd gone to in acquiring it. People said Huxley's brother had some kind of a thing going with Miss Durand the French teaching assistant, which obviously seemed far-fetched and fantastical, but then who knew what to think? People were strange, and wild sometimes, it seemed. Almost anything was possible.

'C'mon,' Stan said to Charlie. 'Let's go.'

'What you talking about?' said Charlie. 'We just got here.'

Huxley's brother was watching them now, pushing his chair back, coming over.

'Did you call my brother a cunt?' he said to Charlie.

'Not really,' said Charlie. 'I mean, technically speaking I did. But I've never met your brother' – he gave Huxley a wave, where he was still sat over at the table. Too cocky, Stan could see, and pushing it way too far already – 'I employed the term merely casually, colloquially, as you might refer to a passing acquaintance or even to a complete stranger. You know the way it is, we all do it. You seen that cunt over there in the funny pastel-coloured sports top? Next to that cunt with the comb-over, and the really dreadful skin? No, the little cunt, the one that looks a lot like the comb-over one but at a different stage of adolescent development . . . really, it's like the seven ages of man. You see? You know how it is. Just like that.'

'You talk too much,' said Huxley's brother. Johnny, his name was. Either Johnny, or Ricky or something like that, Stan wasn't sure. He'd never paid much attention. Whatever his name was, he took a step closer to Charlie, looking much older, suddenly, and taller. 'But you know that, don't you?'

'I don't, I don't, mate,' said Charlie. 'Because that's all we came in here to do, really, you see, me and Stan here. Just talk. Shoot the breeze of a Sunday evening. No trouble.'

'I see,' said Huxley's brother – Johnny, Stan was pretty sure it was Johnny. 'You'd better watch yourself, is all I'm saying. My friends and I over there won't tolerate rubbish from anyone. Let alone from the likes of you.'

With that, Johnny sank his hands into his pockets and stalked back across the pub to his table. Huxley didn't seem too happy to see his brother returned so soon. Probably he'd hoped he'd be back with Stan's entrails in a jar or his head on a spike or something. He hissed something at him Stan couldn't quite catch, but Johnny just shrugged and slid back into his place at the table. Stan breathed out, the constricted feeling in his throat easing off, loosening a little.

'Bloody hell,' he said to Charlie. 'You trying to get us killed?'

'Killed? Those lads? Nah,' said Charlie. 'Look at them. They've not got much bark on them, never mind bite. C'mon. You want a drink?'

Charlie headed off towards the bar. Stan looked over again at Johnny and Huxley, trying to make it look like nothing more than a casual glance around the pub as a whole, hoping to God they hadn't heard what Charlie had just said – but they were too busy arguing with each other, it seemed. Heads bent low, bickering in hushed voices, arms and elbows on the table locked around their pints in uncon-scious mirrors of each other. Stan followed Charlie to the bar.

'I'm sorry,' the barman was saying, an affable-seeming hippy, maybe late twenties, maybe early thirties, Stan found it difficult to tell. 'I'm sorry, man, but it's my job on the line, you know. We're all individually liable. I could get done by like the government and everything, I mean, dude, I don't like the system, don't get me wrong, but I'm only after a quiet life, you know? No trouble.'

*No trouble.* That little phrase again. Why was this barman talking like this to Charlie?

'But I promise you, mate,' Charlie was saying. 'I am actually nineteen. I've always looked young for my age, that's just it. Everyone says it. *Oh that Charlie, such a baby face, but it'll be good for him later, when his friends are all ancient and haggard-looking and he still looks twenty-five, or whatever.* It's ridiculous, I promise you. Happens everywhere I go.'

'What you doing for your A Levels then?' the barman said.

'A Levels? I'm not in school, mate. Got a job, haven't I? Because, like I say, I'm not a kid.'

'That right? What d'you do then?'

'Work at the boxing gym. Assistant to the coach.'

'Boxing? That's cool,' said the hippy barman. 'And who's this? Your younger brother?'

'You being funny or something?' Charlie said. 'Course he's not my brother. He doesn't look anything like my brother.'

'And he's nineteen too, is he?'

'Eighteen. He's eighteen. Aren't you, Stan?'

'Alright okay so that's enough now. It's soft drinks or nothing for you boys I'm sure you realise, so what'll you be having?'

They took their ginger beers to a table by the smoking area – not as far from Huxley and Johnny as ideally Stan would have liked. He half-suspected Charlie had chosen to sit near them like this, to keep an eye on them, maybe, or as a deliberate show of defiance. Why couldn't he just do as he said he would, and try and pass the afternoon with *no trouble*? And yet as Stan sipped the ginger beer and tasted sugar and spice and felt the carbon dioxide burning the back of his throat (he'd actually been quite glad they hadn't got served, he didn't even really like beer anyway) he felt a spark lighting itself somewhere in his chest and floating up to his head with the bubbles. Huxley Edwards's older brother, put in his place by his mate Charlie.

'What was that about?' he asked Charlie.

'What was what?'

'Just then. When you said I didn't look anything like your brother.'

'Yeah, well you don't.'

'You don't have a brother.'

'I've got a brother.'

'What?'

'Yeah.'

'You never talk about him.'

'You never ask about him.'

'That's not the point. I didn't know he existed.'

Charlie shrugged. 'What's the big deal about it anyway?'

'It's not a big deal, it's just weird.'

'No it's not.'

'Yeah it is,' Stan took a gulp of ginger beer to cover for his general sense of discombobulation. It was too big a gulp, though, and he found himself feeling like it was too much to swallow – so he just sat with his mouth full of ginger beer like a hamster-cheeked muppet, staring at Charlie with wide eyes.

'What?' said Charlie, who then burst into a cackle, laughing at Stan. 'Bloody hell, look at you. What's that face for, mate?'

Stan felt himself starting to laugh, too. Please God no. Not with his mouth bursting full with ginger beer. Not with Huxley Edwards a few tables away, probably watching, probably looking for an excuse to come over. Stan controlled himself and painfully swallowed it down, feeling the air bubbles make dents in his gullet as they went.

'You got any other siblings?' he asked.

'Nope,' said Charlie. 'Just my bro.'

'How old is he?' said Stan.

'Thirteen,' said Charlie.

'My age?' said Stan.

Charlie took a sip of his drink and wiped his mouth on the sleeve of his jacket before replying. 'I suppose,' he said. 'But he's not like you at all. You don't seem the same age.'

'What's he like?'

Charlie shrugged. 'It's not important. Now who's that clown at the next table? He's still watching us, I don't get it. He is the one who took your glasses, isn't he?'

'Yeah but don't make a thing of it. Please,' said Stan.

You can't just let people take what they want, though. Never let them tell you where you do and don't belong. That barman, for instance. He would've served us, he would, he was going to I know he was – and then you came over looking so meek and sorry for yourself he could see there's no way you're eighteen and bam, ginger ale, that's us.'

'It's cheaper, at least.'

'Stop looking on the bright side, it's not helping.' Charlie took a huge gulp of his drink, and shuddered. 'I can't believe that guy,' he said. 'Back in Manchester nobody gave a shit. Here they're all so proper, so *careful*, so . . . that's what it is, Stan. I'll tell you what gets me about this place. Everyone's so accepting of authority. Take you and that kid who nicked your glasses. Why defer to him? Why is what he wants law? Why, in your eyes, are you not as important as him?'

'It's not like that.'

'Then what is it like?'

Stan found he couldn't explain. Couldn't even begin to.

'I knew it,' said Charlie. Then necked the rest of his drink, shoved his chair back from the table, stood up, and made straight for Huxley and Johnny's table.

'Charlie,' said Stan, far too loud. And without thinking really at all about what he was doing he jumped to his feet and followed him. Huxley and Johnny were now deep in conversation with the other boys around the table – Johnny's friends, from the look of them. Stan thought he recognised a few faces from school.

'Alright,' said Charlie, slapping a hand down right in the middle of their nest of torn-open crisp packets. 'What I want to know, is why people like you lot think you own this place. Why you think you can come over and mess with me just for walking in the same pub you happen to be drinking in, telling me I talk too much even though you've never even met me before. Why you think you can nick my friend Stan here's glasses—'

'Please, Charlie, it's not a big deal—'

'It is a big deal, though, Stan. It's a big deal to me because I want to know how it is these entitled southern bastards came to think this whole bleeding world is theirs to do with as they wish just 'cause their dad works in banking or what-ever it is and their trainers cost more than my house.'

Johnny was on his feet and had Charlie by the front of the T-shirt faster than you could blink.

'Hey now,' Stan could hear the hippie barman start to say, dishwater-thin, from over behind them.

'Fuck you,' Johnny said to Charlie. 'You think you know all about it, don't you? You think you know everything and the sun shines out of your fucking arse. I could see it the minute you walked in.'

'I've often thought,' said Charlie – still relatively composed, despite being dragged by the scruff of the T-shirt ever closer to Johnny's Action Man jawline – 'that whenever people swear a lot like that, like you just did, my friend, that it comes down to a fundamental lack of eloquence – that, well, in so many words, you're too stupid to express what it is you really mean.'

Charlie's head seemed to snap back and his nose start bleeding completely of its own accord – Johnny was that fast.

'Hey,' called the barman again, from somewhere close to Stan – but then Stan was hardly paying attention because suddenly he was in there, on Johnny's back, before he knew what he was doing – before he'd even thought, even considered whether it was anything like a good idea, clawing at Johnny's face from behind, pulling him off Charlie – or trying to, at least. Trying with all his strength, which, he saw now, was pretty meagre, embarrassingly meagre, now that he was actually pressed to use it. He'd barely even registered with Johnny, it seemed, who despite Stan's efforts still had Charlie in a headlock – Charlie who was punching Johnny in the gut as he squirmed and spun in the bigger boy's grip.

'Go on, Johnny!' Stan heard Huxley's voice from behind him, behind the table, Huxley hanging back – Huxley all talk, maybe? 'Get him,' Huxley said.

'Fuck you,' spat Charlie, from the crouched depths of the headlock. 'Nasty little bastard.'

Johnny heaved his shoulders back, sending Stan flying off, crashing into a table and from there to the floor, into chair legs and bruises and confusion – and in that same moment Stan saw Charlie take advantage of that instant of Johnny switching the angle and force of his grip, by battering him one right in the solar plexus and bursting free, spitting and beetroot, breathing like he'd run a marathon. And then Charlie had put up his fists like a boxer and was on his toes, dancing back and forth like Stan had seen in the fights on TV, and Johnny was coughing and saying, 'You think you're so fucking clever but you look like a prick doing that you know.'

And then a big guy with no hair and no neck for that matter and a dark-coloured shirt had them both by the upper arm, and Stan wriggled round on the floor to see the barman standing by – wearing an apologetic expression and, Stan now noticed, the same shirt as the fat bald guy manhandling both Charlie and Johnny to the door. Which meant they were in uniform and he must work here, then, that bald guy.

Stan scrambled to his feet. 'Charlie,' he called. And fuck, he realised, as he stumbled after them, past the tables of half-consumed pints and affronted customers all scrubbed and polished and so pleased with themselves it seemed to him now, as everyone in this town always seemed to be, so pleased not to be Stan, or Charlie, or even Johnny today. But fuck, he thought, this was his fault. If he'd not let the situation with Huxley back at school get so bad then none of this would have happened. Would Charlie see it like that?

Would Charlie be angry with him? Or ashamed, even? To have inadvertently made friends with such a liability? With someone he couldn't even go out with for a quick drink without getting picked on? The fat barman pushed open the double doors of the pub using the two boys like handles. Stan followed, too close, nearly getting himself hit in the face by a door on the rebound. He emerged into the early evening sunlight to see Johnny being summarily released.

'You,' said the barman. 'Johnny Edwards, isn't it? You walk it off and don't come back until you've got some sense back in you—'

For a second Johnny looked as if he might argue, but the barman grabbed his shoulders, spun him round and gave him a shove down the road – all the office workers and shoppers heading home, young mums with blow-dried hair and double-buggies looking shocked at the commotion.

'But my friends are all in there,' said Johnny.

'Go on,' said the barman. 'They'll still be there when you get back if I know that lot. Probably won't even notice you're gone. Don't argue. Once round the block or you're barred.'

Johnny looked sulky but tamed – younger out in the day-light with a real adult dressing him down than he'd seemed back in the artificial gloom of the bar.

'Get lost,' said the barman and Johnny obliged, hands in pockets, loping off down the hill towards the car park, hunched shoulders looking more sulky than defiant.

'Now you' – the barman still had Charlie by the arm – 'I'll be honest with you. I don't like your lot, and I don't like you being round here. And though there's not much I can do about that I won't have you coming into my place of work, picking fights with the customers, disturbing the peace. I see you again, I'll have to get the proper authorities involved. Right? You following me? You understand?'

'Jesus Christ, yes,' Charlie shook himself loose, recovering a bit of his dignity, maybe, though he really did look a bit stung all of a sudden, Stan noticed. 'No need to be rude about it. I'm a human being too y'know.'

And without another word or even a glance at Stan he'd turned on his heel and was heading off up the street in the opposite direction to the way Johnny had gone. Stan wasn't sure whether to follow until Charlie stopped, and called over his shoulder.

'Stan,' he said. 'You coming, mate?'

'Where you going?' said Stan.

'Co-op,' Charlie said. 'Frozen peas. You could probably do with a bag yourself, too.'

Then he was off again at a pace, and of course Stan was after him, jogging, almost, to keep up, without even a backwards glance at the barman.

It wasn't till later, when it was dark and they were sitting on the bike racks on Spelman Road, shivering and nursing their wounds with the weeping, freezing sacks of peas held to their skin, that Stan felt he could ask.

'What did he mean, back there? Your lot?'

'Fucking pricks,' was all Charlie said. 'People like that. They just expect it. They expect you to take it and do what they say and accept it as right. They expect to win, is what it is. They always just *expect* to win.'

# 7

'Pikey,' Stan heard, making his way through the crush under the corridor's strip lights, on the way to biology next morning. He stopped dead and spun round, causing the girl who happened to be walking behind him – Marianne Lindsay in the year above, why did it have to be Marianne Lindsay in the year above? – to trip over his feet and mutter, *can't you watch where you're going?* without even bothering to properly look at him.

He hadn't even been aware of Huxley Edwards in the between-classes crush around him, had been more preoccupied wondering about Charlie, if Charlie would still want to be friends with him now after yesterday – and then what else there could be about Charlie that he didn't know, as there could be anything, really, seeing as he'd omitted to mention a whole actual living brother. What was Charlie's brother like? He was Stan's age, he'd said, like that had only just occurred to him there and then, in the pub as they were talking. Could that really be the case though, that it had only just occurred to him? Or had he decided not to tell Stan for some particular reason? Maybe he was ashamed of Stan, ashamed of being friends with someone so much younger, so much less cool, someone so pathetic . . . God, the way he had hung on to Huxley's brother's back like that, like some sort of little kid, just shouting and getting absolutely nowhere.

'Oi, pikey' – but there was Huxley's voice again. It was definitely Huxley. Stan would know that voice anywhere – 'Happy Halloween, pikey,' he was saying. 'And bloody hell don't you look a fright. I always forget when I don't see you.' And then Huxley was suddenly on him, and dragging him from behind by the hair.

Stan twisted, bent his spine backwards, trying not to fall over and feeling a bit like some idiot at a party trying to do limbo – until the weight of his backpack full of books over-balanced him, and he stumbled round, whirling clumsily, desperately trying to keep his balance as the bag swung out behind him. He felt it knock into someone, books making contact with soft human flesh, and he heard a yelp and a curse . . . but then he was facing Huxley who had let go of his hair now, and seemed to be without Neil or Eddie flanking him, for once. If anything that only made Stan more nervous. They couldn't, after all, have gone far.

'You alright, pikey? You struggling a bit there, without your pikey friend?'

'Pikey?' said Stan, rubbing the back of his head, wishing he could turn around and apologise to whoever it was he had whacked with his bag but not daring to, not daring to show his back to Huxley, and then realising that Charlie would dare – that that was exactly what Charlie would do now, ignore Huxley completely and clap whoever the wronged soul behind him was on the shoulder – *you alright, mate?* he'd say. *I'm sorry, this prick here caught me unawares for a moment* . . . yep, that's exactly what Charlie would do. Which was why Charlie was someone he wanted to be friends with, and he'd be lucky if Charlie even wanted to look at him now.

'Yeah,' said Huxley. 'Pikey. It rubs off on you, you see, if that's who you choose for your friends. Really, Stanley, God knows I don't think much of you but I did think more of you than that. Still, it was an interesting surprise I suppose, to discover that you do *have* some friends, even if they are all scumbag gyppos. That you're not just sat in the dark with your mum, getting up to whatever you get up to when you're sat in the dark with your mum.'

'What's that supposed to mean?' said Stan.

'What, you and your mum? Use your brain, Gower. Not very with it this morning, are you?'

'No, the . . . gyppos – the gyppo thing.'

Huxley grinned. 'You didn't know?' he said, and then, playing to the invisible audience that seemed to follow him around all the time, 'He didn't know! Well, Stanley, it may surprise you – then again it might not – to learn that that little friend of yours, the one you introduced us to back there in the pub, is a full-on fucking gyppo. Full-on inbred trailer trash, no less. Can't be a very good friend, if you really know so little about him.'

'What?' said Stan. 'What did you say?'

'That your friend's a pikey scumbag? You should really get to know someone a little better before you jump to their defence with such embarrassing loyalty, you know. Really know a few more basic facts before you're willing to try and scratch my brother's eyes out for them. You're lucky my brother's got better things to worry about than remembering to hold a grudge against you and your scabby friends.

63

Then again, he's a smart man, my brother. He's got a very good memory.'

The bell rang out, loud again in the suddenly almost empty corridor – just a few stragglers dashing past now, Aiden Smith from Stan's class, always late, jogging towards biology with shoelaces undone. Stan irrationally hoped he would stop next to them and interject with something, ask Stan if he was coming to class, maybe – a mad hope, really, seeing as they'd barely exchanged two sentences since starting at St Reginald's. Of course Aiden sped on without so much as a backwards glance. And then it was only Stan and Huxley, staring at each other in the ringing aftermath of the bell.

'Go ask your friend what he is,' said Huxley. 'That would be my advice. And think whether you'd like to apologise to my brother – whether you'd like to admit you made a mistake yesterday. That you were acting under nefarious influences and would never in your right mind even dream of assaulting my brother for that sort of pikey scum. He can be forgiving, my brother, if you ask nicely.'

Huxley was threatening him now, that much was clear – Stan had caught up with that much of what was happening. And he should be worried, he knew. Things were escalating. He'd never seen Huxley out of school before like he had yesterday – or no, there'd been that time he'd been sitting on the steps that led down from the library and Huxley had walked past and flicked him the Vs – but it had never been like yesterday, they'd never spoken, never brought the stifling viciousness that haunted Stan's school days out of the walls of the school building and into the outside world. Certainly they'd never brought other people, almost-adults like Johnny, into it. Everything was different now Johnny was involved. And Charlie. *Charlie.*

Stan knew full well he should be careful now, that he should do or say something accommodating, something to make sure this stopped here, stopped now . . . but there was something about the ugliness of the expression on Huxley's face there grinning at him, so smug, so certain Stan would capitulate, those words *pikey scum* still hanging in the air with the ringing aftermath sound of the bell – something that made Stan look Huxley right in the eye for actually maybe the first time ever, and say, 'Go on, Huxley, get lost or we'll both be late for class.'

And then simply walk off down the corridor, not waiting to be discarded or dismissed.

*

It took Stan until about halfway through double biology to stop feeling elated at the backbone he'd discovered in that last encounter with Huxley, and to start feeling worried. What an idiot he'd been, talking back to him like that, because what could honestly be gained from defiance? Surely it'd have been much wiser to have shut up, to have agreed with whatever Huxley was saying and apologised, to have just given him what he wanted and defused the situation. It had already gone far enough. Then again, though, that was a question. Had it gone too far already for that to even be an option? There was so much Stan didn't understand. The whole *pikey* thing. The whole *gyppo* thing. He'd heard them before, those words, but honestly he wasn't really fully sure what they meant. And then the way Charlie's head had snapped back and his nose had bled when Johnny had punched him. Stan had never seen anyone get punched in the face before. Not in real life. Only in films.

*

For once, Stan rode his bike home after school. Helen was finally off night shifts for a while which meant cycling home instead of the endless lifts she still insisted on, and then a free house, if he wanted it, until at least seven o'clock. He whizzed along Woodside Lane, Monopoly houses cheerful-looking tonight, done up with fairy lights and jack-o'-lanterns, and then round the roundabout and up past the hospital where Helen would be right now – and *sweet freedom!* he thought, as he flew past it.

He didn't really expect Charlie to be on the common after what had happened the day before but still, he told himself, it'd be nice to get some fresh air – cold fresh air now that it was autumn proper – and just be outside and alone there in the wide open space of it, with only rabbits and birds for company, and probably moles. It might even be nice to spend an evening by himself for a change. Maybe he'd bring his new Discman along, and then he could sit in the grass and listen to that CD Charlie had found him in the charity shop, the one with the swimming baby on the cover. That's what he'd do, he'd listen while he watched the sun go down – early, very early now, it was getting there already and it was only, what? 4.30? Dusk at 4.30? He felt almost cheated. At home, in his room and out of school uniform, he shoved the Discman with its CD into the front pocket of his hoodie before shouting a vague goodbye to Helen, remembering she wasn't there to hear it, and jumping on his bike.

There was no need for the Discman though. When he got to the common there was Charlie waiting for him, calm as you like, just as if yesterday had never happened. Except from, that is, the expanse of purple stretching over the whole left side of his face, all the way up from his nose to the eye socket – clear as day to Stan even from this slight distance away, in the dim light, still without a pair of glasses.

'Practically dark already,' Charlie said when Stan approached. 'Don't know there's that much point in our being out here. It's getting cold.'

'Your face looks a mess,' said Stan. Probably it was best to try and sound nonchalant about it. Charlie wouldn't appreciate sympathy.

'Thanks,' Charlie said. 'Don't think those frozen peas did much good really, do you? I should write in and complain.'

Stan tried to think of some comment or wisecrack to reply with, to pretend everything was fine, but he couldn't – couldn't think of anything at all. So he just stood there like a lemon, staring at Charlie with what must have been a ridiculous expression on his face because out of nowhere Charlie started laughing.

'Come on,' he said. 'It's not the first time I've had a few bruises, you know. This is nothing. You look like someone's died.'

'Sorry,' said Stan.

'Don't apologise for yourself,' said Charlie. 'And besides, Stan. *Halloween*. If there's a day of the year when it's fine to look awful, this is the one. Saved me a lot of bother, that lad back there. Don't even need to worry about a costume now.'

'I saw his brother at school today,' said Stan. He hadn't meant to say a thing about it, and yet here he was, unable to deal with it on his own like he should have done, spilling his guts when they'd barely said hello. 'He called you pikey. Called me pikey, too.'

Charlie's eyes narrowed. 'Don't use that word,' he said. 'It's a fucking horrible word.'

'Charlie, he said – he said you were a Gypsy.'

'Yeah,' Charlie stared back at him, through the dark. 'And is there anything wrong with that?' he said.

'You're a Gypsy?' Stan said.

'And I asked you if there was anything wrong with that,' said Charlie.

'Course – course not,' said Stan. 'It's just . . . I don't know. You never said. You never told me.'

Charlie shrugged. 'Never came up.'

'That's not fair,' said Stan. 'It could have done. It could have come up. You didn't tell me deliberately.'

'Oh Jesus Christ, Stan, it's not like, it's not like I meant anything *personal* – like I was deliberately not telling you, or anything. It's not even that big a deal. I mean, I'm a Gypsy, a Traveller, yeah. I'm Romany. But it's kind of . . . not the most important thing about me. I'm mainly just a *person*, you know. Come on, mate, you're being weird.'

Stan shoved his cold hands into the front pocket of his hoodie and sat down in the grass. It was cold, and slightly damp. He stared out over to the last line of light above the trees as he tried to figure out just what it was that he minded. It wasn't that he was worried at all about Charlie being a Gypsy, if that was really true. Whatever his mum said about children with scabies, and disorder in the town whenever they arrived again, his own idea of the Gypsies was vague, formed mostly out of children's books – tales of circuses and lion tamers and dancing girls with big gold hoops gleaming at their ears. It was that he'd had to find out this new thing about his best friend – his only friend, really, now that it came to it – from Huxley Edwards, of all people.

Charlie stayed standing and Stan could feel him watching him. And then some kid screamed somewhere off in the distance, making Stan jump. The scream was followed by shouts, and laughter. Because, of course, it was Halloween, as Charlie had said. How had Stan forgotten? Night of sweets, trick-or-treating, fancy-dress parties . . . except he hadn't been invited to anything like that this year, of course. He probably never would be again, now he was at St Reginald's. He turned away from the expanse of the common to look back at Charlie.

'What?' said Stan then.

'What d'you mean, *what*?' said Charlie.

'You're laughing at me,' said Stan.

'No I'm not,' said Charlie.

'Yes you are. I'm staring at your face and you're laughing – or you're trying not to laugh at me. What's so funny?'

'I don't know, mate. You're just – so bloody *sensitive*.'

Stan shrugged. 'What's that meant to mean?'

Charlie sighed. 'Nothing. Look if it's such a big problem . . . I don't know. Come tonight. For Halloween. Meet my family. It's my brother's favourite night of the year. He'd probably like another guest.'

'Your brother?'

'Yeah.'

'The one my age?'

'Yeah course, idiot, I've only got one brother.'

'Well I don't know, do I? You don't tell me anything.'

'God, Stan, you sound like my mum. Would you like to come or not? I'm trying to invite you. To something nice. Or not *nice* exactly because it's Halloween and all but you know. D'you want to come or not?'

'Seriously?'

'Yes, seriously.'

'And your family are Gypsies?'

'Yeah, but it's not – you shouldn't listen to those lads at school, Stan, it's not that weird a thing. It's just me. Just like normal.'

'My mum talks about the Gypsies. She doesn't like them. Says they cause all kinds of trouble. That they think they can do whatever they like and not pay their taxes and then the second someone's ill or something's wrong they come running to the hospital, expecting the NHS to fix it.'

'Bloody hell, Stan, chill out.'

'It's just what my mum says. I don't know if I believe her. But that's you, isn't it? The Gypsies.'

'D'you even know what it means, Stan? Being a Gypsy? Being Romany?'

Stan thought for a moment, then shook his head.

'Ah,' said Charlie. 'Of course. They don't teach that in school, either.'

'Do I need a costume?' Stan asked. 'If it's Halloween?'

'Nah,' said Charlie. 'You're fine like that, it's not like formal or anything. And Nan will have something anyway you can borrow if you want. She's got this dressing-up box with all kinds of weird crap in it. You'll love Nan,' he grinned suddenly. 'She's mental. Honestly, Stan, I can't think why I didn't take you to meet her before.'

'Should I go home first and drop my bike?'

'We can take the bikes,' said Charlie. 'It's only five minutes, but still.'

And Stan was mostly excited, following Charlie like that, the two of them cycling up a long residential street he'd never even thought to explore, lying as it did in the opposite direction to the town centre, away from his house. He was also a little bit proud, maybe, to be spending Halloween with a friend after all, even though everything had gone so wrong at St Reginald's. Especially proud that this friend was Charlie – Charlie who was choosing to really include him in something now. There was only a small part of him that was slightly apprehensive. This was the part that spoke with Helen's voice and called the Gypsies *wild, completely lawless*, that called them *dangerous people*. As they rode up through the quiet streets, passing a clutch of trick or treaters – kids Stan didn't recognise, younger than him and much younger than Charlie, dressed as little ghosts and vampires and witches and one even as a Pokémon – he found it easier and easier to ignore that Helen voice in his head. He would rather have friends, after all, than be constantly suspicious and afraid.

# 8

Charlie turned off at a break in the hedge that Stan had barely even registered – it was so dark now that everything on that side of the road was basically invisible, covered up in patches of darkness with slightly alternating textures, the precise shapes and boundaries blurred by his bad eyes. But here it was. A break in the hedge and a drive leading into a sort of . . . courtyard, Stan thought. Or something between a courtyard and a car park. A stretch of concrete in the fields, filled with caravans and trailers. Not the kind he'd imagined – not old wooden ones, that is, with pictures and paintings all over the sides, rich colours and tassels, mysterious wall hangings and amulets – but white-and-cream modern ones, all fairly uniform-looking, give or take some pot plants or photographs in the windows.

Charlie had braked and jumped off his bike, and was now scratching the ears of a shaggy grey dog who'd bounded up to him immediately their bikes had pulled into the drive. Charlie laughed.

'This is Benji,' he said. 'Fastest dog on the site. And the friendliest too, I reckon. Want to say hello?'

Stan held his bike awkwardly with one hand and stretched out the other towards Benji's head. Animals and young children – he never knew how to behave with either of them. Even when he'd been a young child himself he'd had no idea. But Charlie was right, Benji seemed friendly enough. Or he didn't complain or move away, in any case, as Stan clumsily stroked his long, tangled fur. But here were some children approaching now – four of them, one holding another dog, a tiny puppy, in his arms that Stan had to admit looked kind of sweet but then again small children and dogs – was he prepared for this? What would he do? How would he be? He hung back, tried to vanish into the background, hunched down, pretending to be engrossed in patting the first dog.

'Charlie,' called one of the kids, a little girl with dark hair all tied up in ribbons, who ran up and grabbed Charlie's arm as he was wheeling his bike.

'Whoa,' Charlie said. 'Sarah. Bloody hell. Did you miss me, then?'

'No,' said Sarah. 'But you'll miss it. You'll miss dressing up and then you'll be sorry, won't you? You'll only have yourself to blame.'

The kids surrounded Charlie and seemed to carry him like a wave further into the site, laughing and nagging and protesting, the boy holding the puppy up, right in Charlie's face.

'Charlie, can you look at Luna? There's something wrong with her foot, I think . . .'

'Not now or he'll miss it – he'll miss the Halloween things—'

'I didn't mean now, *obviously*, I meant—'

'Charlie, is it true that if you feed a rabbit stinging nettles it'll explode or something because Jamie says—'

'Come *on*! You're *so slow*!'

'Alright, you lot,' Charlie said then. 'Wait for Stan.'

Until that point they hadn't even seemed to register that he was there at all, still hanging back, petting the dog. Now they turned to him though, eight sets of eyes.

'Careful,' said the little girl to Stan – Sarah, her name had been, hadn't it? 'You'll scare Benji.'

'Sorry,' said Stan, stepping away from him, though Benji was panting and wagging his tail, no sign of being scared at all.

'Charlie,' said the boy, all serious now, apparently. 'Charlie, you know what Martin says. We're not supposed to bring Gorjer friends back on the site.'

'To hell with Martin,' Charlie said, making the kids laugh and look shocked in equal measure. 'Martin says a lot of things. Come on. Come on, Stan.'

They followed Charlie through the caravans, still wheeling their bikes, Stan sneaking a look in some of the windows as he went past – kitchens, mainly, was all he saw, looking much the same as any kitchen – and then getting a long, curious look from a woman about Helen's age, he would guess, sitting on the steps leading down from her front door, smoking a cigarette. Charlie and the kids stopped in front of a white caravan on the far end of the site. He leaned his bike against the side and Stan copied him, noticing as he did so the wheelchair there, standing off to one side.

'Alright, Stan?' said Charlie, glancing back with a grin as he was dragged towards the door by little Sarah. 'Come meet Nan – go on, you'll love her.'

First thing through the door, Stan couldn't help but feel a little confused by the relative normality of it all. He wouldn't have been able to say exactly what he'd been expecting, but when Charlie had stared at him through the darkness on the common, answering emphatically *yes* to the name of Gypsy, and then with the moon coming out as they'd cycled over here, and it being Halloween night – it certainly hadn't been this. They were in a small living room decked out with bright orange Halloween bunting, and elaborately patterned china plates and cups and saucers. And there was the same spotty tablecloth as Helen had at home right there, the table laid out like something at a school fête, with bowls of crisps and sandwiches.

There was a kitchen off to one side, in which some people were gathered, voices and bustle evident through the doorway. Stan was distracted from all that though by the only person there in the main room, sat in the green armchair in the corner. He was a boy of about Stan's age, with light hair and a scattering of freckles across the bridge of his nose that made it look as if somehow, in spite of the English weather, he'd spent most of his life outside in the sun. A huge tabby cat was curled up and dozing in his lap, and he was holding a notepad – sketching something, it looked like. This boy looked up from his drawing as they entered the room, glancing over automatically, with no special interest, as if he were simply expecting people generally to be wandering through. His face lit up completely, though, the second he saw Charlie.

'Alright, mate,' said Charlie, going straight over to the boy and kneeling beside his chair. 'What's been happening? You all good?'

The giant orange cat stirred, and looked up to Charlie with sleepy, hooded eyes. Charlie backed away a bit, eyeing it suspiciously.

'Of course,' said the boy. 'Been drawing. This one's of the pepper pot, in Godalming town centre. What d'you reckon? Remember it?'

He sounded different from Charlie. No strange hybrid Manchester-inflected accent. He sounded to Stan like a farmer's son – and like he'd lived round here, or hereabouts, his whole life.

'Course I do,' Charlie said, bending over to look at the sketch. 'It's good, mate. Really good. Seriously.'

Stan sneaked a glance, too. Charlie was right. On the notepad was a perfect pencil drawing of Godalming's idiosyncratic old market building, the light and shadows falling in a way that somehow made it clear it was an early morning in spring.

The boy flushed, looked away, tried to hide a smile. 'Thanks,' he said. 'Though I'm not sure. Maybe it needs some people in it, or something. What d'you think? Except people are bloody hard though, to get right. I never know what they should be *doing*, you know? You can't have them standing there for no reason, but then . . .' He shrugged, trailed off, turned to Stan. 'Who's this, anyway?'

'My friend Stan,' Charlie said. 'Brought him down to see you, didn't I? Thought he'd have fun with Nan, anyway. Stan, my brother James.'

And he could see it, too, despite the different hair and the tracksuit Charlie wouldn't have been seen dead in. They had the same hazel eyes. Stan felt oddly formal, with that introduction, and though he'd never normally do this in any usual social situation he'd find himself in, he stepped forward to the boy – to Charlie's brother James. 'Nice to meet you,' he said, and he held out his hand for James to shake.

There was a horrible moment – probably only a few seconds, but it felt like an age – when he thought James might leave him hanging. But then, slowly, James stretched out his hand and shook Stan's.

'Alright,' said James. 'You too.'

And though he met Stan's eye with a nod then, and it was a good, firm handshake, he didn't get up. Not that Stan really cared at all about 'good manners', or anything like that. Helen was far too obsessed with all that kind of thing. But it did feel a little odd.

'Where d'you learn to draw like that?' asked Stan.

'Been teaching myself, mainly,' said James. 'I like the way it makes you see things differently.' He glanced between his brother and Stan, then, and bit his lip. 'How did you two get to be friends, then? D'you go to that boxing club in town? The one Charlie goes to?'

Stan shook his head, as Charlie said, 'Stan's not the fighting kind, are you, Stan?'

James laughed at that, a slight edge to the laugh that Stan didn't quite understand. 'That makes two of us, then, these days,' James said.

'Yeah,' Charlie said. 'I suppose it does.'

And then there was some commotion from over by the door to the kitchen.

'Oi, Stan,' Charlie was saying then, 'what you looking at? Stop gawking and come meet Nan.' And then Stan was being towed over to a woman who'd just stepped out of the kitchen – her hair a mass of black and grey, and her face and hands a map of wrinkles. His other main general impressions were that of many cardigans, and of her having precisely the same eyes as both Charlie and James.

'Alright, chavi? Who's this you brought to me, then?' she was asking Charlie. 'This a friend of yours?' She turned to Stan. 'Sastipe! So tutti's lav?'

'This is Stan, Nan,' Charlie said. 'He's my friend, from in town. He's a good lad though, you'll like him. Into stories and books and stuff. Just like you. Just like Mum.'

Stan couldn't help but feel a little surprised – Charlie, understanding another language. Charlie, whose main interests were bikes and cars and boxing and girls and who didn't even go to school.

She stood back a moment, sharp eyes looking Stan up and down. And Stan knew he should smile or offer a handshake or even just say hello – but he found he couldn't move, couldn't speak somehow, under this woman's gaze. What if Charlie was completely wrong, and this was all a big mistake, his coming here? And what had they all been talking about earlier, outside, when the little boy had said something about Charlie not being meant to bring him here, for some reason, when he'd mentioned somebody called Martin? Then though, her assessment apparently complete, Charlie's Nan's face cracked into a smile.

'Stories and books, you say?' she said. 'Dordi. Well, good luck to you. I'm always telling this one here to pay more attention to that kind of thing. Perhaps we'll both get through to him.'

Her name was Susanna, and she spoke quickly and with an accent that, like James's, was pure rural south of England – no trace of Charlie's Manchester at all. She led Stan and Charlie into the kitchen then, where four girls, all clearly older than Stan, fell silent and stared the moment they stepped in.

'Charlie,' hissed one of them, a tall girl with hair that fell in a dark curtain over her shoulders. 'You know Martin's about tonight, don't you?'

But Susanna shook her head at that, and Charlie laughed and chatted and teased in the way that he did, and eventually everyone seemed to loosen up, turning to Stan, asking him all sorts of questions.

'So how d'you get to be friends with this loser, then?'

'D'you actually like Halloween, or did he persuade you it was something worth doing?'

'This the first time you've met any Travellers? It is, isn't it? It's as clear as day on your face.'

'Is it like what you expected? Are we like what you expected?'

'You're not meant to be here, really, you know. Charlie shouldn't have brought you, but he never does what he's told, does he . . .'

'D'you want a biscuit? There are loads here, come on.'

'Kekker, all of you.' This from Susanna. 'He's just got here, we don't want to scare him.'

'Ah, Stan doesn't scare that easily – do you, Stan?'

'But he shouldn't be here, Nan. You know that. He's a Gorjer. And Martin said—'

'You can't just be listening to Martin all your life' – Susanna's voice was final, firm – 'or you'd never do anything. Charlie did just right in bringing his friend here to visit and that's all I have to say about it.'

'How old are you?' This from the smallest girl. She had a long dark plait down her back, and something about the quietly amused look on her face made Stan like her immediately.

'I'm thirteen,' he said.

'I'm thirteen, too,' she said. 'I'm Cindy.'

'I'm Stan,' he said.

'I know,' she said. 'My cousin just told us.'

'So he did,' said Stan. And then before he really knew what was happening Charlie was hustling him out of the kitchen and back into the main room, towards the table with the sandwiches and crisps.

'I'm starving,' Charlie was saying, grabbing a handful of the crisps. 'Come on, Stan, you must be, too.'

Stan reached out and took a sandwich just as Susanna appeared beside them again and said, 'Good. Now you can help me with the little ones. Help them pick their costumes from the box.'

And so he and Charlie sat on the sofa like a kind of theatre audience as little Sarah and the others who had met them on the drive rummaged in a big wooden box of old hats, necklaces, scarves, waistcoats and gloves. Stan gathered that they were somehow all members of Charlie's family. How strange it must be to have such a big family. He could hardly imagine it, it was so different to his own, with just him and Helen, now. And Gran, of course, whenever they went to visit, though that wasn't too often these days, for some reason. Gran with her doilies and her incomprehensible television serials. He tried to picture Gran meeting Susanna, the two of them doing something simple, like shopping, or walking a dog . . . but then Gran hated dogs, and he couldn't, just couldn't imagine the two of them together somehow. Frankly it was difficult to picture Gran just being out of the house. Had he ever seen her out of the house? She was always in the armchair whenever they went to visit her, and she rarely got up, only sometimes to go to the kitchen or bathroom, and then anyway if it was the kitchen Helen would glare at him, give him evils for not springing to his feet instantly, and saying something like, *don't get up, Gran, I'll make the tea.* Susanna was so different, flitting between the girls in the kitchen and them in the living room, laughing her loud, sparkling laugh at one of the little boys – David, his name was, or Davey, as everyone seemed to call him – walking around in a flat cap so big it fell over his eyes.

'Look at him,' Charlie was saying. 'He'll be a man soon.'

Everything seemed unfamiliar to Stan, but everything seemed good, too. All Stan's worries, even fears, in coming here, and all those initial awkward moments, the suspicious looks, and the talk of 'Martin', whoever he might be, finally vanished. And yet as Charlie slouched back into the sofa, slurping tea and making pronouncements on the various sartorial disasters and hilarities of the little ones – *No, Sarah, you look just like a frog. And who wants to look like a frog? Exactly. Nobody. Nobody wants to look like a frog* – Stan couldn't help his eyes drifting, with increasing regularity, over to the armchair in the corner of the room, where Charlie's brother sat on his own, slightly removed from all the hubbub and laughter, still just sketching and stroking the cat. Should he go over and say something? Try and get him more involved? But surely that was Charlie's job, or Susanna's? Anyone else's responsibility, really, but his? He barely knew James, hardly knew anything about him at all, couldn't even say for sure if James would want to come over and join in all the commotion. Still, he did know how rubbish that felt – sitting off to one side of other people's fun. Then James glanced up and caught him staring, and Stan glanced away, lightning speed, not even giving himself time to shrug, or grin.

Sarah had picked up the puppy now, and was tying a scarf round its neck, much to the distaste of little Davey. Stan could sympathise, Davey was right, the dog did look stupid like that, or *like a bloody lapdog*, as Davey put it. The puppy had big feet. Probably that meant it would grow soon.

There was a clock on the wall but Stan didn't look at it, and as he milled around with Charlie, and as the room filled up with more and more people it became increasingly easy to avoid noticing it. There was always some more pressing distraction, people wandering in and out and having cups of tea and Charlie introducing them all to Stan, each meeting a double-take, a sharp look up and down, a confused glance at Charlie, and then more often than not a handshake for Stan, and a grin. Then Charlie's mum appeared, and her face – so much the spit of Charlie's it was almost funny – broke into a smile the second Charlie introduced him.

'I'm very glad to meet you,' she said. 'Charlie talks about you. You're clever, he says. I'm Rose, by the way.'

And Charlie . . . he seemed so at home here, slipping into that language, the one they were always speaking, listening to Susanna's pronouncements and anecdotes, calling *sastipe!* or *lachho dives!* or *alright mush, how're you keeping?* to anyone who came in through the door – and sipping tea, for godssake. Stan had never dreamed someone like Charlie could do something so utterly tame as drink tea.

And then there was Charlie's cousin Cindy again, with her long plait and her wise smile, and it seemed Charlie must have wandered off somewhere, because suddenly it was Cindy who was next to Stan, carrying with her somehow an atmosphere of quietness, as if it were only the two of them somewhere peaceful, not in the middle of this hectic living room at all.

'Where d'you go to school?' she was asking him. 'I go to Eastpoint.'

'You go to school?' Stan asked.

'Of course,' she said. 'But you go to a different school, don't you? Somewhere across town.'

'Charlie doesn't go to school,' said Stan.

'Charlie's older,' said Cindy. 'And don't get me wrong – Susanna and Rose did want him to go, they really, really wanted it, in spite of what Martin and everyone was saying – but Charlie's . . . difficult.' She was watching him now, across the room, as he leaned on the mantelpiece, deep in conversation with an older man – quick words being exchanged, both of them frowning. How much a conversation, how much an argument?

'Difficult?' said Stan. 'How d'you mean?'

'Well,' said Cindy, turning her hazel eyes back on Stan once again. 'Only that he never wants to fall in, or be a part of anything. Not school or anything like that. Not even us, here, sometimes. He's alright now, like tonight. Like . . . he's always game for a chat and a bit of fun, but ever since he got back from Manchester it's as if he doesn't like us, any more, all the time. Or some part of him doesn't, anyway. He talks strangely now, for one thing. He never used to talk like that.'

'I've noticed that,' said Stan.

'That he's changed the way he talks?'

'No, just that – wait. So he never sounded northern before?' said Stan. 'I did notice how none of the rest of you do. You don't, for instance.'

'No, I don't,' she said, and sighed. 'He misses his dad, probably. And then he blames himself, too – or my mum thinks anyway – for what happened with James.'

She shook her head, then looked up, over towards the doorway to where someone new had just arrived. A tall man with heavy boots and a youngish face, though his dark hair was already threaded through with grey. And he wasn't just tall either – from his build and the way he stood he looked impossibly strong, as if whole worlds could be set down on his shoulders and he wouldn't even blink. There was an evaluating, proprietorial look about him as his eyes swept the room, and Stan couldn't help but notice that most people there acknowledged him immediately, nodding him greetings, clapping him on the arm or the shoulder. Stan checked back to where Charlie had been standing, over by the mantelpiece, but he'd disappeared. Glancing around the room then, Stan just caught sight of him heading back into the kitchen.

'That's Martin Evans,' Cindy said to Stan, nodding at the man who'd just arrived. She was keeping her tone low, though there were so many other voices ringing out in the room there was little chance of them being overheard. 'Everyone complains about him being too strict, but I think he's alright really. It's only because he's trying to look after everyone, that he has all his rules. But he and Charlie . . . well. As I said, Charlie's difficult.'

Just then, Susanna emerged from the kitchen and began moving through the room with speed and purpose. It soon became apparent, Stan noticed with mounting nervousness, that she was making a beeline straight for him. Arriving next to him though, she seemed all relaxed, all casual cheerfulness.

'Alright, chavi,' she said, raising her eyebrows at him a little. 'You having a nice night?'

'Yes, thanks,' Stan said. 'It's lovely. All of it.' Stan looked round for Cindy then, but she wasn't there any more, must have gone off somewhere while he wasn't paying attention.

Susanna smiled. 'I'm glad you think so,' she said. And then her eyes shifted to somewhere up and behind Stan, and he turned to see Martin Evans right there behind him.

'Who's this, then?' Martin said to Susanna, eyes flicking down to Stan, eyes which close up now Stan could see were the colour of granite, the colour of rock.

'Friend of your nephew's,' Susanna said. 'And he's very welcome, might I add.'

'Will I be able to guess which nephew?' Martin said.

'Don't start,' said Susanna. 'It's Halloween. Just let them be boys, Martin. They need to have friends.'

'They're boys all the time,' Martin said. 'That's the problem.'

He gave Stan a sharp look before moving off through the crowd, over to James. Stan watched James reach up to greet him, and Martin's brow furrow deeper as he grasped James's shoulder, frowning at the sketchpad on his knees.

Stan didn't get a chance for ages to ask Cindy what she'd meant, when she'd said about Charlie blaming himself for something that had happened with James. Not until after he'd drunk another cup of tea from Susanna, after he and Charlie had re-enacted the fight with Huxley and Johnny in the pub for the benefit of Charlie's older cousins – with certain edits and exaggerations – and after he'd gone over and tried to talk to James, but not done very well at it.

'Charlie never mentioned you before,' James had said.

'Yeah, well he never mentioned you either,' Stan had replied, too quick, without really thinking.

He'd stepped out of the caravan for a bit of air and quiet, and for a look at the night sky – a little cloudy, but with fast-moving cloud, so that the moon was never covered up for long – when he noticed her at the bottom of the close, a small figure holding a bowl of water. He watched as she set it down on the ground and whistled.

He wandered up. 'Cindy,' he said, when he was near, so as not to frighten her – she still jumped though, looking up at him in an almost guilty way.

'Stan?' she said.

'What you doing?' he asked.

'Just some water,' she said.

The shaggy grey dog and another two appeared then out of the dark, trotting up towards her in answer to her whistle. Cindy nuzzled and then stroked all three as they jostled to drink from the bowl of water, nudging each other's noses out of the way. Then she gave Stan a long, calculating stare. At last, apparently judging him to be trustworthy, she reached into her jacket pocket and produced a huge handful of sandwiches, obviously taken from the food table inside. He watched as she tore them into little pieces, hand-feeding them to the dogs.

'I know I shouldn't,' she said. 'But it doesn't seem fair we should get to celebrate with all these treats and things, while they get nothing.'

Stan couldn't help smiling at that. 'I completely agree,' he told her.

'You do?'

'Of course.'

He watched until she'd worked her way through the whole clump of sandwiches, and the dogs were sniffing again at the bowl of water.

'What did you mean earlier?' he asked then. 'When you said about Charlie? That he blamed himself for something to do with James?'

She nodded, slowly, and tucked a loose strand of hair behind an ear. 'It was an accident,' she said. 'It wasn't Charlie's fault. It was only the two of them in the field but plenty of people saw what happened from further away, from the road or from back at the farm. James drove a quad bike into a tree, and Charlie was there. That was all. And now Charlie can barely look at him. He can barely look at any of us. I thought it might get better with him going away for a while, up north. If anything though it's got worse.'

'How old was he?'

'Charlie?'

'No.'

'James?'

'Yeah.'

'Ten. I remember because I was ten, too.'

'And that's why he can't walk?'

She nodded. 'His spine was shattered, the doctor said.'

'Will he get better?' Stan asked.

Cindy bit her lip. 'If you have hope you have everything, my mum says.'

Then, without saying anything about it, as if it were the most natural, casual thing in the world, she took hold of his hand, and led him back through the dark to Susanna's caravan.

And of course Charlie was outside, smoking a cigarette.

He frowned when he saw them together like that, and instinctively Stan snatched his hand away from Cindy's.

'Alright there, Stan, making yourself at home, I see.'

'Shut up it's not like that,' said Stan, in a rush.

'It's alright, I'm only messing,' said Charlie, clapping him on the shoulder again. He finished the cigarette, dropped the butt and ground it out with his heel.

'Charlie,' Cindy said, smile gone, her voice different now. Less self-assured.

'What?' said Charlie. And then, 'Jesus Christ, mate. It's not like I'm going to tell. Just – you watch yourself a bit, is all. Be careful.'

When they stepped back into the caravan the mood was quieter than it had been before, Davey and Sarah were asleep, propping each other up on the sofa, the puppy dozing at their feet, and the conversation amongst the men at the mantelpiece was now reduced to mostly mutterings and mur- murings, noises and nods of affirmation or light objection. The women were still chatting around the kitchen doorway, but their talk was softer now too, less frenetic.

Stan took a moment then to look round at this family gathering. All these people, talking together in one room, with no television serials or awkwardness in sight. Or no awkwardness, that is, that was immediately obvious, but then again, there was James still in his armchair, though it was angled round now to face into the room, and he'd put away the sketchpad and pencils. He was watching Charlie, though Charlie didn't seem to notice – or affected not to notice, in any case.

Stan let himself be led by Charlie to a free patch of floor by the table where they sat down, Charlie raising his eyebrows at Stan, Stan looking round to find Cindy and seeing they'd left her by the door – before noticing the clock again, and reading the time to find that unbelievably, unsettlingly, it was well past half nine.

Stan swore under his breath. 'I have to go,' he hissed at Charlie. 'Bloody hell, it's almost ten.'

'And what happens at ten?' Charlie said, too relaxed for the seriousness of the situation. 'You turn into a pumpkin, do you? The lovely ball gown turns to rags?'

'Charlie, it's not funny, my mum'll be raging. I didn't even tell her I was going out tonight.'

'But it's Halloween. She'll know you're out having fun.'

Stan shook his head. 'My mum doesn't work like that.'

'Yeah but she won't be *raging*. Didn't you say she was always too tired to care about anything properly?'

'Hey that's not – I never said – I don't know. But she's a weird one, Charlie. This'll be trouble, honestly.'

Charlie turned to look at him properly. 'Come on, mate,' he said. 'Look at yourself. You can't let this be the way you run your life. You're your own man. If you're off having a nice time somewhere you're off having a nice time somewhere. You don't have to answer to anyone.'

'It's not like that, though.'

'Then what is it like?'

'She's my mum, Charlie. I don't know. I can't explain. She's all on her own.'

Charlie shrugged, started unloading rolling papers and tobacco from his pockets, laying them out on the table. 'Fair enough,' he said.

'Charlie,' said Stan.

'It's just,' said Charlie, 'I don't get it. It's like you're always going home because she's in charge of you, and not because you ever actually want to. And, well, y'know. No one should be in charge of you. I listen to my mum when she's got decent stuff to say, not because she gave birth to me. And I don't listen to half of this lot here, certainly wouldn't do as they say just because they're family. Because I reckon it's not – that it shouldn't work like that, family . . .' But here he glanced away, and went back to fiddling with his tobacco and papers, seemingly about to let whatever he'd been saying tail off. And though Stan had to leave, and no time was soon enough considering he should have been home hours ago, he found himself really wanting to know how Charlie would finish his sentence.

'Family?' said Stan.

'What?' said Charlie.

'You were saying – about to say. Something about, about what you reckon about family.'

And suddenly Charlie seemed sheepish. He kept on messing with the stuff on the table, rolling a second cigarette now, though he already had a perfect one there, lined up next to the packets of Rizla and filters and the pouch of tobacco.

'Nothing important,' he said. 'I don't know.' He glanced around. 'And it's probably an unpopular idea around here and all but I just think, maybe, that blood ties aren't everything. Or no, that's – not quite what I mean. What I mean is, I think you have to earn them, and keep on earning them. That people have to keep doing right by people. Keep making them laugh, keep helping them out, all that. That's what I think. That it's not enough, just being family.'

Stan nodded. 'Maybe,' he said. 'I'll think about it. But right now I really have to go.'

'Oh come on,' said Charlie. 'Can't you think about it here?'

'Naw, mate, I'm in enough trouble already.'

'So what's another while going to cost you? I mean, if you'll have a nightmare with your mum whenever you go back, you may as well just leave when you want.'

Stan frowned. 'You know, mate, I'm really not sure it works like that.'

'Oh come on, Stan,' Charlie said then. 'Don't go now. It'll be no fun round here without you.'

Stan laughed. 'Now that's a lie,' he said, standing up from the spot where they were sitting on the floor. 'It'll be loads of fun. I'll catch you tomorrow, okay?'

And he only felt flattered by Charlie's attempts to get him to stay until he'd made it through the throng of people to the door, and was turning to take one last glance into the room before stepping out, back into the night. And there was Charlie, the only one not talking to anyone, staring down at the table, and rolling yet another cigarette. His shoulders were hunched and his hair falling into his face in such a way that reminded Stan, somehow, of the way he himself sometimes felt on the school bus, trying to hide in plain sight. It was a strange thing to witness – even slightly confusing, after everything else he'd seen that evening, the warmth and chatter and hilarity, the slipping from English into that other language it was they all spoke, and how at home Charlie had seemed to him in amongst it all.

Stan's eyes drifted from him to take in the rest of the room – the gossiping cousins by the kitchen door, the older women with their cups of tea on the sofa, the sleeping children, the men at the mantelpiece with their glasses of whiskey. That was when he noticed it wasn't only Charlie who wasn't talking to anybody, because there was James of course, still in his armchair. He was occasionally nodding at the things people around him were saying, but really he was still staring right at Charlie – watching his brother, who seemed unaware of the fact, reluctant as he was to look up.

But then there was the clock again, showing almost ten to ten. Stan tried to imagine what Helen might say when he got back, and found he simply couldn't. He'd never done anything like this before, never gone out all night without telling her. And then where would he say he'd been, even? He'd have to make something up on the way home.

He dragged his eyes away from the room, away from everyone still talking, Charlie still rolling his endless ciga-rettes, and James still watching, going to pick up his bike from where he'd left it resting against the caravan outside, next to James's wheelchair. He was taking a hold of the handlebars, cursing himself for not changing down gears properly when he'd pulled in and come to a stop, when he noticed something coming towards him, out of the dark. At first he thought it was a fox, but then he saw it was the same grey dog who'd greeted them when they'd first arrived at the site, and then who'd been among the trio Cindy was feeding, with her torn-up bits of secret sandwiches. What had Charlie said its name was? Benji. That was it. Stan held out the hand that wasn't holding his bike and Benji nuzzled into it.

'Hello,' he said, copying the way he'd seen Charlie scratch his ears when they'd first arrived. 'Hello, Benji.'

Cycling home down the dark almost-countryside roads, he completely forgot to think of any excuses for Helen. He kept coming back instead to what Charlie had said before he'd left – that thing about family, about always having to earn it. And he thought about Helen, and then about Dad, of course, and Gran, and then about Charlie and James. He wondered whether Charlie had even believed what he'd said, and, given what Cindy had told him about what had happened between the two brothers, what it would mean for him if he had.

# 9

It must have been at least ten by the time Stan turned on to the Eastern Road, approaching the house – and he could see right away something was up. All the lights were on, for one thing. And though Helen was off night shifts that only meant she'd be asleep by now, usually. She was always going to bed so early, these days. On the sofa and yawning by nine, in pyjamas and brushing her teeth by half past, lights off and tucked up in bed with magazines shortly after. The lights were even on in the window of the little room upstairs, the room which had once been a spare room for when guests came to stay, but which, in the last year or so, seemed to have organically transformed into a place where Stan and Helen left things they didn't want or couldn't face fixing – a broken Hoover, an old shelving unit, a football with a puncture, a coat stand, some cake tins, a radio with dead batteries. Neither of them ever went in there, except to deposit whichever item it was they wanted to put out of sight, and close the door.

Stan stopped pedalling, slowing as he approached. The continually broken street light meant it wasn't until he was almost right outside that he saw the long gluey streaks all down the front door and windows, and the eggshells on the paving in front of the house.

He wheeled his bike up to the front door and fitted his key in the lock as quietly as he could. Just to leave his bike in its usual spot in the hall, slip off his shoes, grab a glass of water from the kitchen and be upstairs in his room with the door shut – that was all he wished for. That, and for whatever fuss and noise that was waiting dormant in the house, clear as if he were approaching a dragon's lair, postponed until tomorrow.

He turned the key and swung open the door to hear Helen's voice instantly, as if he'd caught her mid-sentence.

'Stanley,' she was saying. 'Stanley, is that you?'

He propped his bike against the wall in the hallway and headed towards the main room. His footsteps sounded inappropriately loud, and the brightness of the harsh lights everywhere felt officious after the evening warmth of Susanna's caravan, and then the dark of the quiet, leafy roads home.

'Stanley?' Helen's voice called again. 'Answer me, Stanley, please. Is that you?'

'Yeah it's me, Mum,' Stan sighed. 'What's up, what's wrong? Why've you turned on all the lights?'

She wasn't in her usual spot on the sofa. She was in her dressing gown, all hunched up, sitting halfway up the stairs. And he knew it was awful of him to think it but she looked so wrecked – so tired-looking, no make-up, the bags under her eyes accentuated by the harsh lighting. And why was she on the stairs like that? Couldn't she have got dressed and sat in a chair like a normal person? It seemed calculated, Stan couldn't help but think, for a certain kind of dramatic effect. A deliberate move to make what he'd done seem like something cruel, something he'd inflicted upon her, when really it was nothing worse than anything any of the other teenagers in this town might have done tonight. Not the sort of thing Charlie's family, for instance, would have cared two pins about, as people said. Not the sort of thing most other people would see as a problem at all. Everything about her posture though made it look as if he'd somehow forced her to get out of bed and sit there like that, waiting for him. Made it look as if him going out and learning something new about the world had been entirely calculated to hurt her.

And something about the feeling of that – the pointed-ness of the waiting on the stairs to confront him the second he came in – made him not want to ask about the broken eggs all over the front of the house, not want to ask how it had happened and offer to help clean it up, and instead say, 'What? What is it?'

'I thought something had happened,' she said. 'Stanley, love. Come up here where I can see you. Where were you? I was so worried.'

'Why are all the lights on?' Stan said, not moving from where he was, in the hall. 'Is there someone else here?'

'No,' she said. 'No one else. Just us.' She tugged at the old dressing gown she was wearing, pulling it tighter around her shoulders. 'Some boys were here, though,' she said then. 'Outside. They knew you, Stanley. They knew you lived here. They threw eggs. They threw eggs at the house. They fright-ened me. And you weren't here, Stanley. I was the only one here.'

'They knew me?' Stan swallowed, feeling the last of the warmth left over from the visit to Charlie's family ebb away. 'How d'you know that?'

'They were shouting for you,' she said. 'Shouting and yelling. They frightened me.'

'What did they look like?' he asked.

She only shook her head.

'Mum? Are you even listening to me? Did you see what they looked like?'

'They had balaclavas on. I couldn't see.'

'How many of them were there, then?'

'Only two,' she said. 'From what I could see, from the window. But there could have been more. I couldn't see very well, Stanley, love, just from peeking over the window sill.'

'What?' he said then, unable to keep the sharpness from his voice.

'There could easily have been more than two,' she said. 'I couldn't see that well from where I was looking, from—'

'Over the window sill?'

'Yes,' she said. 'What? What is it, Stanley?'

'They were egging the house, Mum. Chucking dozens of eggs from what it looks like. Throwing them right at the house and shouting and wearing balaclavas, and you sat here doing nothing about it? You sat here *hiding*?'

'I was frightened, love. They frightened me.'

And Stan knew he wasn't being fair now. He knew this wasn't why he'd come home, or how this was supposed to go. He knew, too, that this wasn't looking after his mum, as he'd promised all of those people at the funeral that he would without thinking at all about what it meant, and yet still the words kept coming. All the rage that should have been directed at Huxley, at Johnny – since that's surely who it had been, egging the house this evening – all the anger at himself and his own inability to stand up to them, to just get it together and do as Charlie would do, for instance, or as Dad would have done, and stand his ground, it all came pouring out of him.

'Mum, they're boys. They're kids. Couldn't you have opened the window and yelled at them or something? Told them off? Told them to go away? Or even just said I wasn't here?'

'Stanley . . .' She edged back up a stair then, her dressing gown catching on her heel and falling open to reveal a pair of faded teddy-bear pyjamas.

'Why couldn't you do something?' he was shouting at her now, fully waking-the-neighbours yelling. 'Why couldn't you make them go away?'

But she only shook her head, and whispered, 'I know, I'm sorry, sweetheart.' And then, gathering her dressing gown tightly round herself again, she scrambled up the stairs and into her room, shutting the door firmly behind her, shutting him out.

He didn't know what to do after that. He tried sitting on the sofa but felt too restless. He tried going into the kitchen but was too impatient to stand and wait for the kettle to boil and he didn't want more tea now anyway – he'd drunk so much tea with Charlie's family that it would feel sad somehow, to make himself a cup like this after everything and sit by himself, alone, drinking it here. He clicked off the kettle and went round the house, turning off the lights. Why had Helen turned them all on in the first place? As some kind of childish show of defiance, after the fact of being threatened? Surely she wasn't afraid of the dark?

Flicking the switch on the wall in the upstairs corridor, plunging everything back into the soothing gloom of night-time in the suburbs, Stan found himself gazing out the window above the stairs, watching the dancing shadow of a treetop in the wind while trying to picture what Charlie might be up to now, and the rest of Charlie's family. Whether they would all still be awake, still celebrating. If Charlie and James would be talking together now, all the awkwardness between them forgotten as they laughed over some old joke. If Cindy was wondering where he'd gone. He hadn't really had a chance to say goodbye.

And then he found himself picturing, too, what it might have been like for Helen, sitting there hiding on the stairs, huddled up beneath the window-ledge. Had he learned it from her, then, this reticence, this inability to stand up and say no to people taking what wasn't theirs? Somehow he'd always imagined that if she saw what happened at school with Huxley and the others she'd be ashamed of him, and embarrassed. That she'd get on at him, even, for not speaking up, and not making himself heard, same as when he was too quiet at the kitchen table, or if they were chatting over the noise of the telly. He'd assumed, now he thought about it, that her lack of commentary on his missing glasses, his bruised skin, his torn, graffitied clothes, had all been down to disappointment in him, for not fighting back. He'd never dreamed though that when faced with exactly the same bullies his mum, Helen, an adult, would be just as unable as he always was to do anything about it.

Still watching that shadow of the swaying treetop outside, but sitting in the dark now, on the stairs, just where she'd been sitting, it was as if he could still hear the way he'd yelled at her, ringing in the space around him, and, worse than that, as if he could still feel the disgust that had driven those words hanging over him now, an unwelcome shadow. It should have had no place here, with either of them, that feeling. It had been given to him by Huxley, he knew, and instead of resisting it he'd let it get the better of him and take over, let it turn him into a bully, even, when God knows that was the last thing in this world that he wanted to be. Charlie would never have lashed out like that. Charlie would have been stronger.

'Nae pasaran,' Stan whispered to himself then, and for the first time saying those words he felt strange and uncomfortable, maybe even ashamed, realising just how far short he'd fallen of the person he wanted to be.

# 10

The next day was Saturday, and raining. Helen wasn't up as she usually was by the time Stan was leaving for his paper round. The door of her room stayed shut, with only silence beyond. He had no idea whether or not she needed to be at work. Maybe he should knock on her door in case she was sleeping, maybe he should shout something through – *Mum, I'm going to work now, I'll be back later* – something neutral like that, not acknowledging last night in any way. Or maybe he should say sorry. He stared at the door for a minute before deciding not to bother. That door spoke volumes. Whatever he might want to tell her, she didn't want to hear it.

Outside, he saw the rain had washed the worst of the egg streaks from the front of the house and crushed the mess of shells into even smaller pieces. It was almost like it had never happened, as if Huxley and Johnny had never even been there. No one would even have to clean up the mess they'd left behind. To think they'd managed to cause all of this anger, all of this misery, when really they were that insubstantial, so easily erased.

*

Hours later, the whole slog of a paper round later, in fact, everything in life felt fun and warm and good again, as Stan and Charlie sat on the kerb outside the chip shop, laughing over the *Newford Echo* headlines wrapped around their chips. *Councillors will lose pints over late rubbish collection, furious pub landlord says.*

It was still raining, hadn't dreamed of stopping today. The sun hadn't even seemed to come up. Still though, in a way, that only made the chips taste better, and life feel all at once more cosy and more intrepid as Stan tightened the cords around the hood of his rain jacket and ate fast, shovelling the hot food in as he shivered, feeling it heat him up from the inside out.

'Fuckers,' Charlie was saying. 'We're going to get them back, Stan. We've really got to. People can't be allowed to get away with shit like this. If you let them, honestly, then the whole world is fucked—'

'Hang on,' said Stan, through a mouthful of batter. 'What you talking about, the world? This is just me. If I don't get them back I'm fucked. Or I'm pathetic, at least. What's the world got to do with it?'

'It's the principle, Stan. All these little things we can't let go without a fight because if we do it means they're okay – that it's okay for thugs like them to come and tell us we're not welcome here.'

'We? Sorry, mate, but it's me they're after. That they've always been after.'

'It isn't, though.'

'What?'

'What did you say that kid called you at school? The little one.'

'Pikey?'

Charlie shuddered, pulling a face under his hood. 'Yes, that.'

'What – what does it mean, Charlie?'

'What does it mean?' Charlie glanced at him a moment, with an expression of complete surprise. 'You've not heard that word before?'

'Not . . . not really. I suppose I've heard people say it before sometimes, but I've never really known – like I never thought it was something that bad . . .'

'That bad?' Charlie's voice had an edge to it now. 'It's a term of racist abuse, is what it is. No debate about it. Pikey, gyppo. Hate-filled, racist words, mate. And people in this country just bandy them about all the time without thinking, without even knowing, sometimes, I think, the hatred that they're spreading. Not that that could be said for that lad from your school. He means what he's saying, I'm pretty sure. Has he ever come to your house before? Ever done anything to get you outside of school?'

'Not really. Only the other day at the pub.'

'Right. Yeah. See? At the pub with me. It's both of us they're trying to mess with, Stan. It's just that out of the two of us, they know where you live.'

Stan considered this as he chewed, watching the reflections of the passing cars' brake lights flash by in the puddles. 'I'm sorry, Charlie,' he said. 'I'm sorry I got you dragged into all this.'

Charlie laughed, without sounding particularly cheerful. 'Not your fault. This isn't new to me, you know. It's not the first time I've dealt with racists. And these lot aren't the worst, either, by any means.'

'Was it any better though, up in Manchester? In a bigger city?'

'I dunno,' said Charlie. 'It was different.' And then, reading off his fish-and-chip paper – '*Merrow vicar's protests at séance woman's success.* Certainly never saw a headline like that, up in Manchester.'

Stan laughed, despite himself. 'Who's the vicar?'

'No idea,' said Charlie. 'Got vinegar on the rest of it, haven't I?' He sighed and sat back, wiped his fingers on his jeans and looked out at the road. 'I don't know,' he said. 'I'm starting to kind of like Newford. I keep finding more cool things about it.'

'You're joking,' said Stan.

'No,' Charlie shook his head, raindrops trailing down the side of his hood. 'I read, for instance, a thing the other day about what people used to do, just over the way in Guildford, on Guy Fawkes night, all throughout Victorian times and up until the 1920s, apparently. The Guy Riots, people called it. Every fifth of November – so next Wednesday, being my reckoning for this year, right? – people would put on masks and just like . . . fucking . . . *maraud*. Or not maraud, that's not quite it. What I mean is that they'd go to the houses or to the buildings of the businesses of anyone who'd wronged them in that year, and wreak havoc. Smash things, wreck things, whatever. And because of the masks, and because it was some kind of fucked-up, yearly tradition, they got away with it. They got away with *decades* of this, Stan, no one even arrested. For one night of the year, a free pass to get revenge. The Guildford Guys, they called themselves. The downtrodden and ill-used. One night every year when they could be on top of the world.'

'Yeah or just thugs in masks. Like what happened at my house yesterday.'

'Yeah, mate, but that's not the *story* though, is it? Where's the romance in that? You hadn't wronged them. They'd wronged you, and were up to more of the same.'

Stan tightened the strings on his hood and tried not to think about his mum, now, getting caught up in this whole situation with Huxley. Tried not to think about the reach of the whirlpool drag of the whole nightmare getting wider, sucking in more and more people.

'Why d'you love this stuff so much?' he asked Charlie then, hoping to change the subject.

'What? Getting back at nasty people?' said Charlie.

'No, the weird local history stuff. I used to think it was because you'd moved around so much, like you found all this stuff out to feel at home in places, or something. I under-stood it, when I thought it was that. But then seeing all of that yesterday, Charlie. Your family are much more from Surrey than mine are. And you've got more of a home, and more of a place to be from, than I have.'

Charlie scrunched up his empty newspaper wrappings and stared at them, balled up in his fist.

'Maybe,' he said. 'Or maybe everybody feels that, or something like it. That everyone else has more of a place to be from.'

'I suppose,' said Stan.

'Although I don't know. It's not . . .' Charlie chucked his fish-and-chip paper under the wheels of the passing traffic. 'I think it's that Mum always taught me to be interested. To keep my eyes open wherever I am, keep reading, keep studying, even though I chucked school. Though don't go getting too interested in my family, anyway. You're *my* friend, remember?'

Stan laughed. 'Come on, mate, don't be daft,' he said. 'You sound like we're in nursery school.'

'I'm not joking,' Charlie said, though he was laughing now, too. 'Seriously, mate. Tread carefully.'

*

It was late when Stan got home that evening, or much later anyway than he usually got back on Saturdays. Helen was up now, curled on the sofa in robe and slippers. Stan felt a stab of guilt, seeing her like that, yesterday's argument seeming suddenly so fresh again now he was home. He wondered if she'd got dressed that day at all.

'Stanley, love, can we talk?' she said. Her voice was so quiet, so tentative that he could barely hear her from the corridor, propping his bike against the wall. He opened his mouth to reply and then closed it again without speaking. In his heart of hearts he knew how unkind he'd been, and he wasn't honestly sure he could face a conversation about it. Still, he went into the living room, where he hovered by the sofa without sitting down.

'What is it?' he asked her.

'It's just . . . is everything alright, Stanley, love? I know I haven't been—' She broke off, looked away, pinched the bridge of her nose and then started again. 'I know it's no excuse, but it's been so hard, this last year, Stanley.' And she looked as if she wanted to say more, but her words faltered into silence.

Stan nodded. 'Yeah, Mum. I know. I know it has. And' – he took a deep breath – 'I'm sorry. For last night. I didn't mean it. I didn't mean what I said.'

Helen bit her lip. 'Who were they, though, Stanley?' she

asked. 'I mean, you're not . . . you're not in any kind of trouble, are you?'

'No. No, Mum. Of course not. It's fine. I'm fine.'

She shuffled herself round on the sofa, to face him more fully. 'I just feel like things have changed so much with you, sweetheart. That I don't know what's going on with you any more at all. Where do you go, every day after school? Who are you with? You're not with those boys, the ones who were here yesterday, are you?'

'No, of course not.' Stan found himself feeling irritated again at the suggestion.

'But you do know who they were?'

He nodded. 'Yeah.'

'Tell me, Stanley, please?'

'For God's sake, Mum, I don't have to tell you everything, do I? They're just some kids from school. Honestly, don't make such a big deal out of it. It's fine.' He turned and crossed the room, heading for the bottom of the stairs.

'Stanley, you never talk to me any more. I am trying, Stanley, really.'

'I know, Mum,' he said, barely looking at her now, swinging his way round the bannister and off up the stairs. 'I'm sorry.'

'Don't you want something to eat? Won't you be hungry?'

'I'm fine, Mum,' he called back. And even if he hadn't eaten already he wouldn't have gone down again. It was awful being around her, suddenly. The air in the house so heavy, everything weighted down and paralysed by so much guilt, sadness and regret.

# 11

Stan spent most of the next day, Sunday, on his own, out on the common or simply wandering about town, looking in Waterstones and Newford's two record shops, wondering whether to spend his paper round money now or save it until there was something he actually needed. Town was busier already with early Christmas shoppers filling the streets. Never something Stan had to worry about, with only Helen to buy for – and Gran sometimes, too, on the years when they went to visit her on Boxing Day.

Maybe he'd get something for Charlie. That might be weird of him, though, and he wouldn't want to freak Charlie out or anything. Then something occurred to him, something strange and new and different. He could get something for Cindy. Nothing too big, or too fancy. Just something tiny, casual. Something he could slip into his pocket, so that he could stroll up to her the next time he saw her, the next time he went to visit Charlie, and say – *Oh hey, I've got something for you. Just made me think of you, is all.* But what could that something be? Flowers were the obvious choice but then who knew when Charlie would next invite him to his family's place? Flowers were unreliable – they wilted, they died. Maybe the whole thing was stupid.

He determined to wait and to think some more about it, and left town going home via the chippy, cycling with the paper bag on his handlebars until he was at the common, the light fading even though it couldn't have been much past four o'clock. No rabbits in sight now, anywhere. Did rabbits hibernate? Who honestly knew? Charlie probably would. Had he been serious, when he'd said that thing, about not getting too interested in his family? Surely not. Charlie was hardly ever *really* serious. He'd only been teasing. Probably he'd been thinking about Cindy.

Rooks flew in dark clouds overhead and Stan laid his bike down in the grass and sat with his back against a tree – oak, he could tell from the leaves. Leaves that were still up there, still hanging on though curled and brown, as if someone had gone through and singed each one with a lighter.

*Seagull menace disgrace to town, local business owner says*, the *Newford Echo* told him as he worked his way through the bag of chips – still hot, miraculously. Or not *miraculously*, he'd cycled fast, but still it *felt* miraculous, the hot food in contrast with the cold air on his cheeks. Food always tasted so much better eaten outside, why was that? And did Charlie's family eat outside, sometimes? Probably the way they lived they did it every night, in summer. Maybe in winter sometimes too, like he was doing now, except with a fire lit – a big bonfire they'd all sit round and talk over, the glow lighting up people's faces and embers dancing like fire fairies for children to chase and catch. He could almost imagine he was sitting there now, at the fireside with all of them. Davey and Sarah and the rest of the little cousins all running around at the edge of the flames, sparks of light dancing around them, and Susanna boiling a kettle and he,

Stan, sitting there watching it all – maybe a snoozing Benji in his lap, and Cindy next to him. Cindy. Well why not? Charlie had only been teasing, surely. After all, he'd always said Stan should meet some girls, hadn't he?

The moon came out and the sun fell behind the treetops, leaving a last line of red that faded all too quickly as the rooks wheeled overhead. And for the first time, Stan found himself really thinking properly about what Charlie had said to him, when they'd first met on the common. *It means they were common land, you know? That they still are, to some extent at least. So this place belongs to us, just as much as it belongs to anyone.*

Was that why he kept coming back here? Why he always felt calm here, more at home here now even than he did when he was actually at home? Because though he'd never really thought of it before, everything in this town and all around it – probably more widely, probably everything in the whole of England, the whole of Britain, even further – everything was someone else's. It was all *owned*, the land they walked on, cycled over, built houses on, whatever. It was always someone's, and anyone else who was there was there on sufferance, being put up with, tolerated, invited on to someone else's territory. Never just simply *there*, without having to answer to anybody, or justify their presence. Not – he thought now, as he looked up at the sky, at the rooks – not like the birds. They were free, he realised, in a way he'd never understood properly before. Sure he'd always imagined the feeling of flying, of zooming like that, to be the feeling of freedom, but it had never occurred to him that being free of the ground and its territories meant freedom in any greater sense than that of just lightness and flight.

It mightn't seem like such a vast realisation, or one that mattered much in practice, but Stan stayed out there on the common far longer than strictly advisable, given the cold – which was intense, now, the night being so clear – trying to get his head around it. But then again, he was maybe also putting off the moment when he'd have to go back to the house, a little. His refusal to stay and speak to Helen last night, and his getting up this morning and leaving before she was awake would only have made the atmosphere between them worse.

He'd never really wished for siblings before, had always thought the idea stupid, whenever anyone asked him about it. It was so huge a thing, after all, that to wish for siblings would be for him to wish not to be himself, to have grown into a different person. But for once, now, he dearly wished he had someone else in his family, someone a little older, maybe, who he could talk to properly about everything. Someone who'd try to understand, who he could talk to about Dad without all the complicated cycles of confusion and blame he always seemed to get trapped in every time he spoke to Helen these days. Someone who'd have time to listen, and just to spend time with him, and stand outside this bank of cloud that seemed to have engulfed him and Helen somehow.

It would be easier, though, from tomorrow. She'd be going back on nights, and then they wouldn't really have to see each other at all, if he simply refused to let her pick him up after school and then stayed out until she'd gone to work. It would be fine, from tomorrow. Almost like living alone.

# 12

'Cindy? Who's that? Your pikey girlfriend?'

Huxley Edwards's bony hands appeared on the desk, either side of the piece of notepaper Stan was writing on.

Fucksake. Of course he shouldn't have written this at school but then he didn't really feel comfortable writing it in the toxic soup of home now, either – and he'd thought he would be safe, coming back to the maths classroom like this after lunch when Huxley and the others were usually out in the playground raising hell and nicking food from anyone who wouldn't cross them by refusing. What was he doing here? And why couldn't Stan be allowed just five minutes on his own? Huxley was getting to be like a wasp in summer if you were eating something with jam, or like a nasty cold you couldn't shake.

'Don't call her that,' said Stan, not looking up, keeping writing, though he could feel his hand start to shake as he did – but why was his hand shaking? He wasn't afraid, was he? For God's sake why was he afraid? What could Huxley do to him that he couldn't do to Huxley? Thinking of Helen – a grown woman hiding beneath the window sill and turning on all the lights – he forced himself to keep writing, and to keep staring down at the page.

*I've never met someone like you before*, he wrote. *When we were together it felt like* – Stan paused in his writing a second, and thought – *it felt like when the lights go down in a cinema. When everything's quiet before the start of a film.*

'Oi, Stanley,' Huxley's voice, too close now, just above his bent head. 'Look at me when I'm talking to you.'

*I know we didn't talk much*, Stan wrote. *So I don't blame you if you think this is strange* – then he paused, and crossed that last part out. No apologies, Charlie always said. *I know we didn't talk much . . . but I'd like to see you again*, the sentence read now – but then Huxley's hand was there, slamming against the paper, just where Stan's pen was about to continue the sentence. Don't look up. Don't be pathetic and let him make you a victim. Stan lifted his pen and started writing again, on the other side of Huxley's hand. It would ruin the look of the writing but he'd have to make another clean copy of this anyway, what with that last crossing-out. Now it was about the principle of the thing, as Charlie would say. About keeping writing, about not letting Huxley win.

*Maybe for a walk somewhere*, he wrote. *Though I suppose that would have to be on a weekend, since it gets so dark so early these days. But have you been to Goshawk Common? I like it down there, and Charlie does too—*

Huxley grabbed the top edge of the paper as Stan planted his hands down on the other side, catching it before Huxley could whip it away from him. It tore right across the middle – right through the '*dark so early these days*'.

'Cindy,' Huxley said. 'I knew it. She is your pikey girlfriend, they've all got names like that, that pikey lot. Better watch you don't catch something. I've heard they start their girls early, if you know what I mean.'

Stan finally looked up at him, got a small kind of satisfaction from the way Huxley seemed to look genuinely angry and not like he was enjoying himself, as he usually did when he was taunting Stan, as if it were a kind of sport.

'What did you say?' said Stan, trying to keep his voice as quiet as possible. 'Say that again.'

'You heard me,' said Huxley. 'Just a piece of friendly advice. Though the thought of it, Stanley, I will admit, does make me feel a little sick. A peasant like you getting with any girl, never mind one of those pikeys.'

'What did you call me?'

'*What did you say? What did you call me?* You're all questions today, aren't you, Stanley Gower?'

These were low blows. Things Stan knew were rubbish. Just so much crap to get a rise out of him. He took a long, slow breath, and then looked down, away from Huxley, back to the piece of paper, now half-torn on the desk in front of him.

*Though I'm not sure what difference that makes actually as Charlie won't be there*, he continued the sentence. *Unless you'd like him to be, of course. We could all go for a walk—*

'Stanley,' Huxley was saying. 'Pay attention when I'm speaking to you. Stanley.'

*Though that wasn't what I was asking, really—*

But then he didn't know what was happening – only noise and shock and sudden agony, Huxley having slammed him face down into the desk. He took a second just sprawled there, eyes shut, letting the sharp pain around the bridge of his nose fade into a slightly more manageable ache. Then he pushed himself up to a sitting position, still not looking at Huxley, picked up his pen and turned back to the letter.

The torn-off sheet was covered in blood now. He realised his face was wet, and put a hand up to his nose to find it was bleeding. He couldn't even feel the touch of his fingers on the bridge of it, that whole part of his face was both throbbing and numb, and then holding the pen it was clear he was shaking again – from the shock of it probably, because he wasn't afraid, or ashamed, or contrite, or whatever it was Huxley wanted him to be. He made himself grip the pen harder to try to stop trembling so much.

'My brother is still waiting,' Huxley said, 'for an apology. From you and from your pikey friend. And believe me it'll be far worse than just some eggs next time, Stanley. I can make your life hell.'

*I was wondering why you held my hand like that, outside the caravan in the moonlight. And if—*

Then pain bloomed again, as with a ringing in his ears he was face down on the desk again, nose bleeding freely, Huxley having slammed him down a second time. Stan's fingers went limp and he felt the pen slip from his grasp.

'You haven't heard the end of this,' Huxley said, leaving now, thank God – halfway through the door as Stan crawled himself back up to sitting in time to see Huxley there, tucking Stan's pen – fucksake that was a nice pen and one of the only ones he could write with without smudging, being left-handed as he was – into his top pocket. 'Not you, not your filthy gyppo mates.'

Stan made himself keep sitting straight and composed for a good ten seconds after the door had shut behind Huxley. Then he was all franticness, searching in his pockets for a tissue to stem the flow of blood from his nose before it ruined his only blazer and his last good shirt completely. And it hurt, of course it hurt, it was agony in fact – but he couldn't help but feel a little bit proud that he'd not given in. *You've got to stick up for yourself Stan*, Charlie had told him. *You can't just let people take what they want. Never let them tell you where you do and don't belong.* Well, he wasn't a push-over. Not any more. His mum had been right about that – he *had* changed. And about fucking time, too.

The half that was left of his letter was still in front of him on the desk, the torn-off edge now soaked through with blood so that none of the words, really, were legible. He'd have to start all over again. He couldn't even really remember what he'd said, or what he'd wanted to say.

Except – could he just go and see her, maybe? Because fuck it, why not? Why did he need to wait for an invitation from Charlie? Charlie didn't own Cindy. Stan knew where she lived, after all, and he was his own man. He'd buy some flowers, that's what he'd do. Or no, he'd *pick* some flowers, from whomsoever's garden he pleased, because though it was late in the season there'd surely still be plenty of good things blooming in the cultivated front gardens of Newford's sub-urbs. He could make it revenge, even, on the nastiest resident or most vicious dog of his paper round. Then he'd go and see her, flowers in hand, and say his piece in person. In fact, he decided, he'd go next Wednesday night, when Charlie would be at the boxing gym, and so not around to laugh at him, or complain.

# 13

Wednesday took forever to arrive, Tuesday dragging by like a whole day of double maths, Stan finding it difficult even to enjoy the evening cycling round the common with Charlie, watching the stars come out. And then he was so agitated by the time Wednesday afternoon finally arrived that he could barely pay attention to the cars on the way home, people blasting horns as he flew by on his bike, an old man yelling at him from the pavement to *watch out* and *be careful*. He couldn't work out if he was frightened or excited. The way his brain chose to interpret the whirling feeling in his stomach and his chest seemed to vary with every gust of wind, every flicker of the setting sun through the now almost bare branches, every click of a gear change on his bicycle.

Reaching the house at last, he dashed in through the front door, ignored Helen, who was clattering around in the kitchen getting herself ready for work, and went straight up to his room, where he swapped his school uniform for jeans and a jumper. Then he flew down the stairs again, grabbing his bike and just yelling, 'Out!' to Helen's half-hearted call of, 'Stanley? Where are you off to, Stanley?'

He hoped Charlie wouldn't be angry. Maybe he wouldn't think anything of it, dropping in to say hi being just a natural thing, something that could be done without all this adrenaline and anticipation, easily, spontaneously. *I was passing*, he'd say, as if it were the most ordinary thing in the world.

In the end he didn't have the nerve to nick flowers from people's front gardens. He'd have felt too exposed while doing it, and anyway there were so few flowers left now it was November it felt mean to tear up the last survivors. He stopped his bike for a second instead to grab a handful of blue things he really hoped weren't weeds from a grass verge, then cycled on through the deepening dark, towards the site.

Like last time, little Sarah was the first to notice him arrive, as if she stood watching there at the bottom of the close all day, like a welcoming committee, or a guard.

'Mum,' she called back over her shoulder, as she ran up to approach him. 'Rose,' she called. 'That Gorjer boy akai. Charlie's friend. You know – the little one, with the squinty eyes.'

'Sorry, what?' said Stan.

'Where's Charlie?' said Sarah.

Stan shook his head. 'Sorry,' he said. 'Only me.'

'Oh,' said Sarah, and then lowered her eyes, looking nervous now all of a sudden.

'Who's this?' asked Stan, gesturing to the little dog trotting up to him from where it had been dozing at her feet. He reached to stroke its head.

'Careful,' said Sarah. 'She's Luna. She was sick when you were here before but now she's better.'

'Oh,' said Stan, lowering his hand, not stroking Luna after all. 'I'm glad to hear it.'

And then Charlie's mum was hurrying up, smoothing her skirt and rolling down her sleeves. Stan noticed a slightly pinched, worried look on her face, and he couldn't help but start to wonder if he'd done the wrong thing, intruding like this.

'Stan,' she said, 'isn't it? Have you got Charlie with you?'

Stan shook his head.

'Never mind,' she said.

'Sorry,' Stan said, quickly. 'Hi, Rose.'

But Charlie's mum didn't invite him in, or anything – she simply stood watching him, looking rushed, and confused. Stan swallowed, looked down at his handful of flowers, which, thinking about it now, he was almost sure were technically weeds. So much for picking flowers outside in November. He probably should just give this all up for lost now, as a stupid idea. It took a monumental effort to collect himself, and to keep talking, keep holding his head high.

'I came – I came to see Cindy.'

Rose treated him to a long stare. 'You seem like a nice boy,' she said, at last. 'But you'll only cause Cindy trouble if you start coming round here looking for her.'

'Trouble?' said Stan. 'No, no. I don't want to cause trouble. Not at all.'

Rose glanced over her shoulder, then back at Stan.

'I know,' she said. 'I can see you don't mean any harm. It's only that there's some others around here who—'

'I don't understand,' said Stan, panicking a little now, and so embarrassed. Wondering if he should simply turn around and leave. 'It's just flowers.'

But then there was a sound of bike wheels on the path behind him and—

'Oi, Stan!' Charlie's strange half-*Coronation Street*, half-something-else accent rang out. 'What you doing, mate?'

'Charlie. But you're meant to be—'

'He came to see your cousin,' said Rose.

Charlie pulled up, braked, and stared at the handful of maybe-flowers, maybe-weeds still bunched in Stan's fist, seeming so awkward now. More incriminating than triumphant.

'Is that right?' he said.

'Yeah,' said Stan. 'Though, though I didn't mean anything by it, Charlie. It was just a stupid whim. I'm sorry.'

Charlie frowned. 'It's what I keep saying to you, Stan. Don't apologise all the time. Don't apologise for stuff that's not your fault.'

'Oh he's alright,' said Rose. 'You leave him alone. He obviously meant no harm by it, Charlie. Anyone could see. She's a pretty girl, your cousin. You can't blame him for it.'

'I'm not,' said Charlie. 'I don't.'

'I thought you'd be at boxing,' Stan said to Charlie, as they followed Charlie's mum who seemed much calmer now Charlie was back, much more like she'd been on the night Stan had first met her. She'd snatched away the flowers, tucking them unobtrusively under the lapel of her coat and the folds of her scarf.

'Boxing? Not tonight, mate. It's fireworks for me. I would have asked you, you know, mate. I would have asked if you wanted to be here, anyway. I was looking for you there, out on the common. Thought you might want to come along.'

'Sorry,' said Stan.

'No apologising,' said Charlie. 'I was even going to ask if you fancied some Guy Rioting. You know, doing our bit to carry on the old Surrey tradition,' he clapped Stan on the shoulder. 'Avenge your broken nose an' all.'

'It's not broken,' said Stan.

They paused, as Charlie's mum ahead of them stopped to reassure a young woman who'd come out to meet her, and seemed worried, or uncertain about something.

'Seriously though, Stan,' Charlie said then, voice low and strangely serious. 'Why didn't you tell me you were coming?'

'I was worried you'd laugh at me,' said Stan, all in a rush.

'Laugh at you?' Charlie looked confused, even saddened by the idea. 'For this?' he said. 'Never.'

# 14

There was fighting, that night. But not fighting like the bully-ing Stan saw at school. Fighting, it seemed, for sport. He sat at the side of the bonfire next to Charlie and James watching boys, some even younger than he was from the looks of it, squaring up to each other, fists up, eyes locked. He stared as they danced on their toes and threw hard punches, shirts off and no gloves or anything to cushion the blows.

'No holding,' Charlie called. 'No kicking,' he said, falling in with the chorus of the other boys and men around them, as the littler of the two fighters caught the shoulders of his opponent and held on to them, pinning his arms to his sides and going for his shins.

'Fair play,' everyone called, 'break it up' – but the little one wouldn't let go. It was as if he was sick of being battered and was now determined to subdue and control his opponent by other means.

'That's enough, Will. You hear me? That's enough, I said,' a voice cut through the rest of the comments from the clutch of spectators by the fire. Martin Evans. Charlie's uncle. The one everyone had been so tentative around on Halloween. He'd appeared with so little warning, seemingly from nowhere. Stan shrank back a bit, away from the flames and into the shadows. Martin, though, didn't seem interested in him tonight, didn't even seem to notice him, his attention fully focused instead on the fight. Martin stepped forward, simply reached in, and dragged the small boy away, off the bigger one.

'Fair play, d'you hear me?' he was saying. 'When I say fair play, I mean fair play. No biting, no scratching, no holding, no fighting dirty. It's a fair fight that we're after here. Always a fair fight. Now on you go.'

The larger boy was instantly back in control, with a blow straight to the smaller one's jaw, and then another to the solar plexus.

'Will he not be hurt?' said Stan to Charlie.

'Not if he defends himself properly,' said Charlie, eyes narrow, fixed on the fight. 'Go on, Will,' he called out. 'Fists up, straight down the middle.'

Charlie's voice seemed to help the boy a little. He straightened up and he put up his fists, and though from the looks of things he was exhausted, sweat dripping off him in the firelight, barely able to hold up his arms, he followed Charlie's advice and drove forward, landing two respectable blows before doubling over, his arms folded over his visibly heaving stomach, spitting into the embers by the side of the flames as the bigger boy regained complete control and came at him, fists swinging, battering his bowed head and hunched shoulders.

'Right,' said Martin, stepping up again, now seemingly the accepted master of ceremonies, the designated referee. The bigger boy stopped punching at the sound of his voice and fell back, out of breath, eyes wide and gazing up at Martin, looking suddenly very young. Martin turned, though, to the little one – Will. 'William Welch,' he said, dead serious, it seemed, in a way that frightened Stan a little. 'What's this, then? You want your dad to be proud of you, don't you? And you give up this easily?'

Then, contrary to all Stan's expectations of what would happen next, little William somehow straightened up, though he was shaking, and raised his fists again. 'I haven't,' he said. 'I haven't given up.'

And then Martin's face – apparently so furious a moment ago – broke into a smile. He clapped William on the back. 'Good,' he said. 'Good man. But you've had enough, it's obvious. Levi wins.'

Some low-level cheering from Charlie and the other boys. James stayed quiet though, a strange expression on his features, as he watched the older boy, Levi, soaking in the praise and the warmth of the hands landing on his shoulders as he shook the sweat from his hair, looking proud, barely a day over twelve but a fighter.

The call soon started up for another bout, for two more young hopefuls to step up and show what they were made of. One of Charlie's cousins Stan recognised from the last time he was here got to his feet, stripped off his shirt, flexed his fingers, circled his wrists.

'Come on, Charlie,' someone said. 'Let's see it – let's see the two of you have a go.'

But Charlie stayed down, cross-legged on the ground in between Stan and James, halfway through rolling a cigarette, as always, and shaking his head, all good-natured refusal – just as if he'd been offered a plate of biscuits or something.

'Nah,' he was saying. 'You know I stopped with the bare-knuckle and all . . .'

'Come on,' Martin was saying now, voice and stance still easy, relaxed, as if he were joking or teasing but his eyes a little sharper on Charlie now. 'Let's see what that place in town has been teaching you then.'

'He's worried it'll mess up his hair,' James called out then. 'Or that he'll embarrass himself in front of his new Gorjer friend. Look at him. I'm right, aren't I? I know I'm right.'

'Jesus, James,' said Charlie. 'That's hardly fair. I'm just watching myself, you know.' He grinned. 'Got to be more careful using my strength these days, haven't I? Now I know I can beat up Martin, if I want to.'

That got some laughs and some shouts and an, 'Alright, you cheeky fuck,' from Martin. 'So that's what they're teaching you in town, then. How to be arrogant, and lazy. On your feet, Charlie. Let's see what you've got.' He nodded then to one of Charlie's older cousins, who grabbed him by the arm, trying to pull him up.

Charlie managed to stay seated, but dropped his tobacco. 'Hey, watch it,' he said, still being jostled as he scrabbled on the ground for it. 'I was just taking the piss, I don't do that any more, you know that. James is the fighting man in the family now, not me—' Charlie froze, as soon as the words were out of his mouth. He'd been in the midst of reaching around on the ground for his dropped tobacco, and so Stan couldn't see his face then, in the shadows. He could see James's though, with the obvious hurt and betrayal splashed across it.

'Jesus,' Charlie said. 'Sorry. I meant – I don't know what I meant. Christ. You'll be alright, mate. You'll be alright.' He reached up and patted the side of James's wheelchair so awkwardly that Stan didn't know how James could bear it. Somehow he did, though, and then Charlie was turning away from him and back towards Stan, forced joviality all over his face.

'What about you, Stan? You want to give it a go?'

This was greeted with general laughter and cheers, and the mood of the evening seemed back on track. People Stan hadn't even spoken to yet were slapping him on the back, maybe just a shade too keen to leave behind whatever it was that had just happened between Martin and the two brothers. And Stan noticed Martin watching him then, the only one not talking or smiling, just a steady gaze through the glow of the flames.

'Ah shit I was only joking,' Charlie was saying, laughing more convincingly now. 'Stan's never fought before in his life—'

And in amidst the melee of friends and cousins and uncles, all offering opinions and instructions on whether or not he should fight, and how he could best go about it if he did, Stan saw James reach out to Charlie and grasp his shoulder, and Charlie freeze, and touch his fingers to his brother's just for a second before shrugging him off, starting on rolling yet another cigarette.

It wasn't until later on that Stan finally saw Cindy, when Charlie and two of the girls from the kitchen last time were playing some music – Charlie doing surprisingly well on the spoons – and couples were dancing and children running everywhere and fireworks going off in the field.

'Rose said you tried to bring me flowers,' she said, sitting down next to him by the last of the fire.

'Yeah,' he said. 'But that didn't seem to go so well. They were pretty, anyway. Or at least I hope they were.'

'I know,' Cindy said, and she reached out for a second, lightly brushing his cheek. 'She gave them to me, you know. Though she told me not to tell you. Or tell anyone.'

'Cindy,' Stan said. 'Why would she say that?'

Cindy shrugged. 'It's difficult. A lot of people wouldn't like that you're not one of us.'

'How d'you mean, not one of us?' said Stan.

Cindy looked at him, wide-eyed. 'Surely you can see it?'

# 15

'Tell me where you're going,' said Helen, from the kitchen doorway. 'You're not leaving this house until you tell me where it is you always go, and who it is you're with.'

'Friends, Mum,' said Stan, lifting his bike, trying to manoeuvre it out the front door. 'What's it to you? A bunch of people. A bunch of different places.'

'Stanley,' said Helen. 'I never raised you this way. I never raised you to be unkind like this. I never raised you to be cruel.'

'You don't raise me to be anything,' said Stan. 'You're always out at work.'

'Stanley Gower, you know that isn't true . . .' Helen began.

But finally Stan had got his bike over the threshold. Stepping out into the rainy night he gave the front door a kick, and let it slam behind him. Then he hopped up on to his pedals and zoomed away, before she tried to follow him.

It had been like this all afternoon, ever since the car ride home from school. He'd got back late again last night after the bonfire with Charlie's family, but instead of trying to tell him off she'd merely stood up from where she'd been waiting on the stairs again, shaken her head, and shut herself away, inside her room. It was as if she'd been waiting for today to do all the telling-off, and to ask him all her questions. *Who was he with? Who were these friends?* It was almost, Stan thought, as if she were jealous.

He cycled to the common on the off chance, just to check and see if Charlie was there. Of course he wasn't though. It was a horrible night, and then all the bickering with Helen had made Stan so late that it was basically dark already – the trees skeletal etchings on an only slightly lighter background, the wind tearing through the open space, ruffling the grass. There was barely even any moonlight to brighten things up.

Stan shivered in his too-thin hoodie and flimsy, leaky canvas shoes. Charlie wouldn't be at the boxing club this late. He'd be at home, surely, where there was shelter and warmth and always cups of tea to drink. Stan couldn't go home, though. Not yet, not with Helen there. To go back so soon would be an admission of defeat, an unacceptable loss of face. He jumped back on to the pedals of his bike, cycled a little way back towards the road – then stopped, hesitating. Maybe this was stupid. Maybe he should wait to be invited instead of showing up again. There was Martin Evans to think about, after all. The way they all talked about him back at the site, and then that look he always gave Stan too, as if he were something out of place, needing to be fixed. And then Charlie himself hadn't exactly seemed keen on Stan dropping in. Although, then again, though it was true Charlie had been a bit weird about him showing up unannounced, that was because he'd gone there asking for Cindy, wasn't it? Surely it would be completely different if he turned up looking for Charlie? And then the whole of Charlie's family knew him now too, now that he'd spent two evenings with them. It wasn't as if he was a stranger any more, was it?

Stan climbed back on to the saddle and turned off the common, pedalling back on to the road to the site.

The roads tonight were a blurry mess of puddles and headlamps, and the strong wind kept blowing him towards unexpected bits of hedge or rubble that flashed into the glare of his lights with only fractions of seconds left to spare for him to avoid them. By the time he was approaching the site his shoulders were locked into a hunched rigor mortis of cold and stress, his hands aching and frozen round his handlebars, and his face dripping with rain. He almost began to hope Cindy wasn't home after all. He must look a mess.

He pulled into the drive without hesitation, too pleased to have finally arrived to think at all about to what extent this was really a good idea. A loud barking started up, Stan couldn't see where it was exactly. The dog must have been behind one of the caravans or just inside somewhere, because, come to think of it – where was everyone? It all looked awfully quiet tonight. Maybe they were all sheltering from the weather? There was no sign of little Sarah, even, coming out to see who had arrived.

Stan would have paid more attention to the nagging feeling of there being something different, maybe a little off, if he hadn't just then noticed the small group on the far end of the site, clustered around Susanna's doorway. There was Martin sitting on the steps in the rain. And there was one of Charlie's older cousins, Stan couldn't remember his name now, standing alongside, and then an older man with a beard and a belly and a loud, loud voice who Stan hadn't worked up the nerve to talk to yet. And then, Stan noticed, with a jolt – there was Charlie. Charlie who he hadn't recognised at first, but who was turning now at the noise of the dog and of Stan's bike, and then leaving the group and coming over towards him.

Why had he not seen that it was Charlie immediately? Maybe it was the dark. It was difficult, after all, to see anyone or anything in conditions like these. But also, Charlie looked different, maybe. Was dressed different. More grown-up, somehow. More like Martin, and the rest of the men in his family. Gone were the black skinny jeans, giant leather jacket and perennial sunglasses, and now here he was in proper shirt and trousers, a flat cap on his head and strong leather boots on his feet. Not only did he look more adult, like this, he also seemed less familiar, somehow. More fully part of the site, and the world of his family. As he came closer too, and the sliver of moon flashed out for a second from behind the clouds, a flicker of something shining, something gold, caught the light on his hand. Charlie, wearing a ring? None of this seemed right. Stan slowed down, instinctively. Stopped in the middle of the yard.

'Best not hang around here tonight, Stan,' said this new, different-looking version of his friend. 'Fucking toxic air, mate.'

Charlie looked over his shoulder at the clutch of men by the steps to the door of Susanna's.

Then, 'Come on,' he said, with a quick gesture off towards the road. 'Best get you out of here.'

Charlie crossed the site, picked up his bike, and then, signalling for Stan to follow, he rode off down the path and out the front entrance. Stan went after him with no more explanation than this, pedalling hard to try to keep up until they were further out from the town than Stan had ever cycled before, turning off down a dirt track into a field – dark and razored to stubble from the last harvest.

They carried on down the track at a pace, until the gate into the next field. Then Charlie braked sharply, still not looking at Stan, staring straight ahead, hands clenched hard around his handlebars. And for a second, Stan felt a little afraid.

'You're not going to ask?' said Charlie. 'Not going to ask me anything? What's happened? What's up? What's different?'

'Sorry,' said Stan.

'What have I told you,' said Charlie, 'about always saying fucking *sorry*.'

And suddenly, Stan almost felt as if he was going to cry. He bit his lips shut and told himself to stop it, to keep it together, to stop being so childish.

'That all you can say?' said Charlie. 'Have you got nothing else?'

'I don't know,' said Stan. 'Charlie, I don't – I don't understand. What's happened?'

'Ah,' said Charlie. 'Now we're getting somewhere.'

Stan shook himself. Forced his mind back into gear. Remembered where he'd seen the group of them – Charlie and the men, clustered at the door.

'Is it Susanna?' he said. 'Is she alright?'

'No, she's not alright,' said Charlie. 'And neither's anyone else, either. Or anything about this whole fucking country. None of it's *alright*, Stan.'

It was such a new thing, this feeling, this situation of Charlie of all people turning hostile. Stan was used to it by now from Helen and Huxley and all of Huxley's stupid friends and even from the teachers at school sometimes, but in spite of himself he'd started to rely on Charlie being different, and, he realised, he had completely lowered his guard. Stan turned away to hide the tears that were escaping now in spite of all his efforts, hopefully blending unobtrusively with the rain. He turned to stare out at the fields and the dark, dark sky as Charlie shut his eyes and took a breath.

'Fuck, I'm sorry. I'm – I didn't mean – I never mean – don't worry about it, Stan. I'm being a prick.'

Stan felt himself nod, though he didn't mean it as affirmation, exactly. 'Come on, Charlie, let's go,' he said. 'We probably shouldn't be up here, anyway.'

'What?' said Charlie. 'What did you say?'

'Let's go back,' said Stan. 'Why are we out here, anyway? It's raining. It's – I want to go back, Charlie.'

'No,' said Charlie. 'The reason you gave. The reason you gave for us going. What was it?'

'I said – I don't know,' said Stan. 'Charlie, you're being weird. What the hell does it matter exactly what I said, I was just . . . talking.'

'Exactly,' Charlie said. 'But that's just it though, isn't it? All the things people say when they're *just talking*. It's *just talking* that fuels all the bullshit assumptions driving everything.'

'Charlie what are you even saying? You've never been – you're never like this, Charlie. Please.'

'*We probably shouldn't be up here, anyway.* That's what you said, Stan. And whether or not you really meant it, that phrase, that assumption – it contains everything that's wrong, everything that's fucked about this whole sorry world, because it's not us that have the problem. It's not us that shouldn't be here. It's—' He broke off then and Stan looked back across the stubble of the cornfield, giving his friend a second to collect himself.

'I'm just sick,' said Charlie a moment later, 'of all these rules, these people telling you where you do and don't have a right to be. How can you say a man's born free when the whole of the world he's born into is already owned by someone else? He might be born free in some abstract, notional way, but what does that mean, Stan, when there's nowhere he can go, nowhere he can just simply *exist* that isn't governed already, that isn't trying to shut him out, move him on, or tell him what he should and shouldn't think – giving him *conditions* all the time? Conditions imposed upon his presence. Where in this world can you go where it's unconditional, Stan? Where the freedom you're technically born with actually means something – something more than just a mood, or a fucking technicality? Where is that, Stan? Tell me.'

Charlie seemed to be genuinely waiting for some kind of answer.

'I don't know,' was all Stan could say. 'Charlie, please stop. I don't understand what you're talking about. I don't know.'

'D'you know what happened yesterday, Stan? Why my nan fell down the steps out of her caravan this morning and is now in bed with a fever and her eyes closed, not talking to anyone, whether out of choice or because she physically can't no one can tell, though I wouldn't blame her, frankly, if it was choice?'

Stan shook his head. 'No,' he said. 'I'm sorry, Charlie. I'm sorry that your gran – that Susanna's . . .'

'Have you heard of a place called Firle, Stan?' said Charlie.

'What?' said Stan.

'Firle,' said Charlie again, as if the word was something nasty he'd bitten into by accident.

'No,' said Stan. 'Never heard of it.'

'Neither had I,' said Charlie. 'But it's not far from here, apparently – an hour or so south-east, Brighton way, where Nan's sister and her husband and her children and her children's bloody children – all these little kids, all the cousins – have been living for years, no trouble, getting on with their fucking lives. Except last night what did this stupid town do? This provincial fucking village?'

Stan shook his head.

'They burned a caravan,' Charlie said.

'What?' said Stan.

'Not a real one,' said Charlie, probably at the look on Stan's face. 'But it was bad enough. The people in this village, right, they built some fake fucking replica of one our caravans, they painted a family on the side of it, looking out from the windows – a mum and a dad and two little kids, Stan, they actually painted that on – then they torched the lot. Stuck it on some huge fucking bonfire and yelled stuff and cheered while it burned up to ash. My mum's cousin was there, with her boys. She'd taken them out to see the Fireworks Night stuff without knowing what it would be. Said she's never felt so frightened. All those people yelling, knocking back the pints, chanting *burn the pikeys* like some kind of fucking – I don't know. And her just there, in amongst the crowd with her kids, there for the fireworks like anyone else and she's thinking *no one here knows who I am – what*

*I am – but if they did . . .?*' Charlie shook his head. 'They painted children on the side of that caravan, Stan.'

'Jesus, Charlie. Where did you hear this?'

But Charlie seemed to have talked himself out. They watched the moon as it appeared from behind the clouds, then vanished again. Appeared, vanished.

'I'm sorry about Susanna,' said Stan, eventually. 'Will she – will she be okay?'

Charlie shrugged. More watching the moon. Appearing, vanishing. Appearing, vanishing.

'I'm sick of it,' he said, at last. 'I'm sick of it and I want to *do* something. Show people like that. Show the whole corrupt fucking world.'

'We should go back,' said Stan. 'You should be near Susanna.'

Charlie shook his head. 'I've been there all day,' he said. 'And James is with her, and I . . .' Moon appearing, disappearing, appearing, disappearing. The wind strong and the clouds fast and Stan so cold now, and soaked from the rain and not knowing what on earth to do or say and just feeling so far, far out of his depth.

'They're just bullies, Charlie. You can't let them get to you. You should go back, and look after Susanna.'

But a strange, fixed expression came over Charlie's face then. 'I've got an idea,' he said. 'I know something we could do.'

And then he was back up and away on his bike, zooming ahead up the dirt track, head down, shoulders hunched, pedalling with a will. His snap into this new decisiveness had been so quick it took Stan a moment to react, looking round himself at the dark and empty field and then at Charlie's bike's retreating backlight, only then realising just how much he didn't want to be left out here all alone in the cold and the dark – where, no matter what Charlie said, Stan knew they shouldn't be.

*

Charlie kept on going, cycling through the awful weather, past the common, past where Stan lived, and on into town, where Stan tried his best to draw up level with him a few times – to ask him where they were going, what Charlie was thinking and what the idea was – but Charlie kept pulling ahead, speeding up, switching gears, until they were all the way past the station, even. And on such a horrible night, too, when no one sane would want to be out in the weather and on a bike, when all anyone would want to do would be to make a cup of tea and sit somewhere warm and well lit, maybe with a good book or a sandwich or a decent CD on. Stan's hands and wrists and even his teeth were aching with the cold of it.

Except where could either of them go for any kind of comfort tonight? *Toxic air*, Charlie had said about the site that evening, and you could use the same words to describe Stan's house – or Helen's house – tonight, easy.

'Charlie,' Stan yelled eventually, using all the breath he had left in his lungs. 'Christ. You don't have to tell me where we're going, but why are we going so fast, at least? I'm fucking knackered.'

And Charlie finally slowed down, braked, pulled in by the kerb.

'People sometimes call my people that,' he said. 'Knackers. Because of the Irish lot. And the horses.'

'What? What d'you mean *your people*? Aren't we all just people, generally? You always said that, didn't you? That this stuff shouldn't matter? That we're all just people in the world and that should be that?'

'I don't know,' said Charlie. 'Maybe that was bullshit, who can say. But Stan, I need your help now, for a minute.'

'My help? Charlie, what can I do?'

'Tell me where they live. That prick who went for me in the pub and the one who smashed your nose and nicked your glasses.'

'What?'

'Where they live. C'mon, it's not like this town is a big fucking place, Stan. You must know where they live.'

And the thing was – Stan did know. Knew from his first week at St Reginald's when his social pariah status hadn't yet stuck and he'd been just another kid – admittedly the new kid who hadn't been with all of the rest of them at the St Reginald's prep school, the new kid with the second-hand school uniform that was obviously too large, purchased for growth . . . but still, he'd been invited, hadn't he? Along with the rest of the year he'd been invited to the start of school party at Huxley Edwards's massive house in Ashbury Down. He'd stood in the corner by the food table for an hour without talking to anyone, then browsed the bookshelves, found something called *Starlit Summer* and had gone upstairs to find a quiet room to read it in – which hadn't been too bad until Cerys Williams and Dean Wright from 8P had come and kicked him out, the two of them all over each other and laughing at the way he was tucked away up there, reading all on his own.

'Well?' said Charlie.

'I' – and for a split second Stan thought about lying to him, saying he had no idea at all where they lived, then – 'Up in Ashbury Down,' he said. 'Come on, follow me.'

# 16

It looked more of a mansion than a house. A huge giant thing with a garage and a vast drive out front, boasting a Land Rover and an Audi TT.

'Fuck,' Charlie whistled. 'Not bad. And how many people live here, d'you reckon?'

'Four,' said Stan. 'Huxley, his brother, both parents. Maybe five if they have a live-in maid.'

'A live-in maid?' said Charlie. 'You mean like a servant?'

'I suppose,' said Stan. 'Maybe we should leave. I think maybe this was a stupid idea.'

'Don't call my ideas stupid,' said Charlie, climbing off his bike and leaning it there against the front hedge. 'It's an excellent idea. And we're carrying on an age-old tradition, aren't we? Guy Riots. I bet these lot have never heard of it. I bet they've grown up in this corner of the world without knowing a thing about what happened in it before they came along. Without even thinking to ask.'

'Shouldn't we have masks?' said Stan. 'Wasn't that part of it? And it's not Guy Riots if it's not Guy Fawkes night.'

'One day late,' said Charlie. 'You're splitting hairs.'

Then with a grin that didn't reach the rest of his face or fill Stan with any confidence whatsoever, he stepped round the side of the hedge towards the house and out of view. Immediately the security light flashed on – glaring out, blurred by the rain and the fact of Stan's still not having glasses.

'Shit,' Stan whispered under his breath. 'Shit shit shit shit shit.'

He glanced the other way up the dark road. There was no one coming, just vast, dark houses, curtains drawn and front gardens artfully illuminated. Some of these places were more lavish than Huxley's, even, with conservatories and trees with swings on them and even something that looked like an observatory tower on one of them. There were iron gates with intercoms, lush hedges, clean pavements and vast, spreading trees. And still the road was completely deserted – no one around to know he'd ever even been here. He could just cycle away, abandon Charlie to whatever stupid madness he was planning, leave him to face the consequences.

'Charlie?' Stan called.

No answer. Only a clattering from the other side of the hedge and the sound of Charlie laughing. Then a crash – a bin falling heavily on its side, it sounded like, losing its lid, rolling on the concrete drive. And then more whoops and cackles from Charlie. The security light flashing on and off.

'For christssake, Stan, what the fuck are you so scared of? Come *on*.'

With one last glance up into the gloom of the silent road, Stan clambered off his bike, dumped it down by the kerb next to Charlie's, and stepped round the hedge. He was just in time to see Charlie flip over another bin – with gusto, dancing in the rubbish. And there was a whole lettuce, still in the store's plastic wrap, a loaf of Kingsmill that looked like it had barely been opened, a bunch of bananas that under the glare of the security light were spotted with black but still fine, still good, definitely not worth throwing away. *There are children out there not as lucky as you, Stanley, children out there who are starving.* That was what Helen always said, whenever he went to throw anything away. Charlie kicked over a third bin with an almighty clatter, a sound like dropping a drum kit out of an aeroplane, spilling more rubbish everywhere – three full giant bins, for four people? When was bin collection day in Ashbury Down? Did the Edwards family just keep forgetting to put their rubbish out on time, and keep missing it?

'Charlie,' he found himself hissing. 'Come on, that's enough now. Let's go.'

'Enough?' Charlie grinned. 'Mate,' he said. 'I'm just getting started.'

And then, quick and light as a cat in spite of the leather boots he was wearing today, Charlie was up on the bonnet of the Land Rover, the headlights and taillights flashing in the second of his feet making contact, stamping with his full weight on the roof and the alarm going off, so loud it was like a kick in the stomach to Stan, watching Charlie crouching down now, keys in hand, scratching a deep line through the paint with a horrible sound like when the can opener was broken and you had to try and get into the beans with a bread knife. But fuck fuck fuck fuck they'd gone and done it now. Huxley's dad would be here, and Johnny and Huxley and even the police, of course the fucking police. And then remembering the way that bouncer had been at the pub, the way he'd let Johnny off with just a walk round the block and told Charlie to never come back, well, Stan couldn't trust that being caught by the authorities with Charlie would bring anything good. But now Charlie was standing up, seemingly relaxed as anything, hands in pockets. He was still on the roof of the car like it was a stage or something, and he was laughing, saying something now to Stan. It took a second to decipher what on earth it was, over the relentless scream of the alarm.

'Stan – Stan. They're out, Stan. The house is ours.'

And while a little bit of him was thinking *neighbours, police cars, what the hell would Helen say* – the rest of him followed Charlie as he leapt off the car and onwards, approaching the house. And then Charlie was turning back and coming over to him, clapping a hand on his shoulder, and suddenly he was laughing too as Charlie ran off ahead again, laughing first with a kind of appalled hysteria and then in simple luxuriant abandon – because Charlie was pissing in a flowerpot. And not just in any flowerpot, but in Huxley Edwards's flowerpot, in Johnny Edwards's flowerpot, in their stupid, smug, wasteful parents' flowerpot – in the biggest, grandest-looking flowerpot, for that matter, amongst the array on the drive. He cackled at the triumphal banner of steaming, stinking yellow piss arcing out through the cold and the rain and the dark into that stone pot as tall as a two-year-old and twice as wide, bursting with ferns and with vast white flowers Stan couldn't even begin to name.

'Just watering the flowers, Stan,' Charlie was saying. 'Just seeing to the garden a bit. Really I'm doing them a favour, they won't have to water them for weeks, now.'

And then Stan was struck by an idea. Cindy. These flowers all around them now were way better than those ones he'd given her. In amidst the scream of the alarm and Charlie's whoops and a *hey Stan, mate, watch out if you don't want to get pissed on* he was on his knees by the lesser flowerpots, hoodie sleeves rolled up to the elbows, trying to see in the strange-coloured flashes of light from the car what colours the flowers were, which ones she might like, which ones here were really beautiful as opposed to merely ornamental. Charlie was cackling again.

'What the fuck you doing, mate? You gone mental? Picking flowers? Honestly only you, Stan, would come here just to pick the flowers.'

And then Stan had his cold hands round their wet stems and was yanking them up from the soil, roots and all, earth spilling out everywhere and working its way into the spaces under his nails – and suddenly he felt incredible, stronger and breathing easier than he had done in weeks, months, even, certainly since he'd started at St Reginald's. It was that same kind of joyous feeling of deep-flowing health that comes in the moments after being copiously sick – that same release, the full discovery of just how good it could feel to be a human being in a human body, outside and alive *right here*, this November evening *right now*.

Then Charlie was behind him, hands landing heavy on his shoulders.

'What you doing?' he was saying. 'Leave that. We haven't got time.'

And then Charlie was over at the apple tree by the front door, jumping up, catching and holding on to its lowest branch, swinging with the toes of his boots just brushing the floor, hauling himself sideways in the air, walking his feet up the trunk like it was some kind of vertical footpath leading up to the sky and then . . . *shit*. The sound of splintering wood cut though the wail of the alarm as with a frothing, tossing chaos of leaves Charlie landed back on the concrete

– landed on his feet, somehow, back on the drive, apples and bits of broken branch and bracken and foliage tangled and scattered all around him.

'Shit, you're bleeding. Christ. Are you okay?'

But Charlie was still grinning, wiping away blood from the cut just above his left eye with the heel of his hand.

'It's no good, mate,' he was saying. 'I'm too heavy. You'll have to do it.'

'Do what?' Stan was saying and yet, even as he was asking, still dumping the flowers down on the concrete and rushing over to Charlie, over to the tree – ready, so ready, to do whatever he could to be of service.

'That one,' Charlie was saying, pointing to a branch slightly higher than the one he'd gone for, though not by much. It looked hardly any stronger at all, maybe even a bit spindlier.

'Come on, I'll boost you up.' Charlie had untangled himself from the fallen branch already and was next to Stan, hands out, fingers linked together into a cradle.

'Come *on*,' he was saying, not grinning or laughing any more. 'Some nosy neighbour will work up the nerve to investigate soon. This has to be *quick* – a quick operation. You'll be fine, I promise. I'll spot you from down here.'

'But what . . . ?'

'The windows – the windows, Stan. Smash those goddamn windows.'

And he saw what Charlie meant, what he was after. While the ground-floor, first-floor and second-floor windows of Huxley's house were relatively normal – square, modest, basically unremarkable – the roof the house, just above the apple tree, boasted two irritatingly large and fancy-looking circular windows – stained glass, both of them, and with all these colourful, elaborate patterns. They sat spaced apart amid the tiles almost as if they were the house's eyes. It was those windows, surely. Charlie wanted to smash those windows. Practically works of art, Stan could see, and a much bigger act of vandalism than simply knocking over some bins or keying a car.

'Alright,' he said.

And almost without thinking about it, he went back to where the flowerpots were and picked up one of the large ornamental rocks lining the path. Then he was back at Charlie's side and before he knew really what was happening his right foot was in Charlie's hands, and he was being propelled upwards into the tree. His left foot flailed out, instinctively, searching for the next step in the air that obviously wouldn't be there as he stretched up with the hand that wasn't still gripping the rock, reaching for the branch.

'Fucking hell, mate, you're so light. Need to get you going to the gym more, after this,' Charlie was saying.

But Stan had no interest any more in *after this*. He got the branch, grasped it and pulled himself up until somehow he was clambering up, scrambling until he was crouched on it. And he didn't even care about the scratches from the bark on his hands, or the leaves and the twigs making a mess of his hair. Though the branch bent beneath his weight, still it *held*, and the rock was still in his hand, the windows still gleaming above him. And now he was edging along back towards the trunk, and manoeuvring himself up one-handed, to the next branch higher up.

'Yes, Stan, yes!' From Charlie on the drive below.

And he was nearly there, nearly at the first stained-glass window. Just one more branch up would do it. He stretched again, pushing his way through the leaves. More scratching and tangling and some last late apples – tiny, they'd hardly be worth picking at all – shaken off, landing below with surprising audible heaviness. He must be quite high up now, for them to sound like that. And then a moment of teetering balance – *Fuck, watch yourself, watch yourself, mate* – and he'd done it! There it was, so close now, the first window with its huge, swirled mosaic of blue and green and red coloured panes. He could hear Charlie cackling again.

'Go on. Fucking do it, mate. Fucking do it.'

But the tree was further away from the glass than it had looked from the ground, and as Stan hefted the rock it was clear to him he'd never be able to do it – never be able to throw it up and quite that far, weak as his arms were, small and young as he was . . . oh but fuck that, *fuck* coming so far and then giving up, for no reason other than being weak and young. Before Stan quite knew what he was doing he'd scrambled all the way out to the narrow end of the branch, and stepped one foot out, on to the guttering of the house.

Both branch and guttering bent underneath him, but it seemed as if the weight was balanced, or Charlie was right and he really was abnormally light. Because by some miracle, both held. And then there he was – a rock in his hand and Huxley Edwards's stupid lavish window right above him – or Huxley Edwards's dad's window, as it probably technically was, but how much did that matter, honestly?

He was definitely close enough now that he could easily do it if he wanted to. And of course he wanted to – Charlie wanted him to, and aside from that *he* wanted it, Stan wanted it, because fuck Huxley and fuck being scared, and, 'Come on,' Charlie was saying from below on the ground. 'Stan, we can't hang around for much longer.'

Except what was that though? Through the window, what Stan could just see now in spite of his bad eyes and the kaleidoscope effect of the stained glass? Stan craned forward as far as he possibly could, standing like this, half in the guttering, half in the tree, and then flinched back at what he saw – at *who* he saw through the glass.

'Stan, Christ, what the fuck d'you think you're doing?' Charlie yelled, below.

Except, looking again, having caught both his balance and his breath, Stan saw it wasn't Huxley's dad at all there in the room, as he'd first thought it was. Gripping the flimsy branch above him for support, fingers tightening in the foliage, twigs sharp on the soft skin of his palm, he stretched up, as far towards the window as he could without losing his balance, standing on his toes now.

'Fuck, Stan, what are you waiting for? We've got to leave. We got to leave now,' Charlie was saying.

'He's got a portrait,' Stan called back. 'Huxley's dad.'

'What?' he could hear Charlie yelling. 'He's got what?'

'A portrait,' Stan shouted, twisting round, rock still in hand, turning to look down at Charlie on the drive. 'A full-on oil painting of his own face.'

'Are you actually serious?'

And in spite of the lights and the night and the awful weather and his lack of glasses Stan could see the grin spreading over Charlie's face there, in the flashing light from the car.

'I'm serious,' said Stan. 'A full-on fuck-off portrait.'

And then he turned to the window again, towards the hulking, larger-than-life image of Huxley's dad on the other side, his pose suggestive of the very essence of the businessman at leisure, leaning back against the edge of a mahogany desk. And Stan couldn't help but remember then why they'd come here tonight, in the first place. Those Romany children, painted on the side of the burning van. And though the connections were loose and tangled like the apple tree leaves in his hair, it all seemed perfect in some kind of a way, all making some garbled kind of sense.

With one last thought of Huxley's awful smug face when he'd called him *loser*, called him *peasant*, called him *pikey*, Stan gripped the rock hard in his right hand, and launched himself out of the tree, catapulting himself with something that was almost a jump, and almost falling upwards, towards the window, towards the portrait. A moment of pause, of awful suspension in the air – and then he'd done it, he'd landed on the sloping ledge of the roof. With grasping hands and scrabbling feet on the tiles he regained something like his balance just as a second alarm started up, higher and more piercing than the one from the car. Ignoring it, Stan reached and hooked the tips of his fingers around the curve of the window sill, and began scrambling up the tiles.

'Go on, mate. Fucking do it,' Charlie was saying now from the ground below – and a new kind of edge, a new kind of glee had crept into his voice, Stan was sure of it. 'Smash the window, grab the painting.'

So that was what he was here to do. Of course. Of course it was. Stan raised the rock again, pulling it back like a javelin, like the shotput in the Olympics on telly, getting ready for the biggest throw of his life . . .

'Go on. Fucking do it, mate. Fucking do it,' Charlie was yelling from somewhere below.

And he was about to, he was, he was just about to hurl that stupid rock with everything he had when for some reason his eyes drifted up to meet the painted ones of Huxley's dad through the glass. And he faltered. And something about the suddenness of that, of that stopping still, right in mid-throw – it set him wobbling a little. Not too much, he was basically fine, could still recover his footing, easy, he wasn't even worried about it, everything was alright, he was almost more concerned with being embarrassed at what Charlie would think of him, stopping short like that of actually smashing the stupid window – until his left foot found a loose tile.

It slipped out from under him, giving under his weight with a feeling like the bottom dropping out of the world. He heard it shatter on the ground below as his fingers turned slack with the shock and lost their hold on the window sill. He fell forwards then, chin slamming hard as he slid down the uneven slope of the roof, fingers scrabbling for a grip on tiles that were suddenly both too smooth and horribly rough, so harsh and sandpapery and sore as he slid down their length. And he had to get a proper grip somewhere, he knew. Had to find a foothold or handhold, had to find some-thing that wasn't just tiles. There was still the tree behind him, wasn't there, and all the branches? Maybe he could still reach, reach backwards to grab on to one of those . . . Except what was happening now? Somehow his internal spirit level was shifting, his precious centre of gravity swinging like a pendulum, forwards to back. What was he doing? Charlie would never have done something like this, this would never happen to Charlie – and Mum would absolutely kill him. He was falling backwards, stepping backwards almost – a blind footstep back into thin air . . .

. . . and then *impact* – on the drive. No time to brace, no time to prepare in any way. Lashing shock waves through his bones and sharp crunches of grit on the ground behind his head and the shock of being completely winded. Eyes flicker open. Only bright whiteness. Don't panic. Eyes shut. Eyes open again.

Flashing lights from the car, still. The security light turning off, turning on. And then Stan's fingers feeling something wet on the ground, spilling out next to him. Eyelids flicker, flutter back shut. Then hands, urgent hands gripping his shoulders. Eyes dragged back open. *Charlie.* Lights, still. And more alarms, even – sirens. Sirens coming. How long had there been sirens?

'Jesus Christ,' Charlie was saying, no, shouting into his face. Hands too rough on his shoulders, shaking him, almost. Why? When he was already all shattered? What would his mum say? Who would explain to her?

'Jesus fucking Christ.'

Why so loud? Why so violent? Why were they here at all? But there were his flowers, there. Flowers for Cindy. That was it – that was right. Flowers for Cindy. He reached out towards them. Charlie holding him. Charlie lying on his chest now, almost. Full weight. Stopping him moving, breathing. But the flowers. Sorry, Cindy.

'What's happened?' he asked Charlie. 'What will happen to me now?'

And asking that made him frightened. Hearing his voice registering how in question this was, how broken he'd got

– *all the king's horses and all the king's men*, sang a stupid, unhelpful part of his mind – before he'd really quite caught up with it, caught up with how bad things seemed to be now, so suddenly. And Charlie gripping him too tight and swearing loud . . . why so violent? Why does everything always have to be so violent? Even friends?

'You'll be alright,' Charlie was saying, head up now, squeezing shoulders, tears running off his face and on to Stan – Charlie crying? But surely that was wrong.

'You'll be alright,' he was saying. 'I promise you, you'll see. You'll see, Stan. I promise—'

'My flowers,' Stan tried to say, wanting to ask him to give them to Cindy, rather than just let them die on the drive and this whole thing be pointless. His heart felt so fast so loud in his ears, flashing lights headache and sirens and sirens and sirens.

'Nae pasaran,' Charlie was saying, shouting at him. 'Nae pasaran. Don't let them win, Stan. Don't fucking let them win.'

But Stan let his eyes close again then – giving up on sirens and Charlie and on lights and on flowers – giving up on it all, just for now.

# 17

As Stan lay unconscious in the hospital, Charlie visited every day, waiting until it was visiting time, chain-smoking roll-ups outside on the front steps while trying to ignore the dirty looks people kept giving him.

Which is how he met Helen. Only once – her job as a nurse meant that mostly she was too busy to be able to see Stan in visiting hours. Instead she went in her breaks, at the end of her shifts, whenever she could. Her one day off came four days into Stan's being there like that, unconscious, hooked up to machines. She and Charlie ended up arriving together, 3 p.m. prompt, at Stan's bedside.

Charlie introduced himself only as, 'A mate of Stan's,' and gave her his hand to shake – tobacco stains, smoky fingers, his grandad's gold ring. She didn't take it, leaving him to slip it back into his jacket pocket, all awkward, just squinting out at her from underneath his Uncle Martin's flat cap, which he always wore these days for some reason, even inside, sometimes. It just made him feel safer, somehow, though he knew that was ridiculous.

The two of them sat down after that, beside unconscious Stan. He was still hooked up to all these machines that seemed to be beeping and flashing and measuring things. Charlie didn't have a clue, really, what it was they were doing. He thought Helen might though. She was a nurse, Stan had said, hadn't he? He wanted to ask her, ask about what the readings might mean, what everything was doing and how it was helping Stan, but she wasn't even looking at them, or even at Stan at all, really. Just staring down into her lap instead, clenching and unclenching her hands.

Soon Charlie was feeling twitchy. He couldn't seem to stop himself coughing, and shifting in the uncomfortable plastic chair. And then at last, when the silence and the weirdness of watching his friend's strangely peaceful, unconscious face got too much, he pulled the Rizlas and filters and tobacco from his pocket and began to roll a cigarette. Obviously not to smoke inside the hospital, he just needed something to distract him for a moment, he needed something to do with his hands. He was just licking the paper, folding it down, when Helen finally spoke to him.

'You were with him, weren't you? When he fell. It was you he was with, wasn't it?'

Charlie froze, rollie in hand, halfway to tucking it behind his ear, and found that for once, he had absolutely no idea what to say.

'What was he even doing up there?' Helen was saying now. 'How could you have let him? Or did you *make* him, even? Did you send him up there?'

And Charlie found he had never in his life wanted to run away or disappear as much he did now, faced with this small woman, practically half his size.

'What were you doing, even hanging around with my Stanley? What would someone like you want with a boy like him?'

Those words. *Someone like you.*

'How old are you?' she asked him then.

'Sixteen,' he managed to choke out.

Helen shook her head. 'He was just a boy,' she said. 'A child—'

'Alright,' Charlie cut in there. 'Hold on. Don't be talking about him like he's already dead or something. He's tough, Stan is. He'll be alright.'

'Why didn't I see it?' Helen seemed to say almost to herself, before turning on Charlie again. 'And who do you think you are to speak to me like that, anyway? About my own son?'

She stood up then, and fully stepped forward, blocking Charlie's view of Stan's unconscious form on the bed. 'You just stay away from him, okay? Do you understand me? You stay away from us both.' She spoke deliberately, slowly, as if she really meant it.

'What?' Charlie stammered. 'Hang on. No. Stan's my friend. He'll wonder where I've got to, as much as anything else, when he wakes up, when he's better. When he's up and about.'

'Do you not realise how serious this is, what you've done?'

'I didn't—' Charlie stood now too. Instinctively he reached out towards her, a conciliatory gesture, trying to make her understand. 'It wasn't my fault,' he said, just as she raised her arms up, in front of her face, as if to protect herself against him.

He stepped back then, let his hands fall, and he opened his mouth to speak, but then realised he couldn't find any words to explain himself. The whole thing was too much of a mess to untangle with poor Stan still lying there, out cold on the hospital bed. And so he swallowed down the indignation that part of him still felt so strongly – the part that insisted that this wasn't actually all his fault, that it was unfair to blame just him, completely. The part of him too that was still smarting at those words she had used, *someone like you.*

Helen shook her head. 'Just stay away from him, please. I've already lost my husband. I can't lose Stanley, too.'

'Tell him I came to visit,' Charlie said. 'Will you do that?'

She didn't reply, though. Didn't move from where she was standing like that, right in front of the bed, as if he were a threat and Stan might need protecting from him. And so, again ignoring the sense he still had that this was all wrong, and that he was making some awful mistake in accepting it – in seeming to agree, almost, with her accusations – he walked out and left them to it. Just Stan and his mum, and all those machines, keeping him alive.

\*

Charlie didn't quite stop going to the hospital. He was just more careful after that, turning up halfway through visiting hours, checking there was no one else there to see Stan already before he went in. Then, on the sixth day after being admitted, Stan woke up. Charlie showed up at four o'clock, the same old routine, up the steps, through the sliding doors and up to the woman on the desk – 'Mate of Stan Gower's' – then over to the duty nurse. Dascha, it was, today. Young, gentle. Big, kind eyes.

'He's awake,' she said. 'He's talking and everything. Come and see.'

A quick almost-laugh of relief, then hands back in pockets, not quite meeting her eye.

'He's alright, then? He'll be okay?'

'Yes, yes. Dr Hartley was worried his brain would be damaged but he is fine, completely fine . . . you must be so glad!'

'Yeah. God, yeah. I am. That's great.'

Except though, instead of following her to Stan's ward, he was off, away back down the corridor with just a nod and a, 'You look after him, alright?'

Then through the hall, out the doors, off down the steps.

\*

And that was that. Charlie stayed away and heard not a thing of Stanley Gower beyond the cold formalities – the arrival of the police report, the hearing at which Stan wasn't present, for some reason, though he was mentioned several times, the community service completed alone.

December and Christmas came and went. Then New Year's Eve came around, Newford suddenly alive with people, dressed up in their best, braving the freezing temperatures to sing in the first hours of 2004. Then January got under way with adverts for gym memberships plastered everywhere. And for the rest of that month Charlie kept his head down, reading in the public library – newspaper articles about soldiers killed in Iraq, about the conservation of Guildford Castle, about a set of photographs that had been taken somehow on Mars.

# 18

The still-cold, still-damp days of February rolled around, bringing with them light dustings of powdery snow and early cherry blossom.

Every afternoon now, Stan would take himself for a walk. Or he called it 'a walk'. And he did his best, limping along, covering a little more ground every day, edging past those same old rows of Monopoly houses, the same silver hatchbacks and windows with net curtains, negotiating the demands of his crutch, his sore back and his still-shattered ankle and femur.

It was important for his strength, both Helen and the physiotherapist kept saying. Essential, if he wanted to be ready to start at the new school in September, because September might feel like a long way away, they kept telling him, but it wasn't, not really, given how badly he'd been injured. And so he had to keep moving, had to keep trying to get back on his feet if he wanted to recover in time. To be honest, Stan wasn't even sure he cared that much. He hated school, and surely things would be even worse at the new place, repeating the year, being a whole year older than everyone else in his class.

It was difficult, too, using his muscles like this when they always seemed to be so sore and so tired these days, aching after so long in bed, first at the hospital and now back at home where he was more or less stuck in his room – and with basically no visitors either, as who would visit him? He'd half-hoped Charlie might stop by, but then he seemed to have disappeared off somewhere or something, seemed to have forgotten Stan altogether. Only Gran came to see him, which had surprised him at first. But it was actually kind of nice, having her there, once he'd got used to it. And he had lots of books to keep him occupied, so it wasn't all bad. Helen seemed better these days, too. Easier to talk to – after the initial awful lecture about how he needed to learn to choose his friends more carefully, anyway. She seemed generally so much more present and alert, though. Maybe even as if his falling off the roof had shocked her awake somehow, had jolted her into being closer to the way she'd been in the years before everything had got so bad with Dad.

So they were getting on better, these days. Finally settling into the fact of it just being the two of them left, at home. And it felt good, it did, having his mum back like this. Even if it was getting a bit much, the way she kept going on at him about how important it was to keep doing his exercises, and walking around all the time. As what really, what honestly, Stan found himself wondering as he limped around the neighbourhood one Tuesday evening at dusk – what was honestly the point? When it was only cold and exhausting and it was getting dark now anyway and then how did he even know this new school he was meant to be going to later in the year would be any better than the old one? It just didn't seem like there was anything to look forward to, when all the newness and excitement – all the fun, even – of his autumn with Charlie felt like another life now, with his body all different these days, and the wings his trusty Falcon Stealth had granted him vanished as it gathered rust under a tarp in the back garden. His world had become so much smaller. Even the end of the street felt like an achievement.

Except – what was that? A funnel of smoke, billowing upwards into the night from over in the direction of the common. The evening suddenly smelled completely different, with the wood smoke on the breeze. Maybe even a little bit like spring. And why not, with early blossoms on the trees, and snowdrops and crocuses, and even daffodils poking up through the soil of the suburban front gardens?

He was all the way down Avenue Road already. The common wouldn't be too much further, after all, would it? He was almost halfway there already. And it wasn't as dark as it had been at this time even last week. And then they were always saying he had to use his muscles. He couldn't lose anything just by going to have a look, could he?

*

It took him the best part of half an hour just to cover the short distance, trekking towards the smoke – there like a signal fire across the suburbs – and wondering all the while if he could be right, if his suspicions were correct about who might be burning what was probably an illegal bonfire out on Goshawk Common in the February weather.

At last he was there, and stepping off the paving stones on to the grass, into open space and vast sky. The night air looked thick and almost enchanted, the last of the light slanting through the smoke and the dust of the bonfire.

New glasses. He supposed that was something to have come out of the last two months. He recognised Charlie immediately, even from this far away – sitting at the edge of the trees, hunched by the side of his fire, poking it with a stick. He saw Charlie clock him, too, though he didn't get up from the ground or anything – just stared at Stan as it took him forever to get across the vast expanse of grass and uneven, stony winter ground between them with his crutch and shattered leg. And God, it felt uncomfortable, that endless, extended approach.

'Charlie,' Stan said, as soon as he judged he was within earshot.

'Alright,' said Charlie.

Just one awkward nod. Was that all he got after all this time had passed? After everything that had happened? He thought of the last thing he remembered before blacking out on the Edwardses' drive – Charlie shouting *nae pasaran* at him, as if all things depended on it. It felt so long ago. A different Charlie. A different Stan.

'Bit cold to be out here tonight, isn't it?'

'Burning things, mate. Makes all the difference.'

Stan nodded. Tried to think of what on earth to say. 'The rabbits'll be back, soon,' he said. 'There's always loads in spring.'

'Don't doubt it, mate,' said Charlie. Then, 'I won't be seeing them, though.'

'Sorry?'

'Getting out of this shithole, aren't I? My family's moving on. With the cousins, the lot from down south, over Lewes way.'

'Where to?'

'London, mate. Or the outskirts, anyway. Some place called Hollytree. Near Amersham.'

'Amersham? But I thought you said you always stayed round here, though. When you moved. When your family moved. That you moved sometimes but apart from when you went to visit your dad in Manchester, which was different, it was never far away.'

'Yeah, well.' Charlie prodded at the fire and a draught of wind caught a patch of embers, sending them skittering through the night towards Stan's trainers. *Fire fairies*, he remembered thinking of them once. 'There's this hospital there, apparently. Some guy who's good with spines and that, word is. You know. For James.'

Stan nodded. They were moving for James. It made sense, of course he could see that.

'When?' he asked Charlie.

'What?'

'When are you going?'

'Sometime next week. Get settled for the spring.'

'Oh,' said Stan again. 'Okay.' Then he tried to sit down on the ground – but it was all too awkward, his leg and his ankle and his back too sore, too weak both to manipulate the crutch and to lower himself down to the grass without injury. And then suddenly Charlie was up on his feet next to him, taking the crutch and Stan's arm.

'Sorry,' Stan said.

'Don't apologise,' Charlie said, not quite looking at him properly but still taking the weight on his arm as Stan adjusted his complaining limbs into a relatively comfortable configuration on the ground. 'I always told you, didn't I? Don't apologise for yourself. Especially – well.'

'What?' said Stan.

Charlie let go his arm, went back to sitting where he'd been, just as if nothing had happened.

'How is he, Charlie?' Stan asked then.

'How's who?'

'James.'

'Oh you know,' Charlie grinned, a bleak kind of grin, met Stan's eyes for a second, the first time this afternoon. 'No worse. You two really are peas in a pod now, almost. Funny how things go.' Charlie laughed, but it sounded all wrong. Stan didn't join in.

'The doctor said I could have died, if I'd braced as I fell,' he said. 'Lucky I was so slow to notice I was falling.'

Charlie threw the rest of his stick on the fire. 'How many stitches?' he said.

'Thirty-two,' said Stan. 'Twelve in the back of my head.'

'Jesus,' said Charlie.

'Yeah,' said Stan.

There was a commotion in the dark canopy of the trees, and a cloud of rooks fluttered out – some irresistible signal or silent predator having sent them up like that, all of one mind.

'Listen,' said Charlie. 'I wanted to say – I wanted to tell you—' But then he coughed, and seemed to change his mind, and started patting his pockets instead. 'Oh but there was also a thing – there's a thing I kept for you. You might – I don't know. It's no explanation I know, no excuse, but you might—' And then he was thrusting a rolled-up newspaper at Stan.

Stan took it without thinking, unfolded it, glanced over the page in front of him, and for a second he was back on the kerb outside the chippy again, him and Charlie flattening out bits of greasy chip paper against their jeans and laughing at the local news headlines – all things about vicars, traffic lights, community halls and noise pollution. Harmless stories, harmless laughter, harmless times. But no – of course that wasn't what this was. Charlie's face was set and this wasn't the *Newford Echo*, anyway. *The Argus*, Stan read. *Race Row Over Bonfire Effigies*. And of course he'd heard the whole thing from Charlie before but still – seeing it written down like that.

'How's your gran?' he asked Charlie.

'Oh,' said Charlie. 'She – she had a stroke. She's old. Probably nothing to do with any of—' He gestured at the paper, then seemingly more widely, at the woods, the fields, the countryside as a whole. 'She's doing okay though, now. She'll be okay.'

'I'm sorry,' said Stan.

'Well,' said Charlie. 'You know.'

'You were keeping it for me,' said Stan.

'What?'

'The paper. You said that you were keeping it for me.'

'That's right.'

'You could have come and visited. If you'd wanted to see me.'

'Ah,' Charlie said. 'Don't know where you live, do I? You never told me. And besides, I thought it was your turn to come and see me.'

'My turn?'

'Yeah. The hospital. Hang on – did she not tell you?'

'Tell me what?'

'I went every day. To the hospital. Until you woke up.'

'Why did you stop?'

Charlie shrugged.

'I did wonder,' said Stan. 'My mum made me promise something about you, you know. And the way she said it – it was like she knew more than just what happened at Huxley's house, you know? She said it like she knew you.'

'What did she make you promise?' said Charlie.

'Never to speak to you again,' said Stan. '*A friend like that*, she said, *will ruin your life.*'

'Well,' Charlie stared into the fire. 'And do you believe her?' he asked.

The question took Stan by surprise. He'd expected anger, self-justification – hoped for Charlie to come back with some good reason not to listen to Helen, why that promise could and should be broken. And the surprise shocked him into thinking – actually thinking about that last question of Charlie's, his brain fully alert now in a way it hadn't been for months, stuck in bed scanning the pages of novels that didn't feel real enough for him to care properly about, without a real lived life to supplement them and switch on their significance. And he wanted to say *no, of course not* – of course he did, because he missed Charlie, missed having a friend, missed having someone to look out for him, and the adventures that occurred in his proximity. And yet . . .

'I don't know,' was all he could say. 'Maybe.'

'Fair enough,' said Charlie, and he dug up a handful of earth with his fingers and threw it into the fire.

And then suddenly, there seemed to be nothing more to say. They sat with just the crackle of the flames for a while, and the sound of birds in the trees, before Stan reached for his crutch, and tried to stand back up – and there was Charlie, again. On his feet, at his side, supporting the crutch and taking Stan's weight on his arm and his shoulder, avoiding his eyes all the time.

'Enjoy London,' Stan said, when he was up.

'Listen, Stan. I should say. I . . .' For a second, Stan thought Charlie might say something almost ground-breaking – something that would reset everything back to what it had been before and make it all okay. But he didn't. Just fell back into silence, fiddling with that old gold ring he wore now, twisting it around and around on his finger.

'I gave those flowers to my cousin,' said Charlie. 'To Cindy. You could come and see her again, since we're going soon. If you like. Say goodbye.'

Stan tried to shrug, but it was too painful with his back and his shoulders still all messed up, and with holding the crutch. 'I don't know,' he said, instead.

'It never could have worked, Stan. My family. It's nothing personal, you understand. They like you well enough. It's just . . . historically, getting involved with outsiders has never brought good things for my people. And Cindy, well. She'll be looking for a husband, soon enough.'

Stan shook his head, feeling so stupid, redness starting to burn up over his cheeks. 'Forget it,' he said. 'The whole thing was stupid.'

'It wasn't stupid,' Charlie said. 'Never say that.'

'Why not?' said Stan. He just felt so embarrassed. Embarrassed about Cindy, and about everything else, too. All that blundering around all autumn, following Charlie almost blindly, without seeing or understanding almost anything clearly, it suddenly felt like.

Stan found then that he really didn't want to be here any more. That he could hardly bear even just to look up at Charlie. He turned to go, starting the long limp back, through the darkness, over the common. Some part of him in spite of himself wondered still if Charlie might try to help him, or if he would shout something at least – call something after him.

He didn't, though. And so when Stan was back at the edge, where the grass met the pavement of Goshawk Road, he took one look back. Charlie was a silhouette now, standing outlined against the light of the fire, tearing and crumpling up pages of something – of that newspaper he'd kept for Stan, maybe – throwing them into the flames.

And Stan wondered what he would do here, now, with Charlie gone. The one person since Dad had died who'd been able to make everything feel almost alright again. The one person, too, who Stan had actually liked himself around. Hanging out with Charlie for those few short months, he'd felt like he'd been growing into a better version of himself, into someone he was almost proud to be. And now Charlie was leaving. Leaving to help James. Which made sense, of course it did, Stan could understand that. It was just . . . London. It seemed so distant. With no way for him, a broken thirteen-year-old in the suburbs of Newford, to even think about getting there.

Still, as he limped on, though – the ache in his ribs and his ankle feeling all the worse now for having sat like that with Charlie on the cold, damp ground – he wondered again about what Helen had said. If on some level it could even be true, and whether he and Charlie had even been meant to be friends, really. And as he kept on walking – slowly, not looking back until he was finally turning off Goshawk

Road and into the network of smaller, residential streets that would eventually lead him home – part of him was wondering whether, though he would miss Charlie of course, this might in fact be, in the end, for the best.

# PART TWO

# 2012

# 19

He'd run to fat, that much was clear, sitting like this, belly out on the sofa. Belly used, in fact, as a kind of tray table for his drink and his arms to rest on as he sat here, drained of all energy, trying not to listen to Kate in the kitchen behind him. She was obviously complaining about something, probably about the fight on Saturday, since that was all she ever seemed to talk to him about these days. The fight, the family reputation, not being an embarrassment and not letting down James. She was worried he wouldn't show up. She'd never say as much to his face, but that was obviously what was behind all this. She thought he was going to let them all down by flaking out, wandering off, and not being there when he was needed. He knew she thought that, of course he did. He knew she thought he was a quitter.

Not that he could really hear any of what she was saying from over here, anyway. He could only catch the odd crash of a plate as she unloaded their dishwasher, and then the occasional rise in pitch of her voice, cresting the music playing in his headphones. Sennheisers, over-ears and noise-cancelling, but nobody could cancel Kate. He'd loved that about her, once. He still did. He just needed a break sometimes, was all. A break from the way she always looked at him these days, from the way she spoke to him, and from how she made him feel, always wanting something from him that he only ever found himself powerless to give, or even understand.

They'd been eighteen, when they'd got married. She'd been sweet, back then, with long red hair. She'd made him laugh, and well, you know, you think you're getting older and *time you settled down*, everyone was saying. Mum and Dad and all of them, even Nan. Poor Nan. It had been Nan especially in fact who'd told him *find yourself a nice girl, you'll want to slow yourself down and have some little ones to take care of, it'll be good for you and you'll enjoy it, no don't look like that of course you will, you'd be surprised, and then, Charlie boy, you'll make us all proud.* So what else could he have done? Listen to your elders, isn't that what they always say? Listen to your elders and it'll all turn out fine?

More crashing sounds from Kate back in the kitchen, stacking plates with a level of frustration strong enough to make itself heard even over his *Best of the 00s* NME compilation – the Foo Fighters now, blasting out into his ears. Ah but those had been good days, hadn't they? Good times, riding along on his bike, Discman whirring, this song sound-tracking the journeys and making him feel a right slick badass as he'd whipped down those green country lanes. Where had that been? He'd had that leather jacket then, hadn't he? The one with all the patches. Farnham? Or Newford maybe. And where had that jacket gone, anyway? It'd never still fit him. Or it might kind of but he'd never be able to do it up properly. He'd only look a fool.

Surely it was neither of their faults though really, what had happened to him and Kate? Surely no one could have guessed that what had happened would happen, and then that in the aftermath of it they'd be like this, hurtling off

down this track they seemed irrevocably stuck on now, left
with each other in the ruins of it, having to face up to the
horrible mess of what it had done to both of them every
single morning they woke up alongside one another. Not
even Nan could have imagined this, and, well, it was probably a terrible thing to think, he knew, but even though he
missed Nan like hell, every day, he was even almost glad
she'd never lived to know about it, that she'd departed this
life seeing the two of them still happy, still laughing and
knocking around together as they used to do, the expectation
still being happy noise and little tricycles and lunchboxes,
or whatever it was. And not this, not all this shite, anyway.

And certainly not this trap of a flat either, with their useless faceless landlord raking in the cash when he did fuck all,
as far as Charlie could tell. Although in fairness of course it
had made sense at the time. Selling the Transit, finding the
flat, signing the tenancy and all of the contracts.

He lifted the tin of Tyskie to his lips and drained the last
just as the Foos switched to the Arctic Monkeys in his ears
and Kate swung into view in front of him, brandishing a
plate, one of the nice Crown Derby ones. Not that he cared,
but that had been Nan's, hadn't it? Jesus, how he wished
Kate would calm down a bit, stop yelling at him, stop talking
to him about the fight this weekend like he'd already fucked
up, already let everybody down.

He raised one of the cans off his ear, lifting the seal protecting the *Best of the 00s* and letting a little of this evening
in. This evening nearly a full decade after all those songs
came out, and after those days of riding around the green
roads of Surrey on his bike. This Monday evening in March,

stuck in his and Kate's stupid rented flat in London, with less than five days to go now until the fight.

'. . . that's your problem,' she was saying. 'That's your problem, Charlie Wells. You think you can get away with it and then when you find you can't, you just pretend it isn't happening. Head in the sand. Get everyone else to deal with it until it goes away. No, don't let me bother you – you keep those headphones on, and keep the real world out. Because isn't that it? Isn't that what you want? Except it's not going to work this time and you know it.'

Strands of her hair, shorter these days, were falling into her face. She had circles under her eyes, and the London winter seemed to have bleached all the colour from her cheeks. Just looking at her made him feel so unbearably guilty, though surely not everything here was his fault? Surely some things just happened, outside of anyone's control. He dropped her gaze, shifted on the sofa, picked up another tin of Tyskie from the carpet by his feet.

'It's fine,' he muttered. 'I'll be fine. I've got it all sorted.'

'How? How, Charlie? When have you ever had anything *all sorted*?'

Charlie started to speak but Kate silenced him with a wave of her hand.

'No, Charlie, I'll tell you. I'll tell you what'll happen on Saturday because it'll be me picking up the pieces, clearing up the mess, stitching everything back together again—'

'Stitching? Oh c'mon, you don't know how to do any of that . . .'

'I was *speaking*' – her voice effortlessly soared over his – 'metaphorically.'

'I'll be fine, Kate. It'll be fine, you'll see,' Charlie said, finally pressing pause on his Discman, silencing the music.

'When did you last go to the gym, even?' Kate was asking now. 'When did you last train?'

'Yesterday,' he said.

'Liar.'

'No,' he said. 'Yesterday. After work. I went, I did.'

'Oh?' Hand on hip, head jerked to one side. She was a harsh woman, these days. All sharp angles and no softness to appeal to, or to hide himself in. 'And how did that go?'

'Fine,' he said, swallowing another sip of beer, giving himself time to think. 'I mean I've got stuff to work on, of course. Davey nearly gave me a run for my money towards the end, but yeah – it was good, overall. Nothing that won't be okay for the weekend.'

'Is that right?' said Kate.

'Yeah,' he said. 'It is.'

'You're a liar, Charlie Wells, and you always have been. You were at the George last night with Tommy Campbell and I know you were because he told me so when I saw him in Wallace's this morning—'

'What were you doing in Wallace's? I thought you were meant to be looking for jobs?'

'*Don't* – she raised her finger up again – 'change the subject. Apart from anything else you should care about, think about James, Charlie. He's relying on you, that boy, God help him. He's relying on you and you'll fail him, going on like this with Tommy Campbell and the George and all your stupid carrying on. All your endless *drinking*' – she lifted up one of the empty cans and sniffed it as if it were six-day-gone-off budget dogfood or something and then threw it across the room, where it hit the far wall and clattered to the ground, dregs spilling on to the carpet – 'd'you not realise it, Charlie? It makes you *slow*.'

'Fucksake,' he said. 'That's not ours. That's our landlord's carpet.'

'I fucking hate our landlord,' she replied.

'Jesus,' he said. 'Fine.' Getting up from the sofa now, he could feel the heaviness of the day of work behind him, of the beer, and of the whole atmosphere of the flat tugging at him, trying to drag him back down as he slid his feet into his trainers. 'I'll go. I'll go to the gym. See? I'm going. Happy? Will that make you happy?'

But she started crying. He couldn't deal with this, now. Never knew what to do with Kate these days, everything he said or did only seeming to make everything so much worse, even just to look at her a reminder of how useless he'd become, how powerless he was to fix anything, and make things okay again for her. He grabbed his keys and his wallet from the ledge in the hall and cut off the sound of her sobbing, slamming the front door behind him.

# 20

He hadn't been lying, when he'd told her he'd go to the gym. She was right, after all. Probably a bit of a run around wasn't a bad idea. Bit of a run around, lift some weights – just oil the gears for the fight on Saturday, and he'd be right as rain when the time came. Adrenaline, that was it. Amazing thing. Reliably works wonders. Especially if you happen to be being beaten up by a distant cousin down some country lane somewhere in the middle of godforsaken nowhere. No one to hear you scream. Ha.

But he'd outsmart the other guy, that's how he'd do it. The Holland kid might be trained up, ready, but he'd be like one of those old footballers, Teddy Sheringham or whoever it was. Never in the starting eleven, but called from the benches when they're most needed, jogging on to the field with no appearance of rush but eyes going everywhere, darting back and forth, brain calculating like lightning, all the angles, all the avenues of approach . . . and then the game kicks off again and *bam!* He's barely run a metre, barely even moved from the spot, and yet through sheer cleverness he's equalised, even before injury time . . . and then *bam*, again! Another goal! His team winning safely now, and him still just standing there in the middle of things, barely even running, as if to say *me? Nope, nothing to do with me*. Except of course it had everything to do with him, didn't it? Because he had the *brains*, that was it. Had the brains, did the research. That's what'll get you ahead in this life, after all. Much more so than anything you could do at the gym. Still, though. Maybe Kate was right in that a little bit of a stretch-out couldn't be bad. A warm-up. Just to get the blood pumping.

Still, it occurred to him, turning down Mount Street towards the main road, that maybe he wouldn't go to Martin's gym today – maybe that was a step too far. And he hadn't told Kate he was going to Martin's, in fairness. He'd just said 'the gym'. What she understood by that was up to her, after all, and God knows he couldn't face Martin and all that lot now, not when he was three beers in already. They'd make him work, make him skip and jog and take their stupid punches until he was sick all over their stupid floor. Then they'd laugh and tell him to clean it up. Yep, that's exactly what they'd do.

And anyway, aside from that, it might sound weird but there was just this other thing, right now, where he didn't want them seeing him, if that made any sense? As in, he'd be fine when it came to the actual fight. The adrenaline, the satisfaction of having a genuine opponent, the challenge of it kick-starting the cogs into action . . . and yes, he supposed the sight of James watching him from the sidelines would help. So he knew he'd be fine when it came to it. He just didn't want all of them at the gym, Martin and the rest of them, he didn't want them seeing him *practise* – because then they wouldn't see how it would really be, in the moment, with the adrenaline and everything. They would see instead how he was now, dog tired after work and having had another fight with Kate. And they'd shake their heads at him and mutter amongst themselves and then Martin would probably give him a beating if he hadn't done already, and then a talking-to of course for good measure as if Charlie were still a kid or something . . . and it would all be unnecessary and completely unfair, because it'd be alright on the night, of course it would – or on the morning, as it were. But whichever, night or morning, the case still stood.

No, if he went now they'd only get him all worked up and nervous when of course he'd do fine, how could he not? How, after all, could he be faced with the prick who had called his little brother a *waste-of-space cripple*, and not beat the fucker to smithereens? The prick who had gone for James, even. Beaten him royally even though he was still in his wheelchair and everything. And at a wedding, too. Jack and Ellie, meant to be a day of celebration. Blushing bride, beautiful cake, slap-up meal and all the rest of it. James all excited too, dressed up, hair slicked back, ready for the day – and sure James had been a bit sharp with the Hollands, maybe, could have been a little too clever for his own good. But that was just James, wasn't it? That was just his sense of humour. And anyway since when did being a bit sarcastic justify that kind of reaction? No, it was impossible that Charlie could be faced with the Holland kid on Saturday, and not want to give him the beating of his life. What kind of man would he even be, after all, if he didn't?

He walked past the stop for the bus he'd take to Martin's gym whistling, hands in pockets, as if he'd been off somewhere else entirely and was only passing by – then jumped on a different bus, where he sat by a window on the ground floor, fiddling with the lace on his trainer and watching the old woman sat on the pair of seats opposite him. A wholesome, grandma sort. He'd never seen her before of course. This was London after all, you could go out every day and never see the same person twice, but something about her though seemed somehow almost achingly familiar . . . ah but imagine Kate turning into someone like that. Ha! She'd sooner die, probably.

Then the glass heights of the leisure centre were pitching into view and with a cheery 'Cheers, mate!' to the driver, though it wasn't like anyone else ever thanked bus drivers in London, or like the drivers ever replied, he skipped off the bus, across the street, and through the shiny sliding doors, heading up to the front desk.

'Alright, love,' he said to the girl there. She looked so young. Almost a different generation, now, to him and Kate. 'I'm here to use the gym, if that's alright.'

'Sure,' she said, smile automatic, eyes blank. 'That'll be nine pounds, for a peak session.'

Charlie nodded like he'd expected as much though in reality he thought it'd be like a public library – just wander in, browse around, use what you need. Of course it wasn't like that though. Nothing was, these days, especially in this city. Not even libraries, sometimes. He put a ten-pound note in front of her on the counter and he couldn't help but notice how she picked it up carefully, as if he might've done something nasty to it.

'You're alright, love,' he told her. 'I've not poisoned it or anything.'

'I'm sorry?' she said. Same blank look but not even with the smile this time.

'I've not poisoned it, I said.'

She frowned, looked at him like there was some kind of

food stuck on his face. Then at last she opened the till and gave him his quid change.

'Up the stairs and on your left,' she said. 'Lockers are a pound.'

'Oh I've not got to get changed or anything,' he said.

'Well,' she said. 'Then you're more prepared than most.' Then she turned back to the computer screen she'd been gazing into when he'd come in, wearing a slight frown now, as if concentrating now on something complex – or on something more interesting than he was, anyway.

He went up the stairs, hands in pockets, whistling something from back in the day just to pick himself up a bit, prove to himself that she hadn't got to him. Bloc Party, that was it, that was what he was whistling. She'd couldn't have been more than a kid when this had come out. Ah except what did any of it matter, really? He was through the double doors now, and out on to the main floor.

It was quite crowded for a Monday night, though oddly silent. Just one man in the corner, letting out a harsh grunt with every pull-up. Everyone else, more or less, seemed locked into a machine. Cross-trainers, treadmills, steps, rowing . . . He'd never liked these kinds of gyms, Charlie remembered now. These places with no windows, only mirrors. And then there was the air conditioning, too. Christ on a bike, that was fierce.

Looking down at his trainers so he wouldn't accidentally catch anyone's eye, he wandered over to a free rowing machine, and was just crouching down to it, just reaching for the handlebar pulley thing, about to clamber on, when this lad walked up, all smiles, good-looking in the same squeaky-clean way as the girl on the desk.

'Sorry, sir,' he said to Charlie.

Charlie paused, halfway through the procedure of manoeuvring himself into the rower, limbs and belly and shoelaces everywhere.

'Yeah?' he said to this shiny-new man.

'Sorry, sir,' the man said, again. 'Is this your first time here?'

'Is it that obvious?' said Charlie, trying to laugh.

'I'm very good with faces,' said the man.

'No, I was – I was kidding. Sort of. You know. I meant, like . . . is it that obvious? As in, am I really that unfit?'

Charlie was aware of his words echoing out into the concentrated quiet of the gym as the squeaky-clean man just blinked. 'If you'll just fill this in for me, *sir*' – he flourished a sheet of paper under Charlie's nose in a way that Charlie couldn't help but feel was somehow pointed – 'then that would be fab.'

'Right,' Charlie said, taking the paper and the biro the man had apparently produced from thin air and was pressing on him now. He shuffled round to sit on the floor next to the rower, and started to read.

*Do you have* – the form asked – *a history of heart disease? Of fainting spells? Of Blindness? Of high blood pressure? Low blood pressure? Epellepsy? Constipation? Do you have any known reason why exercise may not be a recommended avenue for you, personally, reasonably to pursue?*

'Who wrote this?' said Charlie.

'What?' said the man.

'Whoever wrote this spelt epilepsy wrong,' said Charlie.

'I'm sorry?' said the man.

'They spelled – they spelled epilepsy . . .' Charlie pointed with the biro to where it appeared misspelled at the top of the form. 'You see it's actually with an "i",' he said. 'And only one—'

The man smiled. The man blinked. Charlie let the biro fall.

'Don't worry about it,' he said. 'I'll just be a minute filling this in.'

And then for the full amount of time he spent ticking boxes, signing dotted lines and writing down pointless details like his blood group and his date of birth, the man remained crouched next to him, his whole posture and attitude reminding Charlie uncomfortably of some healthy younger man who might have stopped and crouched down, concerned, next to someone who'd keeled over on the pavement.

When he was done, he handed the form back. The man scanned it, a placid nod of contentment greeting every section properly filled in.

'No fixed abode?' he said, when he reached the *Tell Us How To Reach You* section.

'Yeah, well, I'm between places,' Charlie said with a shrug. Why had he written that, though? When he wasn't really between places at all? Hard to explain, but it had felt like a small gesture of defiance, somehow. A reassertion of how things should be.

The man frowned but let it pass, just carried on reading, although with less of a contented aspect, now. 'You'll need an induction and a tour,' he said – finally standing up, about to leave Charlie alone – 'before you can use one of those,' he gestured at the rowing machine.

'So I can't just use it now?' said Charlie.

'Afraid not,' the man said. 'Not without the induction or the tour.'

'But couldn't you just give those to me now though?'

The man shrugged. 'Why don't we wait to see how you get on, first?' he said. 'Those are fine for you to use,' and he pointed to a scuffed-looking row of treadmills by the far wall, lined up in front of a bank of flashing TV screens. They were all empty, apart from one occupied by what looked like a teenage girl, running fast, a hard, miserable expression on her face.

'Okay,' said Charlie, wondering if he should mention the nine pounds he'd just paid to come in here, and then thinking better of it.

'My apologies, sir,' said the man, not sounding sorry at all.

'That's okay,' said Charlie. 'You're only doing your job.'

Feeling foolish and lumpen under the man's gaze Charlie headed over to a treadmill, stepped up, pressed some buttons on the peeling plasticated dashboard, and found himself surprised when it started to work, the belt moving and rolling under him, easy as that.

And suddenly it felt good, it did. Surprisingly so, given the beers in his system, and the heaviness over his body from the long day at work before that, and then of course given the way he just always felt kind of heavy and out of condition these days, even when he hadn't been working or drinking or anything, just out of a simple lack of sleep. Because who would be able to sleep, really sleep, in his situation, lying there every night next to Kate, with everything that had gone wrong between them just hanging above them over the bed, souring the air? But he was walking fast, now.

Pressing the little plus button on the dash, legs keeping up, breath just about keeping up, too.

Ah but it would be fine on Saturday. He didn't know what Kate was on about. He was feeling so fine now in fact, the fast marching pace so easily managed, that he was almost bored. He picked up the pair of flimsy headphones hanging from the dash and slipped them over his ears. It took him a moment to figure out what he was listening to. He'd instinctively expected music, but instead it was three voices, one woman, two men, talking about July. *The world's eyes on the capital*, they were saying. The Olympics, again, it had to be. There was a particular way they always talked about London on these kinds of things, he was starting to notice. Technically it was the same city as the one he lived in, but honestly? Sometimes it felt like they were discussing a different world.

He scanned the TV screens looming above him, neck craned like a man trapped down a well, searching for the one that corresponded to the sound in his ears. Why put the screens up so high, when they were this close up to the treadmills? He found the right one at last – a panel show, everyone in suits – and then pressed a few more buttons, trying to change the channel. Instead though something on the dashboard started to flash, and the belt began to move faster, before tipping so that he was half-marching, half-jogging on an incline. He pressed a few more things, sending the belt moving faster until he was legitimately jogging – feeling less comfortable now, it hadn't been so long since he'd given up smoking and his breath was still catching uncomfortably in his lungs – until finally he hit upon the button for switching the channel in the headphones. *Flick* – he sent it on to the next screen. Another news programme. That prick George

Osborne this time, going on about freezing allowances. *Flick*, again. Next channel. 'Gangnam Style'. That mad dance they all did on the screen up above him as the headphones blared and the treadmill kept on going nuts, still on an incline and speeding up now, apparently of its own accord.

Charlie set his fist down on the big red emergency stop button, right in the centre of the rest of the controls, sending the treadmill juddering to a halt, and as he did so catching in the corner of his eye the sight of the shiny-faced man from before glancing up at the noise and beginning to stride over. Enough, now, thought Charlie. That was enough of all this. He'd put up with enough for one day.

'Sir,' called the man, advancing through the ranks of serious-faced Londoners on gym machines, solemnly working their muscles while taking up a bare minimum of space. 'Is everything okay there, sir? Do you need help with something?'

And the words were fine, of course. Almost friendly, even. But Charlie wasn't an idiot. He hadn't been born yesterday and he knew the way this customer service talk worked, asking questions like, 'Need help with something?' when really that meant, 'Start behaving properly or get out.'

'It's alright,' he said, stepping off the treadmill sharpish, wiping his forehead on his sleeve, even though he hadn't been there long enough to break a sweat. 'Don't bother yourself, I'm off, anyway.'

*

He stepped back on to the pavement and into the coldness of the early spring night, wondering about the emergency stop button on the treadmill. Imagine, he thought, if somewhere there were some wider, more general, cosmic emergency stop button that he just hadn't found yet. Imagine if he suddenly saw it lurking, like in the corner of his field of vision, and he could run right up to it, grab it before it disappeared again, and just stop time for a bit. Not for forever, but just long enough, maybe, to get a few gym sessions in before the fight this Saturday.

It could be like a training montage from a film, in fact. Stretching, jogging . . . then over to the boxing gym and Martin, getting beaten badly there but still getting back up on his feet, hauling himself off the ground, hero in the making, then back to jogging round the block, look of flinty resolve in his eye this time, then another spell in the boxing gym, this time old Martin yelling *yes, Charlie boy, you'll bring him down* and then sit-ups, press-ups, the lot.

The bus heading back in the direction of home rounded the corner and drove right past where he was walking, disrupting his daydream. He'd been planning to catch that bus, and just go off back home, to Kate. But now he saw it, though . . . well. The whole idea of the emergency stop and the training montage had cheered him up a bit, made him feel stronger, almost as if he'd actually done the whole thing instead of just daydreaming it. And, well, though he might not exactly feel it all the time these days, he was still young, wasn't he? And this was London, for God's sake. And it had barely just got dark.

The bus signalled and pulled up at the stop just a little ahead, down the street. And Charlie lingered, walking perhaps a little slower than necessary as he watched people pile on. A little old lady counting out her change held up the queue and he realised he could easily catch it now if he wanted to, he wouldn't even need to run for it. He stopped walking. The old woman finally seemed to pay her fare, and the queue started moving again. Then the bus pulled away, leaving him behind on the pavement.

Charlie slipped his hands into his pockets and turned around, walking away from the bus stop now and heading towards the city centre, weaving his way through the evening crowds . . . People in work clothes, runners in gym clothes, evening shoppers laden with Tesco bags, and a few people still dragging tired kids along by the hand. That was one good thing at least, Charlie supposed, about not having kids. You could still go out and about whenever you wanted.

And then there were all the big groups of young people, too, the young professionals and students – though come to think of it he didn't know why he should think of them as young people, specifically, when it wasn't like most of them could be any younger than he was. They just had that air about them, maybe – it was something about their clothes, or the way they moved in groups, or simply the way they carried themselves. There were just so many of them too, heading to the bars and the pubs. And it was a funny thing, he found himself thinking then, how no one really seemed to dress up at all to go out in this city, as if it weren't quite the done thing to be seen to be making an effort.

And yet still –

'No trainers,' said the bouncer at the first bar he tried, mouth turned down in a thin line of dour disdain as, at the same time as stopping Charlie, he waved through a bunch of lads, who as far as Charlie could tell were dressed just the same as he was.

'What?' Charlie said. 'Sorry, mate, I know you're only doing your job and all but weren't some of those just in trainers, same as me?'

'Not really,' said the bouncer.

'Sorry?' said Charlie.

The bouncer just shook his head.

'But surely trainers is trainers though, right?' said Charlie.

The bouncer appeared to think about this for a moment, then said, 'No. These ones' – indicating the shoes on Charlie's feet – 'these aren't the same thing at all.'

# 21

Ah but this was the place! Half empty and tiny, a dark basement somewhere, central-east. But how far, exactly, had he wandered? There had been the gin bar after that first place, and then the old man pub by the river too before he'd wandered up here, to the part of the city he never went to. He'd just never felt like it was for him round here, really, all art students and people in berets and whatnot – very middle-class, hipster Gorjer – but fuck it, why shouldn't it be for him? Why on earth shouldn't he feel at home and at ease among these people? He was as legit and worthy as anyone else, wasn't he? He'd been forgetting that a bit recently, maybe.

He stepped up to the bar, nodding his head to the tune that was on, and ordered a whiskey. Poor Kate. She needed a better man, that was the honest truth of it. Someone who'd know how to deal with everything, and keep on top of stuff. Someone calm and in control, who wouldn't let her down all the time. Someone stronger, smarter, someone who saw the bigger picture. Someone capable. Not like him. If only he could take her back to Hollytree, that would be something. If only he could take her back in time, to the open air and the swallows and skylarks. He might not know what on earth to do as far as she was concerned these days, but she'd like that, he was sure of it. And there'd be swallows everywhere at Hollytree, this time of year, wouldn't there? Or maybe it was still too early yet, still a couple of months until they came.

It hadn't always been the easiest life at Hollytree, not always warm and not always that steady financially either – or not always predictable, at least – but still, they'd had some measure of control over things back then. Or it had felt like it at least. And there'd just been this comforting, concrete sense that this was their place in the world and that was that. In the mornings especially, it had felt that way. Him and Kate sat on the steps of the van, huddled together with the cold, cups of tea in hand, and she all moody – though not moody in the way she was moody all the time these days, no way, not by a long shot. Just moody in a way that he could enjoy trying to tease her out of. Moody with nothing more serious than the morning.

The girl behind the bar handed him his drink and he gave her a tenner and she only gave him back two quid change, and then he sipped the drink and realised she'd poured him a double though he hadn't asked for it. He supposed it didn't really matter. It was payday soon and anyway he needed this, he really needed this evening out. He never came out like this, did he, just for fun? He never did this any more.

He closed his eyes a moment, nodding along to the music, then turned to lean against the bar, thinking back again to Hollytree, remembering Kate, the swallows . . . you'd get that particular kind of really clear early morning light sometimes up there, too. That beautiful clear light, especially in spring. Exactly this time of year, in fact. Not that you'd realise it here in the city, with concrete and brick as far as the eye could see.

But back to those memories of grumpy Kate in the mornings, dragging the quilt off their bed and round her shoulders. Dragging the quilt and then coming to sit next to him all wrapped up like that, a caterpillar in a cocoon, frowning as he blathered on about some crap to her, God knows, probably something about skylarks or gooseberries – or something even about the way Travellers had stopped there, on that land, for centuries. From the sixteenth century at least, he'd found out from his forays into that old library on Green Street, maybe even before that. Just to think of that, families like theirs watching the skylarks since possibly even before the UK was the UK. Certainly long before passports and councils and 'injunctions to protect land from unauthorised encampments' . . .

Ah but then the world had changed of course and so had Kate and there was no sense in going over all that again. And where even was that quilt, these days? He had to stop losing things. Why was he always losing things? It'd been one that Nan had made, too. Poor Nan. In an effort to shake off those thoughts he rubbed his eyes, and took another gulp of whiskey.

This place, though. This place he was in, this felt almost right, tonight. This unlikely basement in the usually obnoxious hipster end of London somehow felt close to being somewhere he actually wanted to be, because it was taking him back in time, just like he wanted – except back way further than Hollytree and the days when Kate had smiled at his jokes and all that. This place . . . this place was like a bloody time warp, like there was some fucking *Doctor Who* shit going on or something, because the music! Muse, The Strokes, Bloc Party, The Killers, that 'Are You Gonna Be My Girl?' song he could never remember the right band name of.

Gorjer music, Martin called this, always telling Charlie it wasn't for him – that there was no place for people like Charlie in the world of this music, and he was kidding himself if he tried to believe otherwise. The people who wrote these songs would probably shudder at the thought of them being played on a Traveller site, Martin said, as when did you last see a Traveller in an indie band, after all? It was just posh Gorjer boys showing off, and what did Charlie want to do with that shite, anyway? Yeah, that's absolutely what Martin said. But then again, Charlie had never quite listened, had never quite believed him. As surely music was just music, wasn't it? And surely this stuff was bigger than all that. Bigger than arguments over whose music it was meant to be, and whose music Martin thought it was. Bigger than Gorjer or not Gorjer, Traveller or not Traveller. It meant more, didn't it? It was the magic of the old indie rock 'n' roll dream and everything – all the hopes and expectations – that had gone with it. And somehow, here, tonight, it was still alive in 2012. Sure the place was more than half empty, but it was only, what, twenty past eleven, if his watch was right? It'd warm up.

And he didn't much care anyway if nobody else arrived. This music, these few people dancing and drinking here, this atmosphere of swagger, of righteous anger, of fuck-off defiance and even of arrogance . . . he'd missed this, this mood, this philosophy. Because where had it gone, recently? What had changed?

This place, it felt like the old days. So much so, in fact, that he'd happily stay for another drink . . . except of course he probably shouldn't as he'd spent way too much already and in any case there was work tomorrow, and Kate to face as usual and he didn't want a hangover, no way, not with Saturday on the horizon . . . but then again, he wasn't ready to leave just quite yet, and were the bar staff giving him the evil eye already? Wondering when he'd fork out for something else to justify his presence here a little longer? That girl who'd served him, for instance, she was definitely looking at him funny. This city. It never stopped asking you for stuff, never stopped demanding you pay up just for the right of continuing to be wherever you happened to be, for the right to breathe the air, and take up your corner of floor space. He headed back over and ordered another whiskey.

People were filtering in now, the place filling up fast, and with some pretty girls among the crowd and all. He'd stay for one more drink, maybe even a bit of a dance too, because how good would it feel to dance to some of these old songs? To all the fucking tunes . . . Intellectually he knew that at twenty-five he was still young, and that no one could possibly call him otherwise. But then these songs, this music, it made him *feel* young, in a way he hadn't really felt for ages. Made him remember how it had been, back when he'd felt like all the unspoken rules and divisions that seemed to govern other people's lives might not apply where he was concerned. Back when he'd felt so many avenues of possibility stretching ahead, wide open – so many different ways his life might yet still go.

When had that been, when he'd last truly felt like that? Before London, certainly. Before all that shite with Kate and the hospital and everything going so wrong. Before losing Nan, too. It would have been the early days in Surrey, most likely. Farnham, Godalming, Guildford, Newford, Woking, Cranleigh, Dorking . . . places that weren't far away, really, but which felt like another world now. And that had been back when James had still been alright too, of course – which wasn't to say he wasn't alright now, but, well, you know, back then he'd still been able to walk and everything, and the two of them had gotten on like peas in a pod. In those days, Charlie had always been taking him out places, to show him stuff. Nothing too wild, just old churches or pubs with a bit of weird history, or random, cool, interesting things, like that pond he'd found round the back of the Travelodge in Dorking with all the frogs and tadpoles and water boatmen.

'Can we take one home?' he still remembered James asking of the frogs. 'Can we keep one? As a pet?'

James had always been good at looking after living things. He seemed to have the knack for it. That gnarly old tabby cat of his, for instance. He'd had her for a lifetime, it felt like – since they were kids. Charlie had said no to taking a frog, that day. He couldn't remember why. Probably he'd been trying to show off a bit, play the older brother, lay down the law. He wished he hadn't, now.

Ah but he'd been such a good kid, James. All wide eyes and listening, sketching everything he came across, that pencil of his creating whole new worlds on the paper. He still was a good kid, really. That wheelchair kept him young, in a way. Poor James. Ah but there it was, the fight on Saturday sidling back into his brain again. He'd be fine. Adrenaline and all of that.

Charlie necked his drink and stepped away from the bar to dance. There were people everywhere now, moving all around – and here were some of the old clothes, too. Leather jackets and skinny jeans and plaid shirts and everything. Where on earth had that old jacket of his gone? The one with all the patches? He'd worn it for years and it'd only got better with age. He must still have it somewhere. It hadn't been all *that* long ago, after all, all of that, had it? Maybe at Hollytree. Maybe he'd lost it at Hollytree. Ha. Like everything bloody else.

The chorus kicked in of the song that was on. Fuck knows what it was, he couldn't name it, hadn't bloody heard it since 2003 or something, had he? But still his hands were up in the air with everyone else's and he found he knew all the words.

It was funny, the way things turned out. Back then, late nineties, early noughties, whatever, it had seemed like there was a whole magical world just waiting for him to inherit it, a world of both family and outsider, Gorjer and Traveller, all mixed up into a particular version of adulthood that would have a place for him in it. A grown-up life that chimed with the rock 'n' roll dream, with Saturdays whiled away at record shops and getting shitfaced on cheap cider and talking life and deep philosophy while riding bikes around the common. And then he'd finally grown old enough to live the adult life he thought he'd been promised, only to find it had vanished, somehow. Disappeared without trace.

And instead, it was all family obligations, Iraq War, Starbucks, financial crash, austerity, the coalition and the fucking BNP. All racists and councils chucking you off the land where you'd made your home without so much as a visit to give notice, only stupid fucking letters in the post that they should have realised no one would read, anyway. And then miscarriages – or not exactly miscarriages, but you know – and town centres all paved over and turned into identikit shopping malls with not a record shop in sight and *Big* fucking *Brother* and *I'm a* fucking *Celebrity* and ketamine and shit jobs and electronic dance music and . . . but who the fuck was that?

That girl, dancing in a group next to him. Singing just as loudly as he was, even, and the same way, like it was important to do so, like they were in church or something, at some remembrance service, maybe. As if it were important to sing along with the guitar solo like this to remember exactly what they'd once dreamed they could have been. And she looked, well, she looked like every girl he'd ever fancied before Kate. Skinny, long messy hair, plenty of black eyeliner . . . but really that wasn't important at all. It was the way she sang, the way she sang the words of the chorus now like they were something that mattered, the way she moved as if she didn't care how she looked. How she danced there in a crowded room of people just as if no one were watching.

He waited until Nirvana had segued into Maximo Park and into The White Stripes before he told himself fuck it, Charlie, you used to have a way with girls, a certain swagger, a confidence, that way you could make them all laugh, and the world may have changed unrecognisably since then, but you haven't, prove to me now that you haven't, too. And so he stepped up, right into the centre of the group of girls she was dancing in, and plonked himself in front of her in a way she couldn't ignore. And then he leaned over and shouted in her ear, over the strains of 'Seven Nation Army'.

'Is there any way at all,' he said, 'that I could have your number?'

She frowned, looked genuinely pained – and his heart, which had been previously jumping up and turning somersaults between his throat and lower stomach plummeted to his stupid trainers.

'I'm sorry,' she said, this girl, in an accent posher than he'd imagined her having, somehow – and she really did look sorry, at least that was something. 'I'm sorry,' she said. 'But there isn't, really. There isn't.' And she shook her head and looked at him with something awfully like pity that was just too terrible to be around, and so which sent him off, away from her and back towards the bar. Fuck it. He was fat and old and married and he hadn't shaved or even dressed himself up properly and he stood out here like a sore thumb, how had he ever kidded himself otherwise? And probably anyway she had a boyfriend – some fucking twenty-year-old with a university degree and a bunch of cocaine in his pocket or whatever was fashionable these days, who knew.

'Whiskey soda please,' he asked the barman, and he'd just paid the full eight quid it was for a double and necked the lot of it when he felt a soft hand between his shoulder blades and turned, thinking it might be her, the girl come back to talk to him again – only to find it wasn't, wasn't at all. It was some emaciated dark-haired bird with an undercut and lots of piercings.

'I've been watching you,' she said, this girl – some sort of accent, a soft twang, not all that pronounced but there, definitely. Australian. Or American, maybe. 'You interest me.'

And then before he knew what had happened he was snogging her and it didn't feel at all bad, actually. There was just something about human contact, wasn't there? And it'd been so long since he and Kate had got together like this and then even when they did once in a blue moon well it was all screwed up now, wasn't it, after . . . well. Poor Kate. But don't think about Kate. It's this bird with the piercings now, and they'd been kissing for what felt like ages, three or four songs at least and he was drunk, he could tell, a bit sloppy but she didn't seem to mind. He didn't even know her name but she'd linked her fingers through his and was leading him through the room of dreamers dancing to 'Disco 2000' now and over to the exit. She was ballsy, that much was clear. It was a bold fucking move, the whole thing. The kind of thing he himself would never have dared to try, not even back in the day when he'd been good with girls and understood the whole game – or not that he'd tried more than once or twice, from what he could remember. Maybe she was just extremely high? Whatever was happening he followed her willingly, letting himself be led like a lamb up the stairs, out the fire exit, through the smoking area and with her into a cab.

They didn't talk on the drive. Or not much, anyway. This girl seemed wild, like she was on some kind of mission – and he just went along with it. Went along with her kissing and groping like it wasn't unexpected or strange at all, like they'd been talking in the club for hours, like he'd asked for her number and they'd got chatting and he'd charmed her in the simple old-fashioned way, whatever that was, and then one thing had led to another . . . that's what he would assume if he were witnessing this from an outside perspective. If he were the taxi driver, say, glancing in the rear-view mirror to see the road and catching their antics in the foreground. But he didn't know the first thing about her, this madwoman.

The only thing she said the whole journey – which seemed to last forever in the strange quiet of it, the cab driver's tinny radio and this girl's murmurs and groans the only sounds breaking the silence – was *48 Crofton Street*, when they got in. And God knows where this Crofton Street was but he hoped it was near, as it was getting awkward now, kind of weird, the girl's exaggerated porn star noises that would have made him burst out laughing if he hadn't been so drunk and unable to extricate himself to a safe distance from this claustrophobic scenario, this myopic perspective, and *mmm baby, yes, I want you*, she was actually saying – who actually said stuff like that though? Maybe he'd got trapped in a horror movie and she was some kind of flesh-eating alien come to kidnap him. She'd digest him and then hang the remains of his dried-out corpse on a meat hook in her basement – in the basement of this 48 Crofton Street where they were headed right now.

The car pulled up outside a house on a dark residential street, and then they were tumbling out the door on to the pavement, she dragging him, the taxi guy saying something. And then her chucking a note at him through the window and detaching her lips from Charlie's for a second to say, 'Keep the change.'

*Keep the change* and *48 Crofton Street*, the only things he knew about this woman. She didn't worry about money, or at least she wasn't worried about it tonight – and she lived here, at 48 Crofton Street. Because surely that's where they were now? She leading him up to a doorway, keys out of her pocket and into a lock at the same moment she grabbed his crotch, and then they were tumbling through the door up a squalid set of stairs – bad carpet, he noticed as he tumbled, threadbare and cheap, needs a hoover, and paint chipped on the bannisters – then up through a second front door into what must be this girl's flat, and then through the first door on the left . . . and crashing through now on to the merciful, merciful softness of a beautiful, wide double bed.

And as soon as they landed, the cloud-like marshmallow structures of the duvet and pillows and mattress surrounded him, supporting his weary limbs and catching that spot just between his shoulders, the bottom of the back of his neck which so often felt like where the key slotted in and wound him up tighter and tighter, as if he were a wind-up toy, little teddy, wee teddy Charlie marching up and down, round in circles, stuffed limbs moving faster as the key twisted tighter, oh but it got him right there, the softness, right at that spot on the back of the neck and though this madwoman from the club whose bed he supposed this must be was scrabbling at his crotch now, trying to undo his buttons and zips with her teeth, he had to say, had to admit, he was only dimly aware of her. Because what really felt good – what really was the best – was this wonderful, nurturing softness all around. It had been so long, so long since he'd been able to sleep without the guilt of Kate lying there next to him. So long since he'd had somewhere soft and neutral like this to be by himself, where nothing that he'd ruined or that had simply gone wrong all by itself on his watch even mattered. Ah and the club had been good too though, hadn't it? It had been a good laugh. He'd needed that. All the old songs, all the old fucking tunes. He batted the strange girl away, yawned, wriggled himself into a hollow in the duvet, and passed out.

# 22

He woke slowly, with an awareness of warm sunlight across his eyelids, and the sense of the rest of his body being cold. Then a catch of smoke in the air . . . cigarette smoke, when he hadn't smoked in months. Given up right after Kate did, with the baby on the way before the – but hang on. Smoking? Who was smoking, then? And why did he feel so bleeding awful, thumping head, pain coalescing around his left eye, scratchy throat, sick stomach . . .

His eyes flew open and fixed instantly on the girl sitting in the window – for girl she was, that was evidently clear. She'd looked older, definitely, last night in the dim light of the club. God, the club. Jesus Christ. What had he been thinking? He'd just been meaning to go out to the gym for an hour or so, maybe two, and instead he'd gone and . . . gone and *what*? And he had work today – he had to be at work, he was already on some kind of warning. They had eyes on him, Kenny had told him, though goodness knows what for, whatever it was it had surely been no fault of his own. Judging by the colour of the light, though, the way it was strong and quite golden and streaming through the open window with a hint of actual heat in it . . . judging by that it was long gone half eight, when he had to be arriving at the warehouse. Could be late morning, even midday, who knew?

She probably would, in fact, this girl with the funny hair and all the piercings and last night's make-up. She'd probably have some rough idea at least about what time it was.

'You looked more interesting in the dark,' she said, before he could speak, staring at him steadily through her cigarette smoke. 'I'm an artist,' she continued. 'I look out for a certain quality in people. It interests me. Something I lack myself but which I need in quantities for my work.'

She still sounded American. So he hadn't imagined that last night, had been a little compos mentis at least.

'Yesterday, I thought you had it. But now . . .?' She shrugged and took a huge inhale of her cigarette.

An artist? Surely not. He didn't have too clear an idea in his head of what an artist looked like, but still this seemed unlikely. She was too young, too . . . he glanced around the room. Shelf of battered black Penguins. Rag rug. Posters for black and white films he didn't recognise stuck straight on to the walls with tape, or Blu Tack.

'You're at art school?' he hazarded.

She nodded, once. 'You?'

'I – work at a warehouse. You know, forklift stuff. I'm sorry,' he said. 'I have to go.'

She laughed, once. Not kindly.

'Be my guest,' she said, blowing smoke, nodding towards the door which stood ajar at the foot of the bed.

*

He felt briefly better when he hit the outside and the cold air and the warm sunlight. Then he felt dramatically worse on the bus ride home. Twenty past twelve, the bus driver had said when he'd asked him. Work was a lost cause, then. He'd have to go in tomorrow and plead food poisoning and hope no one was mean enough to question it. And it wasn't totally a lie. He *felt* food-poisoned, at least, because God was it hard keeping the contents of his stomach down in the heat and endless swinging back and forth of this bus. He'd ended up all the way across town, way on the other side of the river. How had he even walked that far? That was exercise, at least – not the gym, exactly, but not too bad for the fitness at least – ten thousand steps a day didn't they say? And he must have taken hundreds of thousands of steps last night to get all the way up here. That had to count for something. He looked out the window for a moment at all the city people – not hung-over, not exhausted, simply going about their innocent business in the sunshine, the fuckers – and felt pleased with himself for a moment, before remembering they'd taken a cab.

He got home to find Kate crying. Couldn't blame her, though, really, him vanishing off like that, no word, phone battery dead, no point in calling – probably thought he was dead or off with some other lass or just upped and left her, not coming back.

'Kate,' he said, keeping his voice as soft as he could. 'Kate. I'm back now. Got held up a bit but it's okay. I'm back, I'm back with you.'

He edged his way round the sofa to where she was sitting curled up, weeping over some bit of paper in her hand, and he reached out and tried to put an arm around her shoulders. He wasn't altogether surprised when she slapped it away, though what she said next came as a bit of a shock.

'You,' she said, shoving the bit of paper right up in his face, so close it caught up on his eyelashes when he blinked.

'You've got some nerve coming back here with all *this* going on. When were you going to tell me, Charlie? Did you think I would never find out?'

Oh he was tired. And sick. Sick as a dog. He needed water, food and sympathy. Not this. Never this.

'What's happened now?' he said, taking the letter and sitting down next to her on the sofa, only scanning what it said at first, then reading it more closely.

'Default on payments?' he said. 'Upkeep and cover charge for communal areas? But this is bullshit. I didn't know about this. Who's this even from? Who are these, these Curren and Edgeley Limited?'

Kate just shook her head, and kept on crying.

'Oh Kate, Kate,' he said. 'It'll be alright, you'll see. It must be some kind of mistake . . .'

'Nine hundred and seventy-eight pounds,' she said. 'How did you think I wouldn't find out? Charlie? How?'

'I didn't – I swear, Kate, I don't know what this is. I've never heard of these Curren and Edgeley people. For all we know it's bullshit.' He reached his arm round her shoulders again.

'It's not bullshit' – she slapped him away again – 'I phoned the man, the man up at the estate agents, and though it took me hours to get through, almost, so help me God I held that line and he said, he said . . .' But she only collapsed into tears again. Softer tears than before, though, maybe. And then she was leaning into Charlie – burying her face and soaking the folds of his jumper. 'I don't know, Charlie,' she said. 'I don't understand. You know I'm no good at understanding things like this. You know I've never been any good at all this kind of stuff . . .'

He nodded and hushed her though he knew that was a sad rewriting of the truth. She had been good at money, and all of this stuff. Had been able to see right through sharp practice and had had her head screwed on about everything much better than he'd ever had. She'd kept their whole operation running, in fact. Saved him from quite a few bad decisions, back in the day. It was since what had happened with the baby, was all. It had turned her all paralysed and panicky.

'Hush, Kate, it'll be alright, you'll see. I'll give them a call tomorrow and work out what's what.'

'Call them today,' she said, into Charlie's shoulder. 'Not tomorrow. Today.'

Then she was lost to crying and rocking again. He stroked her back. Skinny shoulder blades like little wings jutting out beneath the thin layers of skin and T-shirt.

'I can't stand it, Charlie,' she was saying. 'I hate it here. This flat, it's like a prison. This isn't what I wanted. This isn't what I ever wanted.' She looked up, a brief moment of clarity in her grey eyes then, shining through the fog of confusion and grief that always hung over them these days. 'What's happened to us, Charlie? I want to go home. D'you remember how the sky looked over the woods at Hollytree this time of year? How we'd sit out on the steps of the old van and listen to the birds?'

'I do remember, Kate. I do.'

He kissed her forehead, then her lips. And my God the feel of her, the relief of it, the way it was like old times almost, strangely, today. The first time it had felt like that in months. What had he been thinking last night with that lip-piercing, tongue-piercing girl? When here was Kate, his Kate, and shared memories and kisses that were like spring rain now, almost, spring rain soft and clear on the fields.

'I want to go home,' Kate whispered.

'I know,' he said. And there were tears on his cheeks now and, speaking honestly, he wasn't even sure that they were just hers any more. He held her then, but he had to be so careful, it felt like, fragile as she seemed these days – his wild Kate now turned so frail and breakable.

# 23

When he woke again he was still on the sofa, Kate was gone, and there was a smell of frying bacon from the kitchen. The curtains were open on the far window though it was past sunset – vestiges of light left in the world outside, but not much.

'Kate?' he said. 'Katie?'

He could hear her singing in the kitchen as she cooked. Wordless, tuneful humming he hadn't heard from her since . . . well. It was always just the same old story, wasn't it?

'Kate?'

She stopped singing and stuck her head round the door frame to look at him. She was smiling, which somehow only made her look more exhausted.

'What you cooking, Kate?'

'Breakfast? Dinner? Who knows? I didn't have lunch, either, so it could even be that.' She ducked back out of sight. There was a sound of clattering pans.

He rubbed his forehead. Sat up. Physically he felt a lot better than the last time he'd woken up. This was good. But what had happened? With Kate? It had been almost wonderful and yet now he felt strange, like he'd agreed to something he knew he would only screw up, like he seemed to screw up everything. Except that now it would be worse because there'd be that fraction of hope involved, the hope that this time round he might manage to be different. That he'd be stronger, wiser, that he wouldn't let her down . . . except then of course, right on cue, there was the fight again, back in his thoughts with the persistence of a cough he couldn't shake. Poor Kate. And poor James, landed with a brother like him. What was he even doing, sleeping the day away when it was in less than a week, now? Less than four days?

'Kate,' he called again. 'Katie. How long did I sleep for?'

'You were out for hours,' she called from the kitchen. 'Like a corpse, you were.'

'You didn't try and wake me?' he said.

'I tried but there was no doing it, so I thought I'd just leave you. You must have needed it, to be so far deep as that.'

'You thought you'd just . . . Kate.' He got up, chucked off the tartan blanket it seemed she'd laid out over him, tucking him in like a child. He went to stand in the kitchen doorway, watching her as she bustled back and forth with her pots and pans – not looking at him any more now, though, avoiding his eyes again, focused on what she was doing on the stove. This way of things, this felt more familiar.

'You do realise, Kate, it's under a week till the fight, now – less than a week till I have to stand in a fucking field somewhere and look the young prick in the eye who insulted my brother and make sure it's him who goes down bleeding and not me, and now you're letting me sleep the day away? Not even trying to wake me? Putting blankets on instead?'

Kate turned down the gas on a pan of eggs that were going to be scrambled. Otherwise she did nothing, said nothing, kept her eyes down.

'What?' said Charlie. 'What, Kate? What even is all this?'

She took a deep breath, wiped her hands on her apron, then turned around from the stove to look him dead in the eye.

'This morning,' she said. 'It was like you coming back to me. I thought – maybe something had changed again. That we were less lost than we've been, maybe.'

He didn't reply immediately. Was aware of letting her words, offered out to him in the warmth and the steam of the cooking food all around him, fall slowly down to the linoleum floor.

'Less lost?' he said, eventually. 'Less lost? This whole thing started because we owe some Curren and whoever it is almost a grand in cash, and we're less lost? And now we're having some sort of – fucksake, Kate, smoked salmon? *Avocados?* When did you buy avocados? We can't be having fucking avocados when we're in debt, Kate.'

He turned on his heel and left the kitchen, then he picked up his jacket. He'd go to the gym now, that's what he'd do. The day wasn't over yet, it was fine – it would all be fine. But Christ what had he been thinking with that girl last night, the one with the lip piercing, the student? Poor Kate. But then seeing as he'd spent a whole night gone AWOL, why hadn't she said anything yet? Did she not even care what he did any more? Or was this just what she expected of him nowadays? He patted his jacket pockets, checking – keys, phone, wallet . . . wallet? But there it was, not in his pocket but on the arm of the sofa.

'Kate,' he shouted through to her over the noise of the pans. 'Kate, did you go through my things?'

'Didn't go through them,' she said. 'Just took a bit of cash so we'd have some nice food.'

'Just took . . . so you refuse to work then you complain about this Curren and whatever thing and then you steal money straight out of my pockets, and then still somehow it's my fault?'

She appeared in the kitchen doorway.

'That's not how it is,' she said. 'You know that's not how it is.'

He shrugged his jacket on.

'Where are you going?' she asked.

'The gym,' he said.

'Like last night?' she said.

'Yeah.'

She watched him in silence as he pulled on his trainers, laced them, patted his pockets one more time, and headed over towards the front door. It was only when he was halfway through it, about to swing it shut, that she started yelling.

'You're so angry about me using a couple of quid for a decent meal for us both? When maybe if you pulled yourself together and found some better work we'd have plenty for weeks. We'd have enough to even get out of this shithole and back on the road again. But you won't, will you? Of course you won't because you're a drunk, Charlie Wells, and you just don't want to admit it—'

He slammed the door, cutting her off mid-rant.

'Ah Kate,' he whispered aloud to himself as he beat his retreat from the house, trying not to think about the way she'd said *I want to go home*, and the way that had caught at something deep in the core of him, and made it into something they both felt, both of them together, this wanting to go back to somewhere they'd felt like they'd belonged, and that everything was right, even the hardships and the problems. Somewhere they'd felt like their hardships and problems were their own hardships and problems, at least. And not those of alien people from some TV soap or something, thrust on them from somewhere else.

How had she done that? he wondered as he walked on towards the gym. How had she made him feel that way, turning it into something both of them were suffering? How had she moved herself in his head from being a symptom of the problem to being a fellow victim of it? Just like that she'd somehow made everything more complicated again, when really? Fuck, he didn't really want to fight or work, he wanted to be driving – driving their old Transit with all their stuff stashed in the back, towards somewhere he could breathe clear air again. Driving to somewhere with trees, and where there was wide sky above them, and long Roman roads stretching this way and that. Driving back in time, too, even, back to James before the accident so he could tell him to never ride that quad bike in that field so he'd be fine today, completely fine which meant of course the fight wouldn't even be happening – and even if for some reason it still were, it would be James fighting, James defending himself as it should be, as it always should have been. Poor James. Maybe, in fact, that's where he'd go now – he'd go and visit James, because that was part of preparing for the fight too, wasn't it, kind of? Getting psychologically ready. And it was too late for the gym, he was too wrecked. He'd only perform badly and have Martin knock him out, probably, knowing Martin, as well as knocking everyone's nerves out of place for the weekend. He walked on as far as the bus stop, and jumped on the first bus that appeared.

It had been ages since he'd caught up with his brother. More than anything to do with getting ready for the fight, he honestly just wanted to see him, and chat to him. Ask him, even, maybe, what he thought about this whole situation with Kate, because they'd never really discussed it, had they? He'd never really talked to anyone about what had happened with the baby. There was never a good time, and it was just too complicated, too difficult to get his head around, and so much easier to simply shut down whoever was asking, sharpish. Except things had never got this bad before – things had never gone this far. Since they'd been married, he'd never gone off with some other bird, not getting home before the morning. Maybe talking about it all with someone, with James now, for instance – maybe it would help?

Ah but who was he kidding, he and James didn't talk about stuff like that. It wasn't how they worked, as brothers. And it wasn't James's problem to worry about, either. Charlie was the older brother, he should be able to handle this on his own. It would be pointless, bringing it up with James. It would be worse than pointless. He didn't need James doubting his strength or his reliability this week. Not before Saturday. It would still be good to see him, though. Just for a chat. They could watch TV together maybe, or head out for a bit to the pub, or just for a walk even. Say hello to Mum, if she was in.

What a trek it was though, all the way across the city, even further than where he'd been that morning, at that American girl's house. This bus wouldn't even take him half-way there. That was the other thing about losing Hollytree. It wasn't just about skylarks and treetops and whatnot. It was about family. He liked seeing his brother, despite what he knew people said, despite how he knew it must seem sometimes. It'd been good when James had been just across the way from him. Him and Kate in their caravan, and James and Nan in the one across so that they'd bump into each other and spend time all the time without having to arrange it. It was this thing now of having to take over an hour to cross the whole city to do it. It wasn't that he couldn't be bothered with the journey, that wasn't it. It was just that the fact of him having so obviously gone to that effort, made him look so much more . . . well.

'Charlie!' he could just remember James yelling now, out the window, across the way. 'What's the opposite of hollow?'

'What?' he'd hollered back. 'Why?'

'Eight down, ten letters,' James had said.

'You're doing the crossword?'

'What d'you think?'

'What the fuck you doing that for? You turned into an old lady now or something?'

'Don't think I didn't hear that—' Nan's voice, chiming in. Christ, Nan. How he missed her. This feeling that had been swamping him recently, this sense of losing his anchor, of no one with any power fighting his corner – surely he could never have felt like this while Nan had still been around.

'The opposite of hollow,' James had yelled again.

'I dunno, full? Filled-out?' he'd said.

'It's ten letters, though.'

'Meaningful. How about meaningful?' Charlie had called back then, sticking his head out the window to see his brother doing exactly the same, arms resting on the ledge in the caravan opposite, cheeky old grin lighting up his face, freckles standing out in the afternoon sun.

'Thanks, mate,' James had said.

'No bother,' Charlie had replied, grinning back. And though it had only been a stupid crossword clue he'd felt a weird stab of pride, as James had lifted that mad tabby cat of his up in the window, waving one of her paws.

'Tiger says thanks, too,' he'd said.

'Well, then, tell her it's no problem at all. Anytime . . .'

Suddenly it felt so cold on the bus. Charlie was shivering now, genuinely properly shivering. You'd never guess it was almost spring. Or maybe it wasn't actually as cold as it felt, and that was just his hangover kicking back in again. He looked about himself, leaving the memories of Hollytree behind to take in the fogged-up windows, and all the other passengers standing in the aisle around him. He suddenly felt kind of claustrophobic. As if the walls and all the edges of things were closing in on him, and his chest and his stomach felt strange, too. All freezing and empty. Maybe it was food he needed? When had he last eaten, after all? Fish and chips, maybe fish and chips would sort him out . . . remember when fish and chips had still come in newspaper? And the newsprint used to come off on your fingers? And as you ate you could read whatever weird local news headline was on your bit of the paper that you'd been given, like some strange parochial lucky dip? The *Newford Echo*, that had had some good ones, hadn't it? God. Right now though, he really needed off this bus.

He went to push the button for the next stop just as the bus lurched round a bend, and he stumbled, and the old lady opposite him sighed and tutted. Nan would have been about her age, if she'd still been around. He couldn't imagine Nan tutting at people on buses though.

Out on to the pavement, finally, and watching the bright lit-up box of the bus pitching away, out of view, he didn't feel the sense of relief he'd hoped for. He could still hear James's voice, too, from all those years ago. *The opposite of hollow.* And yet he didn't think he could face seeing James now after all. Not when he was feeling so shite. So unprepared for Saturday, hung-over and in yesterday's clothes. But where else could he go? Not the gym. Not home, back to Kate. He didn't even feel hungry, any more. The gnawing feeling in his stomach was still there, but now it didn't feel fixable with anything so simple as food. He needed something different. Something completely outside of this nightmare of the flat and facing Kate and James and the gym and the fight on Saturday. Just a break from it all. A window on to something else completely different. Windows and differences, windows and differences . . . what did that remind him of?

And he thought again then of that American girl smoking this morning, laughing at him when he'd told her about the warehouse he worked in. And, trying not to think too much about what he was doing in case it would seem too insane and he was forced to think better of it, he began retracing his steps from the morning, back to where he'd begun this whole long, confusing day. To 48 Crofton Street – one of the only things about last night he could recall with clarity.

# 24

It wasn't like he was interested in the American girl – not *interested* interested. And he certainly wasn't kidding himself she'd look twice again at him either, or even that there'd been any particular rhyme or reason to them getting together in the bar last night at all. Though he couldn't say quite why he'd come here, that definitely wasn't it. Still, out of some strange impulse, thinking it might make her like him better, maybe, or make him showing up here seem somehow a touch less insane, he slipped his wedding ring in his pocket just as he heard the bolt of the front door slide back.

'You,' she said, opening the door not even halfway, just enough to stick her nose through and look him up and down. He wished he wasn't still wearing the same clothes as this morning. Wished he'd showered at least. He decided to pretend he hadn't noticed the edge to her tone there. Tried to pretend it was five years ago, when girls had still smiled at him in the street and he'd never had to ask for a number twice. Tummy in, shoulders back, easy smile – that wasn't so hard now was it?

'Haven't forgotten me already?' he said.

She seemed to shudder, maybe a tad theatrically, and in doing so widened the opening of the front door a little. Unlike him, she had changed her clothes. She had a whole new look going on – still with all the piercings, but with some kind of dress on now, some trailing floral number with shoulder pads like what his mum had worn in pictures from the eighties. That probably meant she had showered, too. Scrubbed away any traces he might have left on her skin. That was fine, though. He'd gone home to his wife. If this was a competition as to who was less bothered he'd still be winning – even with her looking at him like that, and the front door held firm against him, even with him waiting out like this on her doorstep, trying to pose as his better self from what felt like a lifetime ago. He wasn't trying to impress her, exactly. It was more like . . . he was pretending that he might be someone a bit like her, maybe. Someone who might also reply with a blank look and a laugh to the words, *I work at a warehouse. You know, forklift stuff.*

He was here because he wanted to look at the posters on her walls. Because he wanted to ask her what films they were for, and to listen to her as she talked on about those old actors and directors or whatever they were like they were people everyone knew. He wanted to go through her kitchen cupboards and see what brand of tea bags she bought, what the crockery looked like, and what CDs were stacked up on her shelves. He needed out of his own head, that was all. Out of his own life.

'Obviously I haven't forgotten you,' she said. 'I don't forget my mistakes so easily.'

'Mistakes? Ah . . . to be fair, it wasn't all bad now, was it?'

She shrugged. 'That was not what I meant. Only, that I was wrong about you. My first impression wasn't correct.'

'The old beer goggles will do that to you, definitely. I was quite surprised too to wake up where I was this morning.'

'I don't drink.'

'Right.'

'It gives me a headache.'

'Well, it gives everyone a headache.'

'Why did you come back here?'

'I don't know,' he said. 'Listen, I don't – I don't wake up at strange women's houses too often. In fact, it's something I never do – something I've almost never done.'

She was watching him more closely now. He decided to keep talking.

'And just . . . well. I've had a bit of a rough day' – her eyes glazed over – 'and I'm interested in you' – he tried to pull it back – 'I don't want anything. I just want to talk. To know a bit more about you. Who you are. What your name is, even, for a start.'

'Hippolyta,' she said, not smiling.

'Good, strong name,' he said.

She shook her head. 'I hate it.'

'I'm Charlie, by the way,' he said, and hesitated just a second before offering his hand for her to shake. She stared down her nose at it for a long moment, before slipping hers into it. Bony fingers. He remembered the touch of them now, from last night.

'Come on,' he said. 'Just a conversation, I don't want anything else. I promise. I'll take you out for a cup of tea, even.'

She looked uncertain, and seemed to be about to say something else when a shout came from behind her – 'Polly!' – and a tall girl with waist-length blonde hair and a face like a model appeared in the hallway behind her. Hippolyta instinctively opened the front door a little wider, including Charlie in the moment even if he wasn't yet inside the building.

'Oh,' the blonde girl said. 'Who's this?'

Her accent was English, but not English like Charlie's which was still resolutely Mancunian in its foundations. Her English was cut-glass BBC, boarding school, those old wartime movies his mum so loved to watch, where everyone had a stiff upper lip and an old-fashioned hairdo . . . and he'd never really met a real person who talked like that, he realised now. He wondered if it had come naturally to her, or she'd had to be taught.

'Sorry,' she said to him, wide-eyed through the gap in the doorway. 'Only I thought you would be someone else.'

'We have friends here this evening,' said Hippolyta, by way of explanation.

'Don't get cold,' said the blonde girl. 'March is no time to be lurking on doorsteps, you know. You'll only catch pneumonia and then you'll be sorry. Come on in. Tea's on in the front room. Have you seen Hippolyta's samovar yet?'

She turned on her heel, and swept down the corridor in that way common to very posh, very beautiful people – something to do with their never entertaining the possibility they might be challenged, or ignored. And it worked, though, because wasn't he walking along behind her into this place he'd almost fled from this morning? Even nodding as she prattled airily about different types of tea, with Hippolyta sulking along behind them.

'But weren't you expecting someone else?' he said, finally snatching a word in edgeways as she paused in her chatter to take a breath. 'You'd invited somebody else, not me.'

'Oh but that doesn't matter,' this blonde girl said, turning her round blue eyes on him, seeming almost surprised he'd bring up such a thing. 'He'll be along in a minute I'm sure and besides, we *love* meeting new people, don't we, Polly?'

He looked round to check Polly's reaction to this. She had a face like thunder – a real hatchet-face, Nan would have called it – but still, she only shrugged.

'Oh, don't mind her,' the blonde girl said, stopping in front of the door at the top of the little flight of stairs they'd just climbed. The building was much bigger than he'd thought it was this morning, and an odd shape, slightly rabbit warren-y, extending out in ways he hadn't quite got his head around – all badly lit corridors, threadbare carpet, patches of damp and high, high ceilings. 'She has to be hostile and challenging, you see – it's part of how she conceptualises her identity.'

'What?' Charlie began to say – but it was swallowed up in the moment of this blonde girl pushing open the door in front of them to reveal a whole living room filled, more or less, with chattering students. Because obviously they were students – it was clear as day from their ages and clothes – all fresh-faced kids in velvets and vintage with heavy kohl eyeliner and well-practised expressions of world-weariness. Clear too from the way they all stood or sat or leaned with such self-consciousness, from the way they held their glasses of red wine or their flowered teacups and their saucers as if it were completely natural to them – and then from the words immediately leaping to the surface of the general wash of conversation in the room . . . *somehow glorious, don't you see . . . the urgency of the brushwork, the rawness of it . . . very disappointing, I thought, utterly facile . . . so hung-over honestly I feel like death, can't think why I even came . . .*

Charlie didn't mind students, really. People talked shite about them, said they were a nuisance or ruined the vibe of a bar or whatever it was when they all came in in a pack in that way they always did – but then he'd always thought they must generally be alright people, underneath it all. As who else would be curious enough to keep on studying for years longer than was legally necessary? Curious enough even to get themselves seriously in debt to keep on doing it, to keep sitting in libraries and reading books?

Watching from the doorway of the living room, though, he was reminded again of how there was always something about the way they were. Something that felt so alien to him, too. They all seemed so much younger than he was, for a start, held in a mysterious kind of second childhood that made him stop short of conversation. That even made him feel a little spooked, for whatever reason. A little nervous. And sure he'd wanted a window into a different world when he'd left Kate that afternoon, but this? This wasn't what he'd been after, surely? He must stick out here like anything. And yet no one in the room had given him so much as a second glance.

He found himself looking back to Hippolyta – for reassurance? Surely not. What was it that he wanted? Her blessing? She just shrugged, in a clear *whatever, knock yourself out* kind of way. Not friendly, but not like anything particularly surreal was happening, either.

'I'm Charlie, by the way,' he said, introducing himself to the posh blonde who was still next to him, for some reason, and offering her his hand to shake.

'Oh,' she said, taking it as if a handshake was some utterly antiquated gesture. 'How charming. I'm Flo. And how do you know Polly? Or shouldn't I enquire?' She flashed him what she probably thought was a sly smile as he unconsciously slipped his free hand into his pocket, worrying his wedding ring with fingers and thumb – and then there was another buzz at the door. Hippolyta sloped off to answer it, and then Flo had a hand on his arm and was propelling him towards a group of people standing by the fireplace – no fire, though. He wondered if the chimney had been blocked off, or if for some reason it just hadn't occurred to them to light one.

'Felix, Asha, Gabe – meet Charlie. Polly's latest discovery.'

'Ah well, you know. I was about for a little while at least before she discovered me, believe it or not,' he said. And then instantly hated the way he'd chosen to say something that made it sound like he knew Hippolyta better than he did. All three of them laughed though, these Felix, Asha and Gabe.

And then one of them, Asha it must have been, said, 'Your accent's interesting, isn't it? Did you grow up abroad or something?'

'Nah, mate,' said Charlie. 'Grew up not too far from here, over Surrey way. I'm a Traveller, though. So I suppose I did kind of grow up all over.'

He didn't know quite why he'd told them like that, exactly. It had somehow just felt necessary to assert the fact.

They all laughed again.

And then when he didn't, Flo began, 'Are you really? A Traveller? You mean like a Gypsy? How *fascinating*.' And she really did seem fascinated for about half a second or so until her eyes slid off his to focus somewhere behind him, and her expression completely changed, like a girl waking up from a dream. 'Oh but he's here,' she said. 'You're here!' And she was off, fluttering away and around him like some sort of songbird off to a higher, brighter treetop.

'Oh he's here, is he?' Charlie found himself saying to the three students in front of him, raising his eyebrows as if this were so typical of Flo it deserved some affectionate ribbing . . . but then what the hell was he doing? When he'd barely met her five minutes ago? And who knew who this *he* of hers was anyway? Why was he grinning along like it was some kind of old joke? And why were the three students duly tittering? God, they were so easy to convince, to come out on top of, to entertain. Just like children, the lot of them. Though they couldn't have been . . . what? Less than twenty-one, twenty-two? Jesus, they were nearly James's age, must have been. Would James be like this if he'd stuck with school, and then gone to uni like Nan had wanted him to?

He slipped his hands nonchalantly in his pockets, riding the wave of the knowing laughter around him – laughter that he'd triggered among these strangers as easy as pushing a laugh-track button – and looked around with the rest of them, watching Flo flit her way over to whoever this *he* was that she was obviously so keen on. And he was actually a little bit curious, because she was weird, Flo, admittedly, a bit posh or sheltered or something maybe but she also seemed kind, and that definitely counted for something . . . except his thoughts were soon stopped in their tracks, and the false, easy smile wiped clean off his face.

Because there she was – birdlike, arty, posh-girl Flo, dashing up to throw her arms around the latest arrival to the room. And he wasn't how Charlie had pictured he would be at all. Because this was someone grinning such a famil-iar grin, trying to hug her back but not quite managing to seem as natural as she had done – all awkward angles and self-consciousness. Someone, in fact, that he, Charlie, would recognise anywhere – even here at this weird student art party in the strange end of London. Because surely that was him? Taller, certainly. Battered tweed jacket and tortoise-shell specs instead of those funny old dinosaur T-shirts and broken NHS numbers with the nose-piece all wound round with tape. But he'd grown up, that was all. And grown up well, from the look of things, from what you could tell like this, just at a glance across an unfamiliar room. And Charlie found in himself all at once a great rush of pride to see his old friend looking so well like this – and also, at the same time, a violent urge to disappear.

Except somehow there was his voice yelling out, almost in spite of the rest of him. Too loud for this party, for this confined space, these people, this room.

'Stan!'

And it was – of course it was. However weird and fucking unlikely, it *was*. Because Stan had stepped back from Flo at the sound of his name, searching the room for its caller, and then at last he saw Charlie, and as he did his face lit up like a child's at some sort of amazing surprise – and thank God it did, in fact, come to think of it, because how had they left things? It hadn't been great, from what Charlie remembered. There had been the hospital, and the roof, and poor Stan bleeding out on the drive right in front of him, and it had all been his fault, really, of course, because it always was. But Stan was fine now, it seemed. Fine and laughing, even, to see him. Disengaging from a puzzled Flo and crossing the room, here was his old friend here again, this boy, this man who'd once been *like a brother, like a brother to me*, as he'd told people for months, for years after even, whenever they'd asked about his growing up in Surrey.

'Alright?' he said. 'Long time no see.'

'My God,' said Stan. 'Is that really you?'

And then they hugged, and Stan felt whole in his grip like that, undamaged, as if he'd never even fallen off that roof at all. And Charlie found himself wishing that he'd shaved that afternoon before coming out. That he'd worn better clothes, or just fresh clothes, even. That he hadn't put on so much weight. That he had some actual friends here and hadn't only washed up in this living room because he was running away from his real life.

And yet fuck it. It was what it was. Stan was here. He'd got his old friend back. Found him again, here of all places. And that was something, wasn't it? One beautiful piece of dumb luck in this washed-out let-down of a world.

And so, suppressing the instinctive urge to apologise for himself, he just said –

'Bloody hell it's good to see you, mate,' and clapped him on the back just as at the same moment Stan said –

'God, Charlie, what happened to you?'

And even though Stan was laughing – it was clearly meant as a joke – Charlie found himself reacting a little, as if it were some kind of challenge. Swallowing the urge to defend himself, he took a step back from Stan, and theatrically looked him up and down.

'Looking well, mate, looking well.'

Stan pushed his hipster specs back up the bridge of his nose with what was clearly a well-practised gesture, and grinned with obvious pleasure.

'Thank you,' he said. 'But how did you – have you met Flo?'

Suddenly she was back at Stan's side, arm slung round his

shoulders. 'But how marvellous! You two know each other already?' she said. 'What a small world it is!'

'Not that small, not really,' said Charlie, under his breath.

'Sorry?' blinked Flo.

'Sorry, I didn't . . . But fucking hell, Stan. I just – it's a shock to see you, that's all. In my head you were still a thirteen-year-old kid.'

'Yeah well in my head you were still . . . sixteen, wasn't it? If I was thirteen.'

'Yeah and I was way cooler back then,' said Charlie. 'Better looking. You wouldn't believe it now' – he found himself saying mock-confidentially to Flo – 'but back then I was the better-looking one of the two of us, by far.'

Flo laughed, a little nervously. 'How do you two know each other, Stanley? Were you at school together?'

'I didn't go to school,' said Charlie. 'But what are you up to these days, mate? You moved to London, then?'

'Master's in Journalism,' Stan said. 'UCL.' He looked proud as he said it, and while Charlie hadn't really registered the actual words he'd spoken at all, was too busy taking in this grown-up, whole-looking version of the friend he'd left a beaten-up, sad child on a common in Newford, he made himself grin, nod, and say, 'Good for you, mate. Good for you.'

'What about you, Charlie?' Stan said.

'Me? Oh I – well. This and that, this and that.'

Charlie found himself restless, suddenly, looking round the room, searching maybe for a quiet corner, unpopulated by these people in their coloured scarves and velvet and fucking berets for godssake and whatever else. But it was great to see Stan, though, great to see how well he was obviously doing. Uni, master's or whatever it was. Beautiful girl like

Flo on his arm – who actually seemed to have her head screwed on too, not just a pretty face. But why did it have to be here? Now? His hangover was kicking back in, maybe that was it, and he needed a cold beer. Hair of the dog and all that. Or fuck it, maybe a cigarette, though it had been months. A cold beer and a cigarette – then he'd feel normal. Or maybe he needed neither of those things at all and just some honest to goodness fresh air, because he hadn't smoked in ages now and that was one good thing, wasn't it, that he'd managed since the last time he'd seen Stan? One genuine achievement. Everything else had gone to shite, but at least his lungs were clear.

'I've stopped smoking,' he told Stan, hopefully.

Ah but then what did that count for, really? Kate was right, he was a fat, useless drunk, these days.

'Anyway, mate,' he found himself saying, 'I was just heading off. Got stuff to do tonight and all. But it was cracking to see you. And I'm glad – I'm glad you're doing so well for yourself.'

And Charlie turned on his heel and began to navigate his way through the little clusters of people . . . *really the narrative voice is all wrong, you'd think he'd never been to New York in his life . . . about the feminine experience, I guess, you'd love it, I'm sure* . . . back towards the door, ignoring Flo's words – 'Oh but you've only just arrived! Polly will miss you' – ringing out behind him. It was sweet of her, but Polly would most certainly not miss him.

He was out the door and halfway down the stairs when he heard footsteps, and turned to see Stan catching up with him – same old expression on his face as he'd worn all those years before, always chasing after him back then, too.

'Hang on, Charlie, wait,' Stan said. 'I've just . . . I mean – isn't this a bit too much of a coincidence to simply ignore? I never thought I'd see you again. It's been years.'

'Yeah,' Charlie said, stopping on the stairs, looking up at Stan and not enjoying the irony of the switch in their height differences. 'It has.'

'So,' said Stan, grinning again. 'Let's catch up. Stay for a drink, at least.'

'No I . . . I don't know any of those people up there, Stan. This whole thing is mental. We weren't meant to meet here tonight. I ended up here by accident.'

'Ah everyone feels like that at Flo and Polly's parties.'

'No, really, mate. I've got stuff – stuff I've got to get back to.'

Stan sobered a little, the delighted grin he'd worn since catching sight of Charlie fading a little.

'Sure,' said Stan. 'But let's not just . . . I mean. This is amazing, Charlie. I've often wondered about how you are, you know.'

'You don't really want to know.'

'Yeah I do.'

'Well, I've got a death sentence on my head for this Saturday, so it's not really worth your while.'

'What?'

'Sorry. I'm just – I'm just messing.'

'Right.'

'Yeah.'

'Charlie, are you alright?'

'Fine, yeah. I'm just – I've got to get on with some things, and – I don't know. Stuff like that up there always makes me a bit antsy, you know?'

Stan nodded. 'Yeah, I see that.'

Stan's face had got kinder with age, and yet Charlie wasn't sure he liked it – wasn't sure he liked the way Stan was looking at him, now.

You don't understand, he wanted to say. I may not be a student like you, but that doesn't mean I haven't done things. I've lived. I've been places. I've explored and I've worked all over the country. I've slept out in sand dunes under the stars and been woken by the strange, pale light of an East Anglian dawn, the sun coming right over the sea. And I've fallen in love – I fell in love twice, in fact. The first time ill-advisedly and the second time – well – I married her, didn't I? I'm married, Stan. I married her up in the hills, and under the open sky. And I sat by Nan, keeping vigil when she died, and I sat with my wife on the steps of our caravan when she was just back from a swim in the river, her hair still wet and shining all down her back and her eyes sparkling, because she'd come to tell me she'd felt it, felt the kick inside her belly while she'd been in the water. I've fought men and won, I've fought men and lost. I've been knocked out a few times. I found a home for myself that, yes, was cold and not exactly easy in its way but there were skylarks there, and if you'd seen the way Kate looked in the light from our window when she woke – the smile on her face in those mornings, you'd never believe it now. I've just done so much, Stan, since we last met. So much has happened. And I've been battered around and all the rest of it but God knows I don't deserve *pity* for that, if that's what that look is, in your eyes now. I don't deserve pity at all. I've seen more of life than anyone can see in a university, I'm sure of it, or why else would I feel so much like a fraud among those people up there? Pretending to know less than I do, and to be less than I am, just to trick them into believing I fit there?

But he didn't say any of that – of course he didn't. He just shrugged and turned to carry on, on his way down the stairs.

'Oh come on, Charlie,' Stan said. 'Let's go for a beer at least. Tomorrow. This week. Whenever you're free.'

Charlie stopped, considered it. And then, 'Okay,' he said.

'Great,' said Stan, that same old childlike smile right back on his face again.

They exchanged numbers, and Stan told Charlie a bit more about himself these days – without prompting, as if he didn't doubt Charlie's interest and couldn't wait until the pub to give him the full rundown, had to offer a sneak preview now, just to prepare him. He was doing this master's degree, yes, but he was also a cub reporter for *Writing Left* and actually preferred that to all the uni stuff because it was *just a bit more real, you know?* Flo wasn't his girlfriend, though she seemed pretty keen and, well, she was a bit posh and everything but she was still gorgeous, right? And he lived in Maida Vale but really it wasn't as swish as it sounded – he says Maida Vale at parties but really it's more like Kilburn.

'Best be off then, mate,' Charlie told him. 'Listen, it was – it's been good seeing you again, Stan, mate. Great to see how well you're doing.'

'Yeah, so you already said. Listen – Charlie?'

Charlie was already off down the stairs. He stopped again, looked up and over his shoulder to see what Stan wanted.

'Just – well. Nae pasaran. Remember?'

'I – yeah,' he said, though the words were, in fact, coming back at him like something from out of a dream, something snatched from the very edge of his consciousness. 'Yeah. Of course I remember.'

He made it the rest of the way down the corridor without meeting anyone, and was just starting to relax, heading down the building's central staircase when he saw Polly leaning on the door frame of the main door out on to the street, smoking a cigarette. She turned at his approach.

'What happened?' she said.

'What?' he said.

'Your wedding ring,' she said. 'You're not wearing it today. Was it a fake one yesterday? Or did I get you in trouble with your wife?'

'Neither,' he said, and brushed past her, out into the clear air of the street.

She shrugged. 'So long!' she called behind him, as he walked into the night towards the river, looking for a bus stop.

# 25

Next morning, Wednesday – only three days now before the fight – it looked as if his day of skiving work had gone unnoticed. Everything seemed fine, no one even mentioning that he hadn't shown up, just one *feeling better today, Charlie?* from kind Alice at the till of the staff canteen when he was buying his breakfast. Everything stayed fine until mid-morning, when John Anderson showed up just as Charlie was unloading a pallet from his forklift – the twenty-fifth one he'd done that morning already, according to the meter by his work station. It never let him lose count, that meter, relentlessly measuring the number of pallets moved per hour, beeping and flashing with each completed job, never letting him just slip into a trance with it, turn zombie for the day until 5 p.m. and homeward bound.

For an awkward-looking middle-aged man, John Anderson was extraordinarily light-footed. That was one of the main problems with him, you never knew when he'd materialise beside you. It could even happen while you were driving across the floor, him falling into step beside you with that silent tread of his. And it wasn't just that he wore soft leather shoes when everybody else around here wore boots, there was some other quality behind his surprise appearances too that made them so unsettling. John reminded Charlie of a cat, and he'd never understood cats, not even James's crazy tabby. They weren't like dogs or horses. He knew dogs and horses, and there was a certain honesty to them. Cats, though – they always had some agenda of their own going on, and they never fully let you in on it until they'd already pounced.

'Well now, look who it is,' said John Anderson, his soft tones starting up too close to Charlie's ear, making him jump and nearly switch the forklift into reverse before he was ready, forcing him to brake suddenly – which of course made it look as though he didn't know how to do his job properly, when in reality he could have done it in his sleep. He'd just been given a shock, was all.

'Now that's just it, isn't it?' John Anderson said, sighing at Charlie's clumsy manoeuvring. 'It's your *attitude*, Charlie. Approximate. Sloppy. *Unreliable* . . .' He leaned on that *unreliable*, rolling it around and around in his mouth.

'Is that right?' said Charlie, pallet fully lowered now, ready to reverse but waiting for John to finish. It was stupid, this sitting still like this, wasting so much time. His meter would probably register him as having worked slower than the target now, and then he'd be in for another, worse earful from John at the end of the day when really the hold-up was John's fault, and nothing to do with him at all. Except John wouldn't see it that way of course.

'Don't think I didn't notice you missing from my team yesterday. I had to get Alfie Morrison to pick up your slack, you know. And he's a good boy, Alfie, he did as I asked, even though it meant him staying three hours after time. And him with his young family at home, and everything. You should think more, Charlie, about the inconvenience you put people to, with your unreliability.'

'Yes, because it was definitely me who made Alfie Morrison work three hours longer than he should have done,' said Charlie.

'But this wider question of unreliability,' John continued, either oblivious or choosing to ignore Charlie's heavily sarcastic tone. 'That's really what I wanted to talk to you about today, Charlie. We both know you've been under review for a while now, that's no secret. And though I do hate to say it, that leaves me with no choice, Charlie. I don't want this any more than you do, believe me, but even so. You should consider this, this conversation today, as your final warning, I'm afraid. One more trick like yesterday, that is to say, and you're out.'

'What?' Charlie said. 'Final warning? Seriously?'

Because sure he'd been on this review type thing recently, though he wasn't even sure why, but he'd never even been given a proper first-time warning. John was erratic, everyone knew that, but this was a bit much, surely, even for him.

'Honestly, mate, I was sick,' he told John. 'It happens to everyone . . .' and in his confusion and the stress of the moment he found himself reaching out then, out of the forklift, towards John's heavily starched shoulder. Conciliatory, the gesture was meant as, but still—

'Don't touch me,' John said, flinching away and brushing off his shirt, though Charlie's fingers had barely made contact.

He fancies Kate, that was the main problem, Charlie thought as he watched John's retreating, sharp-suited form stalking its way up the loading shelves, tapping lads on the shoulder and making them jump. He'd seen the way he'd looked at her that last Christmas drinks. It had been so creepy and blatant that he and Kate had laughed about it, even. One of the few things they'd laughed about since everything had gone wrong, in fact.

And yet this was the man, Charlie reflected as he finally clocked in that last pallet, seeing the dial on his meter flick up to twenty-six and turn green again, back from its previous impatient red, this was the man who held sway over him now, who could fire him, if the mood happened to take him, and leave him and Kate with no income, sending him back into the debilitating, uncertain circus of looking for work. This was the man he had to listen to and obey, even – this ridiculous, petty clown.

As he carried on through the morning, loading and unloading pallets, driving back and forth and watching his counter go from twenty-six, twenty-seven, twenty-eight all the way up to forty-three, forty-four, forty-five – almost always happy green now, amber only once or twice and never red, not another red all day, because he was good at his job and fast, no one could argue with that – his thoughts drifted to Stan, yesterday on the stairs. To the earnestness on his face as he'd said that *nae pasaran*. Charlie snorted as he thought about it. The noble struggle. Right and wrong and enemies worthy of resistance. Surely Stan hadn't managed to avoid seeing it for himself already, though? Why it was funny, why it was sad? Surely Stan saw too that this world now was no place for nae pasaran any more – no place for it at all.

He glanced up to see John Anderson checking his posture in the reflective surface of a shelving unit's side. And he had a spectacular expression on his face, somewhere between affected nobility and severe constipation. What was the good of the old battle cries when these were the kinds of villains they were up against?

*

In the end he was the one to call Stan's number, standing outside the warehouse gates in the light drizzle of early evening. If he was honest, partly he was ringing just because he was tired, and Tommy Campbell was busy for once, and he couldn't face going home yet. Stan picked up on the second ring.

'Alright, mate?' Charlie said as soon as he did. 'How about that pint you mentioned, then?'

'Charlie, hi, yeah. Look, I'm so glad you called. Listen. I was thinking—'

'Whereabouts are you at, then? I'm out east but I'll have to get a bus somewhere anyway because nowhere here is decent for a drink really, so I'm happy to come to wherever you are or to wherever you think will be good and not like the kind of place you have to sell both your kidneys for a pint of something . . .'

'What, you mean now?'

'What was that, mate?'

'You mean meet up like, right now?'

'Yeah. Why else would I ring?'

'But Charlie, I can't just . . . I'm at work. There's the paper to put to bed before tomorrow, and, well, I was thinking maybe sometime next week? Or how are you fixed on Sunday?'

Sunday, ha. The day after the fight with Holland. The way things were looking he'd probably be in hospital on Sunday. In a fucking coma, probably. That or stepping off a flight in Mexico or somewhere else far away and warm where he could run away to and where there wouldn't be this fucking awful drizzle all the time.

'Ah come on, mate,' he said into the phone. 'Just an hour – half an hour! Where do you work? I'll come to you. You can just nip out for a bit. Dinner break.'

'But we're not having dinner, are we?'

'Liquid dinner. Come on. It'd be great to see you, Stan. It's been a lifetime.'

'I . . . but Charlie. I have a job. I can't just' – long breath, laugh, then a sigh as if his arm had been really twisted over it, when Charlie had barely had to ask, and – 'fine. Fine,' Stan was saying. 'It's a quietish day so they won't miss me for half an hour, I'm sure. I'll just tell them I've had a surprise visit from a long-lost family member. I'm in Old Street, so . . . is the Tap House alright? On the corner of Spixworth Street and Judges Lane? You know the one, where all the reporters drink. It's just round the corner from my office.'

'Sure,' said Charlie, 'I know the one.' Though honestly he had no clue what Stan meant by that *where all the reporters drink*. 'Forty minutes?' he hazarded.

'An hour. I've got some stuff to finish up here first.'

'Right you are. In an hour, then.'

# 26

It took Charlie longer than he'd thought to find the Tap House. For a start there were two separate places called Tap House in the four streets or so around Judges Lane, and he ended up in what was definitely the wrong one first – so rowdy and plasticky a sports bar that the idea of the new Stan drinking here, with his hipster specs and uni mates and tweed jacket, almost made Charlie laugh aloud, in spite of the cloud that was hanging over him this week, getting thicker and darker with every second the time ticked closer to Saturday.

The second Tap House was an awkward little place in a basement – no sign at street level or anything, definitely not easy for just anyone to find. It was almost like you needed to know it existed already, or else you couldn't drink there. And yet even despite all the kerfuffle in finding it Charlie still arrived early enough to drink most of a pint, frowning at the dingy decor, before Stan finally showed up. A good thing that, too. He always needed that first pint after work these days, to unwind him, to decompress, switch his mind back on again and lift his thoughts off the repetitive back-and-forth track they always got stuck on during the hours at the warehouse. Load pallet. Drive and drive and unload pallet. Faster, faster, faster.

'Charlie,' Stan clapped him on the back and pulled him into a hug. They'd hugged yesterday, too. Maybe they were friends who hugged now, though he never remembered any of that back in the day. Back in those long afternoons on Goshawk Common, with the sound of the wind in the canopy and all those fucking rabbits jumping around all over the show, in front of your bike wheels and everything, so you had to be careful and keep your eyes sharp while you were riding around so you didn't end up beheading one of them or something. And you did see the odd dead one. No self-preservation instinct, those rabbits. Always bounding headlong into trouble.

'Good to see you, mate,' Charlie said. 'Sorry about yesterday. I was – well. I wasn't feeling my best.'

'No problem, no problem. Can I get you a drink of anything?' said Stan. And then, 'Ah no, I see you've already got one . . .' he carried on, at exactly the same moment Charlie said –

'Wouldn't say no, mate, if you're offering.'

Stan got himself a ginger ale and Charlie another pint of bitter, and then they settled at a table in the corner where Stan sat down luxuriously on his spindly wooden stool as if it were the most comfortable armchair in England.

'Man, I love this place,' he said. 'It's a proper old dive, isn't it? Rumour has it so many stories have had their origins here. People meeting up under the radar, swapping info, getting scoops here since the fifties.'

Charlie raised his eyebrows. 'That so?' he said. It was the beginning of the second pint, and there was a good hour, now, between him and anything that had anything to do with John Anderson. And then Stan's face looked almost alarmingly open, his enthusiasm for their somewhat bleak surroundings so obvious that Charlie began to feel his mood genuinely starting to lift a little, in spite of himself.

Stan was nodding now, all earnestness and seriousness. 'Yep,' he said. 'Julius Green leaked all his intel to Nadine Robeson here. Well, that could be apocryphal of course, but I'd believe it, why not?'

'Exactly mate, why not?'

'You taught me that, you know.'

'What?'

'To value the history of places. To make the effort to find out what happened in them before we all came along. You know. Do a bit of digging and find the interesting stories.'

'Oh, sure. Right enough.' Charlie tried his best not to look puzzled. 'Hang on. You say I taught you that?'

Stan blinked, as if he hadn't really thought about what he'd said that first time he'd said it, and had to reconsider it afresh now he was asked. 'Yes,' he said. 'I think so. Anyway,' he tapped his hands down on the tabletop, decisively. 'I've got to get back to work in a minute so let's get the boring bit of catching up out the way fast. I'm a journalist, a master's student, live in Maida Vale . . . oh but we talked about that already, didn't we? Anyway I got out of Newford years ago, thank God. Did my undergrad in Bristol, of all places – good fun but some heavy nights out, if you know what I mean' – he lapsed into a weird, nervous giggle that he certainly hadn't had when they'd last known each other – 'but that's enough about me,' he said. 'Tell me, what's been happening to you?'

It took Charlie a second to catch up to the fact he'd even been asked a question. Stan had been talking so fast and in this weird sort of glazed-over way, not that he was glazed over while he was talking, more that the *words* were, the sentences, all behind panes of glass like in a museum or like with shop windows – as if everything he said wasn't for Charlie, particularly, but had been compiled and prepared in advance for a more general kind of presentation, ready to be wheeled out whatever the context, listener or occasion. Charlie covered his confusion at the new pace and delivery of his old friend's words with a slow sip of his drink.

'Sorry, what was that?' was all he found he could say.

'Oh I just – I just asked what had happened in your life, was all. Since we last met. It's just I've been gabbling on so much about myself, and then I realised I know almost nothing about you, and it's been – what? Nearly a decade?' That same nervous laugh again.

'Yep,' said Charlie. 'Yep it has.'

What a question. Summarise the last decade of your life in a few sentences. He wondered if Stan had learned to think like this at work – that journalist thing of taking a long, messy story and somehow fitting it into a few snappy paragraphs. The years of his own life, though, swirled around his head in a kind of soup, all emotions and memories of isolated incidents and dead dogs and weddings and funerals and people who'd been around for a while then just vanished. How had Stan summed up his own last ten years? College in Woking. Bristol for uni. He'd made it look easy, but thinking of his own experience Charlie knew he'd never be able to make it fit. And he did know, of course he knew that that didn't make his life or experiences any less important, or less valuable than Stan's, but then something about the way Stan had framed the question made it almost seem so. As if he'd taken it as a given that it was important for a life to fit into these artificial stages, somehow. Charlie drained his drink, washing down a flash of indignation.

'Hang on,' he said. 'I'll just get another. You want another of those – what is it? Ginger beer?'

Stan's glass was still nearly full. He'd just taken a few token sips off the very top.

'That's kind of you,' he said, 'but no thanks. I'm afraid I'm still working on this one here.'

Charlie got a Guinness this time – slower drinking, to help him better keep pace with Stan. When he got back to the table Stan was staring at his phone, thumbs flying across the screen faster than Charlie had ever seen anyone type before.

'Sorry,' said Stan, without looking up. 'Just realised I'd forgotten to . . . there's just so much . . . Jesus. Right. There. That's done. I'm back with you. What's been happening? Are you alright? I must say you're looking very tired.'

And Charlie took a gulp of Guinness, and maybe it was because this man sat in front of him now looked so much like his boyhood friend – maybe it was because in the minutes it had taken him to ask for the Guinness, pay for the Guinness, and have a jovial exchange with the barman while they both waited for the pint to settle before he topped it up again, he'd had a bit of a chance to think about what really was the summary headline, the true Most Important Thing of Charlie Wells's Most Recent Decade. Or maybe it was because he was a little resentful of the way Stan's eyes were roving the bar now, flitting between the door, the people at the other tables, and his phone screen, not really looking at Charlie at all. Maybe he wanted to be a little dramatic. It was what journalists liked, after all, wasn't it?

'My wife and I got kicked off our site by the council. The whole thing was cleared. We thought we had a kid on the way at the time so I got myself a warehouse job and found us a bricks and mortar house. She didn't want to move into it at first, hated the idea it wasn't ours, that we were renting. Hated not being on the move, too. But I don't know . . . I thought I'd like to try it for a bit, you know, living like Gorjers and all that. Got to be something to it, I thought, since so many people choose to do it and then, well, I also thought it might be better for the baby, I suppose. But then of course she lost it, and now we're still just *there* and kind of trapped because we signed all these contracts and now we owe a bunch of random companies a bunch of money for a whole load of stuff they never even said we had to pay.'

Stan nearly dropped his phone, fumbling it and catching it at the last moment before it clattered on the sticky table-top. He was looking at Charlie now, really looking at him, paying attention.

'Seriously?' he said, with an odd kind of intensity Charlie couldn't remember from the old days. 'Interesting. I mean, terrible – that's terrible, Charlie. Why didn't you say so immediately?'

'Dunno,' said Charlie. 'I mean, I kind of did, didn't I?'

'But Charlie, you realise that kind of injustice – for injustice it is, there's no doubt about that – you realise it's not only what happened, what's happening, to you. It's symptomatic, it's endemic – you're a victim of this whole political project of the past three years – or longer, in fact, if you read some of my colleagues, though I'd argue that's all a bit paranoid – but in any case, do you see? It's just so typical, what you told me just there. It's this thing they're doing, the buggers, of trying to enforce and sustain the existence of a superior tier of society alongside a constant, hopeless underclass—'

'Hopeless underclass?'

'Oh God, Charlie, I didn't mean it like that. You see the thing is I'm just so . . . I'm all over the place at the moment. In fact, really I shouldn't even be here. There's this story I've got to get back to the office for – it's on page eight tomorrow and needs urgent proofreading. You might find it interesting, actually, in the light of . . . I'll print it off for you, anyway. But listen, what you've told me, it's . . . I'm interested. And well, I don't want to speak too soon, but I might be able to help you. In fact' – Stan stopped, halfway into his coat, checking something on the screen of his phone – 'are you going to Polly's thing later? That is happening tonight, isn't it? I might just be able to swing by, after we've finished up for the night, if you're going?'

'I don't – I don't even know . . .'

'The Birdcage, Shoreditch, tenish. Though she says that, of course, but no one'll be there till more like eleven. Please come, I'll actively look forward to it, then. I can't really be bothered, you see. Much rather be at home with my feet up, but, well, Flo's expecting me.'

Then with a clap on Charlie's shoulder and a 'Cheerio!' to the barman, he was off, disappearing into the chill of the evening. Who the hell said *cheerio* like that? In 2012? In London?

Charlie contemplated leaving too, but ended up staying to sink another pint while he weighed up which of his two options would ultimately depress him least – going straight back home and giving this whole evening up as a lost cause, or sticking around for a bit, maybe a couple more drinks here before wandering on to the Birdcage, wherever that was. Just for a look, really. Just to call in and see what it was all about.

# 27

The lights had all been covered with red and pink filters, giving everything in the bar a rosy tinge that reminded Charlie of a butcher's shop. Polly stood on a raised platform in the corner wearing nothing but a garland of flowers in her hair. She was reciting some kind of ritual chant, from what he could tell. None of the words were in English, or even any language he recognised. Every so often she would break off to pour water over herself from a plastic bucket, which was also adorned with a flower garland. How odd that after the manner in which they had met this should be the way he ended up seeing her naked body. Here in public, in this bar full of students who were all only half watching, eyes sliding over her as if maybe a little bored, while they talked to their friends or bought more wine, Polly's nakedness and chanting just background noise, just wallpaper to their evening out. Though Kate seemed to be past caring what he did these days, it did still somehow make him feel a bit better about going home with Polly, being part of this big crowd of strangers she was presenting her body to now in this way, nothing private or truly intimate about it at all.

Stan, for instance, was hardly paying attention – as if the sight of his naked friend dousing herself in water were a mere commonplace. He was more interested in telling Charlie all about his interpretation of the state of the nation.

'It's happened under the cover of the financial crash,' he was saying, shouting over the general hubbub of chatter and the drone of Polly's chanting – she was miked up, her reverb-laden voice echoing over the PA, from speakers all around them. 'They've used that as the excuse. And it is the perfect excuse, I'll give them that, no wonder people buy into it, the poor mugs. But what they're doing, it's not really necessary at all, do you see? It is, in fact, the exact opposite of necessary in many ways – the exact opposite of what would help this country recover. It's almost Orwellian, in fact, if you think about it. Frightening stuff.' Stan grimaced theatrically. 'But can I get you another drink? It seems you're running short.'

Charlie glanced down at his glass, whiskey soda now, to see that Stan was right and somehow it was empty, though he'd only gone to the bar five minutes ago it felt like, and he couldn't remember drinking any of it – not really, just a couple of sips. He was starting to feel a little woozy, though. Almost drunk, in fact. Probably he should take a break. But Stan was offering now, and how much had he spent tonight already?

'Sure,' he said to Stan.

Ah but probably he shouldn't drink any more tonight. He had to go to the gym tomorrow. Get himself in shape. Had to get himself down to the gym, training hard, because—

'Whiskey soda, was it?' Stan said.

'Yeah mate, much appreciated.'

The fight, again, resurfacing in his thoughts in spite of his best efforts to forget about it. Christ, of course he couldn't forget a thing like that, who was he kidding, thinking he could just ignore it? Still it had been a relief, though, hadn't it, even pretending not to think about it, even for an hour or so. A relief not to have Kate's voice going on in his head about gyms and debts and failure, not to be worrying about James all the time . . . But then what time was it, even, and how long had he been here? It seemed like Polly had been going on like that over there for ages now.

'Thanks, mate,' he said, as Stan reappeared – very quickly, it felt like – and handed him a new glass. He took it and clinked it against the side of Stan's red wine.

'I was serious though, Charlie,' Stan said then. 'About what I said before, about the paper. Your story of what happened to you. What they did to you and your wife. Do consider it, won't you?'

'Yeah mate, course I will,' said Charlie, though if he'd been asked he'd have had to admit he honestly had no idea what Stan was on about now. 'Listen, what d'you reckon about this?' He gestured towards Polly. 'I can't understand a word of what's going on.'

'It's Sanskrit,' said Flo, who was somehow there too now, arm linked through Stan's, a cloud of paper butterflies artfully arranged in her hair. 'She's so talented, Polly. I've never met anyone like her. She's so knowledgeable, so interested in other cultures. And so brave.'

Charlie wasn't sure if she was joking, but before he could laugh Stan had cut in.

'Yes,' he was saying. 'I mean, it's clearly juvenilia of course, but even I'll admit there's something powerful about it. You can see echoes of Marina Abramović, I think. Somewhere in the visceral nature of it, the urgency.'

'Stan's such a philistine,' Flo laughed, turning to Charlie, mock-lowering her voice. 'He doesn't see the point in art unless it's got an overt political purpose, or message. Can you believe it?'

But Charlie had had too many drinks for this. It was very hot, too, and very crowded, and then of course the lights were weird and maybe stopping at the offie back there for that six-pack of Tyskie had been a poor idea. He felt sick. Maybe like he needed to sit down. If Polly would stop chanting that would certainly help. Just some music would be nice. Something soulful that cut straight to the heart. Like Pearl Jam, maybe.

Flo was laughing. 'You don't agree with him, do you? Oh but Charlie, you *can't*!' She swiped him playfully on the arm. 'You absolute beast!'

He let his eyes drift back over to Polly, and he made himself really question – what on earth was the point of all this? Of what she was doing now? He sincerely tried to answer that, but he couldn't help but draw a blank, thinking only that she must be getting cold, like that, even despite how bloody warm it was in here. That someone should just give the girl a towel and a hot whiskey and tell her to get a real job. He turned back to Stan and Flo. Flo was playing with one of Stan's lapels now as he sipped his wine.

'If you look at the work of Artaud, though,' Stan was saying to her, 'and the whole principle of Theatre of Cruelty, you'll see another possibility, as it's not propaganda, exactly, but it's also not aimless, not vacuous, either—'

'But that's just it, Stanley!' Flo squealed then. 'Vacuous? Look at your choice of words!'

This way they talked. This way Stan talked, now. When did they learn it? When they went to university? Or before, as a kind of preparation? And what was any of it about, really? Was it really as highfalutin and important as it was dressing itself up to be? Or was it just so much empty posturing, like all those idiot politicians talking on the news all the time, for instance, or even like Polly in the corner there, because Flo said she was talented and brave, but looking at her eyes now Charlie could see the fear in them, and then as for what she was doing, was he really the only one to see that the Emperor had no clothes? Empty posturing, all of it. Like a young kid talking big before a fight he was certain to lose . . . oh but he didn't want to think about fighting, that wasn't why he was here. And surely there was more to Stan these days than just this paper-thin chatter about abstract things – about nothing?

'What about your mum?' He asked Stan, interrupting Flo, probably quite rudely in fact, but kind of beyond caring. 'I met her, you know, back when you were in hospital. She keeping alright these days?' Because so what if that encounter with Stan's mum hadn't been a great one. She'd been worried . . .

Stan blinked. 'I don't really know, I'm afraid,' he said, shortly, sliding an arm round Flo now, who was looking between the two of them, apparently a little put out.

'You were in hospital?' she said. 'Stanley? When were you in hospital?'

'How d'you mean you don't really know?' Charlie asked Stan.

'No, I – sorry, that sounded flippant. We just don't see each other as much as all that, is all. But listen, Charlie, it's not a very interesting story. I don't want to bore you with it.'

'I asked about it,' said Charlie. 'I'm not bored.'

Stan shrugged. 'I am. I'm tired of thinking about it, in fact. D'you know,' he said then, looking for a second much more like the old Stan, as opposed to just someone else wearing a slightly aged version of his face, 'she once made me swear never to speak to you again?'

'Yeah, you told me. At the time.'

'Did I? I'd forgotten that. I wish we hadn't lost touch, Charlie, after that. Newford wasn't the same without you, you know.'

'Stanley,' said Flo then. 'Will you come with me to congratulate Polly? She's on the last lap now and I think we really ought to be there for her when she finishes. She must be spent, poor thing.'

'You go on,' said Stan. 'I'll catch you up.'

Flo gave him a puzzled look, no anger in it – if anything, she seemed a little concerned. Then she shrugged and swept off through the crowd, dress and paper butterflies fluttering out behind her as she went.

'Listen,' said Stan then. 'I'm afraid you'll think I'm being utterly heartless.'

'What?' said Charlie. 'She seems okay, mate, but really it's up to you—'

'No,' said Stan. 'I meant about my mum.'

'Oh,' said Charlie.

'She just . . . it's just complicated. And, well. I've come to think that family isn't necessarily who you're born with. That it can be who you choose to have around you, as much as anything else. The movement, for instance, around

252

*Writing Left.* It's become my family as much as anything else, Charlie, and I really do mean that. It's based on something more than blood, in a way. It's based on shared values, do you see?'

'I don't know,' said Charlie. 'Honestly I don't, mate. I know your mum wasn't always easy to get on with, but your family's your family, whether you like it or not. I don't think you can just up and get a new one like that, however much you want to, however hard you try.'

Stan, though, didn't seem to be listening. 'I really meant what I said before,' he said. 'I really think *Writing Left* could help you. I mean, it's awful what happened there. Really outrageous. And I'm not pretending to be some big cheese now or something, but the others on the editorial team – they really do respect me, Charlie. Just let me talk to some people, make some enquiries. But I really think . . . you know I never forgot that story you told me, about those warehouse workers up in East Kilbride, refusing to mend those engines? It's stories like that that show the best of humanity, don't you agree? It's stories like that that show our saving graces.'

And Charlie was drunk, he realised now. He really must be, because he was nodding and saying, 'Jesus Christ, are you sure though? That they'll want to help me. Because honestly, mate, at this point if someone could help that would be – I mean that would be . . .'

And Stan was clapping him on the back. 'Of course I'm sure,' he was saying. 'It's a big story, Charlie. We could be on to something really key, here . . .'

And suddenly Charlie found himself caught between grinning and weeping because despite the crap art and all the student pretension, here was a flash of his old friend, a flash of the past and the world they both remembered from before it all went tits up – and, more than anything, here was someone, finally, someone else other than his own fucking self who thought that what had happened to him, all this shite over all these years, was unjust, was wrong, was not what he deserved or what should have happened.

'I didn't want any of this,' he said out loud to Stan, only realising he was echoing Kate as the words fell out of his mouth. Kate. Left all alone at home. He should go back, really. He should go back now.

'I know, mate, I know,' said Stan, grasping his shoulder.

'Listen,' said Charlie. 'Will you have another?' He held up his glass, waggling it so it caught the strange coloured lights, turning pink.

'Wouldn't say no,' said Stan. 'Same again, mate, but listen – I'll give you the cash. Just take my wallet and—'

'Fucksake, Stan, I'm not on my uppers yet,' he said, trying to smile, maybe half managing it. 'I can stand you a drink, at least.'

When he got back from the bar Polly's chanting had miraculously stopped, and Stan had vanished from the spot they'd been hanging about in before. It took Charlie a second of scanning the crowd, eyes narrowed, to find where it was he'd disappeared off to. Of course, there he was – at the side of the stage, lips locked and arms entwined with Flo. Charlie tried to grin, then took a swallow of his drink. Why was it, he wondered, that though there weren't that many years between them he'd had to grow up and get so fucking old while Stan had been allowed to stay like this?

To hell with James, and the fight, and work and saving money and going off home to Kate. Was he not allowed some fun, some hope, some irresponsibility? He downed the rest of his whiskey in one, went back to the bar for another, then piloted himself and the drinks through the room, through all the milling, clustering, chatting, shouting people towards his old friend. Maybe this was just what he'd needed, finding Stan again like this. Maybe life had provided, as Nan used to say it would. Maybe against all the odds it had finally surprised him with a silver lining, or a lifeline, even, from the past. Maybe, at last, his luck was on the turn.

# 28

He still felt good, felt hopeful the next morning – in spite of the dry mouth, the looming headache, the sweatiness, his guts churning and Kate lying next to him awake, staring up at the ceiling with an expression he could only describe as hollow resignation. He turned to her, tangling himself even further in the sheets in the process – he was already all wound up in them, must have been tossing and turning something dreadful in the night.

'You alright, mate?' he said to her. 'Sleep okay?'

'I never said a word,' she said, still staring at the ceiling. 'You were away doing God knows what with who knows who all night and I never said a word about it. But that didn't mean I just expected you to go and do it again.'

'What?' he said. 'No. I came back. What was it? Eleven? Midnight? And you were asleep, anyway.'

'It was after two,' she said. 'And of course I wasn't asleep. What do you think? That I could sleep through all your crashing around and your whining and your flicking on and off with the lights? I just didn't want to have to speak to you, was all it was.'

'So you were pretending, is that what you're saying?'

'I was closing my eyes,' she said, 'and hoping that way the whole situation would just disappear.'

'Ah Kate,' he told her. 'You should never do that. Got to face up to things, grab the bull by the horns, and all that – it's the only way to get anything done in this life.'

'That so?' she said. 'Jesus Christ, you should listen to yourself.'

Choosing to ignore that remark, Charlie yawned, stretched, unravelled himself from the covers, and checked the time on the clock – twenty past six, so four hours' sleep, roughly, if Kate was right about when he'd got back. That was fine, that was grand. And he'd actually be on time for work, too.

He rolled out of bed, feet landing squarely on the floor, rubbed his eyes, and looked down at Kate, lying there, a floating head above the duvet, haloed with her red hair spread out against the pillow. Suddenly she looked really awfully small. She needed chivvying along a little, reminding that things weren't completely hopeless all the time – that they were still at the beginning of their lives, that there were plenty of great things for them to do yet.

'You've got to stop hiding from things,' he said. 'You've got to stop letting things get on top of you like this. It's time to kick against the world a little, Kate. Time to take control, remember what's possible.'

They were grand words for an early morning in a small and untidy bedroom. But then again, why not? Why not have a plan, and a sense of direction? Why not decide to hope that something went his way for once? He padded barefoot to the shower, turned on the water, twisted the dial to cold and stepped in. And *nae pasaran*, he thought, as the freezing water hit, shocking and bright on his skin.

*

The canteen at work, breakfast time. He'd said hi to Alice and then, keeping eyes out for John Anderson, he'd taken his tray and sat down next to a group of four lads from the heavy loads team who worked just across the floor from where he loaded the pallets. They were understaffed, chronically, and John was on their backs almost as much as he was on Charlie's, always telling them they weren't moving fast enough, that the rest of the whole operation was relying on them speeding up, reaching targets, that they were holding the whole business back – all that sort of stuff. The easy solution for John, of course, would be to simply hire enough people to get through the work at the pace he wanted in the available time. But of course he chose not to – too proud of his low overheads to compromise that on an extra salary. He relied on his bullying and chivvying instead, threatening pay cuts, probationary periods, weekly reviews and simple dismissals. Charlie figured these lads would be a good place to start.

'Alright,' he said, as he sat down, plonking his tray next to theirs on the table. 'Charlie Wells,' he said. 'From over on the forklifts. Don't know if I ever introduced myself properly before.'

'Aye, we know who you are,' said one of the lads, a grin spreading over his face. Charlie hadn't known how this would go, but a grin was a good sign, surely?

'Good,' said Charlie, pushing on with it now, thinking he'd take the plunge and see how things went. They didn't have much time before they had to be back upstairs after all, and anyway what was the sense in faffing around? He was seizing the bull by the horns today. 'Look, I won't bother you lads for long, but I wanted to run something past you, scope out some interest, see what you thought about something I've been considering for a while.'

All four of them nodded, but none of them spoke – just carried on chewing their breakfasts and staring at him. Not men of many words, these, then.

'It's no secret John doesn't like you lot,' he said. 'Or – he doesn't treat you lot well, anyway. I can't help what I hear across the floor when I'm working, and I'm not saying it's your fault – in fact, quite the opposite. See, he's on my back, too. All the time. Put me on some final warning thing even though I never had a first warning, and I never had a proper meeting, even, for him to tell me. He just spat it out at me when he was walking past yesterday, as if on a whim, almost.'

The lads were nodding, now, the one who seemed the youngest of them, just going on looks, had stopped eating, even, and was looking at Charlie intently. Amazing, if it could just be this easy. He'd kick himself for having let himself be pushed around for so long.

'So I was thinking,' he continued, 'that he shouldn't just be able to do that. That it isn't fair, it isn't right that he should have so much power over our lives. He's our boss, sure, but he isn't God, is he?'

One of the lads snorted – a kind of mirthless snort, Charlie would have called it. 'He certainly isn't that,' this lad said.

'Right!' said Charlie. 'But that's just it. It's ridiculous the way he stalks around this place like he owns it. He doesn't own it any more than we do, and it's not like he ever does a lick of actual work, either.'

More nodding.

'I'm going to organise some kind of meeting,' Charlie continued, sounding definitely more certain than he'd felt when he'd first sat down, 'of all the workers on the floor who feel like something's up. Would you lads be interested? Should I keep you in the loop?'

Still nodding but getting to their feet, now, eyes on the clock, gathering up trays and plates and cutlery.

'Sure,' said the young-looking one, who was apparently their chosen spokesman in spite of his years. 'Sounds good.'

And then the bell was ringing, they were gone, and Charlie hadn't even started on his breakfast. He contemplated just sitting there as everyone else filed out – these full-grown men jumping to the sound of somebody else's timetable. He imagined eating it as slowly as he pleased, taking his time, easing his headache with the hash browns and bacon still hot on his plate in front of him, taking soothing sips of his tea. He seriously considered it, but in the end he stood up just like everyone else, picked up his tray and tipped his food into the bin. And he didn't relish doing it at all, but there were better hills to die on. He couldn't afford to be late again, and that had been a good strong response to his first canvass. Things were looking hopeful – looking exciting, even. Stan had been right, last night. It was possible to make things better if you didn't just take them lying down. And to think he, Charlie, had actually taught Stan that back in the day. How much he had forgotten of himself, of the way he used to think.

*

Charlie's good mood lasted until lunchtime, until, back in the canteen, sitting on a table by himself and focusing on filling up, just for a moment – taking just a minute to refuel the engine before going to scope out the room again and ask a few more people what they felt about having a go at making some changes to the way things worked around here – the chair across the table in front of him was pulled out, and none other than John Anderson was suddenly sat opposite him. It was a rare occurrence, seeing John down here. Charlie had no clue where he generally ate his lunch or spent his breaks, but it was certainly never in the canteen with the rest of them.

'I hear you've been stirring up trouble,' John began. 'Trying to create discord amongst my team members. Is that right?'

So that's what this was about, then. For Christ's sake. For some pretty outstandingly taciturn lads they'd clearly wasted no time in spreading the word. Charlie put down his knife and fork, and studied John's face. It was funny, normally when talking to Charlie, John just looked like he was enjoying himself, having fun lording it over him, nothing more than an overgrown playground bully. Now though he looked almost injured, and as if he were genuinely waiting for an answer. For want of any better ideas for how to deal with the situation, Charlie decided he would try, just try and be straight with him, and talk to him honestly.

'It's not right,' he told John. 'I've got my wife to support, and rent and bills to pay. You can't just tell me I'm on some final warning out of the blue, without any kind of proper meeting about it, or any proper review. I rely on this money, John. You can't just mess with people's lives like that.'

But John's face only hardened. 'I'm not *messing with your life*, Charlie,' he said. 'Don't you understand? I pay you to do a job, and provide a service. If I judge that you are failing to do that job and to provide that service up to the expected standard, I have every right to do as I see fit. I don't know what else you expect. It's not up to me to *look after* you. This is the professional world.'

'I'm not asking to be looked after,' Charlie said, a bit of indignation creeping in at the edges, in spite of his efforts to keep sounding calm, collected, reasonable. 'I'm just asking for you to be fair. I mean, come on. We're not even paid the living wage here—'

He was stopped in his tracks there though by an odd look coming over John's face. A smug sort of expression, a thin-lipped smile, as if he were somehow one step ahead of Charlie here. As if he knew something Charlie didn't.

'What?' Charlie said. 'What is it? Why're you looking at me like that?'

John shrugged. 'No reason,' he said. 'It's just . . . you might not find it all that easy, rounding up comrades to fight your corner on that one.'

And just like that, Charlie knew. He'd never even suspected that John – that this whole fucking company – could be so messed up. He felt blindsided. As if the whole workforce had played some kind of huge trick on him. John suddenly started looking more sheepish, and less smug.

'And why would that be?' Charlie said, abandoning all attempts now to keep the hostility he felt from his voice.

'Forget it,' John said. 'I shouldn't have said anything.'

'You pay me less, don't you?' Charlie said then. 'You pay me less than everyone else in this place, for doing exactly the same job.'

'I didn't say that.'

'Oh but come on though, mate. It's obvious. I'm not stupid. Be honest. It was written all over your face.'

For a moment, John looked as if he might try to deny it. Then he just sat back in his chair – as if he were lounging, almost – and shrugged. 'I pay you what you're worth,' he said. 'Market price. As I told you, you're lucky to be here. You should be grateful. Not everyone would be so open to the idea of employing someone like you.'

And with that – obviously determined to have the last word as usual – John pushed back his chair, stood up and stalked off, carving a smooth path through the lunchtime commotion of the canteen.

And Charlie didn't know what to do. He stared down at his food, but though he hadn't eaten since yesterday he'd lost his appetite, the hangover he'd been keeping at bay all morning with his rediscovered optimism threatening to crash through his defences and engulf him. He needed to speak to Stan, he realised. Not because Stan would have any particular wisdom or insight as to how to deal with this situation – he didn't want Stan's *advice*. It was just that in speaking to him last night, it had reminded him of who he'd once been, and of the man he'd once hoped to become one day – a hope that only this morning had felt like something that could almost be back within his reach.

He had ten minutes left until he had to be back on the warehouse floor. He abandoned his food, left the canteen, and stepped out into the smoking area to phone Stan. Again, Stan picked up on the second ring.

'Charlie,' said Stan. 'Good to hear from you, mate, was just about to ring you myself. Good night last night though, wasn't it? You get home alright?'

It took Charlie a moment to process what Stan was talking about. Last night felt a thousand years ago, even despite the headache thumping behind his eyes.

'Yeah,' he said. 'Yeah, got home no problem.'

But Stan seemed to have already lost interest in the answer to that question, and to be on to the next thing entirely. 'Listen though, Charlie,' he was saying. 'I pitched your story to my boss at *Writing Left* this morning and she was keen, very keen. It could be just what we need, in fact, she said. The social side of the whole issue. Real coalface stuff about how these policies are affecting real people's lives, you know? How they're intrinsically geared towards persecuting minorities, all that kind of thing. Really it's perfect. And – well. If we properly get behind it, give it some welly on our socials and everything, I honestly do think it might have some effect, Charlie. That it might help you. I read about this kid, in fact, who was having trouble getting his hospital treatment for some chronic thing he had. I forget now what it was he had exactly, but the whole thing was because of some funding cuts to some NHS trust somewhere, surprise surprise, and the story just blew up – like right overnight. Someone even started a crowdfunder to help him, but, get this, he didn't even need it because the NHS turned around the next day and apologised – said of course they could continue the treatment, and it had just been some sort of clerical error, some admin thing. Isn't that incredible? The power of a good story, mate. It's an amazing thing. Clerical error my arse.'

'Right, yeah, sure. That does sound good and everything, but I wanted to ask – I'm just . . . I don't know. It's been a bit of a rough week and a weird day and, well, you wouldn't be up for a pint later on, would you?'

'Sure,' Stan said, immediately. He seemed to think and talk so fast these days, making whole decisions about things before Charlie could blink. 'You're right, in fact. It would be better, easier to talk about this all in person. Tap House again? Does that work for you? Six o'clock? Half five, even?'

'Have you not got work?'

'Ah well, you know. My editor's pretty pleased with me right now. She's not going to mind if I skip out for a bit. Oh but one thing, Charlie, mate?'

'Yeah?'

'We might need just a few more things for the story, like . . . I don't know. Something to bulk out the whole minority discrimination side and build that whole argument up. You know – that society is rigged in favour of the establishment, and discriminates against the rest. D'you think you could find a few bits for me, maybe? It could just be anecdotal, I guess. Or maybe I could talk to one of your family or some-thing – just to get a corroborating voice in there. D'you think that might be possible?'

'I've just found out I'm paid less than everyone else in this place,' said Charlie, 'because I'm a Traveller, basically, I reckon. Does that count?'

'What?' said Stan, so sharp and so loud Charlie nearly dropped the phone. 'Bloody hell, mate, that's perfect. I mean, it's awful, obviously, but yeah – God. You think you know the system's corrupt and then you hear something else that makes you appreciate you had no idea how bad things were. I mean, Charlie – that's really just *awful*. Are you sure it's true?'

'Pretty sure, mate, yeah.'

'Look, I have to go, but is there a way, do you think, that you could find me some hard evidence of that – of discriminatory pay? It could even change the whole angle of the story, give it a wider scope by far . . .' Stan giggled – that nervous giggle Charlie still had a hard time getting used to – then put on a weird fake American accent. 'This, my friend, might go all the way to the top.'

And Charlie tried to laugh along with Stan, but felt weird doing it. The connection over the phone was over too vast a distance, somehow, and they were talking from such different spaces. Charlie standing outside in the drizzle in oil-stained overalls, watching the last few smokers working their way through their roll-ups as quickly as possible before lunchbreak was up. And Stan? Well. Who knew where Stan was. Charlie could hear a general hubbub of voices and keyboards tap-tapping and telephones ringing down the line, but really that didn't say much.

'Stan?' asked Charlie then.

'Yeah, mate?' said Stan.

'Look, I know you're all excited about this and everything, and I appreciate what you're trying to do with your writing and your stories and all – but, well . . .'

'Charlie?' Stan sounded worried. 'What is it?'

'Do you think it really could help?' Charlie said, trying to sound as offhand and not really bothered as possible, worried as he said it that the question might just sound embarrassingly pathetic – and from him, too, who Stan had looked up to, back in the day.

'Of course! Of course I think so, Charlie,' Stan was saying. 'D'you think I'd be doing any of this if, ultimately,

I didn't truly believe it could do something? I get caught up and gabble away about all sorts of crap, I know – Flo teases me about it, says I talk all the time but say nothing really – but the thing is really that that's ultimately the point of all this, Charlie. To change things, to help. Because why tell these stories if they don't do that? If they didn't have that ultimate aim? I think it's terrible what's happened to you, Charlie, really. And I think others would agree with me too, if only they could see what I'm seeing.'

Charlie tried to laugh again. 'I'm not doing too badly, mate. Way you put it makes it sound like I'm on death's door, or something.'

'No that's – that's not what I meant, of course it's not. But Charlie? I've got to go, I'm sorry. I'll catch you later on, alright?'

'I – yeah, sure. In fact I'd best be off too, now that you mention it.'

Actually he should have gone ages ago, that last smoker long since having dropped his half-finished cigarette on the ground and disappeared back through the double doors into work.

'But – well. Thanks, Stan, mate. Thanks for helping me out like this.'

'Least I could do for an old friend. Now, you will think about that pay bracket thing?'

'Sorry?'

'Evidence of discriminatory pay.'

'Oh sure. Yeah. Of course. Though listen, Stan?'

But Stan had already rung off.

# 29

Stan took a large gulp of his ginger beer, and slammed the glass down on the table – the fizzy, cloudy liquid just avoiding slopping over the rim.

'That's it,' he was saying, so excitably that Charlie was worried maybe he was reacting to having had too much sugar or something. This was his third ginger beer of the evening, after all – keeping pace with Charlie's pints in cans of fizzy drink. 'That's it *exactly*. Stories have power, Charlie. As much power as – I don't know. As engines, as weapons, as fists.'

'I don't know, mate,' said Charlie.

'But I do know,' said Stan. 'I believe in it, totally. So much of history is just us as humans telling stories about ourselves, and then making changes when we don't like what we hear, when we don't like what we discern from those stories. We're narrative beings, Charlie. So it follows that narrative itself is powerful, that narrative wins hearts and minds – and when you've won those hearts and minds? You're there, Charlie. You're sorted.'

'You reckon?' said Charlie.

'I know it,' said Stan. 'And don't forget you taught me this stuff, Charlie. The way there's a story behind everything. Every pub, every chip shop, every, I don't know. Every bit of wall, even. Every street corner. A whole network of stories behind everything, a whole web of them that's really as important as . . . as the paving stones, as the bricks and mortar of the buildings. Or more important, even. Because stories become the essence of a place, don't they? They can show us how we see ourselves, and from there – where we want to go.'

How did he find the energy to come up with all this stuff without even a drink or two in him? Charlie had never known someone to go on like this so insistently and so, well, so *passionately*, without being royally hammered first. Usually this kind of ranting was a sign that whoever you were with needed a glass of water, a pat on the back and the quiet suggestion that it might be best they headed off home now. And how had they even gotten on to all of this? Charlie couldn't remember. He picked at a bit of candlewax that was dried on to the streaked, sticky tabletop. It came away slowly, in tiny shavings that embedded themselves under his nail.

'I taught you this, eh?' he said. 'Doesn't seem likely. Sounds more like university stuff to me.'

'Oh come on, Charlie, don't be obtuse. You remember.'

'Obtuse? I'm not being obtuse.'

'Yes, you are,' said Stan. 'You remember it just as well as I can. We used to laugh about it, even. About those weird local stories. When fish and chips still came in newspaper.'

'Yeah,' said Charlie. 'It's just that sometimes all that feels like another life. Like that happened to two other people. We're both so different now. So much has changed.'

Stan paused, his glass halfway to his mouth – then replaced it on the table without drinking from it.

'Yeah,' he said. 'I know what you mean. I didn't even recognise you, for a minute, when I first saw you at Flo's.'

'Because I've got fat?'

Stan laughed – or he nearly did. It was somewhere between a sigh and a laugh – and he met Charlie's eyes properly for the first time that evening. 'No,' he said. 'It was more than that. You seemed different.'

'I have got fat, though. That can't be denied.'

'You're a bit heavier, sure, but I wouldn't say *fat*, exactly . . .' Stan was grinning, sipping his ginger ale.

And Charlie couldn't help but say, 'Remember that time we tried to get served in that pub and they would only give us ginger ale? The barman nearly chucked us out.'

'He did chuck us out, from what I remember,' said Stan.

'Little did you think back then that one day you'd actually be ordering ginger ale by choice.'

'Not exactly by choice,' Stan said. 'I'm working later, remember, after this. Going to do a bit of digging for you, about land clearance stuff, council policy on rehousing Gypsies—'

'Ah but we did have some good times though, didn't we?' Charlie interrupted, sick of discussing the story, sick of hearing Stan evangelise about the importance of his work – and anyway feeling warmed up now, lit up by these shared memories of the fish and chip shop paper, and the trying to get served in that shitty Newford pub. Why had they been chucked out again? 'Remember how you fell for my cousin?' he said. 'And how you kept following her around all moony-eyed, trying to give her flowers and things?'

That got a smile out of Stan – finally wiped away that

earnest look he always seemed to wear these days, and got him grinning.

'Of course,' Stan said. 'Cindy. I wouldn't forget her. Whatever is she up to these days?'

'Married some lad from near Yarmouth, didn't she?' Charlie said. 'He was alright, I think – least he seemed so. Some Colby boy, I don't know. Think they've got a kid now, last I heard.'

'Seriously?' said Stan, smile faltering a little.

'Yeah,' said Charlie. 'What? Is that such a surprise?'

Stan blinked. 'I suppose not, no,' he said. 'It's funny,' he continued. 'When we were kids, I just didn't see it – I didn't see the differences between us. I suppose kids don't.'

'I saw it,' said Charlie. 'Wasn't such a baby as you were back then, was I? Didn't think it was much of a big deal though, was all.'

'And is it, do you think?'

'Why should it be?'

Stan nodded. Picked up his drink, and then put it down again without drinking any. He stared at the glass. 'I'm sick of this ginger rubbish,' he said.

'Can I get you a real drink?' said Charlie.

'Probably I shouldn't,' said Stan, though he didn't look so sure.

'I shouldn't either,' Charlie found himself saying then – airily, comfortably, as if it were just some vaguely interesting, not very important aside. 'I'm fighting next week. Or – well. Day after tomorrow, actually.'

'What's that?'

'Got a fight, haven't I? On Saturday.'

'How d'you mean?'

'Oh I don't know. Nothing much interesting. Some distant cousin or other insulted my brother at a wedding – and now I've got to fight him.' He tried to laugh. 'Defend the family's good name and all that.'

'Excuse me?' said Stan.

'So really I shouldn't be drinking at all. Really I should be at the gym.'

'When you say fighting,' said Stan. 'You mean like boxing?'

'Yeah, yeah. The bareknuckle. That's the one.' He kind of wished he'd not brought this up. Stan was looking so shocked – and that didn't exactly boost the confidence levels for Saturday, seeing him look so worried like that. Then again though, it kind of did feel good to talk about it, actually. To take all that dread that was just knotted up in his belly and to dump it like this, its full ugly self, on the table in front of Stan.

Stan seemed to be about to say something, then stopped. Then opened his mouth again like a goldfish – and still failed to say anything. And Charlie kind of wanted to fill the silence then, make it all seem a bit more normal for a moment, more casual, make what he'd told Stan less of a big deal, but now he'd spoken aloud about the fight he found somehow he couldn't crack a joke or laugh it off. Until he'd just said it in fact he'd kind of forgotten that it was quite so soon as the day after tomorrow. So they just sat in silence, staring at each other with only the noise of the radio on in the bar, and the barman clattering glasses.

'But that's barbaric,' Stan said at last. 'Medieval, Charlie. You're not going to go through with it?'

'Oh I dunno if barbaric is the word. I mean, it's organised. And it's not like there's weapons or anything.'

Stan didn't look convinced – didn't look convinced at all.

'You're actually going to fight your cousin to defend your family's honour?'

'Well that's not' – Charlie lifted his pint, then put it down again without drinking – 'I just have to, don't I? I don't like the idea any more than you do – less probably, since I'm the one getting beaten up in a couple of days. But I've got no choice.'

'Bullshit, Charlie, you always have a choice.'

'Easy for you to say.'

'No, it's not – I know it's not always easy. God knows I know that it isn't. But sometimes you just have to say no, and not let yourself be pushed around by people. Jesus, Charlie, I never thought I'd have to say this to you.'

'Look, it's more complicated than that,' said Charlie. 'I tried – I tried to get out of fighting, years ago. I tried to take a step back from my family even, I did, but then there's James, Stan. And I can't leave him there with the rest of them . . . and family's family, anyway, isn't it? I owe them all too much to just fuck off somewhere and disappear. They're probably the most important thing I haven't lost yet.'

'It's always complicated. But they can't make you do this if you don't want to. You're a grown man.'

'But that's it, exactly. I have responsibilities. And I care about my brother.'

'So you want to fight, then?'

'I – don't know.'

Charlie realised he was twisting the remains of a crisp packet the previous occupant of their table had left behind around and around his finger, cutting off the blood supply.

He unwound it – and then for some reason carefully folded it up and laid it to one side.

'It's just not as simple as all that,' he said, not quite able to look at Stan and so staring at both of their hands on the tabletop now instead – his calloused and still grubby with oil and dust from work, covered in little nicks and scars, nails short, wearing his uncle's saddle ring, his grandpa's ring, his wedding ring. Stan's hands pale, skinny, cracked and dry over the knuckles like he washed them too often, broken nails, smudges of biro and of newspaper ink, no rings on his fingers at all. And to think he'd felt once that they were almost like brothers. 'I have to show up,' he said, still staring at their hands on the table. 'Even if I lose, I have to show up, and face him.' He sighed, and then found himself admitting out loud for the first time, 'Kate, my wife, she thinks I won't, you know.'

'I do understand,' Stan said then. 'About how difficult it can be. When it's family. You might think I don't, but I do.'

'I get what you said,' said Charlie. 'And I've seen it in a million films and TV shows and books and, Christ, even in adverts – the idea that you can win just by talking, by explaining yourself properly, and that stories and words have just as much power as fists, that the pen is mightier than the sword, all of that. That if you can somehow get people to listen to you then they'll understand and it'll be okay. But in my world,' he said, 'it's not like that. Or not for the men, anyway. There's so little space for words. The majority of my family don't read – can't read. My mum's the only one, really, and she – well. It's not like people didn't think she was strange because of it. It just feels like . . . like the old ways are the only way to get by, sometimes. And either you carry on and accept them, the good and the bad, or you're against them, and you run away and lose everything. And that's that.'

Too late, he realised his eyes were sparking. He dragged his sleeve across his face, trying to cover himself with the pretence of wiping his nose, and then raised his glass to drink – before realising it was empty.

'I never asked,' he said, more to change the subject than anything else. 'What happened to you, with your mum? You said the two of you didn't speak much any more.'

'Oh,' said Stan. 'That. Well. It's probably not worth dredging up.'

'I'm interested,' said Charlie, and realised he really was now. What had her name been, Stan's mum? *Helen*, that was it. That awful afternoon at the hospital. So strange to think that Stan had been there, but completely unaware, still unconscious. He'd never told Stan about that day. He wondered if she had.

'Something happened to her, I think, when my dad died,' Stan was saying now though. 'And as I got older, it got worse. Every time she looked at me I just felt like a disappointment. Like, she was so sad all the time, and I was always letting her down in some way by not being able to help her more, you know? Sometimes even as if she were angry with me, almost, for not being him.'

'I'm sure that's not true though, mate.'

'I don't know,' Stan said.

'So what happened? You just moved out, and went to uni?'

'No, it happened after that, really. We had an argument. An argument that felt sort of final, in some way. I walked out and after that . . . things were just never the same.'

'What? How did that happen?'

'I just snapped, one day. I don't know how it happened. I was back for the holidays, from Bristol, and one minute we were just bickering over something utterly normal, and then we were talking about Dad, suddenly, except she was still refusing to have a proper conversation with me about him even though it had been all these years . . . and yes, I suppose I ended up saying some horrible things to her. I apologised afterwards, of course. But – I don't know.'

'You seen her much, since?'

'We email, sometimes. In a way, though, I can't help but wonder if she's quite glad to be shot of me.'

'Oh come on, mate, I doubt that's true.'

'You don't know her, Charlie. She's difficult.'

And as Stan said that, Charlie could just picture her, standing there in front of him in the hospital and blocking his view of Stan on the bed, her jaw set, telling him to stay away from her son. Difficult seemed fair, but even through her hostility that afternoon it had been easy enough to see just how much she had cared about Stan, and just how much she feared losing him, too.

'I don't know,' Charlie said then. 'But look at you. She'd be proud to see you, surely.'

'Honestly, who knows?' said Stan.

'She should be proud though. I mean, you're doing well for yourself, mate, really. University degree, good job, living in London. I'm sure she'd like to see that.'

'You think?' Stan said, looking so uncertain as he said it, pushing his glasses up his nose.

'Of course,' Charlie told him. 'Absolutely she would.' And then, because Stan was looking so down now, and he wanted to do something for his old friend – wanted to cheer him up a bit and couldn't really think of anything else right now at this point – 'How about I get you that proper drink, then?' he said. 'What d'you fancy? I'm buying.'

Stan grinned – a melancholy sort of grin.

'Just whatever you're having,' he said. 'And thanks, Charlie.'

'It's just a drink,' said Charlie.

'I didn't mean the drink,' said Stan.

'Yeah,' said Charlie. 'I know.'

# 30

'Adios,' said Stan, heading off into the rain – back to the office, apparently, though it was late, already nearly ten – full of talk about researching the legal background to Charlie's situation, squatter's rights and land law and minorities' protection and precedents and protests. Really it was all a blur to Charlie, what Stan was on about – he couldn't see how it connected, really, or how it was relevant to what had happened to him, but Stan seemed to have rallied, cheered up no end since that moment of worry or whatever it was back there and that was good enough for Charlie, to see his old friend lit up like that and more himself again.

'No prisoners,' he said, calling after Stan, who was already off, halfway down the street.

Stan raised his fist in the air. 'Nae pasaran,' he called back.

Ah but he was a good lad, Stan Gower. Always had been, ever since he was a kid. Charlie turned and headed the opposite way down the pavement, not drunk but still too far gone to bother with dodging puddles. His shoes were soaked within five paces. The street lighting was shite too, that was partly it – he couldn't see where he was putting his feet. Back at Hollytree they'd strung lights up around each individual plot – those LED ones that work by battery, and didn't even have to hook up to a generator or anything. And they'd lit fires, too, most nights. Or some nights, anyway, when it had been warm enough to sit outside. The point was though that there had been light everywhere, back at Hollytree. In the middle of the countryside, almost, fields and space all around and London just a hum of traffic in the distance. It had felt like a whole city of their own, with the lights and the fires, and all the talk.

Really, he knew, he should be heading now to Martin's gym. *Come on*, he told himself. *It's the day after tomorrow, this is getting beyond a joke.* And what could the old fool really do to him anyway? When you looked at it properly, Martin was only some stupid uncle with a bit of a temper and a half-decent right hook on him. That was all. Was Charlie frightened of him, was that it? Surely not. He stopped dead in the street, stared at the rain, at the passing cars on the main road just ahead of him. He was at that particular level of drunkenness when everything seems very clear, suddenly – the sweet spot where everything you've been letting get on top of you resolves into simplicity, and after all the agonising it's suddenly clear to you what you really think, what you really want to do.

He started walking again, this time with more purpose. Drunk hen night, drunk students . . . why were humans always drunk? Give us some free time and that's what we do with it, it seemed – we go directly in search of oblivion. Properly out in the bright lights now, going down Hoxton Street to the bus stop, and then on to the number 108 and out towards the gym, man on the top deck raving, strange shit about judgement and God, everyone else either pointedly ignoring or just not caring, even kids and everything, no one asking questions, shouting men so normal it seemed in this city that no one felt it was worth bothering. How he hated buses, though. Why was he always on buses? Any self-respecting Traveller man would never even think of taking the bus. Would never have sold the Transit, or would have got some new wheels by now, at least, when Charlie didn't even have a bike . . . and then somehow he was stepping off again, and it was still raining, still icy even though it was March – and then, quicker than he would have liked, he was turning into Rowan Street, and had stopped outside the gym.

Shouts from inside, still. Part of him had slightly hoped, he realised now, that no one would be there – that they'd all have gone home to their dinners and their wives and their television sets, or whatever it was these men did of an evening. Not to say that he occupied his time with anything better – not that anyone in this world did, really, far as he could see. Except Stan, maybe. Stan was different, working away, reading books, writing things. The power of a good story, eh? Maybe he should have brought him here – brought him along, shown him just how different the real world was from what he learned about in university.

Ah but he didn't want to be bringing Stan along to somewhere like this. They'd have him for breakfast – tweedy Gorjer boy with all his clever talk and horn-rimmed spectacles. No, Stan was too gentle somehow to be dragged into this, because hell, now he was here even Charlie, who'd known this the whole of his life, on and off, found himself nervous, apprehensive, not wanting to be here at all.

The sounds of punches – gloved punches, these were – landing on pads. The sound of a punchbag being pummelled. Male voices laughing together, shouting, posturing . . . *What was that, you little bastard? You think you're really some-thing, do you . . .?* General laughter, and whoever was being goaded talking back. *Alright, alright, very funny*, he was saying, whoever he was – except it wasn't so funny, really, not funny at all because then Charlie heard the sounds of the two as they began sparring, the others cheering them on, all of them at once offering their two cents as the fight-ers dodged and danced and spat and as punches landed. Standing outside on the street like that, the whole scene was painted for Charlie in sound. He even recognised the voices of the fighters, and of the people standing by. Martin was there, sure enough. That was his voice, yelling . . . *No grab-bing like that*, he was roaring over the general melee, *fair play, no holding*. And the two fighters, who were they? Leo Smith was one of them, definitely. The way he kept trying to fight dirty, people shouting every time he tried to kick or bite or scratch, even the sound of his grunts and his shouts were familiar. But who was the other?

Charlie listened a little longer, but he still couldn't tell. It was only when the fight dissolved with laughs and curses and cries of *that's enough, he's had enough*, that he recognised the voice of Davey Evans, his young cousin on his mother's side – fifteen, now, and everything an Evans lad should grow up to be. Not like Charlie, who even at that age had been ducking out, avoiding Martin and ignoring his mum, too interested in books or music or chasing Gorjer girls for his own good. Really Davey should be the one fighting next week and not Charlie. If only that could be the way of things. If Charlie could just disappear somehow, leaving Davey as the closest fighting man to James. Davey would beat that Holland kid easy, no problem – or he'd be in with a good chance, at least.

Still, no sense in dwelling on what obviously never could happen, and Jesus, who even was he, fantasising like that about ducking out, running off, and throwing young Davey under the bus in place of himself? Charlie pulled his stomach in, pushed his shoulders back, slapped a lazy grin on to his face and held his chin high as he pushed open the double doors, and stepped inside.

'Charlie boy,' said Martin, the second he was in the main room – fewer men in there than he'd expected, from the noise. Just Martin and Davey and Leo Smith of course and a couple of others. It was late, after all, half ten almost now, Charlie saw, glancing down at his watch.

'Alright, mush?' continued Martin. 'Looking well, mate, looking well.'

'Hello, Uncle,' Charlie said, going over, giving Martin the obligatory clap on the shoulder. 'You alright?'

'Look, lads,' said Martin, amid a general blur of greetings from the others – a nod and proper smile from Davey – 'it's the bonny prince. Bonny Prince Charlie. What a rare treat. I practically brought him up, good as, and these days I hardly see him from one month to the next. Why be such a stranger, eh? Forgetting your old uncle?'

Martin always talked this way, as if to an audience – as if his whole life were some TV show and every new person to wander on to the set needed a proper introduction, even if nobody else around was caring or paying attention.

'Nah,' Charlie said, trying to laugh. Martin was only messing, after all. Only a bit of fun. 'Been busy with work, haven't I? Bringing in the cash, supporting Kate.'

'And how is she, Kate? Another little one on the way?'

'No,' said Charlie. 'No, not yet.'

Martin gave him an odd look.

'So – what have I missed?' said Charlie, trying to take control, change the subject, most of him wishing he'd just gone straight home after leaving the bar. That he'd just said goodnight to Stan and got straight on the bus back. But at least he'd be able to tell Kate truthfully tonight that he'd come here – that was something.

'You don't want to wait too long,' said Martin, not having any of it. 'She's not all that young any more, Charlie. Neither of you are. And a woman like her – well. You don't want to let her dwell on it, on what happened to the two of you. Give her something else to occupy her mind, eh? Time to get back on the old horse.'

He found himself joining in with the general laughter, because it was easier than doing anything else. And it actually felt alright, to be laughing about something that had haunted him for so long, just with this old lot in the gym. Was he really letting himself get pushed around here, as Stan had told him he was? Or was this in fact what he was meant to be doing? And all that stuff Stan had said, about words being just as strong as fists – and everything Mum had taught him for that matter, getting him books and signing him up to local libraries and all of that – maybe that was all . . . not bollocks, exactly, but just something from a different world, and not for him to worry about?

He cracked a few more jokes with the lads, squared up to little Davey just for a laugh – who wasn't so little any more, actually, by any means – and then when the others had started to lose interest in the novelty of him showing up like this, Martin focusing back on training up young Davey, and Leo and Pete grabbing their towels and their bags and setting off home, he stripped off his shirt and just wandered around like that for a bit. He tried not to feel too self-conscious about the mass of his belly, tensing and sucking it in as much as possible as he threw the odd punch at the odd punchbag, and did some press-ups and sit-ups, counting himself out in sets of twelve and feeling the alcohol come out in his sweat. Then he went and sat on the far side of the room. What the hell was he doing here, really? Was he just here to say he'd been? So he could go home and tell Kate that he'd done something useful for once? He was hardly here to spar, or even to train seriously, was he, turning up half-cut like this, not even having brought any gloves or anything?

He found some tape, anyway, and began winding it around and around his knuckles – slowly, slowly – watching as Davey and Martin carried on, everyone else fallen away now, talking shite and packing up and pulling on sweaters. Martin with the pads on, held out for Davey to punch – Davey in grappling gloves, hands of steel already, only fifteen – landing each punch square in the centre of each pad again and again, still so light on his feet after ages of training, sweat beading up at his temples but no signs of being at all out of breath. And then Martin with that look in his eye, watching Davey's every move, not even talking, just moving back and forth, shifting the pads, seeing what Davey could do, very occasionally giving a quick, satisfied nod – challenge met, good, on to the next one.

So Davey was Martin's new project, now. His new talent, his favourite and his protégé. There was always one. Martin had even tried to make it Charlie, way back when. Back when his boxing gym had been so much smaller than this one, just a dusty room with a couple of mats spaced on the hard floor and a few free weights in the corner. Not like this place – you could tell Martin was doing well with all the mirrors, weights, mats, machines and the vast, framed pictures of him with various boxing semi-legends on the walls. There was even a water cooler, for christssake. But even though so much had changed, all those years ago back in Farnham with Charlie he'd had that same look exactly. That same knife-edge focus as he had with young Davey now. Charlie remembered it like it was yesterday. The thrill of it, at first. Going from being the kid with the useless dad who'd run off back up north to live like a Gorjer, to having Martin, the toughest man on the site, right behind you. The knowledge that you were doing him proud, doing your family proud. But then the hell of it, too, when you hadn't slept well or you were late or slow from drinking – or even if you were found in the gym by yourself as Charlie had been once, going at a punchbag while listening to *that wailing Gorjer poofter music*, as Martin had called his Muse CD. The anger of him then, when you had let him down. His favourite, not living up to expectations – worse than simply being mediocre from the off.

But Charlie had stood his ground, hadn't he, been a bit more reckless, way back when. Because of course there had been one occasion that, for all their banter and their gestures towards civility, neither he nor Martin would ever forget. The time Martin had gone for him too hard one training session, and Charlie had fought back, wild and kicking and with teeth and with nails, and had somehow managed to bring Martin down and bleeding. Charlie had sworn after that he'd never go back, never go back to train with Martin again and that he'd be off to the Gorjer boxing club instead with the lads from school. And for whatever reason, after that, Martin hadn't even tried to tell him *no*. He couldn't have been more than fourteen, when all that had happened, surely. And still, back then he'd been a man who could stand his own ground.

Davey was showing clear signs of tiring now, eyes still focused but bulging in their sockets, face red as beetroot and breath catching all raggedy in his lungs. 'Come on, lad,' said Martin. 'You've not done more than a minute now, hardly – you want to be a proper fighter you're going to have to do better than that.'

Davey looked spent but he kept on going. Charlie undid the tape from his left hand and started winding it again, as he'd gone and done it a bit too tight, the first time. Not that he was going to use it, really, he didn't know why he'd even wrapped his hands like this, it wasn't like he was here to properly fight anyone, or anything.

After Charlie, anyway, Martin had moved on to James. And that had gone alright, for a while. Really it should be James out there fighting for himself. Fucking Holland boy – typical coward, choosing someone like James to pick on, who couldn't defend himself any more. He'd been a great fighter back then, James. Only a kid but still great, could have been great. Charlie hoped the Holland boy knew that. But then that Holland kid was – what? Nineteen? Eighteen? He'd never have seen all that, probably.

But then Davey was even younger than Holland, and with the strength of a man twice his age was only slowing up now – and it must have been, what? Five, even ten minutes that Martin had had him going like that? And after a whole evening of this, too, and after sparring with that Leo earlier.

'Fucksake, Martin,' Charlie yelled out. 'That's enough. The kid's had enough.'

Martin stopped moving, lowered the pads, raised his bristling eyebrows at Davey then turned to Charlie. It was only the three of them left in the gym now, and everything quiet. Charlie hadn't paid attention to the others melting away.

'You telling me how to run this place now?' said Martin.

'Naw, Uncle,' said Charlie – easy grin, teasing voice, trying to keep the tone light – 'I'd never dare. But the kid's been at it all night, hasn't he? He's shattered, look at him.'

'I'm fine,' said Davey, but he was bent double, stomach heaving, voice rasping.

Martin looked at Davey, seemed to think about it. 'You here for a reason, then?' he said. 'Or are you just here to watch?'

It took Charlie a moment to realise Martin was speaking to him. Martin was still staring at Davey with an odd expression on his face – a straight split between pride and wishing the boy had done better. 'You fancy taking his place?' Martin said.

Charlie almost refused. Almost insisted that ten years ago he'd sworn he'd never let himself get beaten up by Martin Evans again, and that nothing had changed, his resolve still stood and Martin couldn't bully him into changing his mind, not even to distract him now, and save young Davey's skin. Except there was that question again – that question of what had he come here for tonight, really? Because surely it hadn't just been to watch, peacock a bit and go home. Time to put his money where his mouth was.

'Go on, then,' he said, getting to his feet all casual, like it hadn't been over a decade since he'd last trained with Martin. 'Let's have it.'

Davey sloped off to the side, grabbed a towel, obviously grateful to no longer be the focus of Martin's attention, as Charlie came forward, stepping up to face Martin in the centre of the gym. Martin dropped the pads, kicked them away to one side, and then he looked at Charlie, really looked at him, gave him this horrible once-over, up and down, that seemed to take in his failure to train for this fight properly, his failures with Kate, with work, with the flat, with James and Mum and with Martin himself, as well as the sag of his belly, and the drinks he'd had in the pub with Stan earlier. Charlie half expected Martin just to put up his fists then, just as they were, but instead Martin sighed and turned, heading to the far side of the gym where he took two pairs of gloves from off some hooks, up above one of the mirrors. He put one pair on himself, and chucked the other down at Charlie's feet.

'Can't have you getting too done in before Saturday,' was all he said.

'What do you care?' Charlie replied, feeling like a child as he said it.

'Shut up, Charlie, of course I care,' Martin replied as, square in front of Charlie again now, he raised his gloved fists and levelled his gaze, ready. And just like that, all the usual forced joviality with which he'd dealt with Charlie since that last day at the gym together all those years ago had vanished, off out the window now, into the London night. And apart from the grey hair on his head it was like no time had passed at all – as if this was only the day after, or something. The rematch.

'Go on then, bonny prince,' he said. 'Let's see what you've got in you these days.'

Christ. What had he been thinking? Coming here so late, so out of condition, after work, even – after drinking with Stan. But then it was all that with Stan, maybe, that had made him do it, all that standing up to the man shite, all that nae pasaran. What was honestly the good if this was where it always got you? But Martin was dancing on his toes, now, and there was no time for regrets. Charlie tugged on the gloves and stretched out his neck as the rest of the room around them – young Davey watching and all the mirrors and mats and things – all blurred into the background. Only Martin his focus now, the ugly old bastard. Charlie was hardly a small man, but Martin was still somehow huge, looming ahead of him and seeming sharp too, in spite of the passing years, his eyes on Charlie's now, still alert as anything.

Charlie went at him, got there first, landing a fist on the side of Martin's neck, another coming in quick to the lower ribs right near the liver – except he'd not thought about this, just gone in swinging and not covering himself, because then Martin was in there, swarmer that he was, making the most of Charlie's stupidly leaving himself open. And now Charlie was trying not to back away, trying to stand his ground at least – but Martin somehow still fought like he was twenty years younger than he was, faster and lighter on his feet than Charlie remembered, even, from back in the day and hammering blows, now, on Charlie's ribs and his jaw and his temples, his kidneys and his gut. And he was just too fast for Charlie – or Charlie was too slow, and too taken aback to dodge or block the assault. He took a step back, at last, thinking strategy – he'd get away from Martin, keep the fight outside, make the most of the more considerable weight that was behind him these days and not even try to compete in this dancing and jabbing game, this showering of blows . . . but as he stepped back, stumbling a little from the sheer power of Martin's last punch to his ribs, he managed to trip over his own shoe, somehow – just as Martin landed another fist to his cheekbone, sending his gaze all off kilter. And though he tried to catch himself, he couldn't help but fall, toppling like a game of Jenga – slow motion, it felt like – on to the cold, hard boxing gym floor.

He was shaking, skin icy yet licked with sweat already after only that short bout. He knew he couldn't stay on the ground – knew that he should raise his chin, look Martin in the eye, pull himself to his feet and try and save face with fighting talk. He knew he should drag his fists up into the air again and go another round. Except Christ he was tired – and what was even really the point? This was just what happened if you tried to fight after a night at the pub, wasn't it? There was no sense denying the drink did slow you down. And now his head was slamming and his vision swimming and he felt sick, too, like the whole area between his chest and his groin was like a fish tank or something, just a big old bubble of liquid with all these weird things floating about in it. And what face did he have to save, anyway? It was only young Davey here watching, and Martin had made up his mind what he thought of him years ago, surely. He'd only be kidding himself if he thought tonight could make any difference.

'Get up,' said Martin. 'Charlie Wells, you get up now or you're a disgrace to this family – d'you hear?'

Finally Charlie pushed himself up from the floor so he was at least sitting, and looked up at Martin.

'Why?' Charlie said then. 'What's the point when you're only going to knock me down again?'

'Get. Up.' Martin's eyes were at their narrowest, voice so low it was almost not words at all, just a strange kind of growl.

And, formidable as Martin was, who could avoid noticing, though, that there was something kind of almost funny about the whole situation, too? The extreme seriousness of everything, the way no one in this gym would ever crack a smile at this old man dancing back and forth on his toes like that, at the distorted fury in his face like a cartoon grotesque, at the way he was deliberately making himself more and more crimson in the face . . . ah but probably it was no laughing matter. God, Kate would be furious, if he burst out laughing now. *You never take things seriously*, she always told him. *But life is no joke, Charlie Wells. Living is a serious business.*

And yet was it, though? Really? Because even like this, on the ground, battered and bruised and humiliated and knowing now, for certain, he had hell to face at the hands of young Holland next week – or no, not even next week, in fact, the day after tomorrow – you still had to laugh, really. That was the problem with the men round here, Charlie thought. They lived life too solemnly, never saw the humour in anything. Stan, now, he would understand why Martin was funny – maybe only after he got over his Gorjer distaste at the so-called brutality of it all, but he would see it, Charlie was sure. Ah if Stan were here, now, how they would laugh.

'What's wrong with you?' said Martin. 'Get up off your arse – now, Charlie Wells.'

'Ah you're alright,' said Charlie. 'Think I'll give it a miss, really.'

'What?' said Martin, not dancing any more, stock still instead. 'Say that again. Look me in the eye and say that again.'

And so Charlie stared into Martin's furious gaze and said, 'Yeah I've got better ways to spend my evening, really. I've' – he thought of Stan, in the pub, the look on his face as he'd said those words, *stories have power* – 'I've got some research to do.'

'Research?' said Martin, as if the very word was disgusting – dog vomit, faeces, fungally infected toes.

'Yeah,' said Charlie, really trying not to grin now at Martin's outraged face, at how easy it was to wind him up like this. 'Why not?'

Then he pulled off his gloves, and got to his feet – thankfully convincing, he hoped, as steadier than he actually felt – and wandered off to pick up his sweater from where he'd left it on the floor, next to young Davey. Davey was staring between him and Martin open-mouthed, and Charlie couldn't help but tip him a wink.

'Alright, chavi?' he said.

Then he pulled on the sweater and headed off, towards the doors, back into the night.

'You think you're better than us, Charlie Wells?' Martin roared after him. 'You always thought you were better than the rest of us because of your useless poshrat father and your reading and your *research* and all of that shite but you'll have your arse kicked on Saturday, no mistake, no matter how much you think the sun shines out of it—'

Charlie stepped out of the double doors into the damp, drizzly night, letting them swing shut behind him. So what if maybe he did think he was better than that? Better than angry, shirtless men brawling with each other because they had no better way of setting themselves against everything wrong in their lives? Maybe Stan was right, and it was bar- baric. Charlie had other fish to fry now, anyway. Maybe Stan was right that that article could make a real difference. Because who ran this world, after all? People who wrote and read newspapers, in their suits and their offices? Or Traveller men shouting unheard, ignored by the rest of society, turning their fists on each other?

Charlie shivered, and set off into the night, still unsteady on his feet after being so roundly beaten but feeling weirdly better, in spite of himself. Because he'd gone to the gym and had a go, hadn't he? And what more could he do now? What more could Kate ask? He'd even made it out relatively unscathed, which was more than he'd expected, frankly. He even had the strange feeling of having got one up, almost, on Martin. Everything was good. He only hoped Martin didn't go and take it out on young Davey now, seeing as he was the only one left in there with him.

# 31

Charlie was messing with the forklift's loading mechanism, which was playing up as usual, when he spotted John Anderson again, pacing into view between the warehouse shelves, clipboard in hand. As if this day could get any worse. Not only was it Friday, meaning the day before the fight, a mere twenty-four hours until he had to face Holland and not leave in an ambulance, but he'd woken that morning not to his alarm clock, as usual, or to the sound of next door's dog barking, but to Kate crying. And as he'd rubbed the sleep from his eyes and yawned and stretched out towards her, doing his very best in his sleep-heavy state to think of what might be troubling her now – after all, if anyone had cause to be waking up weeping this morning then God knows it was him – she'd just thrown off his arm and scrambled straight out of bed and shut herself in the kitchen. Hadn't even let him in when he'd hammered on the door, cajoled, begged, just asked her straight out – *What do you think you're doing, Kate? D'you not think I've got other things to worry me today? Let me in, why don't you? Why won't you let me in?* She'd just yelled back through the plywood – *If you can't figure it out, there's something wrong with you.* And it wasn't even like he'd woken her when he'd got back in last night, or anything. He'd been quiet, after all, considerate.

John Anderson, though, was still coming closer. He seemed, in fact, to be heading straight for him. Why, though? Why this time? Why this morning? When it wasn't like Charlie had said another word to anyone else about organising a meeting or anything. He'd shut all that right down, straight after that last run-in in the canteen.

He was just thinking back through the last couple of hours since arriving at work, trying to think of what he might possibly have done wrong now, when he happened to notice how John's shirt matched his eyes exactly today, making him look all the more like a corporate upgrade on the standard human. And in spite of the bleakness of the day so far Charlie found himself laughing at that, at the idea of them all chucking in their usual work to make clones of John Anderson. How John would love that.

'Sorry,' said John, stopping right in front of Charlie, leaning in uncomfortably close, 'but I'm afraid I can't see what's quite so funny.'

'I'm just happy to see you John, is all.'

John's eyes narrowed. 'I don't like to say this so soon after having our last little chat, but I'm afraid you give me no choice in the matter. Because if you honestly think that on top of everything else you can keep arriving at work so late – late as many days this week as you've been on time, in fact – well. I'm afraid to say you've got another think coming.'

*Another think coming* – what kind of person uses that as a genuine threat? People who couldn't think of anything specific to threaten you with, that was who. People who were all bark and no bite. This stupid little man with his ridiculous shirt and fancy accent thought he could intimidate him, when if he knew how pathetic he seemed in comparison with the other things Charlie had to face down and deal with he would head for the hills. Compared to Martin last night, for instance. A red-blooded man going at Charlie with a will – and he hadn't let that rattle him, had he? He'd come out more or less on top, even.

'Ah come off it, John,' said Charlie. 'I'm trying to get my work done, aren't I? You're only slowing me down, with all this chatter.'

John's eyebrows shot up, zooming a surprising distance towards the crown of his head.

'I am your line manager, Charlie. And this is not *chatter*. I don't know how things work where you come from, but in a professional context you stop and you listen to your superiors.'

'You're not my superior,' said Charlie, turning back to the forklift, giving the apron guard a shove in the hope it might jam something back into position. He could actually feel John's breath, hot on the side of his face now.

'Look at me when I'm talking to you,' said John, in a rush, voice tight – an elastic band stretched to maximum tension. 'You're lucky to be here, why won't you understand that? You're lucky even to work here.'

'Do you want me to thank you, then, is that it? For paying me less than everybody else?'

John was very red in the face now, hackles up, clearly. He was opening and shutting his mouth like a goldfish, no sound coming out. 'Who do you think you are?' he spat, eventually. 'No qualifications, no schooling. Probably you can't even read. I just don't understand it. Outside of this room you have no prospects, do you understand me? Outside of this room you're worthless. Nobody else would hire you.'

'Bullshit,' said Charlie. 'And I'm not illiterate. You don't know a thing about me.'

And, just like that, he took off his helmet, stepped away from the forklift, and walked out – going the whole long way across the warehouse floor to the doors, never pausing, not looking back once.

\*

He spent the rest of the morning jogging round the park – feeling pretty good now, actually. Maybe the bit he had done last night in the gym had warmed him up, reminded his body what it felt like being in condition. And they did say after all, didn't they, that if you'd ever been really fit in your life then however much of a slob you got to be later on you'd be able to get right back to full capacity much more quickly. And Charlie had been pretty on it as a teenager, after all. Sharp, a decent fighter. Even after he'd stepped away from the bare-knuckle stuff – getting laughed at and lectured by everyone else on the site, almost, for going off with the Gorjers – he'd still been a solid opponent for any kid in Newford. All those skinny boys from suburban houses, worried mothers waiting at home with antiseptic wipes and steaming plates of dinner. Ah but they'd been alright, those lads. He'd had a laugh with them. Hadn't taken fighting too seriously, any of them. It had been a bit of fun, then, a hobby – just as it should be. Important enough but hardly the be all and end all.

He slowed his pace to a walk, and then sat down on a bench in the sunshine. Finally today it was starting to feel like spring. The sixteenth of March, and birdsong in the trees again and daffodils springing up everywhere. Maybe, just maybe, he let himself consider then, eyes shut with the sun on them making red and orange patterns on the back of his lids, maybe things really were on the up. Stan would write his article and something would happen with Hollytree. They'd get themselves a lawyer to help them get it back, or get compensation, or something at least. And him and Kate would pay their debts, and then they'd buy themselves a nice van with whatever was left over, so they could get out of the city to somewhere the air was clear and you could see the stars at night. And then who knows? Maybe in a year or so they'd have another little one who'd live, this time – and all of this here in London would just be a blip, a time they'd shake their heads and sigh about, or even laugh about in the future, Kate in the kitchen frying up some breakfast and kids running all over and playing and fighting and yelling and doing what kids do. And Charlie would be out of godawful warehouse work forever, because he'd set up as a mechanic on his own, maybe – fixing cars or even just bikes somewhere on their land so he could stay at home most days, be near Kate and be a good dad to the kids, not like his own dad had been – he'd be around to keep eyes on his little ones and they'd grow up strong and Kate would laugh again at their antics and grow her hair long, just as she'd had it before, before she'd started pulling it out and all of that – and well, basically, he couldn't wait, he couldn't wait to get started.

Maybe he'd even win the fight tomorrow. He wasn't in with a bad chance, he didn't think, now. Far from it. He'd felt great jogging around a minute ago, hadn't he? And apart from that, he'd been to the gym twice in the last week. And he'd got back a bit of his old spirit too, hadn't he? A bit of his old sharp tongue, of being able to see the funny side, and bounce back – a bit of the old nae pasaran. He wouldn't just show up for James and take a beating. He'd do more than that, he'd do him proud, and James would look at him again in that way he'd always done before, back before Hollytree, before Newford, before that stupid quad bike and Charlie ducking out, disappearing off to Manchester, leaving James when he'd been at his most injured and frightened, all the way back in Surrey.

He stayed on the bench a little while longer, then wandered off to find himself some lunch – not cheap, out in the city like this. London was getting ridiculous these days, £12.50 for a cod and chips? But proper fish, this, and so good once everything was drenched in vinegar. So much better than that canteen food, by a long way. Was he ever going back there? After what he'd said to John? It didn't seem likely.

He sat on the kerb to eat in spite of the dirty looks he got for getting in the way of passers-by, and thought back over the altercation with John that morning – shaking his head at the arrogance of the man, at the prejudice, and then at the way he'd let himself put up with it for what was nearly almost a year now.

Then he scrumpled up his greasy fish-and-chip paper, lobbed it out into the road, and phoned Stan to tell him the good news.

'I've quit,' he said, the second Stan picked up. 'I've finally done it, mate. Told my stupid boss where to go and walked the fuck right out of there. I'm free.'

'Charlie? Where are you? Are you okay?'

'I'm great! Haven't felt this good in years – not since my fucking wedding day or something and d'you know what, Stan? It's because of you.'

'What? Me? Did you just say you quit your job?'

'I did, mate, I did.'

'Why?'

'Put up with enough crap, hadn't I? Boss was mental and they weren't paying me fair.'

'But will you be okay, Charlie? What will you do for money?'

'Okay? Of course I'll be okay. I *am* okay. You worry too much, mate, you know that? I've got plans. Grand plans.'

'Right,' said Stan, still sounding worried. 'Listen, Charlie, I was going to ring you anyway – you're not around this evening, are you? After work?'

'I'm around any time. I'm free, like I said.'

'Actually in that case, are you around now? To meet up?'

'I suppose so, yeah mate. Not got much else on this afternoon.'

'Tap House at three?'

'Don't see why not.'

# 32

Same table, same two chairs, same barman – did that guy never have a day off, or did nobody else work here? – same combo of ginger beer and a pint, same grubby tabletop, same sticky floor. It was becoming quite the routine.

'Cheers, Stan,' said Charlie, lifting his glass and clinking it against Stan's still on the table. 'To sweet freedom, three p.m. pints, old friends, and the future.'

Stan sighed. 'Listen, Charlie,' he said, not sounding celebratory at all. 'There's something I wanted to talk to you about.'

'I know you're worried it was a bad idea, Stan. I could tell from the second I mentioned it back there on the phone. You were sceptical, definitely. Even concerned. But you've got to trust me. I know what I'm doing, now. It's for the last year or so up till now that I haven't known. Losing money. Losing my sense of self, sense of humour, all my friends. It was you going on about the old days that did it – about not taking any crap from anyone and all that. You reminded me, Stan – you reminded me of who I really am.'

'Yeah, look, Charlie. It's not that—'

'You forget, Stan. I'm older than you. I've seen a lot of this world. I've suffered, yes, but I've done stuff. I've learned stuff—'

'Charlie, I've got some bad news.'

'You don't have to worry about me, Stan.'

'Charlie.'

'What?'

'The article, Charlie. I've been trying to tell you. I pitched it to the editor this morning and he said no.' Stan looked terrible, Charlie only noticed now, as if he'd aged fifteen years since yesterday, all drawn and pinched around the eyes.

'What was that, mate? Are you alright?'

'Yeah. No. I'm so sorry, Charlie.'

'That's – that's okay,' said Charlie. 'Of course it's okay. Don't worry yourself about it, Stan. Don't worry yourself about me.' He was still processing what Stan had said, it had come out in such a rush. *Editor said no*. 'I thought you'd already talked to your boss though? I thought she told you it would be huge, just what everyone needed and all of that stuff?'

'I – I'm sorry, Charlie,' Stan said, again, looking worse.

'No, no it's just – what happened? You said it was an important story to tell, my story? The power of words and all that?'

'It is, Charlie. I still – I firmly believe that. But I spoke too soon. I'd talked to my boss, but not to my boss boss—'

'What?'

'The guy who runs the whole paper, the whole of *Writing Left*.' I shouldn't have told you all that stuff, it was too early. I shouldn't have said anything to you until we'd had the full go-ahead.'

'But – just like that?' said Charlie. 'That's it? You're not going to argue?'

Stan shrugged. 'I did,' he said. 'He was pretty final. Told me to get out of his office.'

'But it was an important story,' said Charlie. 'Your other boss thought so.'

'Yeah,' said Stan. 'And maybe we will still get to run it sometime in the future, but for now, for the time being—'

'But why not?' said Charlie. 'Why did he tell you to get out?'

Stan put his head in his hands, rubbed his eyes, then looked at Charlie properly – and the expression on his face, then, it almost broke Charlie's heart to see his old friend look-ing so defeated. 'Oh Charlie,' he said. 'It's not important.'

'No,' said Charlie. 'Why? I – it's okay, Stan, really it is. I just want to know why not.'

'Gypsies don't sell papers, is what he said,' said Stan then. 'And apparently everyone's suspicious enough of *Writing Left* already "without us getting mixed up in all of that", as he put it. He told me we had more important battles to fight.'

'More important,' said Charlie.

'I know,' said Stan. 'He's a bastard. I'm sorry.'

Charlie stared into the amber liquid of his glass. Just a minute ago they'd clinked glasses to freedom and the future. He'd quit his job. What had he done? And he'd toasted old friends, too, when here was Stan looking like the world had ended. Poor Stan. He was young yet. Not so much in years, maybe, but in that Gorjer, student way of his. He just didn't understand how fucked up the world was, that was his problem. He'd expected it, thoughtlessly, to be better, more easily fixed. And then – it wasn't even a complete disaster, not running the article, was it? There were other ways of making money, and getting things untangled. And it was still a good thing, to be free of John Anderson and that hellhole warehouse prison, wasn't it?

'Ah Stan,' he said. 'Don't look like that. It'll be alright.'

'I feel so awful, Charlie. Like such a fool. I was complacent, that was the problem. I just thought – I don't know . . .'

'You really did think my story was important,' said Charlie. 'That's nothing to be ashamed of.'

'I've been such an idiot, Charlie. Chatting on about the cause and standing up for what's right and not letting yourself be pushed around—'

'But you've got to believe in that stuff, mate. For as long as you can. For as long as the world lets you hold on to that stuff, you've got to believe it. That's the only way anything good gets done.'

'You really think so?'

'Course I do,' said Charlie. 'Now stop all your navel-gazing and drink up.'

'Charlie—'

'Don't worry about it,' he said. 'I've had plenty of bad news in my time, this is minor in comparison. Believe me, I'll be alright.'

'You're sure?'

'Of course I'm sure. I'm always alright.'

'No, I mean – you're sure you're not angry with me, or anything?'

'Angry? No,' said Charlie.

And maybe he should have said something more to Stan. Maybe he should have given him just a flash of an indication of the feeling threatening to engulf him now, that feeling of the bottom having dropped out of things – everything floating everywhere, like when one of the airlocks breaks in a spaceship in a film and everything goes haywire, TVs and sofas and toothpaste and stuff getting sucked out into zero G, all things contextless, everything scattered about in the void. But what good would it have done? It wasn't Stan's fault, any of this. He'd only been trying to help. And you had to make these mistakes to learn in life, didn't you?

'Nah, I have to tell you, mate,' Charlie said, 'I'm not even massively surprised.'

They spent the next four hours in the Tap House, Stan graduating from ginger beer to IPA after the second round. Eventually, when it seemed to be getting dark outside, Charlie asked the barman for the time.

'Getting on for half seven,' he told them.

'Can I ask you something?' Charlie found himself saying to Stan. 'Kate'll be at home and I can't face her alone. Not like this, not when I should have been at work all afternoon, shouldn't even have been drinking at all, with the fight tomorrow – and then my job, Stan, mate. Kate won't understand it's a good thing, now that I'm free. I can't tell her alone, mate, please. Come with me?'

Stan seemed to hesitate for just a second, but then he nodded. 'Of course,' he said. 'Anything I can do to help.'

# 33

Kate was silent when they got back – just sat on the sofa and staring at the TV, which was playing a rerun of that *Strictly Come Dancing* she loved so much. Not a *how was your day?* for him, not even a word of hello. Or, for that matter, any acknowledgement that Stan was here too – and it was surely worth commenting on, this impossibly rare occurrence of his bringing a friend home, and a Gorjer friend at that?

That was funny, how it still felt a bit like a rebellion having Gorjer friends, in spite of them living in a Gorjer house now, and everything. It almost made him smile now, to think of the first time he'd brought Stan to meet his family, all those years ago in Newford. How shit-scared he'd been, just relying on Nan and the way nobody in the family would ever dare cross her to keep things from blowing up. And though it had been a gamble, certainly, it had paid off, hadn't it? Or it had been fine, anyway.

But back to now, back to London – and though it was only Kate he was facing tonight he found he only felt, if any-thing, more awkward and more nervous than he had back then. In Newford, he supposed, he'd still assumed there'd be a way out for him, a special set of more relaxed rules by which he could still be a member of his family, and yet have a different life, too, in a different world. And then Kate was such a wild card, that was the other thing. There was no telling how she'd respond. This, for instance, was odd. He'd expected to come back to her crashing pots around the kitchen, clattering and clanging and swearing away like nobody's business at him being late, him not going enough to the gym – or about the fight tomorrow.

'Alright, Kate,' he said.

He could feel Stan hovering behind him, and could just picture his self-consciousness, his bumbling awkwardness, and the expression on his face – as if he expected a handshake and a glass of wine just for stepping across the threshold. *Stop it*, he wanted to tell him. *Act normal, why can't you?* Teenage Stan had been so much more presentable somehow. And yet Kate acknowledged neither of them. Just kept sitting there curled like a cat, cushion on her lap, face blank, with the flickering light of the TV playing over her features. Whatever was happening in the programme came to an end and people broke into whooping applause. Still Kate didn't smile, didn't move, didn't look up.

'Okay,' he said, eventually. 'Suit yourself. Come on, Stan. Welcome home. You hungry or anything?'

'It has been a while since I last ate, I'll admit,' said Stan, sounding, again, as if he was at some tittering bohemian dinner party. Did Stan feel like this, he wondered then, when they were with Flo and all of the rest of that lot? As if he had to explain his friend to them, and make excuses? Kate, though, stayed quiet.

'Hungry, Kate?' he called to her, on the way into the kitchen.

No response. Just more noise from the telly. That old geezer was saying that thing he always said – *nice to see you,* with the audience all laughing and chanting back to him, *to see you nice!* . . . If only everything were that easy. Every interaction. If there were just a simple way to reciprocate everything anyone ever said or did to you, with no misunderstandings or unexpected cruelty. No violence. A simple call-and-response way of life. He opened the fridge to find it empty, more or less. Just a few jars of pickled things knocking about in the door and half an onion on the top shelf. He scanned the rest of the room. Nothing on any of the surfaces, really. Just a mostly demolished pack of corn chips and a mouldering loaf of bread.

'I'll be fine with just a cup of tea,' said Stan.

Charlie turned around to look at him. He'd taken his shoes off, he noticed, and was wearing socks with cartoon dinosaurs all up the sides.

'Haven't got any milk,' he told Stan. 'Haven't got any tea bags either, I'll bet.'

He edged past Stan, through the doorway back into the living room.

On the TV, a tall Scandinavian-looking bird in some glittery outfit was leading an awkward old fat man round the stage in what looked like some kind of salsa-type thing. Still Kate was blank-eyed. Her unresponsiveness was starting to freak him out.

'Kate,' he said. 'What you playing at? Why've we got nothing in?'

'If you don't do anything to show you're my husband I'll do nothing for you, either.'

'What? Kate. But that's not fair. You've been in the house all day while I've been – and I do. I do plenty, Kate.'

'What do you do, Charlie? Tell me. Because really I would like to know.'

'I suppose – well I don't know. I can't think of a list off the top of my head, can I? And anyway don't be an idiot, Kate, you know that's not how it works.'

'How does it work, then? Tell me. Because from where I'm sitting it looks as though I may as well not be here – except to feed you and make sure your house is clean. I can't remember the last time you listened to me, or asked my advice, or showed the slightest bit of interest in me, even. Asked me a question about what I've been up to. Or noticed the taste of the food on your plate, let alone thanked me for it.'

'Come on, Kate. I talk to you all the time—'

'It's tomorrow, Charlie. The fight is tomorrow morning. And you're not ready, I can tell. In fact it's as clear as fucking day because you've been out every night this week drinking until God knows when and the one time you went to Martin's he beat you so badly you had to turn and run, didn't even finish the fight—'

'Hang on, wait a sec. Whoever told you that was a liar—'

'Really, Charlie? Because tell me, what did they make up?'

'I didn't turn and run. I told him where to go and left of my own accord. In my own time—'

'And is that what you're going to do tomorrow? Tell Holland where to go and leave of your own accord? Fucking marvellous, that would be, Charlie, you'd make us all proud.'

'Shut up,' he said, sounding like a child and hating himself for it. 'You're always on at me about everything – do this, do that, go to the gym . . . when will you understand?

I'm tired, Kate. When you don't see me, when I'm not here, it's not like I'm lying dormant in some cupboard somewhere, just switched to standby mode. I'm at work. And I'm tired when I get home.'

'Oh?' she said. 'Is that where you've been today then, at work?'

He stopped, halfway through the process of turning back into the kitchen.

'Red in the face, stinking of booze?' she said. 'Where have you been, Charlie? Because sure as hell it wasn't work.'

'I – not today, no.' He went over to her then. Reached out to her, for some reason, seeking what, he didn't know. Reached out and put his hands on her shoulders. She scowled, but she met his eye at least.

'I'm sorry, Kate – Katie. I think I'm going to have to look for work again. I – I don't know. I had a disagreement, sort of, with my manager.'

'Great,' she said. 'A disagreement. And d'you know what? I'm not even surprised. You're useless, Charlie. If there's any way to wriggle out of something, to avoid taking responsibility, you find it. It's the one thing about you I can rely on.'

'They weren't paying him fair,' Stan piped up then, from where he'd been stood up till now in the kitchen doorway, gaping like a fish and staring between the two of them. 'It was pay discrimination. Paying him less than everyone else doing the same job, exactly.'

'Great,' said Kate, pulling away from Charlie, scrambling over to the other side of the sofa, away from him, to turn on Stan. 'That's just great. But you know what? You can shut your stupid Gorjer mouth because you know *nothing* about my marriage. You don't know or understand anything at all. I mean look at you – just like an overgrown child, following this waste of space around and taking his word for everything, just because he talks big? But what do you know? This man, I tell you, has done *nothing*, nothing at all to help me. Eight months ago I gave birth to a dead child. Our baby, a boy, dead in my womb with two weeks to go until the due date. I held him for all of five minutes – tiny, lifeless, getting colder in my arms before the people at the hospital took him away from me. We had to name him for the post mortem, for the birth and death certificate – but guess what? This man, this man you dare to try and defend here, he wouldn't even help me choose a name. And now, of course, he treats me like I'm spoiled goods. Isn't that right, Charlie? Why you barely even touch me any more? See – he won't deny it.'

'Jesus, Charlie, is that – did you really lose a child?'

Charlie nodded. 'Yeah,' he said. 'That we did, Stan. That we did.'

'I'm sorry,' Stan said, speaking to Kate, now. 'I had no idea. He never said.'

'No,' she said. 'Of course he didn't. As far as he's concerned, it didn't happen.'

'Come on, Kate, that's not fair—' Charlie began.

'What name did you choose?' Stan asked Kate then.

'Eli,' she said. 'After my father.'

Stan nodded, but didn't seem to be able to say anything else after that, just stood there, eyes wide, mouth shut.

'That's shut you up, hasn't it?' said Kate, not completely unkindly.

'Come on, Kate, he didn't know. I asked him here, asked him to come back as a guest. Leave him alone.'

'So loyal to his friends,' she said then. 'Leaping to everybody's defence but mine. All the boys, closing ranks. Bringing
your mates back here so you don't have to face me alone,
isn't that how it is? *She's crazy*, I bet you tell all of them. And I
bet you tell them nothing else. You're a coward, Charlie, and
you need to learn to grow up, step up and take some responsibility for your own life. Because d'you know what? I'm sick
of it – I'm sick to death of worrying about you. In fact, I hope
you lose tomorrow. I hope Holland gives you the beating you
deserve and that James never looks at you again. It would
teach you a lesson.'

'Jesus Christ, Kate, shut up,' Charlie said, an odd, distorted expression on his face – as if he were trying to grin,
to laugh it off, to make light of what she'd said, but just
couldn't quite manage it.

'Don't tell me to shut up, you've no right,' said Kate.

'Say it again, then. Tell me again that you hope that I lose.
So I know you really mean it.'

The TV erupted once more in flamboyant applause, but
Kate didn't take her eyes off Charlie.

'I hope you lose,' she said simply.

For a second Charlie didn't move, just stared at her, face
frozen as if he'd been halfway into making a joke before the
wind had changed. The TV screen flickered with colour –
some eighties power ballad started up, and a couple started
whirling around the stage in a waltz. Kate stared right back
at him, chin held high, cushion still clutched in front of her
like a shield. Then Charlie blinked, looked away.

'Right,' he said. 'C'mon, Stan. We're off.'

# 34

'Where to now, then?' Stan asked, after the door had slammed behind them and they'd both stared at it a while.

'Don't know, mate, I'm afraid,' said Charlie.

Stan was staring at him so expectantly, as if this had all been part of some kind of plan, underneath it all – as if Charlie had it all under control and would know exactly where next, what next on the programme for the evening.

'Think she'll let you back in, in a bit?'

'I don't want back in,' Charlie said. 'I can't relax, can't breathe in there. Can't sleep with her next to me. I've got to be right for the morning, Stan. Going back in there will only drain me of every last bit of fight I've got in me.'

Stan nodded. Checked his watch. 'You could come over to mine,' he said. 'It's on the other side of the city but it's not that late, yet. We'd be there by nine. Could get a takeaway or something.'

'Seriously?'

'Yeah. Normally I'd clear it with my flatmates, but they'll be fine with it I'm sure.'

'Who're the flatmates?'

'Just some other students – or wait, no. Dan's a photographer now, not a student. But the others are students. They're all nice, I promise.'

Stan's student flat. Probably all books and wine and newspapers. Weird posters on the walls and conversation in the kitchen. Back there for a takeaway, small talk, explanations, Stan gritting his teeth and putting a brave face on it, but probably feeling just as he himself had felt back there, bringing Stan home to Kate – as if his friend made no sense at all in this context, was just one huge walking target for contempt and misunderstanding, impossible to protect, or fully explain.

'Come on, Charlie, you've got to go somewhere. And you've never even seen where I live. It'll be fun. You can meet my friends, we'll have some food. I'll even turn the heating on – special treat.'

'Right,' Charlie said. 'No, mate. Thanks very much for the offer and all but I don't feel I've got it in me, somehow.'

'Don't say that. I'd love to have you over, Charlie. And you'd love my flat, I'm sure. It's nice, I promise you. I made us sound like proper cheapskates with that heating thing but it's a nice place, I swear. I'll even make you dinner, if you like.'

'Nah, mate, I couldn't ask that . . .' Charlie said, hands shoved in jacket pockets, flimsy hood up against the rain, the wind, the London night – and he began to walk slowly, to drift away from the doorstep, away from Stan.

'Come on, mate, where're you going?'

'Sorry, Stan,' he said. 'I can't face it. Don't worry about me, I'll be alright.'

Stan was following now, keeping up with him. 'Do you have somewhere else to go?' he said. 'Honestly, Charlie. Tell me.'

Charlie stopped walking. Turned to Stan, tried to grin.

'Course I do,' he said. 'Got plenty of places to stay, haven't I? Friends all over the city.'

'You're sure you don't just want to come over to mine?'

He nodded. 'Yeah,' he said. 'I'll go to my brother's. That'll be best.'

'James?'

'Yeah. Only got one brother, haven't I?'

'How is he these days?'

'Not bad, mate, I'd say. Not bad.'

And then they just stood there in the rain, apparently with nothing more to say.

'I'll be off, then,' said Charlie.

'Alright,' said Stan. 'If you change your mind, you've got my number.'

'Yeah, I know,' said Charlie.

'And Charlie?'

'What?'

'Good luck tomorrow, alright?'

'Thanks, mate.'

'I hope you win. And I'm sure underneath it all, she does, too.' Stan nodded his head back in the direction of Charlie's front door.

'Thanks, mate,' he said again. 'That's good of you. Thanks.'

And then he turned and walked away, leaving Stan staring after him, face filled with uncertainty, boots filling with rain.

\*

Charlie felt better now he was on his own. That was the thing about other people. You owed them a particular version of yourself. You had to make them laugh, or feel safe, or whatever else they expected from you. You had to seem like you had the whole thing under control. On your own you could let all that go a bit. Be who you were when there was no one there to see you. No longer a good husband, a good mate, a good brother, a good colleague, a good team member, whatever. A good son, a good man. By himself like this he could just be Charlie. Capable of being anything he wanted, free to break all the rules, if he wanted, wriggle out of expectations and say and do whatever the hell he fancied. He could yell up to the moon, if he wanted – that slip of a crescent moon, appearing and disappearing behind the clouds, right there.

He stopped dead in the street and howled up at it, through the rain, through the night, through the city's light pollution. He got a few odd looks. It was a pretty quiet street, mostly residential, but there was still some young guy in a suit walking past and a woman further up, getting out of her car. But who cared what these random strangers thought? He could be the madman singing and staggering around in the night, if he wanted. And it's not like he'd be on his own. This was London, after all, anything was possible, and howling at the moon felt so good he did it again. It seemed to put some life back in his blood, like the first bars of a good tune coming over his headphones on the Discman. It would have been good if he'd had his Discman with him, was the only thing. Just to have some music in his ears as he wandered around, to reset his mood before the fight.

Ah but it was alright, wasn't it? Walking like this in the fresh air and the weather, getting out of that prison of a house and the ruins of his marriage. Except was it ruins really? Maybe Stan had been right about Kate. He hoped

Stan was right. He and Kate, they'd really had something once. And though everything was messed up now – and he hadn't been the best, maybe, at dealing with what had happened with the baby, he'd admit that – surely she couldn't really have meant what she'd said? Surely all that shared history, all that love, couldn't just have died and disappeared somewhere, without leaving even a trace?

He wouldn't go to his brother's, anyway. He'd never really intended to, he realised. It had just been something to say to Stan. He jumped on a bus instead, heading up in the direction of the river. Buses, why was he always on buses, these days?

Then he was off the bus again, and walking out on to the concrete-landscaped path by the Thames. He sat down on one of the empty, identical benches and looked out, watching the city, and the boats drift by. The water was fast-flowing tonight. High tide. And the river might be iron grey, urban sludge down here, but still it comforted him to know that this same water in front of him now had flowed all the way from somewhere where there were hills, where the air was clear and the skies were huge. Somewhere a bit like where he and Kate had got married, even, maybe. He and Kate. Kate and him. Happy pair. Happy day. Happier times. Nan still there. God, how he missed her. All the old crowd. This river in front of him now seemed almost to flow all the way to him here from back then, all the way through all the intervening days and weeks and years, through all the hills and fields. Past Hollytree, too. What would be there at Hollytree now, if he were to go back? A power station? A warehouse? A housing complex? Or was it just blank? Cleared of them all for no good reason?

But it was cold tonight. He could feel his feet starting to ache with it in his trainers. He'd stepped in some puddles back there, not looking where he was going and then not able to see properly in the dark in any case, and he was soaked through to the socks. He had to keep walking, leave the river behind him now and get the blood pumping, the circulation firing. He had to keep moving. Then he'd be fine, no problems. As he'd said to Stan, he'd be alright. He was always alright.

*

He walked all the way up the river into the city centre, in time to see Big Ben strike midnight. That had been his plan, sort of, from when he'd reached Tower Bridge onwards, and he'd hoped that the moment of it, of being under the clock to bear witness to the first official moments of Saturday, would somehow feel portentous, essential, like something from a film. And maybe it would have done too, if he hadn't been so tired and soaked through to the skin, just in trackies and trainers and his definitely-not-waterproof jacket.

Trying not to feel too downcast at the anti-climax of it though, he wandered over to Westminster station, and sat down on the steps to watch the street. It was funny, it felt like the night had gone on for hours and hours, but it still wasn't even late yet in the normal world. People were wandering around as usual, heading to and from bars, getting in and out of taxis and buses.

'Oi, mate, got a light?' said a voice from behind him. He turned to see a sour-faced man in a suit with a girl on his arm, all shining ironed hair and discreet designer logos.

'Sorry, mate, don't smoke,' he said, turning back to the street.

'Course you do,' said the man. 'No need to be difficult. That's all I want, mate, just a light.'

'Yeah I wasn't lying,' Charlie said. 'I really don't smoke. Gave up last year.'

'Shut up, mate, no you didn't.'

'Leave it, Jamie,' said the girl.

'Leave fucking what?' said Jamie.

'Alright, mate, no need to turn on her,' said Charlie.

'You telling me how to speak to my girl?' said Jamie. 'Come on then, let's have it.' He bent down clumsily, drunkenly, to give Charlie a shove. He smelled of cigarettes and aftershave, after-coffee mints and sour sweat. Violence everywhere, in life. You couldn't sit down for a minute, you couldn't peacefully occupy even the few square centimetres of space you needed simply to continue existing before someone else was there, talking shite, trying to provoke you.

'Jamie!' said the girl.

'It's alright,' said Charlie. 'I'm going. I'll get out of your way. You get him home alright, okay?' he said to the girl.

She just stared at him.

'Don't you fucking talk to her, you pikey scum,' said Jamie.

'I'm leaving,' said Charlie, hands up, backing off, turning, striding away now. 'Believe me, I'm not interested.'

'Get back here, you little coward,' Jamie was yelling after him, but Charlie just kept on walking.

\*

'Sorry, sir. I'm afraid you can't stay there.'

He was a young policeman, younger than Charlie, certainly, maybe even younger than Stan. Spotty, round-faced, uncertain smile. It must have been an hour or so after the encounter with Jamie. He'd got tired of walking about again, and had stopped in Floral Street, more in the shopping zone of the city. It was quieter round here at this time of night with all the shops closed, and he'd figured he'd have more chance of being left alone, that there'd be less likelihood of a run-in with another Friday night drinker, restless and bored and spoiling for a fight. But now here was this young lad with his ill-fitting police uniform, gazing at him like he wanted a pat on the back for being some kind of ideal citizen when Charlie had been doing no harm to anyone, just sitting on a stone-cold bench opposite the vast front windows of Superdry, staring vacantly at the overpriced hoodies lit up in the window, and thinking his own thoughts.

'Why's that?' he asked, half-hearted. He didn't want a fight, especially not with this kid. He looked so tentative, for a policeman. So naturally affable.

'It's just this area, here, with all the shops. I'm meant to move anyone on who hangs about for a concerning amount of time. It's to stop people nicking things and smashing windows and all that, meant to be.'

'Fair enough,' said Charlie. 'Is it working?'

'Don't know,' said the kid. 'I'm new on the job. Not really sure what I'm doing yet, to tell you the truth. It's dead exciting though. I only got my uniform last week. Still need to take a photograph, to show my gran.'

Charlie thought of his own grandmother – Nan leaning out of windows and yelling *the gavvers, the gavvers are here!* every time any police siren passed vaguely within earshot.

'Listen,' said Charlie. 'Aren't you lot meant to work in twos? Like you're meant to have a partner with you, maybe someone more experienced, so you're not just wandering about on your own in the night?'

'Oh I do – I mean I have got another guy on the shift with me. Only he went for a piss and to buy cigarettes. It's been dead quiet, tonight.'

'First week on the job, then?' said Charlie.

'That's right,' said the lad, grin lighting up his face like sunlight.

'And you need me to move on?'

'If that's alright with you, yes, I do.'

'What happens if it's not?'

The smile faltered, slightly. 'Oh, well. I suppose. I suppose I'd have to take your details, give you a caution – or I'd call the station, maybe. Ring for a car to come and pick you up.'

'Lock me in the cells, is that it?'

'I'd hope I wouldn't have to do that, sir.'

He was so earnest, so madly unspoiled. Charlie could just see him now in his granny's living room, cup and saucer balanced on his knee, being told how proud of him she was, what a credit to the family.

'Don't worry,' he said. 'I'm just messing with you. I'll go. I was getting cold, anyway.'

He stood up. Brushed himself off, started walking.

'Thank you,' called the kid, after him. 'Thank you, sir.'

'Best of luck now,' he called back. 'You make your nan proud.'

He didn't stick around to see it, but he could just picture the boy's face, glowing with pride. And why not? Whatever you thought about the police, at least the kid had something to show for himself – qualifications, probably. Foot on the ladder to a decent career.

Still though, he thought, as he walked away from the vast, silent shops and back towards the river via shit clubs and echoing basslines and twenty-four-hour supermarkets with alarmingly bright strip lighting – maybe that only made it worse. To be moved on like that by someone so optimistic, so full of faith in the direction life was taking him. To be moved on by someone that he didn't even have the heart to tell to go to hell – because honestly? For once he actually wanted to do as he was told, and get out of the way to help this young and likely lad. That was the fucked-up-ness of it all, really. He was always being shifted, told to move on – told that everyone else was more important and that whatever space there was in the world was for them to take up, and not him. Maybe he was starting to get used to it, starting to accept it, even.

# 35

Clocks across the city chimed two, and the last clubs started disgorging whoever was left dancing – the drunk and the high and the simply deliriously happy and the people who were having a bit of a shit night really but were out so late because they were hiding from home. Charlie walked among these late-night stragglers, aware that it was time he went home, too. He should have gone back hours ago, really. Just given Kate an hour or two to cool down and then showed up in time for a square meal and a decent night's rest before tomorrow and the fight . . . ah but fuck that. He'd go in a bit, when almost definitely she'd be asleep. Then he could sneak in without waking her, maybe kip under a blanket on the sofa or something, and then slip out in the morning before she'd even figured out he was back. He couldn't face another confrontation. Couldn't face explaining, apologising, justifying. Couldn't face the way she looked at him.

He kept walking, wandering on as the night deepened, and as London's streets began to grow increasingly empty around him. Eventually, when the city was quiet enough that he could hear the birds singing – though he never could get over the way so many London birds sang at night – Charlie found himself in Hoxton Square. He hadn't meant to come here, really. It was just where his feet had brought him.

He carried on, following the impulse, stepping down narrow streets, now, through vast imposing buildings, everything feeling like a back entrance, or a loading bay or a car park – until he had turned on to Spixworth Street, and from there into Judges Lane, with its crap street lights, line of parked cars, and broken paving stones. And then there he was suddenly, standing on the pavement outside the Tap House. It was closed, obviously. Even that one perennial barman had decided to go home to bed. He took one long look at its peeling pub sign, then sat down on the kerb right in front of it.

Then a door swung open from out of the line of parked cars up the street, and Charlie found himself sighing. *Here we go*, he thought. Never allowed a moment of peace in this world. Never allowed just to sit still and think. Except—

'Charlie,' whoever it was was calling. And then Stan was there. Stan just as he'd left him, back outside the flat hours ago. Same clothes, same shoes, same anxious expression. Charlie found he didn't even have the energy left to be surprised.

'Alright?' he said.

'Charlie,' said Stan again. 'I've been looking for you. I've been looking for you everywhere.'

Charlie spread his hands wide. 'You found me.'

'Are you drunk?' said Stan.

'No,' said Charlie. 'Should I be?'

'Bloody hell, Charlie,' said Stan, sitting down next to him on the pavement, 'I was worried. I've driven all round the city.'

'Looking for me?'

'I thought you would call. I thought I'd give you a while

to go off on your own and work out whatever you needed to work out, and then you would ring and come over and we'd have dinner and I don't know – that it would all just be fine.'

'You don't have to look after me, Stan. Really you don't. I'm fine.'

'Are you, though, Charlie? I was close to giving up. I only came here as a last resort. Thought you might be here if you'd – I don't know. If you'd lost my number, or something.'

'I do have other places to go, you know,' said Charlie. 'I wasn't lying, before. When I said that.'

'I know,' said Stan. 'I know you weren't. Shall we get going now, then? You must be freezing.'

He jumped to his feet but Charlie stayed put, shook his head, shoved his hands deeper into his jacket pockets.

'You go. I'm fine here.'

'What?' said Stan. 'That's ridiculous. You need some food, Charlie. A hot shower. A good meal. This – well. This isn't doing anyone any good.'

'I want to be outside,' Charlie said. 'Where I can feel what the weather's like, feel the wind on my face.'

'What?' said Stan again, holding his car keys, all poised to head off.

'I'm fine,' Charlie said again. 'You go.'

But Stan sat back down next to him on the kerb instead.

'What are you doing?' Charlie asked him.

'Sitting down.'

'Why?'

'Because you don't want to go home.'

Charlie sighed. 'Don't be an idiot, Stan.'

'I'm not,' said Stan.

And the way he said it – he spoke lightly, but something there stopped Charlie from arguing. He shrugged, instead. 'Suit yourself.'

'I will.'

'But I was just going to stay here now, I think, until it's time to get going.'

'Get going?'

'Northhill. Where the Holland lot are stopping.'

Stan looked blank.

'You know – for the fight.'

'What? You're not still going to go?'

'Yep.'

'You shouldn't. Not like this.'

'Why?'

'Charlie. You'll get destroyed.'

'Thanks.'

'No, I didn't mean—'

'I know what you meant.'

They both stared out at the puddles on the tarmac, at the quiet line of parked cars, at the torn, empty crisp packet blowing back and forth on the breeze.

'Listen,' Charlie said then. 'You didn't have to come and find me like this. You don't owe me anything, you know. I know you feel bad about that article and everything but really you shouldn't have come. It was nothing, really. No harm done. And anyway, if anything – I owe you, in fact.'

'How d'you mean?'

'Way back. Newford. My fault, Stan. I haven't forgotten. Keep track of my debts, at least.'

'Doesn't work like that, though,' Stan said. 'Friendship doesn't work like that.'

Charlie nodded, and then found he couldn't really look at Stan, so kept staring at the road instead. 'You said once you weren't sure whether it was true what your mum said, that I would ruin your life.'

'Ha, yeah,' said Stan, and then didn't say anything more.

Still Charlie didn't look at him, just stared ahead at the rain pooling in the gutters, and at the toes of his soaking wet shoes.

'You decided yet?' he asked, eventually.

'Course, mate,' said Stan, sounding surprised. 'I was thirteen. That was all rubbish.'

'Oh come on. You've got a nice life, Stan. Good job. Studying for a fucking degree, wandering the hallowed halls of the university, cosy flat, nice friends, all reading books and late night tea and toast and chats about Marx or whatever it is. And look at me. Stuck out here on the pavement in the weather with nothing, Stan. Nothing. And look at you now. Stuck out here with me.'

Stan shrugged. 'Like I said,' he told Charlie, 'I don't think it works like that.'

Eventually the sky started to brighten, and Charlie broke the silence, getting to his feet.

'Right,' he said. 'Time I was off.'

'To Northhill?' said Stan.

'Yeah,' said Charlie, narrowing his eyes at the dawn.

'How're you getting there?'

'Bus, maybe?' said Charlie, like he'd only just thought about it. 'Really I should drive, but I sold my van.'

'Listen,' said Stan, before getting to his feet, too. 'I could take you, if you want. I still think you shouldn't go, but if it would help I can do it.'

327

'I'm going,' said Charlie.

'I know,' said Stan. 'So will you accept a lift, at least?'

Charlie stared at him a moment, then nodded.

\*

They didn't talk much in the car. Charlie just lay against the window with his eyes shut, and Stan thought it best to let him sleep. He needed whatever strength he could salvage before the fight, after all.

He understood so little of this – of Charlie's world, and whatever code of obligation was now leading him to drive his oldest friend down a dusty B road to the dead zone of green space behind a power station, where no one he knew, at least, ever went – all just to take a beating. But then again, maybe Charlie was better prepared for this than he thought? He was a Traveller through and through, maybe he'd been raised for this. He'd boxed for most of his life after all, hadn't he? And sure he'd had a rough night, but who knew how these things worked, and what Charlie was really capable of? Probably he should have more faith in his old friend.

Just as he thought that, the sun broke through the mist and the cloud as if to agree with him, to chime in with his mood – and Charlie yawned and opened his eyes.

'Bloody hell, mate, I tell you,' he said. 'I don't feel half bad, considering. Not at all bad.'

'Seriously?' said Stan, turning off a roundabout. *Follow signs to the power station*, was all Charlie had told him.

'Seriously,' said Charlie.

'Are we going the right way?' said Stan.

'I don't know, mate, where are we?'

'Near Halgrove, I think. Coming up to the station.'

'That'll be fine, then. That'll be fine.' Charlie yawned and sat up in his seat, looking alert now, scanning the world outside for landmarks. 'It's a left here, mate, if that's okay?'

They turned off the B road on to a road that narrowed, after ten minutes or so, to something little more substantial than a country lane.

Charlie stretched, then said, 'Actually, mate, here's good. Just here would be great, in fact.'

Stan slowed the car – going even slower than the thirty-mile-an-hour speed limit until they were moving at a crawl – but he didn't stop.

'Here?' he said. 'But I can take you all the way to the place, wherever it is. It's no bother. I've come this far, haven't I?'

'Nah,' said Charlie. 'Don't worry about it. Right here is great.'

'Come on, Charlie. Don't be ridiculous. I'll take you to wherever you need to go.'

'I'm not being ridiculous,' said Charlie. 'I'll walk the rest of the way. It's not far.'

'How far is it?'

'Not far at all. Look, I – I don't want them seeing I came in your car.'

'Why not?'

'Listen, Stan. Things have changed since we were kids and believe me, it's just – easier this way. Please. It's a tough enough morning as it is.'

Stan stopped the car, cut the engine. Then they just sat there for a bit.

Until Charlie said, 'Listen, Stan. I want to thank you – for staying, outside the pub last night.'

'That's alright,' said Stan.

'And – look. Well. I . . . God, I don't know. I'd better go,' said Charlie. He rubbed his eyes and stared out the wind-screen for a moment, then opened the car door.

'Charlie?' said Stan.

'Yeah?'

'This guy insulted your brother, right? That's why you're fighting him?'

'Yeah. What of it?'

'It's – it's good of you. To go through with it.'

Charlie shrugged – outside the car now, standing on the path looking in. 'It's just what you do,' he said. 'Isn't it?'

'Good luck,' Stan said. 'Give him hell. Sounds like he deserves it.'

'Nae pasaran,' said Charlie, and slammed the car door, raising his hand in a wave.

'Nae pasaran,' said Stan, though Charlie wouldn't hear him reply.

*

He drove down the road until he thought Charlie was a safe distance away, then pulled the car into a lay-by, and stopped while he studied his road atlas. Then he turned around, heading straight for the back lanes behind the power station.

He saw the cars first, going in one direction. Pick-ups, souped-up Transits, Mercs and a BMW convertible – horse-shoes and miniature boxing gloves dangling from the mirrors. Too much traffic and of too specific a sort to be usual for such a sleepy area. Stan kept his face as calm and blank as possible and carried on driving, trying not to dwell on how conspicuous his poky Citroën was amongst this company. It felt like he was encroaching on forbidden land, stepping into a world in which he had no right to be . . . but then hadn't he always said – hadn't he always been determined never to let anyone make him feel that way, as if he had no right to go and be wherever he pleased? Hadn't Charlie taught him that? *Never let them tell you where you do and don't belong*, he'd always said.

Stan still hadn't the courage, though, to turn off down the narrow dirt track that the other vehicles seemed to be taking. Instead, he drove straight ahead, carried on for what he hoped was a safe distance, then parked up just off the road. He couldn't see anything from here, but he was close, still, he knew. Just a road away, really, and behind a hedge from the action. He rolled the windows down, and sure enough – there they were, carried to him on the breeze. Voices shouting instructions, threats, cracking jokes.

It was stupid, probably. Probably he should go home. And yet there he stayed, ready to drive off at any moment, but still waiting, ears tuned to the noise of the field beyond, windows down. Eventually the general wash of noise took on some direction, and he was able to pick out Charlie – hurling threats and insults and sounding strong, violent, keyed-up and ready, so much so that he almost didn't recognise the voice of his old friend, and even would have assumed it belonged to someone else, if it hadn't been for that distinctive accent – that old touch of the Manchester twang. And he felt a little afraid to hear Charlie like that, in that context, so much the fighter, so much the Traveller. He also felt a little more hopeful, though – that same feeling he'd had as he'd said goodbye to Charlie back there in the lane. That hope that this would all work out after all. Charlie was tough, hard as nails. He knew this world. He'd win.

And then it started. Charlie's opponent, that Holland guy, whoever he was, snarling and yelling and Charlie giving as good as he got – and then the voice of some older guy soaring over the two of theirs, refereeing the fight, it sounded like. And for a second it still seemed fine, like everything might still be okay. And then Stan heard the blows landing, and Charlie yelling – not with defiance this time, clearly, but with pain. And then the ref was calling *fight fair lads, c'mon, fair play* but still the sickening sounds of the blows and Charlie swearing and crying and so many voices all laughing or shouting at him to get back on his feet.

'Have you had enough?' came the ref's voice, after this had gone on for what felt to Stan, sitting there frozen, hands on the wheel, like truly forever. 'Have you had enough?'

And there was a pause – a lull in the general hubbub of shouting and calling. And God knows what was happening. What was Charlie doing? What was going on?

Then Charlie's voice, sounding so ragged, so unfamiliar, utterly torn-up and alien, came echoing through the morning.

'Not fucking likely,' it said.

And then Stan couldn't listen any more. When he had driven round here, part of him had planned, maybe, to wait until the fight was over and most of the people had dispersed to drive up and surprise his friend. To either congratulate or console him, and then give him a lift back into town and take him to A&E or to breakfast or to whatever seemed most appropriate. But this – this now – this was not what he'd thought it would be. It was too much, too savage, and just – far too *complicated* for him to cope with.

He sank down in his seat behind the wheel, and for the first time in his life he felt just how unfathomable other people's lives could be. And for a moment, then, he felt really, truly afraid.

Then he rolled the windows back up against the yelling – Charlie's screams just a part of the melee now, unrecognisable, lost among the rest – before starting the car and driving away, back into the city, back to home and to his own Saturday, planned-out and waiting for him. Uni and the library and then an afternoon at the paper and then home to cook dinner and maybe read or catch up with his housemates – who would have all been doing things like finishing up essays or meeting girls for coffee and going to water polo club. He needed to get away from all this, from this violence and tragedy. He needed to get safely back to the real world.

*The real world*, Stan thought, as he drove – and after a while he was comforted. But even so, a part of him still couldn't quite believe it, not really, not fully. Couldn't forget that feeling he'd had back in the lane with his car windows down. Couldn't quite shake the suspicion that maybe this was it, and that in some way, maybe this was all anything came down to in the end – just two tired men beating each other up in a field. That complicated, that simple, and that impossible for him to fix with naive good intentions.

# PART THREE

# Two weeks later

# 36

Stan handed in his notice at *Writing Left*. It seemed odd to think he'd once been so in awe of everyone on the staff, and of the newspaper itself. He'd really thought he'd made it, on some level, working there. Really believed that he was using his mind and his words and his writing to do something important. The whole thing seemed so hollow now, after what had happened with the article, and Charlie. More than hollow, it felt prejudiced and morally corrupt. And he felt like such an idiot, too. Embarrassed, ashamed even. He'd been so keen to show Charlie just how much he'd grown up since the old days that he'd been careless, and promised more than he'd had the power to give.

On his last day at the paper, Stan packed all the bits and pieces he'd left in his cubbyhole in the office into a cardboard box – just old books, mainly, and a broken Dictaphone – before going to meet Flo. It was April now, still bright at five o'clock and warm enough to sit outside, if you had a decent jacket. She was waiting for him in Gordon Square, just round the corner from the university library, where she'd been revising for exams. She was sitting on a blanket on the grass reading a book, frowning and chewing a thumbnail. This was how he usually found her these days, with finals approaching.

It was funny, he found himself thinking then, watching her across the square. When he'd first met her, he'd not really understood her, at all. He'd made all sorts of stupid judgements based on her accent, her clothes, and the famous boarding school she'd been to. He'd assumed she'd be frivolous, insubstantial, someone who lived life lightly and took nothing seriously. He'd even seen dating her almost as a form of social tourism. It was only in the last few months that he'd realised quite how unfair he'd been, and quite what an unfair approach that was to take to people, generally. He hefted his cardboard box and walked over to meet her.

'That a present for me?' she asked, nodding at the box as he approached, looking up from her book to squint at him through the evening sun.

'Can be, if you want,' he said. 'If you'd like a broken Dictaphone.'

'I'd love one,' she replied. 'Let it never be said you don't spoil me.'

He plonked the box next to her on the grass and sat down, giving her a kiss hello.

'Long day?' she said, probably at the look on his face.

'Last day,' he told her. 'At *Writing Left*. That was my last shift.'

'Finally,' she said. 'And how does it feel?'

He shrugged. 'I'm so excited to begin my future as a Students' Union barista.'

'Don't be sarcastic,' she said. 'It doesn't suit you. And the Students' Union will be one hundred times better than working for a bunch of stupid racists.'

'They're not all racist,' he said.

'Yes, but then what was it you told me your boss had said, again?'

'He's not my boss any more.'

She rolled her eyes. 'Your old boss, as of ten minutes ago. What was it he said?'

'Gypsies don't sell papers.'

'Exactly.' She nodded, emphatic, her point proved. Which it was, of course.

Stan sighed, sat back on the blanket, and stared at the cardboard box full of his things. 'I wish all that had never happened,' he said then. 'I wish I'd never promised him that article.'

'Your boss? Your old boss?'

'Charlie.'

'Oh,' she frowned, chewed her thumbnail again. 'Have you heard from him at all?'

Stan shrugged. 'A bit. Not much. He rang the other day. I was in the library though.'

'How is he?'

'I don't know. I didn't pick up.'

'Stan.'

'I know. I'll phone him. I'll get in touch soon.'

'You should.'

He was surprised to see how serious she suddenly looked. 'Why d'you care so much, all of a sudden?' he asked her.

Flo only shrugged. 'You've got to stick by people,' was all she said. 'It's important.'

And yet, although he agreed with her, he didn't call Charlie back. He meant to, of course. But then he just kept on with coursework deadlines and his new barista job and with cheering up Flo through her finals, putting off the moment of getting back in touch. Until, without him quite knowing how it had happened, it was the final week of May, and London was suddenly alive with colour and life, the whole city a riot of summer clothes and roses, of wisteria spilling over the confines of window boxes, and people spilling out of restaurants and bars on to pavements as songbirds and bright green parakeets chirped and squawked between the trees.

It was around this time that a small green envelope arrived in the post, hand-addressed like a birthday card. Stan tore it open without thinking, the neat, curly writing on the front not anyone's he recognised, only to jump at the small cloud of confetti that fell out, bright against the scratched laminate of his desk. Hundreds of tiny green shamrocks. He picked one up on his fingertip and stared at it a moment before unfolding the note that had been inside. *Kate and Charlie's Leaving Party*, it said, in the same painstakingly neat handwriting – which must be Kate's, he realised now. *We're off on the road again. Come raise a glass with us next Tuesday.*

Stan stared at the words *leaving party*. Why hadn't Charlie phoned him, or messaged him even, if he was really leaving? And leaving where? Stan frowned at the invitation a while longer. At least it meant that Charlie and Kate were still together. He'd wondered, after that awful night at their flat, before the fight.

Stan closed his eyes, and tried to push away the feeling that was now threatening to engulf him. Because it was perfectly understandable, his falling out of touch for a while, wasn't it? It wasn't like their lives were genuinely that interconnected any more. They might be in the same city, but they lived in different worlds, really, didn't they?

Even to himself the excuses sounded thin. He folded the invitation in half, and then into quarters, and then into eighths, and slid it into his pocket, before sweeping all the green confetti into the bin.

# 37

Stan arrived at Charlie's place just after half past four – a nice, neutral time to arrive, he hoped. A perfectly reasonable hour to assume from such an unhelpfully general invitation as 'next Tuesday'. Still, he couldn't help but feel a little nervous as he approached the front door to the building, and rang the buzzer for Charlie's flat. *Don't apologise for yourself*, Charlie had always told him, and now, this time – when it really mattered and he really did actually want to apologise – he found himself worried that he wouldn't be able to somehow, that he wouldn't be able to find the words. A woman's voice answered through the intercom. He couldn't tell if it was Kate or someone else. He couldn't even really hear what she said, the speaker distorted the sound so much.

'It's Stan,' he said, feeling nervous, never so much like an interloper, as the front door buzzed and he stepped through into the hall.

The door to Charlie's flat had been left on the latch, and there was one green balloon dangling from the letter box. Stan pushed it open and saw that so far, at least, there weren't many people at this party at all. There was Kate of course, who nodded hello, thankfully, though she didn't smile. Still, he'd take that, given how they'd left things last time he'd met her. And then there was a man Stan didn't recognise but who looked, as his mum might have said back in the day, like a bit of a hard case. Then a young guy Stan was sure he'd seen somewhere before though he couldn't place it now, and another woman Stan recognised after a double-take as Charlie's mum, except now with grey hair.

Then Charlie appeared in the doorway from the kitchen, holding a six-pack of beers, and his eyes met Stan's, and for a second nobody said anything. His face had healed up, at least.

'Alright, mate,' Charlie said. 'Started to think you weren't coming.'

'Course,' said Stan. 'I – Charlie. Of course I came.'

Charlie only shrugged, headed on into the room, and put the beers down on the table. He separated one off and held it out to Stan.

'No I – won't, actually,' Stan said.

'Suit yourself,' said Charlie, eyes flitting away as he cracked open the beer and took a gulp himself. 'Just trying to make you feel welcome.'

'It's only,' Stan said, 'that I have this essay. Due in on Friday.'

'Yeah, on Friday,' Charlie said. 'Not now.'

Kate came over at this point. 'Should we start again?' she said, offering her hand for Stan to shake. 'I'm sorry we didn't meet in a better way, before.'

'Not at all. Thanks so much for asking me, today,' Stan said, wishing he sounded less like a child at a tea party.

'Of course,' she said, eyes flitting up to Charlie in a way he couldn't quite read.

After that, Stan shook hands with the other guests. The slightly scary-looking one introduced himself as Tommy

Campbell, with a broad smile and a handshake that nearly broke Stan's fingers. Davey Evans was the other, Charlie's younger cousin, and it took Stan a moment to blink and recognise the boy's features in this man's face – that same little kid from the site all the way back in Newford, parading around for them in his pretend adult clothes.

'Stan' – Charlie's mum recognised him immediately – 'how are you? Still reading all those books?'

'I am,' he told her. 'I'm at uni now, here in London, doing my master's. How have you been?'

'Oh you know,' she said. 'This and that.'

Charlie was watching him as he talked, standing a little apart from the others, leaning in the doorway to the kitchen. Stan excused himself with a quick nod, and went over to him, finding, as he did, that he was a little nervous, and couldn't think of quite what to say.

'Looking good, mate,' he began. 'Looking well.'

'Yeah,' said Charlie. 'Well. Although. I don't know. That's not really true though, is it?'

Stan shrugged. Charlie did look stronger than the last time he'd seen him, more or less recovered from his injuries, but still, there were dark circles under his eyes, and the Guinness T-shirt he was wearing looked too tight, as if he'd put on even more weight since the spring – which, Stan reminded himself, probably anyone would have done, stuck in the house like that, injured, with no job and nothing to do. And something, some feeling, then, threatened to well up from Stan's stomach into his throat. He swallowed it back down as determinedly as he could.

'I'm sorry, Charlie,' he said then.

'What for?' Charlie said.

'You know. Being so rubbish recently. I didn't mean to be.'

Charlie didn't say anything for a while, just sipped his beer and stared at the living-room wall. Then he rubbed his eyes and said, 'Ah it's nothing, really, Stan. You had exams and that, didn't you?'

'Coursework,' said Stan. 'Yeah, I did. Still though.'

Charlie shrugged, still not looking at Stan properly.

'Where are you off to, then?' Stan asked him.

'What's that?'

'You're leaving, right? Where are you leaving to?'

Charlie nodded, slow. Had another long drink of his beer before replying. 'Ireland, Stan,' he said, at last. 'I'm going to figure things out, out there. Going to stop drinking and everything.'

*Ireland.* Suddenly it clicked. The shamrock confetti, the green balloon on the door, Charlie's Guinness T-shirt.

'Stop drinking?' said Stan, staring at the Guinness logo. 'In Ireland?'

'Ah Christ, mate, it's only a T-shirt.'

Stan felt himself frowning, not sure if he wanted to cry or laugh.

'Ah come on. I'm just getting into the spirit of things, aren't I? It was all I had to wear that was Irish.' But Charlie gave him an odd kind of look then. 'You don't believe me, do you?' he said.

'What?'

'Don't believe I'm going to clean up. Stop the drinking and everything. I am though. We're going west, Katie and me. Not to the city or anything but to the middle of fucking *nowhere*, Stan. Imagine it. Just the two of us and no one else to fuck things up or let us down or get in the fucking way.

We're going to Kerry, and the mountains. And we're going to drive the Wild Atlantic Way, and wake up like we used to with the birds.'

'I – no I do believe you, of course. That's – that's great, Charlie.'

Charlie nodded, looking unconvinced.

'Why didn't you tell me before?' Stan asked him then.

Charlie stared, and then laughed, a little. 'Tried to, didn't I? You were never around.'

\*

Out in the corridor a little later on, Stan was surprised to see Charlie and Kate's bedroom door ajar, and a light on inside. Without really thinking what he was doing he wandered up, and pushed it gently open. And there was James, frowning into a computer screen, tapping away at the keyboard.

'Sorry,' said Stan, as soon as he'd opened the door.

'S'okay,' said James, without looking away from the screen.

Stan nearly turned around to go back to the living room then, to Charlie and the rest, but for whatever reason his feet seemed stuck to the ground. 'What you up to?' he asked James.

'Research,' said James. Then looking round to Stan and flicking his hair out of his eyes, he said, 'Or – I don't know. Just some shit on Facebook.'

'Oh,' said Stan. 'Right.'

'Just got sick of not really knowing stuff, you know? About how everything worked. Got sick of trusting other people all the time then watching it all go to shit.'

'Makes sense, I guess.'

'I was looking up about "unauthorised encampments"' –
the quotation marks were strongly audible in James's voice
– 'about the law for how they get people evicted. Bringing in
the bailiffs and all that.'

'Charlie told me what happened at Hollytree. I'm so
sorry, it sounded really awful.' Stan was aware of just how
hollow those words sounded as soon as they were out of his
mouth, like someone reading a line off a sheet of paper –
*here's some vaguely appropriate thing I thought I ought to
say to fill the space here.* James had obviously picked up on
it too, from the expression on his face.

'Yeah, well,' James said. 'It's happening everywhere. All
these families being turned out on the side of the road. And
then instead of anyone saying something should be done
about it, the internet's full of fuckers mouthing off that they
got what they deserved, those families, that they got what
they had coming to them. But how can they really think that
that's true though? When they've been sending in the riot
police?'

'The riot police?'

'People keep going on, saying Travellers have all these
*problems*,' said James, as if Stan hadn't even spoken. 'You
even hear this lot round here doing it sometimes, complaining about the Irish – about the kids running wild and all
that. But *everyone*'s got problems, haven't they? Not just us.
As far as I can see the only difference is that our problems
happen because no one who's in charge of anything ever
seems to accept we exist – so like, it's not a surprise if there
are a few things, you know? And then it's not even like ours
are the bad ones, anyway. When we're not the ones starting
the wars or fucking up the planet.'

'Yeah,' said Stan. 'That's true I guess.'

'Where was it again,' James said then, 'where we first met you?'

'You mean Newford?' Stan said.

'Yeah, Newford,' James nodded. 'Things were better then. It isn't only Charlie who hates it here, you know. Though as usual he's the one who makes the most noise about it. When was the last time you went back?'

The sudden change of direction in James's question caught Stan off guard, and for a second he could only blink back at him. 'To Newford?'

'Yeah.'

Stan found he had to think about it, actually count the months, he didn't know offhand. 'I suppose it would be two years now, nearly.'

'Still got family there?'

'Yeah. My mum. She's still there.'

'And you haven't been to see her in two years?'

'I suppose that means I haven't, no,' Stan said, and only felt even more awkward.

\*

'So, why Ireland?' Stan asked Charlie, back in the living room with James now, who was over by the sofa with Kate, trying to tune the radio, flicking through music and static, fragments of words and conversation.

'Don't know really,' Charlie replied, 'but we're running away, aren't we? Felt only right we should leave the country. And anyway it's beautiful there. So beautiful it could break your heart, Stan.'

'Running away?' said Stan.

'Yeah. Well. Just . . . getting away from it all and starting again. No expectations or obligations. Certainly no bleeding landlords, letting agents or debts. Just disappear for a bit, that's all. They'll forget us soon enough.'

'Charlie, is that – what d'you mean disappear? You're not actually *running away*, are you? From your landlord?'

Charlie shrugged. 'How else d'you think we're ever going to get out of here?'

'But Charlie, you can't just . . . I mean you can't just *go*. It's not possible.'

'Got to look after ourselves though, haven't we, mate? No one else is going to do it, and you're wrong if you think I'm going to waste my life away waiting here just because I owe some prick some money. He can afford it, at the end of the day. I can't.'

'But surely, Charlie, if you got a job or something – if you made a proper plan and budgeted. You could set a date to leave next year.'

'Can't do it, mate,' Charlie said. 'Can't stay here any longer.' And for a second then he seemed to come into focus, and look a little sharper, more like the Charlie from the old days. 'I can't stay here, Stan,' he said. 'Don't you see? I'm dying here. It's killing me.'

Stan opened his mouth, ready to tell his friend he was overreacting, then closed it again without speaking. 'Yeah,' he said eventually. 'I do see.'

'So if anyone asks you,' Charlie said with a faint kind of grin, 'you never saw me, you don't know me. Alright?'

Stan laughed at first.

'I'm serious though,' said Charlie. 'Can you do that for me, Stan?'

'God,' said Stan. 'I suppose. Yeah, alright. I guess. If anyone asks, I don't know you.'

Charlie nodded. 'Good,' he said.

'Is it?' said Stan then.

And Charlie's face broke into what looked like the first real grin Stan had seen from him in a while, even if it did have a kind of desolate edge. 'I don't know, mate, but it's what we've got,' he said.

# 38

For those early weeks of summer, the two of them lived off whatever Charlie managed to scrape together, helping out on the farms. And he liked the work well enough, in those early days of stopping drinking. It distracted him, gave him something else to focus on in the days and then left him so worn out he'd fall asleep like a child every evening. No one was able to pay much though, or had more than a few days' work for him. It was different from the old days, all the farmers told him, each of them saying more or less the same. Things were tight enough now with just themselves, never mind with taking on long-term extra help. And then there were the Irish Travellers, too. Charlie managed to get along with most of the lads he came across just fine – he was still pretty good at making friends after all, wherever he found himself – but there was always that first conversation though, that first argument, that first set of assumptions that he'd be not much more than some kind of stuck-up arsehole who thought he was better than them. So it wasn't easy. Not like a holiday or anything, as he'd sort of hoped it might be, back when they'd fled their debts in England.

Then there was one particular bright July day just outside of Tralee, picking strawberries alongside some bored local lad who seemed determined to pick a fight whatever Charlie did or said, and the charm of that whole kind of life started to wear off, after that. And so Charlie and Kate had driven back out of Kerry, up the cliffs and then over to Clare on the ferry – which was more or less how they'd ended up here, stopping in these late summer days in the car park of the Asda superstore, just outside Galway City.

Charlie woke to the sound of the rain on the Transit roof. Kate's eyes were still closed, her red hair spread against the pillow. And it suited her, being on the road like this. She was getting stronger, more sure of herself again, even in spite of the new types of hardship that they'd discovered went along with this version of the old travelling dream.

Things were better in Galway though. Not that they'd been all that bad on the farms, nothing like the hell of London, no way, he wasn't complaining – but there was simply more money here in the city, and that certainly made everything easier. After not even two days of asking for work he'd landed a decent job working shifts as a kind of roadie, helping set up and pack down rigs at the local music venue. All the bands, passing through. And that was an amazing thing to find, on top of everything else – Ireland hadn't forgotten what music was, certainly hadn't relegated it like so many people back home into being nothing more than a background buzz in a bar, or just another way to sell clothes or phones or whatever. People here still wrote lyrics that meant something, even the young ones, and he got to watch the gigs most nights. Kate even came along sometimes too, if she wasn't too tired, and if she liked the sound of the band that was on. Maybe even sometimes just because she wanted to see him.

Because that was the other thing. Their experiment seemed to be working. Experiment, because though they'd told no one of course when they'd left – made out all happy couple, united front and riding off together hand in hand into the great unknown – the reality of it was they'd given themselves one year. One year on the road trying to make things right again, to get back what they'd promised each other nine years ago on the day they were married. One year, or that would be it, and they'd agree to part ways. Not even ten months left now.

He shuffled himself up under the covers and reached over Kate to slide open the blind on the window a little. It might not have been sunny out, but it was bright. One of those gentle days you occasionally seemed to get in Ireland, with the rain so soft and clear, and everything in different tones of grey. He lay back and shut his eyes again, enjoying the light playing on his lids and the sound of the rain outside. When he opened them again, Kate was wide awake and watching him.

'Morning,' he said.

'Morning,' she replied, and she smiled back at him – more properly than she'd done in ages. And what did that look like? Like the sun coming out after a long spell of darkness? No, that wasn't quite it. More like the first drops of rain, hitting parched ground after a long, dry summer.

'You off to work again today?' she asked him.

'I am,' he said.

'Anyone good playing later?'

He thought a moment. 'I think you'd like them, yeah.'

'Really?' she said.

'Nah,' he said. 'In fact I think you'll probably hate them. I was just saying that though 'cause I reckon it'd be fun if you were there.'

'D'you know,' she said, 'I'm really not sure which one of those to believe?'

'Which would you rather believe?'

And she shrugged, and she smiled. 'I'm actually not sure,' she said.

# 39

The place looked different, somehow. Neater. There wasn't a single weed growing in the small front garden, the cracked paving slabs had been replaced with stones of a warm, buttery golden colour, and the window panes were polished and gleaming. The whole front facade in fact looked as if it had been recently power-washed. Stan unlatched the gate, and ventured up to the front step. The bell resonated inside the house in a recorded doorbell sound that echoed, as if the rooms beyond were mostly empty. No one answered. He stood listening to the birds in the suburban trees a moment, pigeons and blackbirds and robins and finches, and made himself count to ten before ringing again.

This time Helen opened the door before the bell could finish its full flourish, almost as if she'd been waiting there, quiet this whole time. And Stan knew it had been a while, well over two years since he'd seen her last, but still. He was almost shocked at how different she looked. She was wearing eyeliner and her hair was blow-dried and highlighted with blonde, but that wasn't the half of it, really. She just seemed more . . . in focus, somehow. As if all her edges were sharper.

'I wasn't sure you'd come,' she said.

'Of course I came,' he told her.

'You're later than you said you'd be.'

'I know, I'm sorry. Signal failure outside Epsom.'

'It's good to see you, Stanley,' she said, at last.

'Thanks, Mum. It's good to see you, too.'

They hugged then. Tentatively, still keeping each other at a distance. It was something though, and Stan even found himself wondering if all the worries that had been churning through his thoughts on the train could be unfounded. Maybe this would be fine. Maybe Charlie was right, and she did want to see him. Maybe this whole afternoon would be okay.

The inside of the house was different, too. So much tidier than Stan had ever seen it, everything in straight lines, the whole place looking as if it had just been scrubbed clean.

'Tea?' Helen asked, as they hovered in the living room.

'I'd love one, thanks Mum.'

He sat down at the kitchen table while she boiled the kettle, and he tried not to think about how odd it felt, arriving like this as a guest in the house he'd grown up in.

'How've you been?' he asked her, aware of the words coming out all stilted as he said them. 'How's everything with work?'

'Work?' she said. 'Work's fine. I'm fine. I'm well, in fact, Stanley.'

'Great,' he said – and then became aware he was nodding his head too vigorously, and made himself stop. 'That's great, Mum. I'm glad.'

The kettle clicked off and she turned to the counter to pour out the tea. 'That Maureen from next door has a grandchild now,' she said then. 'You remember Beverly, don't you? Maureen's daughter Beverly? She's had a girl, apparently. Very sweet. I've seen the pictures. They haven't been to visit yet.'

'Beverly?' Stan said, the name drifting back from some long-ago time, half remembered.

'No, well I suppose you probably wouldn't remember her. She's a bit older than you. Not by that much, mind. But I suppose at that age it does make a difference.'

And so they talked about the neighbours, and Stan started to relax. It was easier, so much easier, than talking about themselves. They were on their second round of tea, the beginnings of dusk just starting outside, when Helen finally asked him something more personal. 'So,' she said. 'What's new with you?'

And though it felt weird at first, to be telling her about uni, and London, and his flat, and the dissertation he was writing, it did start to feel more *normal* with every word he spoke, sitting here at this familiar-unfamiliar kitchen table, telling his mum about his life. She seemed to be properly listening, too, that distracted look she'd always had when he'd been a kid nowhere to be seen.

'I was even thinking,' he found himself saying – though he hadn't really planned to, not today at least – 'that it might be nice for you to meet my girlfriend. Just sometime. Doesn't have to be soon. Just if you wanted.'

'Your girlfriend?' Helen said, raising her eyebrows, blowing on her tea.

'Yeah,' said Stan, trying not to grin too much now but mainly failing. 'Flo. She's nice, I promise.'

'A student?'

'Yeah. Art history. Also at UCL. She's a year younger than me though so she's just finished finals.'

'Where's she from?'

'Scotland, actually. Though you'd never guess it. She's one of those posh Scottish people who basically have English accents.'

Helen even laughed at that. 'Good,' she said. 'I'm glad. It's a relief, in fact, Stanley. I did often wonder who on earth you'd end up with, the way you picked some of your friends, as a boy.'

Stan stopped, tea halfway to his mouth. 'What's that meant to mean?' he asked her.

'Never mind,' she said. 'I shouldn't have said anything. You'll only get on at me. I know that now.'

'You don't mean Charlie, do you?'

'I don't know. I don't remember his name. That Gypsy kid you used to hang about with, God knows where you met him. The one who pushed you off that roof.'

'Yeah that was Charlie,' Stan said, 'except he didn't push me off the roof, Mum. It was an accident. He wasn't even up there. And I chose to go up there, anyway. That was me.'

'Well, then,' Helen said, her tone light but firm, 'that isn't how I remember it, but I'm sorry I brought it up. Just so long as this Flo is nothing like that then I'm sure we'll get along fine.'

'But Mum, Charlie's still a good friend of mine. He's even the one who told me to come here and see you, who told me to get back in touch.'

Helen pursed her lips. 'Now that I find hard to believe.'

'It's true, Mum. Why wouldn't you believe it?'

'Well until five minutes ago I didn't even know you were still in touch.'

'Mum,' Stan said, only just now processing properly the way she'd called Charlie *that Gypsy kid.* 'How can you still be so weird about Charlie? It was so long ago.'

'Well you shouldn't have brought him up, if you didn't want me to talk about him.'

Stan sighed, closed his eyes. Why did it always have to happen like this, every time he tried to speak to her? 'You once told me he would ruin my life,' he said then. 'D'you remember?'

'Of course I do, Stanley. And I don't regret it. You very nearly died, on that roof.'

'But it was an accident, as I said.'

She only gave an exasperatingly exaggerated shrug.

'Why would you say that though, Mum? That he would ruin my life? What were you afraid of?'

'You always do this when you come, Stanley. You always tangle what I say in knots and make me the bad one.'

'He hasn't ruined my life yet,' he told her.

'Give him time,' she replied.

Stan pushed back his chair at that, and stood up. 'I don't need to listen to this,' he said.

'Fine,' she was saying back. 'I never asked you, Stanley, you know. I never asked you to come here. You were the one who got in touch and wanted to see me. Out of the blue, after going silent for all of two years. I have a life now, Stanley. A whole life I've built without you.'

'I don't have to do this. I'm going now, Mum. I'm going to go.'

She didn't say anything. Just sat there in silence, her head in her hands. She wouldn't even look up at him.

Outside on the front step, the door closed behind him and an atmosphere of miserable finality heavy in the air, Stan made himself breathe as he went back through that last conversation, wondering how things could have escalated so quickly. It had just seemed insane to him that she could hold the same unrevised opinion about somebody for so many years. And then, aside from all that, there were those questions he'd ended up asking her, almost without thinking. *Why would you say that? What were you afraid of?* They'd been more than simply rhetorical. He'd actually found himself wanting her to answer him, and to explain herself. Because really, he was starting to realise, wasn't it something very similar that had led to his deserting Charlie in the weeks after the fight? He'd been scared, was the real truth of it. But scared of what? Scared of their worlds colliding? Of what might happen if Charlie's world started bleeding into his? What a sad, stupid way to abandon a friend. He was just as likely to ruin Charlie's life as Charlie was to ruin his, that had always been the case. And anyway, those fears would only make any logical sense, even, if he was content to accept and enforce the premise that he and Charlie should live in separate worlds in the first place. Charlie had never accepted that. And Stan resolved, in that moment, on his childhood doorstep, that he wouldn't, either.

Walking away from Helen's house now, setting off back to the train station, Stan felt some mad need to reaffirm his apology to Charlie, and so he pulled out his phone and called Charlie's number. For the first few rings he felt almost nervous, uncertain of what he would say now he was actually calling him – but then the phone kept ringing, and ringing, and slowly Stan realised no one was going to answer. He hung up, stopped walking, and typed a message instead.

Just fully understood what a terrible friend I was, back in the spring. I messed up. I'm really sorry, Charlie.

Was it too much? He decided he didn't care, and pressed Send, anyway.

He kept checking his phone all throughout the rest of the walk to the station and the train journey to London. He kept an eye on it for the whole evening, and then for the whole of the following week, too, when he was beginning to regret what he'd done, to wonder if the message had been too out of the blue, too strange. Still nothing, he saw, every time he checked. Still no reply.

# 40

Another evening, yet another cup of bloody tea. The thing was though, Charlie was actually starting not to mind, was starting to relish it even. Not the tea so much, that was neither here nor there, but the increased clarity ditching the booze seemed to grant him. Every morning seemed brighter, more in focus, sharper and benign in a way he could only remember from being a kid, really, when opening his eyes had just been a neutral fact as opposed to a moment of crushing calamity, with worries, debts, anxieties and unfulfilled obligations flooding in on him, filling his brain to throb just behind his eyes with the hangover.

And then there was Kate too, sitting next to him by this fire they'd built together on this beach in Ireland, having driven out of the city for Charlie's night off, pulling up in the quiet of the Connemara roadside and walking down here to the bay. This was more like how he'd imagined things would be when they'd run out of London. Open skies, open fires, open ocean and Kate like this with a smile back on her lips, blanket slung around her shoulders, humming some old tune to herself as she poked at the flames with a stick. Her eyes flicked up and over then, away from the fire to meet his.

'Thoughtful tonight, aren't you?' she said.

'More . . . grateful,' he said. 'Taking the time to say thank you.'

'Thank you to who? Or to what?'

He shrugged. 'I don't know,' he said. 'To this?' He gestured around them at the waves and then at the stretching fields behind. 'A thank you for getting my life back.'

She shook her head. 'You don't owe anyone thanks for that,' she said. 'This is who you are.'

'Thanks to you, then,' he said. 'Am I allowed to do that? I give thanks to you.'

'Come off it, Charlie,' she said. 'I'm not falling for any of your shite.' She was laughing though, and he was glad he'd said it, even if she hadn't taken him seriously.

'I mean it,' he told her. 'I know it hasn't always been easy. I know I haven't always been easy. You never gave up on me, though.'

Her expression changed in the firelight to turn a shade more serious, and she seemed to be about to say something else when the whole thing was interrupted by his phone going off, loud in his pocket.

'Fuck, sorry,' he said, scrabbling round on the ground so he could grab it. 'Thought I'd turned that off.'

But the moment had passed. She was sighing, going back to the fire, whatever she'd been about to say vanished off up into the air with the smoke.

'Sorry, Katie,' he told her as he pulled the phone out. *James*, read the display. He stared at it for one ring, two rings, three and more – before pressing the button to silence the call. He slid the phone back in his pocket and took a gulp of the night air, trying to recover the feeling of peace that had come over him so effortlessly a moment before.

'What was I saying?' he asked Kate.

'Something about how grateful you were for the simple things in life,' she said.

'Was I really? Can't think what came over me.'

He was glad she didn't ask who'd called. He took a gulp of tea and started humming a tune, just something to distract from the leaden feeling that seemed to have snuck up on him suddenly, and was threatening to take hold. Kate started laughing even before he'd got through the second line of the song.

'That old thing?' she said. 'What're you singing that for?'

And it was so good to hear her laugh like that that he started singing the words.

*'I'm a Romany rai,*
*I'm a true didikai,*
*I build all my castles beneath the blue sky,*
*I live in a tent, and I don't pay no rent,*
*And that's why they call me a Romany rai.'*

She was just starting to clap along when his phone went off again.

'Ah Christ,' he said as she frowned. 'What now?'

Though he'd be kidding himself if he said he couldn't guess who it'd be. *James*, the screen said again. Of course. James had no reason to call idly. Surely had every reason to forget he had a brother at all in fact – which meant something particular must be up. Still, he silenced the ringing again and put the phone back in his pocket. When he looked up though Kate was watching him, eyes sharp.

'Who was that?' she said.

'No one,' he said.

'Don't give me that,' she said. 'I thought we were past this. Past the lies and the bullshit.'

'It's not – I'm not lying to you, Kate. Or I don't want to be. It's just that . . . well.'

'What? It's just that what?'

'Not everything's your business,' he said then. 'It was my phone that rang, not yours.'

And the look she gave him at that. It was dark outside now, her face lit only by the fire and the moonlight, all shadows, angles and brightness – but only a fool could miss the disdain, the closing off, the resignation in her eyes. And this wasn't right, was it? This wasn't why they'd done this, this wasn't what he wanted. He took a breath and pulled himself together.

'It's James,' he told her. 'That's all. My brother James.'

'Why're you ignoring it, then?' she asked.

What a question. Wasn't it obvious? 'I just – haven't got the head for it now, is all. We came out here to get away from all that, didn't we?'

She frowned. 'Not really. Get away from all what? Not from James, surely.'

He shrugged. 'I don't know,' he said. 'Away from letting him down all the time. Away from letting them all down.'

Kate dropped the stick she'd been using to prod the fire, folded her hands, and turned to him properly, her expression almost stern.

'Charlie Wells,' she said then. 'I'm going to tell you this one more time, and you are going to listen. You didn't let your brother down. You showed up, and you fought for him. And you took three broken ribs and a broken arm and even in that state you never gave up.'

'But Kate. I still—'

'Being knocked unconscious doesn't count as giving up, Charlie. You didn't. You never gave in.'

'Christ, I was an embarrassment though, Kate.'

'You weren't,' she said. 'He still looks up to you, you know, Charlie.'

He stared at her. She seemed, somehow, to be deadly serious. 'Bloody hell, Kate,' he said. 'I don't know. I don't want to think about this. This was meant to be a fresh fucking start.'

And then his phone began to ring again.

'Charlie,' said Kate. 'Charlie.'

'Oh fucking Christ, okay I'm doing it, I'm answering,' he said. 'You happy now?' He dragged the phone out of his pocket and answered the call. 'Alright, chavi?' he said, trying to sound as normal and nonchalant as possible. 'Everything okay?'

'Charlie, fuck, I didn't think you'd pick up.'

Even the sound of James's voice on the other end made him want to curl in on himself, made him want to hide. Surely what Kate said couldn't be right. She'd just have been trying cheer him up a bit, so she could have a husband who held his head high again, that was all.

'James,' he said. 'I'm sorry. I'm here now. What is it?'

'It's Martin,' said James.

'Martin?' said Charlie. Of all the things he'd feared or expected this was not one of them. After all, the last time he'd tried to speak to him, Martin had let him know in no uncertain terms that he was a disappointment and a failure, that the sight of him made him sick. Definitely Kate's argument that simply showing up and taking a beating was in some way sufficient was never going to wash with Martin. 'What d'you mean it's Martin?'

'He's asking for you,' said James. 'He's in a bad way, Charlie.'

'Must be if he's asking for me.'

'It's not funny. He's in hospital and everything.'

'In hospital? What the fuck happened? Is he ill?'

'He is now,' James said. 'Got beaten up, didn't he? Some lads down the pub. No fucking respect. Dragged him out the Goat and Compasses and beat him in the street.'

'What?' said Charlie. Kate's frown deepened. 'What did you say? *Martin?* Are you serious?'

'Course I'm fucking serious. Think I'd joke about something like this? And he's asking for you, mate.'

'Is he okay?'

'Course he's not fucking okay.'

'But he's – he's not—'

'He's not dying, if that's what you mean. He's still Martin.'

'Christ.' Charlie stared out into the dark. '*Christ.* Who the fuck were they? And how . . .'

*How could they bring down a man like Martin?* he wanted to ask. Because sure, Martin wasn't the youngest any more, but by God he was a match for anyone who dared have a go. *Martin.* It seemed impossible. The whole idea insane.

'I know,' said James. 'There were seven of them. He still gave them a run for their money.'

'But who were they? It wasn't Hollands or something, was it?'

'Christ no,' James said. 'Come on, Charlie. You know as well as I do no Holland would ever fuck with Martin. These lads, they were part of something – so Martin said at least. They'd been having some meeting in the pub, all dressed up in shirts with these badges on them. All St George's crosses and that.'

'St George's crosses? In London?'

'Nah, mate,' said James. 'We're back down Newford way.'

'What?'

'Yeah. After all that shite with the Hollands and then with the two of you going off like that no one felt like sticking round for too long after.'

'Newford though?' said Charlie. 'What the bloody hell d'you go back there for? What's in Newford?'

'These lot now, apparently. England's Shield, they call themselves. I've been doing a bit of research.'

'Bloody hell,' said Charlie. 'And have they got them now, then?'

'What, mate?' said James.

'The lads that did it. The seven of them. Have they got them?'

'What d'you mean?'

'The gavvers. Didn't they arrest them or something?'

'Course not. They just ran off, didn't they?'

'But they're looking for them?'

'Doubt it.'

'Fucking hell.' Charlie rubbed his eyes. This old story again. 'How is he?' he said. 'How bad is it?'

'He's talking now,' said James. 'Still looks fucking awful though, connected to all these tubes and things. It's not safe for him to leave for another week or so, the doctor said.'

'And he's asking for me?' said Charlie. 'To see me?'

'Yeah, mate.'

'Why?'

'Fuck knows. Probably just misses you. You coming or what?'

'I – dunno. I'm in Ireland. I'll ask Kate.'

'Please come, Charlie.'

'I – yeah. I need to talk to Kate first. I'll ring you back. Thanks for telling me.'

'You will ring me back,' said James, 'won't you? You're not just going to fuck off and disappear on me now or something, are you?'

'No. Course I'm not. What makes you say that?'

'Sorry Charlie, I don't know. This is just . . . it's just so *fucked*, you know?'

'Yeah mate, I know. I'll call you in a little.'

'You'd better.'

'I will.'

'What's happening?' said Kate, soon as he got off the phone. She was pulling the blanket tighter round herself though it wasn't really cold or anything. 'What's going on?'

'It's Martin, isn't it?' said Charlie. 'Got beaten up by some thugs in England.'

'Is he alright?'

'He's in hospital.'

She nodded. Stared wide-eyed into the fire. 'We should go,' she said, no hesitations. 'We should go down and see him.'

'What?' he said. 'But Martin – last time I saw Martin he—'

'Martin loves you,' she said.

'Jesus, Kate. You think you know what you're talking about but you really, really don't.'

'I do though,' she said.

'You don't.'

'But don't you care about him? Don't you want to see how he is?'

'God, I don't know. Last time I saw him I thought he was going to knock me out for the second time in one week. Okay so he's asking for me now, but how do I know that when I get there he won't . . .'

'You scared of him?'

'Honestly? No. I don't think I am.'

'What, then? He makes you feel small?'

'Bloody hell, Kate—'

'You'll regret it, you know. You'll regret it forever if you don't go down and see him, whatever happens when you're there. For all his faults, Martin has always looked out for you, Charlie, in his way.'

He rubbed his eyes again – they were stinging with the smoke from the fire – and he opened his mouth to argue, to tell her it was all ridiculous, that what she'd just said made no sense at all. Except—

'I know,' was what he found himself saying instead.

And as soon as it was out of his mouth he knew in his heart it was true.

# 41

On the sofa and still in pyjamas at 3 p.m., Stan was starting to feel restless. It wasn't that he'd got up late, there'd just been no real reason to get dressed, seeing as sitting on his laptop writing laughably paid freelance articles while simultaneously job-hunting and watching the Olympics javelin hadn't really required anything more elaborate. It was strange, this thing with the Olympics. The image of London that all the TV footage and ceremonies and events seemed to be working so hard to project seemed so different from the city's reality that sometimes he couldn't help but feel a little as if it was all happening on another planet. He was jolted out of his stupor though by his phone starting to ring. It was a mobile number, not one he or his phone recognised. He answered it anyway, glad of a distraction.

'Stan,' said the voice on the other end, as soon as the line connected.

'Charlie,' Stan replied. 'Bloody hell Charlie, it's been ages. I was worried. I've been trying to ring you all summer. What happened?'

'Lost my phone, didn't I? Hang on though. You were worried? About me?' And Stan knew that tone of voice, Charlie was laughing at him. And to think he had actually been worrying, too. Worrying alternately that Charlie was angry with him, or worse, that something had happened to him. Still, Stan couldn't help but feel the day brighten around him now in a way that had nothing to do with the weather.

'Fucksake, Charlie.'

'Ah, I'm just messing.'

'I know.'

'Good, then.'

'How are you though, Charlie? You still in Ireland?'

'I am, I am. And things are . . . things are good, Stan, for the most part.'

Something about the way Charlie said that though made Stan shut his laptop, and put it to one side. 'What?' he asked. 'What's going on?'

'I'm coming back to the UK, for a bit.'

'But . . . why, Charlie? Can you even do that?'

'How d'you mean?'

'With your debts. Your old landlord.'

'Christ, him. I don't know, do I? Good luck to him finding me.'

'Charlie . . .'

'No, Stan, listen. It's Martin.'

'Martin?'

'You remember Martin. My uncle.'

'Course I remember him.'

'Well he's in hospital. I'm coming back to see him. Just a few days, nothing major.'

'He's in hospital?'

'It's a long story.'

'Is he . . . okay?'

'I don't know.'

There was a silence on the other end then, and Stan didn't know quite how to break it.

'Will you be about?' Charlie asked him, at last. 'When I'm over. It'd be good to see you, mate. It's all just – well. I don't know.'

'In London?'

'Newford.'

'Newford?'

'That's where Martin is, they're back in Newford.'

'What's wrong with Martin, Charlie?'

'Got beaten up, didn't he?'

'And he's in hospital?'

'Seems so.'

'Jesus.'

'I'll be there tomorrow, anyway. Or the next day. Or maybe Tuesday, actually. We're headed to the ferry now.'

'Okay, of course, yeah. I'll see what I can do.'

Charlie rang off after that, and Stan found himself staring out the window at the deceptively bright London afternoon, at the cyclists zipping by and the green leaves just starting to tinge with red. It seemed crazy, Charlie coming back to the UK and risking trouble for the debts he'd left, just to see Martin, of all people. Martin who'd hounded him for most of his life, it seemed like. Except, then again though, hadn't it also been Martin who'd sort of brought Charlie up, stepping into the gap his dad had left? And then more than that, that was just the thing about Charlie, Stan supposed. He had a certain kind of staying power. Like how he'd insisted on Stan driving him to the fight that morning, all those months ago now, even though surely he'd realised full well by then what would happen, known the beating he'd take.

*Nae pasaran.* The words drifted into Stan's head from some subconscious place as he gazed down at the sunshine on the rain-slicked pavements. Now that he thought about it, he'd never properly questioned what it actually meant. Had always just associated it with Charlie helping him with the bullies all those years ago in school, had assumed it was simply about defiance, about not taking things lying down or letting people get the better of you. Now though, he could feel himself finally starting to understand how it was really about so much more than that. That fundamentally, nae pasaran was about showing up for people. Showing up for people even when a huge part of you might want to close your eyes, and retreat back into comfort and wilful blindness. Showing up for people not out of curiosity or pity but because of friendship, conducted on solidly equal terms. He saw now too how a friendship could sustain you like almost nothing else. And he saw that really, that's what nae pasaran had always been about. So much more than its being about defiance, it was about solidarity, of course it was. Solidarity and friendship.

# 42

There was no denying it, Martin looked like shite. Completely messed up, lying in his hospital bed with tubes coming out of his arm and everything, bandages and dressings and plasters scattered in numbers over his body. Or – no. Maybe it wasn't quite as simple as him looking like shite. Because the way he was slouched there on the bed, the whole back half of it raised up so it was like a chaise longue or something, like he was almost *reclining*. He was still Martin, after everything. So no, he didn't look like shite at all, actually – what had Charlie been thinking? He looked like a warrior, was more like it.

'Fuck,' Martin said, first thing Charlie stepped up to the bed. 'You've lost weight.'

'Yeah well I was a right fat bastard before, wasn't I?'

Martin shrugged, best as he was able to under all the dressings. 'You're the one who said it, mate. Not me.'

'Nice to see you, too,' said Charlie.

'Didn't think you'd come,' said Martin.

'Course I came,' said Charlie. 'Think I'd miss the chance of seeing you like this?'

The anger sparked immediately in Martin's face. A few months ago he'd have been able to take a line like that with a laugh, something quick back maybe and a clap on the shoulder. Now, though, was probably not the time.

'Sorry,' said Charlie. 'I was joking – obviously. I didn't mean it.'

'Yeah you did,' said Martin. 'Course you meant it. Even if you were joking.'

'Look,' said Charlie. 'I came all the way from Ireland to see you. Drove the van on the ferry and everything. Bloody hours it took. And then Kate got seasick, it was awful. I didn't come here to argue.'

'Ireland?'

'Yeah. Did the others not tell you?'

Martin shuffled in his sheets, wrinkled his nose as if wanting to scratch it – one arm was in a cast, and the other looked painful to move, all bandaged up around the wrist. 'I suppose they might have mentioned something,' he said. 'I wouldn't have been listening.'

'We didn't ask you to the leaving party,' said Charlie. 'I'm sorry about that.'

'Ah,' said Martin. 'You're alright. I wouldn't have come, anyway.'

'Sure,' said Charlie.

Then he walked round to sit on the chair by the bed. It was weird being back here. Not just in Newford, though that was weird enough, but back in this hospital, of all places. Like déjà vu or something, waiting on the steps outside for the start of visiting hours then going up to the desk. *Mate of Stan Gower's*, he'd nearly said. Except here was Martin, not Stan – Martin staring at him now that he'd sat down, the old fire in his eyes burning brighter than ever, it seemed, in spite of everything.

'Making yourself comfortable?' said Martin.

'Aye, well you asked me to visit.'

'I didn't *ask you to visit*. I said I wanted to see you.'

'What's the difference?'

'*Ask you to visit*. Makes it sound like I'm some bloody charity case.'

Charlie sighed. 'Why did you *want to see me* then, if the sight of me riles you that much? You should know I've got better things to do with myself these days than sitting here being hated by you.'

Martin gave him a funny look then. Almost pained – though that could have just been something to do with his injuries. 'I don't hate you, mate,' he said. 'Course I don't hate you. Don't know what would have made you think that.'

Charlie wanted to laugh but it got stuck somewhere in his throat. 'You aren't being serious?' he said.

'You're a right drama queen, aren't you, Charlie Wells?' Martin said then. 'I'm laid up here after being put in the fucking *hospital* by some boy scouts with their fancy badges and it's you needs cheering up? Some things never change.'

'What's that supposed to mean?'

'You always thought you were so important.'

'No, I didn't. I don't. That's why I came here today, if you'll listen. Because I thought that what had happened – what happened to you with those lads in the pub – might be a bit more important than all this shite between us, Martin. Maybe I was wrong.'

Martin closed his eyes a while. When he opened them again he said, 'I know I've always been hard on you, Charlie boy. But this is why – d'you see?' He lifted his injured arm with barely a wince to gesture the length of his body, propped up like that in the bed. '*This is why*. I taught you to be strong, which is what a man needs in this world. What any person, man or woman, needs in this world. Any Traveller, anyway. You want someone to humour you, to lie to you and tell you it's going to be easier than it is? You want someone to tell you you're better than you are, that it'll all be fine and work out lovely for you even when you fuck up?'

'That's not what I meant,' said Charlie, quietly.

'Because that kind of *bullshit*,' Martin continued, apparently oblivious to Charlie's interruption, 'is the privilege of the people who run this world, Charlie. Not us. Not you. When they fuck up, it might be fine. When you fuck up, you drown.'

Charlie swallowed, tried to speak and found his voice came out as a dry kind of croak. He coughed and tried again. 'Who were they,' he said, 'the lads who put you here? James said they were calling themselves England's Shield or something.'

'Ah who knows?' said Martin then. 'They're all the bloody same, aren't they, in the end? None of them any better than the others, whatever the name of them is. BNP. Britain First. EDL. Whatever you want to call it now. Even the bloody government, these days – because that lot, that lot are just as bad.'

'No, come on, Martin—'

'We have to fight, Charlie boy. We have to fight and keep fighting because whatever they may say they don't like us, they don't care about us, and no one else is going to help us. We're on our own, Charlie. Completely on our fucking own.'

And Charlie couldn't help but think of Stan, then, driving him out to meet the Holland kid then disappearing, disappearing for weeks. And the worst thing was, Charlie hadn't even been that surprised.

'You will keep fighting won't you?' Martin said. His fingers were clamped round Charlie's forearm now, his grip surprisingly strong in spite of his damaged wrist. 'I taught you that much, didn't I?'

'Come on, Martin, this isn't – I don't know what you mean.'

'Didn't I tell you, didn't I always say to you – you must never let them tell you . . .'

'. . . *where you do and don't belong*,' Charlie joined in, speaking those last words with Martin almost automatically, their two voices sounding surprisingly alike when lined up together like that. 'Yeah,' said Charlie then. 'I suppose you always did, at that.'

'Because you are worth just as much and have just as much right to be here as anyone else. They're the problem, not you.' Martin's eyes were wide now – huge gaping pupils. God knows what they had him on in this place but sure as hell it wasn't paracetamol. And yet still. *Never let them tell you where you do and don't belong.* He'd forgotten it was Martin who'd first drilled that into him. Stuff could get so mixed up and murky over the passing years, all these bits left in your head without you knowing properly where they even came from. All these people drifting through, no one quite remembering who said what, or why, who owed who, and who it was who'd let who down. All the years telling himself he hated Martin. All that wasted energy, when really this was Martin – this man here before him now. Not his enemy. Never his enemy.

'You're right,' said Charlie. 'And I'm going to get whoever did this to you. That's a promise.'

*

'How was he?' Kate and James spoke together, waiting for
Charlie outside in the hospital foyer, Kate obviously just concerned for Martin, James asking something slightly different
– more *how was that?* really, than *how was he?*

'Fine,' Charlie said to them both. 'Mad as ever, but then
he's within his rights to be this time I'd say.'

James flashed him a quick smile – one of those James
smiles, here and gone so fast you had to be bloody sharp not
to miss them. 'Glad you came,' he said.

'So am I,' said Charlie.

''Scuse me,' said a hospital orderly then, pushing a trolley
laden with various medical supplies. 'Could you stand to one
side please?'

'Sure right yeah sorry,' Charlie said to him, and without
thinking he grabbed the back of James's wheelchair, thinking
to move them all over to one side, quick as possible.

'Hang on, mate,' said James. 'There's no need for that.
What d'you think? I can't move around on my own?'

'I – no. Fuck. Sorry,' said Charlie, letting go of the chair.

'Excuse me,' said the orderly with the trolley again, still
not able to get by.

'Christ,' said Charlie. 'Fine, okay.' He shifted himself to
the wall and James and Kate followed.

'Thank you,' said the orderly, his tone rather pointed,
Charlie thought, on the way past.

'That's right. And fuck you, too,' called James after him.

'James,' said Kate. 'For Christ's sake. As if people aren't staring enough.'

'What?' said James. 'I'm sick of being told to get out of the way. We were in the middle of an important conversation.'

'That we were,' said Charlie, keen to change the subject, not liking the way Kate's eyes were flashing now – he hadn't seen that look in a while from her, not in months. He even almost missed it – *almost* being the key word there. 'The guys that got Martin. England's Shield. What do we know about them?'

'Not much,' said James. 'I found their Facebook page. Not too many members. Or not round here, anyway. Most of the posts just bullshit about Muslims. Don't know what they thought they were doing picking a fight with Martin, to be honest.'

'Ah it doesn't matter who they claim to have a problem with,' Charlie said. 'Muslims or not, it's always the same bollocks, isn't it? It always includes Black people, and it always includes us.'

'Charlie,' said Kate, a warning in her voice.

'What?' he said. 'Is that not the truth? What about that isn't the truth?'

She shrugged. 'You're speaking so loud,' she said. 'People are staring.'

'Fuck people staring,' he said.

'Exactly,' said James.

'Fucking Newford,' said Charlie.

'For christssake you'll get us thrown out,' said Kate.

Charlie looked around. She was right. People were gaping at them as if they'd pulled out weapons or something instead of just saying a few words at above average volume. And then that girl on reception was watching them too, hand hovering over her phone – and Charlie knew that look a mile off. She was wondering whether or not to call security. Christ.

'Okay,' he said, in lower tones this time. 'Okay. What my point is though is that we're not going to let them get away with it, are we?'

'I'm sorry?' said Kate.

'This lot, this England's Shield. We're not going to let them get away with it.'

'Are we not?' said Kate.

'I suppose,' said James.

'What the hell?' said Charlie. 'You think we're going to take this lying down? If we do nothing now it's like . . . it's like it doesn't matter. Like Martin doesn't matter.'

'We could go to the police,' said Kate.

'Fuck the police,' said James.

'Alright,' said Kate. 'So what do we do? Because it's all very romantic certainly, all very noble starting up some *war* without even thinking about it, some war with some organisation we know next to nothing about. But is it clever? I don't think so.'

'I don't care about clever,' said Charlie quietly, more to himself really than to either of the other two.

'What? What was that?' said Kate.

He sighed. 'I don't care about clever,' he repeated, as loudly as he could without properly yelling. Ah but of course he'd gone and done it now. The reception girl was on the phone, eyes on them all the while from behind her desk.

'That's all very fine, Charlie Wells,' said Kate, 'but somebody's got to be clever, haven't they? Because when we're not clever, what happens? What happens is these people win.'

'She's right actually, Charlie,' said James. 'We should think about this.'

'What?' said Charlie. 'Since when were you so cautious all of a sudden?'

'Since I got sick of losing,' said James.

'Bloody hell,' said Charlie. 'Look at you two. Fine. Okay. So what do we know about them? There must be some way we can get them.'

'What about the police?' suggested Kate, again.

'The police?' said James. 'You trust the police and you know where that'll get you? It'll be us they're going after, in the blink of an eye. It'll be Martin. Believe me. They'll just . . . twist it around.'

'Not the police then,' Charlie said. 'But what?'

'We need to find out what we're dealing with,' said Kate.

'James found them on Facebook. We know what we're dealing with.'

'No, we don't. Not really.'

'God, how much more can there be to it? Saint George's flag, private money, hatred of everything they don't understand. Am I right, James?'

'Maybe we should go,' said James.

'What?' said Charlie and Kate at the same time.

'To their next meeting. Maybe we should go.'

'What, join them back at the bloody . . . Goat and Compasses?'

'No,' said James. 'It's a different pub every time, I think. I could look on Facebook. See about the next one.'

'And then we'd just . . . show up at it?' said Charlie. 'What for? I thought we weren't going to start a war?'

'Depends,' said James. 'But there's only so much I can tell

from a Facebook page. I say we go look them in the eye, find out what we're dealing with.'

'I don't know,' said Kate. 'Maybe that's what they want.'

'Course it's not what they want,' Charlie said then. 'Think they care enough about us to play those kind of mind games? They want us to disappear, not keep turning up where they're drinking.'

'Then that's what we should do,' said James.

'Just go, have a look, have a drink, show them we're not scared to be there,' said Charlie. 'You in?'

'I'm coming,' said Kate. 'If you're going.'

'Excuse me please,' said the security guy who'd just appeared behind Charlie's shoulder. 'I'm afraid I'm going to have to ask you to leave.'

'For Christ's sake,' said James.

'It's alright,' said Charlie. 'We were going, anyway.'

# 43

'Stan,' said Charlie's voice, as Stan stared out the train window at the passing fields, and listened again to the voice-mail Charlie had left him, part of him still wondering what on earth he was doing, dropping everything and heading to Newford like this in a hurry.

'I didn't tell you what had happened with Martin, really,' Charlie continued. There was some noise in the background behind him now, the sound of a road and sirens and a woman's voice saying something, maybe Kate.

'Don't know why I didn't,' Charlie was saying. 'I think maybe I didn't believe it myself when I heard, or maybe that I was embarrassed, or something. But then that's just their bullshit, isn't it, working its way into my head? They call themselves England's Shield, Stan, the people who put my uncle in the hospital. England's Shield. I've googled them and they're fascists, is the long and the short of it. And we're going to one of their meetings tonight, anyway, to see what we can do about it. Because I don't know, Stan. But Newford's better than this, than this England's Shield bollocks, isn't it?'

The uncertainty on that last *isn't it*. Stan could just sense what the look on Charlie's face would have been in that moment, finding himself brought up short like that, by his own question. Then the sound of the busy road again, then of James's voice saying, 'Charlie, mate, what you up to? We haven't got time.'

'So yeah,' Charlie's voice again, picking up the thread of the message. 'Seven p.m. at the Crossed Keys, if you fancy it. And well, you know' – road sounds, sirens, Kate's voice this time just saying, '*Charlie!*' – 'nae pasaran, I suppose, and all that.'

And that was it, Charlie rang off.

The Crossed Keys. Stan hadn't been there in years. It was on the slightly quieter side of town, not far from the river. He couldn't remember much more about it than that, aside from a particularly grouchy landlord, and going there on a few awkward teenage dates he would rather forget. He put his phone away back in his coat pocket, and then leaned against the window again, looking out. His train was due in at six fifty. If he ran from the station, he could just about make it.

# 44

'This is the one, isn't it? The Crossed Keys?' Charlie squinted up at the sign. It seemed unlikely somehow.

'This is it,' said James, heading on up to the entrance. 'One of you going to get the door for me, then?'

'You're sure it's here?' said Charlie. 'And it was definitely seven p.m.?'

'D'you not trust me now all of a sudden?'

'Course I trust you,' Charlie said, grabbing the door handle, swinging it open for James. 'It's just . . . not what I expected, is all.'

'What did you expect?'

'I don't know,' said Charlie. 'It just looks so . . . normal.'

'That's how they get you,' said James. 'Normality. Their secret weapon.' He raised his eyebrows at Charlie as he wheeled on past through the door.

'Actually, mate,' said Charlie, holding the door open for Kate, too. 'D'you know, I think maybe that's true?'

'Course it's true,' said James.

'Be careful,' Kate said to him then as she stepped past him. 'Be *clever*.'

'I'm always clever,' he said.

'I'm serious,' she said.

'I know.'

He followed her into the pub and let the door swing shut behind them. Inside it basically looked like your bog-standard Wetherspoons, only playing a bit to the yuppie crowd with the flowery wallpaper and all the weird-looking lights round the bar. It was surprisingly full for a Wednesday, humming with chat and with laughter. Loads of people about – or, in fact, loads of men, Charlie noticed on second glance, and most of them dressed in the same football shirt. Yellow and white stripes. Must be the strip of the local team round here, then. He hadn't even known Newford had its own football club, but of course it did, everywhere did, he always just forgot about stuff like that because though he had nothing particularly against football – or nothing until certain fans got drunk and lairy – he'd just never been all that into it. And he'd be lying if he said it didn't make him uneasy, them all being here tonight, all these lot with their pints, dressed the same, having just come from the game. Most of them looked cheerful enough now, though. Probably that meant Newford hadn't lost at least. He hoped it was a good omen.

'Oi Charlie,' said James, calling over to him, making the universal gesture for a pint. 'Drink?'

'Nah mate,' he said. Then, 'Or actually . . .' he began – and he could feel Kate's eyes on him then, sharp as anything, and he found he was even quite enjoying teasing her like this, was that unfair of him? '*Actually*,' he said again, stringing the word out for as long as possible, 'I'll have a lime and soda, mate, if that's alright with you.'

James shrugged. 'Suit yourself,' he said. 'What you having?' he said to Kate.

'The same,' she said, rolling her eyes at Charlie.

'You lot Newford City fans, then?' the football-shirted barman asked Charlie as they waited for the second pour on James's Guinness.

'Got nothing against them,' said Charlie.

'You're not from round here, are you?' the barman said.

'What makes you say that?' said Charlie. Kate shot him a warning look.

The barman didn't answer, just began pouring the lime and sodas. 'So you didn't catch the game tonight?'

'Can't say we did, no.'

The barman shook his head. 'People think just because we're one of the smaller clubs it's not worth the bother.'

'That's not what I said,' said Charlie.

'Yeah, well,' said the barman. 'That'll be four-sixty then, anyway.'

'What?' said Charlie.

'I said that'll be four-sixty mate, unless there's a problem with that?'

'No mate, no. It's just . . . are you charging for the lime and sodas?'

'Twenty pence a lime and soda, four-twenty for the Guinness. Now hurry up about it, there's folk behind you wanting served.'

'Christ. Alright. James,' Charlie called across to him. He'd drifted over to the other side of the pub, scouting for a free table. 'James, you got a quid I can borrow?'

'What was that?' James yelled back, too loud for the room, even in this crowd of football lads.

The barman's frown deepened.

'Have you got a quid? I said,' repeated Charlie.

'For Christ's sake,' said Kate, dropping a pound coin in

front of Charlie on the bar. 'Sorry,' she said to the barman, turning on a bright, conciliatory smile. 'I can't take him anywhere.'

'So I see,' said the barman, without smiling back.

They went with their drinks over to the table James had found in the corner – an ideal spot from which to see the whole room without being themselves too conspicuous. Charlie checked his watch, looked around. He'd left a message on Stan's phone an hour or so ago with the name of the pub and the time they'd be there, but that was likely way too late in the day to be letting him know, he knew. Someone like Stan, he probably had an appointments diary that was all filled up with one thing after another until Christmas. Fuck knows why he was looking around for Stan here, anyway. He could handle this without him, couldn't he? Maybe it was just something about being back here, in Newford, that made it feel as though he should be here.

'Are you trying to fuck this up?' Kate hissed, as they wove their way through all the tables, clustered round with little groups of football people.

It took Charlie a moment to shake off his thoughts and realise she was talking about the barman. 'No,' he said. 'Sorry. He just seemed . . . I don't know. I didn't like the way he'd asked us if we'd been to the match. Like he was trying to make some kind of point.'

'So what?' she said. 'It wasn't worth it, Charlie. He's not someone to piss off. Everyone here clearly knows him. I even heard someone say his son plays for the team.'

'When d'you hear that?'

'Just now. When you were too busy arguing to be paying attention or listening to anything.'

Charlie shrugged. 'Ah what does it matter though? At the end of the day he was still being a prick.'

She raised her eyebrows at him, but left it at that.

'Seven p.m., was it?' he asked James as they sat down and settled in.

'That's what I told you,' James told him.

Charlie checked his watch again – 7:13, now. He took out his phone, double-checked that message he'd sent to Stan, then made himself shove it back in his pocket again and look around the pub. No sign of Stan, no sign of anyone who looked as if they might be England's Shield, either, just tables and tables of guys in football shirts. Everything suddenly felt completely wrong. He would have stood up then, insisted they leave, grabbed Kate's hand and driven her all the way back to the ferry and back over to Ireland, if he hadn't had Martin to think about. Martin in the hospital. Martin who he did know had always tried to do right by him, even if he hadn't always agreed with how he'd gone about it at the time.

'And that's definitely what it said on Facebook?' he asked James, more or less just for something to say.

'No,' said James. 'I invented a false time to piss you off.'

'I can't see any of them though. It doesn't look like any-one's here.'

'They could be here,' Kate said. 'We don't know what they look like.'

'I mean yeah it could probably be any of these lot really, couldn't it?' said James, taking a sip of his drink, glowering round at the rest of the pub.

Charlie made himself slow down then, stopped his thoughts whirring, making a racket in his head. He took a

breath, he narrowed his eyes and he looked around, properly. 'No,' he said. 'I don't think so. Not these.'

'How can you tell?' said James. 'As I said – normality. It's
how they get you.'

'No,' Charlie found himself insisting. 'That's wrong.
These people are . . . they might be wearing football shirts
but look at them. They're just a bunch of dads and – I don't
know. Insurance salesmen or whatever.'

'Fascists can be dads and insurance salesmen.'

'No,' said Charlie again. 'They're not here yet.'

James shrugged. 'This is where they said they were
meeting.'

'Maybe they're running late,' said Kate.

'Maybe,' said Charlie.

'What about that guy?' said James.

And Charlie followed his gaze to the opposite corner of
the pub, to what was the closest thing you could probably
find in this bright, loud, echoing room to a 'quiet table'.
One man, sitting by himself – wearing a yellow-and-white
striped football shirt like the others, but slightly apart from
everything too, reading through a stack of papers on the
table in front of him, pen in hand, marking something down
every now and then. He looked young. About James's age
maybe or even younger. One of those lads whose baby face
hadn't aged fast enough to keep up with the rest of him.

After a few minutes another man arrived at the table, this
one in a suit and tie as if he'd just come from a job in an
office somewhere that fancied itself as a bit swish. Charlie
watched the two men shake hands and exchange a few lines
of conversation – no chance of overhearing that. The pub
was loud now, and they were too far away.

'They don't know each other well, but they've met before,' said Charlie, still watching them.

'What makes you say that?' said James.

'The handshake was formal, kind of. But now look – he's handing him those papers, no explanation or anything. They've obviously done this before, whatever it is.'

'And here we have some more,' said Kate, as two new guys appeared. Older, this time. One of them much more familiar with the first lad, the one in the Newford shirt, grasping his shoulder and cracking some joke that made them all smile. Charlie checked his phone again. Still nothing from Stan. Looking back across the pub at the lads at the table there was one of the new arrivals now, just standing there with his hands in his pockets, looking round at the rest of the bar with something close to disdain. He checked his phone again. Still nothing. Kate was looking at him now with a question in her eyes as he did one last sweep of the bar. No Stan. Not yet. Which was fine. He was fine. *Nae pasaran*, he said to himself.

'I'm going over,' he told her and James.

'What?' said Kate. 'I thought you said we were just here for a look – to see what we were dealing with.'

'We are,' said Charlie. 'I did. But I can't tell a thing from back here, can I? It could be a meeting of the Newford Men's Fly Fishing Society for all we know. Can't hear a bloody word.'

'I'm coming with you,' said Kate.

'We should all go,' said James. 'I want to know if it's them, same as you.'

They made their way through the tables of Newford City supporters. They all seemed to know each other, everyone laughing and joking, slapping each other on the back and buying each other drinks . . . and Kate had been right too, they all seemed to know the barman, from the way they were chatting with him. Small town, small world, Charlie supposed. Maybe his son really did play for the team. He sat down again at a table just one away from the men in the corner. Kate and James followed.

'Eddie Franks,' the first lad in the Newford shirt was saying, introducing himself, shaking the hand of a fifth guy who'd just wandered up to join their table – youngish, suit, signet ring. 'Welcome to England's Shield. Good to have you on board.'

'Cheers,' said the new guy. 'I'm glad I came. You're doing good work, you know. Everyone knows it. Some are just afraid to say it—'

'Things are changing though,' cut in one of the old guys then. 'The country's waking up.'

'I hope so,' said the new guy. 'It can't happen soon enough.'

Christ. Were they really serious? 'Bloody hell,' Charlie muttered to James. 'They're like some evil cult from a film. *Welcome, Citizen, to the chapter. Please prepare for your initiation ceremony.*'

'Don't know what about that seems so funny,' said James.

'Ah you know. Look at them. They're like – I don't know. The evil council in the *Star Wars* films or something. They think they're so important.'

'Exactly,' said James.

'Right, unless anyone has any objections,' said the first one – Eddie Franks, he'd said his name was, hadn't he? 'I'm just going to kick off. We're well past time, and I'm sure any latecomers can manage to settle themselves in, alright?'

Murmurs of assent from the rest of the table.

'Some of you I know,' said Eddie, 'some of you I haven't seen before. It's always good to have new faces round the table. Welcome.'

More murmurs of assent.

'So for those of you who don't know and who are new to this, the focus of this group is very local. We're not technically linked to the main national body of England's Shield – we're an affiliated group. So the aim here is to focus on the local issues, the issues threatening the safety and integrity of our community specifically, and to put some of those values upheld and championed by England's Shield on the national level into action on that local level, in order to combat those threats.'

Nods from everyone around the table. *Community? Safety and integrity?* The effect was bizarre, seeing them all nodding along to these fluffy, positive words while knowing exactly what they meant by them.

'I thought we could talk today,' Eddie Franks was saying now, 'about the GP surgeries, and about the hospital.'

More nods around the table – and then some amazingly out of tune singing started up from the Newford City guys at the table behind. Charlie pulled his chair as near as he could to England's Shield without actually sitting next to them, leaning in as close as was possible without making himself far too obvious.

'My mum tried to get a GP appointment the other day,' Eddie was saying. 'She rang up, just like you're meant to, soon as the surgery opened. Been a patient there for years, and what do they tell her? That they're sorry, but the first available slot they have is three weeks away. Three weeks.

Then they suggest the walk-in service at the hospital. So I drive her there, course I do, because she's not young any more, my mum, and it's not like I'm going to let her get the bus' – that got a few nods and grumbles of approval – 'and what do we find when we arrive? There's over an hour of waiting time. Over an hour. They'd keep an old lady who's lived in this town all her life waiting for over an hour just to see a doctor. And d'you know what? About every single other person waiting in that room, I can guarantee, had arrived in this country within the last year or so – that's the absolute maximum any of them could have been here, I am certain. Different languages being spoken all over. And about half of them in bloody hijabs . . .'

The whole table was nodding now.

'Why does that not surprise me?' said the new guy in the suit with the signet ring, speaking up now, showing off to his new mates.

'D'you want to know why someone like my mum can't get seen by a doctor any more in this town?' Eddie continued. 'It's obvious. They tell us it's not, but it's simple. Pure mathematics. Any *child* could see it. Because it's sheer numbers, isn't it? Newford isn't a big place. And we're overrun, is the long and the short of it. We're overrun.'

'*Bollocks.*' The word was out of Charlie's mouth before his mind had had any say in it – and loud, he'd said it loud too, his voice, that word. Loud enough to be heard clearly by anyone over the songs of the football supporters behind.

'Charlie,' hissed Kate. 'For fucksake.'

But they'd all turned to look at him now, of course they had. The whole bloody table, the whole boy scout team of them, all – he counted, eyes flicking over them quick as you like – all eight of them now, Newford's formidable England's Shield *affiliated group*, or whatever the fuck they were calling themselves.

'Charlie,' said James, a note of warning in his voice.

Except. Except. Fuck it. Look at them, the bastards. Because it was these lot who had gone for Martin, obviously it had been. There were the fucking badges even, their fucking fancy little pin badges, all matching, little St George's flags gleaming out from their lapels and blending in deceptively with the yellow and white of Eddie Franks's Newford City football shirt. And Charlie was sick of it. Sick of being careful and shutting up and putting up with things and being too tired or beaten down to bother telling people they were talking shite when obviously they were.

Both Kate and James were staring at him now too, clearly wary as fuck. Maybe he should pay attention to them. Maybe they were right. But then there was that look on Eddie Franks's face. The sheer smugness of it, as clear as if he were saying right out loud – *well, well, well, what have we here?*

'Bollocks,' Charlie yelled again, this time loud enough for the whole pub to hear. And it felt good actually, in spite of Kate's hand going to her mouth. Felt great not to be accepting things and letting things go, as he had been really for too long now, for too many years. Jesus, it almost made him feel young again.

'What was that?' said Eddie Franks.

'Oh come on,' said Charlie. 'I couldn't help but overhear you, and you're talking bollocks. It's not Muslim people's fault your mum had to wait a bit to see a doctor, it's the fucking government, cutting all the money. Any idiot knows that. It's been happening to the rest of us for years.'

'I never said it was the Muslims,' said Eddie Franks.

'Yeah but you did though, mate, didn't you? *About half of them in bloody hijabs*, were the exact words I heard coming out of your mouth just a second ago. You did say that, didn't you? Or is there something wrong with my ears?'

The rest of the pub was going quiet now, the singing at the next table dwindling to silence and people turning to gawp, confused faces staring between Charlie and Eddie, everyone caught off guard, trying to figure out what to think. Eddie Franks took a moment to sweep a glance over the room before replying.

'I'll stand by that,' he said at last. 'About half of them were in hijabs. That's the truth. People in this country need to face up to the truth.'

'Hear hear,' said one of the Newford City lads at the next table, and Charlie felt something in him slam shut.

'Hang on, mate,' he said, turning to the guy who'd just spoken. 'There's no need for that, is there? I mean, there's no need to be such an arsehole.'

'Charlie,' started Kate. 'Charlie, for God's sake . . .'

'That man there,' said the Newford City guy, 'he's speaking the truth.'

'The truth?' Charlie began – but before he could say any more, one of the old England's Shield guys had piped up, at Eddie Franks's shoulder.

'You're one of that pikey lot. You are, aren't you? Who said you were welcome in this pub?'

'Oh am I not?' said Charlie. 'I mean, what is this, the nineteen fifties? *No Gypsies allowed*, is that it?'

'You're a bloody nuisance,' said the old guy. 'Because this is what you do, isn't it? You come in here and stir up trouble

398

for everyone else. Everyone was having a nice evening, a quiet drink.'

A few murmurs of agreement from around the pub, a few nods from more of the tables now – and Charlie watched as faces that had only looked confused before latched comfortably on to the seemingly innocuous appeal in the words *quiet drink*.

'Yeah while you were in the corner there,' he said, 'spreading your lies about Muslims.'

'Charlie,' hissed Kate again. 'Stop. This is not our fight.'

And he wanted to turn to her, to reassure her or to explain to her, or *something* – but all eight of the England's Shield guys were staring him down with such unbridled hatred he couldn't look away, couldn't turn or dip his gaze or do anything that might let them think they'd spooked him. Anyway though, James got there first.

'Except it is though,' James's voice rang out next to him. 'Charlie's right. Because it's always our fight, isn't it? It's not fair, but it's always our fight.'

'Oh come on,' said the signet ring guy then. 'What d'you think you're on about *fight*? Are *you* really going to fight *us*?'

Eddie Franks started to laugh then, and the other lads at the table followed his lead, as well as quite a few others around the pub. Christ. Jesus fucking Christ. Fucking football fans. This was why Charlie never watched football, this was why he never went to games. Because so often it was *this* under the surface, wasn't it? Nationalism and pack mentality. And now what the fuck had he gone and gotten them into? Would James be alright? Would Kate? And how could he look out for them properly when they were up against so many?

'Yeah,' said Eddie then, riding the wave of the general laughter around them now. 'I mean, what exactly are you going to do, you fucking deadbeat pikey cripple?'

There was a general explosion of voices and noise but Charlie was barely aware of it. He was over there faster than his brain could catch up with the rest of him, the scruff of Eddie Franks's football shirt in his hand, fist held over his self-important face.

'I dare you to try,' Eddie said then.

'Charlie!' He looked up at the sound of Kate's voice to see her, hand reached out as if to leap forward and stop his knuckles making contact – though in actual fact she was too far away to do anything.

Except she didn't need to leap forward though, did she? She didn't need to be any closer, because his fist hadn't yet smashed down into Eddie Franks's face. He was still holding it, clenched above. And *be clever*, she'd said to him, hadn't she? *Because when we're not clever what happens? What happens is that these people win.* Everybody staring now. All these men in their matching shirts, mouths open, fear in their eyes, staring at him as if it were he, Charlie, who were somehow the threat, and not the England's Shield lot at all. He swallowed and lowered his fist.

'I want you to tell me again,' he said, 'what you just called my brother.'

'I'm sorry?' said Eddie Franks.

'Say it again,' said Charlie.

'Are you giving me orders now?'

'Say it again,' repeated Charlie, but Eddie stayed silent, staring back at him, eyes narrowing. He wasn't going to say it, not with all these people watching.

'*Fucking deadbeat pikey cripple.*'

But it wasn't Eddie Franks who spoke. The words rang out from all the way across the floor of the pub. It was the barman who'd said it. That arsehole, of course. Ah and Kate had been right, hadn't she? He should never have pissed him off earlier. He'd probably been waiting for an excuse to chuck them out all evening.

'*Fucking deadbeat pikey cripple,*' the barman said again, so loud and so slow each word seemed to land heavier and uglier than the last. And Charlie had almost given the whole thing up as a disaster, was ready to grab James and Kate and just run before this could get any worse, when the barman turned to Eddie Franks. 'Go on,' he said to him. 'That's what you called him, isn't it? Why don't you admit it? Or does it not sound so good to you, with a little more reflection?'

Charlie's eyes met James's then. He looked as confused as Charlie now felt.

'Bloody hell,' said Eddie Franks. 'It's just . . . something I said. Don't you think this is a bit of an overreaction?'

Sighs, jeers, groans from people around the pub – not all of them sounding so hostile now though. More uncertain faces definitely. Charlie caught James's eye again. He looked uncertain, excited. *What the fuck is happening?* his expression seemed to say. Charlie decided to risk it. He turned back to Eddie Franks.

'Look,' he said. 'Before you got here we were having a quiet drink like everyone else, trying to have a nice evening.'

'Like hell you were,' said Eddie Franks. 'You came out looking for trouble, is what you did. Because that's what you lot always do. You come out into our communities and you fight and you steal and you deliberately stir up trouble. Jesus, just looking at you, honestly. It makes me sick.'

'I'm the threat to the community?' said Charlie. 'Me? Me and my wife and my brother over there? What about you? These people were trying to have a nice evening and celebrate a football match when you came in with your meeting, with your England's Shield fucking affiliated group.'

'Yeah but I also came to celebrate the match, didn't I?' said Eddie, gesturing at his Newford City shirt. 'Came to raise a glass with my friend Matthew over there like all the rest of us in here.' He waved a hand over in the direction of the barman. 'Because guess what?' he continued. 'This is *my* community. Not yours. I mean, look at you. What do you know about this community? Get out. Get out of my sight.'

Charlie made himself take a long, slow breath as he considered what to do next. Eddie Franks was trying to provoke him, that much was clear, and he couldn't rise to it. They were just a hair's breadth from chaos, from the three of them ending up in hospital maybe, even, right alongside Martin. He knew he had seconds to find some way to make Eddie hang himself by his own rope – but how the fuck would he do that? They were interrupted by the barman.

'This isn't your community,' he was saying. 'And I decide if somebody needs to leave my pub, not you.'

Then other people around the pub were nodding at that too, it seemed these lot were impressionable as sheep. And now the barman was coming over, moving with authority, like a man who knew he was among friends and solidly on home turf, no question about it – because he wasn't just the barman of course, Charlie realised then, he was the landlord.

And Charlie had seen a lot of wild things in his life, been confused and betrayed and had to revise his opinion of people on the hoof more times than he cared to remember, but few things had ever surprised him so much as what this landlord came out with next.

'You're a disgrace, is what you are,' he said to the England's Shield lot, right in front of them now, eye to eye with Eddie Franks. 'My son would be ashamed to have the likes of you supporting his team. Get out of my pub. You're a disgrace to Newford City.'

Someone began applauding then, loud, from over on the other side of the pub, by the doors. And as people started joining in Charlie looked across to see who had started it. And he had to stop himself from laughing then. Had to stop himself from swearing or yelling or doing something completely weird that would ruin this whole carefully balanced thing – because if it wasn't Stan over there, tipping him a nod, standing up on a chair now and leading the applause. Charlie honestly hadn't thought he would come. Or actually, it was more like he hadn't been sure which way the balance would swing. Back in London it had almost been like there were two Stans. The one he recognised, and then a new version too, who seemed cold, far away, off in some different world. And Charlie had wondered at times – especially in those long weeks after walking out of his job, and then after the fight with Holland, too – he'd wondered if he'd only been deluding himself about his old friend, and that really Stan had changed irreparably, and hadn't really cared much about him at all. He'd wondered if all that stuff with the article had just been messing about, nothing really serious. But then there'd been that night on the pavement outside the

Tap House too, and why would Stan have stayed there if it had all just been a game to him?

Stan wasn't looking at Charlie any more though, he was staring down Eddie Franks instead, and with a look in his eye Charlie was surprised to see there, generally mild-mannered as Stan usually was. And then there was Eddie Franks too, staring back at Stan for all the world as if he'd seen a ghost. Charlie didn't have long to wonder what on earth that look might mean though because Stan was shouting something now – chanting, even. Singing, almost. Singing something to the familiar strains of *Glory, Glory Hallelujah*, and though a few others were getting up, pushing chairs back, shaking their heads, heading for the doors in obvious disgust, most of those around him were joining in. What was it? What could Stan be chanting to get that kind of reaction?

'*You're a disgrace to Newford City,*
*You're a disgrace to Newford City,*
*You're a disgrace to Newford City,*
*And so are all your mates . . .*'

A football chant. But Christ, it was brilliant! Why hadn't he thought of that? People in this country bloody loved football chants, would chant along with anything at the drop of a hat in almost any situation, regardless of the words, no questions asked. *Stan Gower, you are a genius*, he wanted to yell across all the people, almost everyone who was left in the pub now on their feet and singing along.

'*You're a disgrace to Newford City*
*You're a disgrace to Newford City . . .*'

He jumped up on a chair and joined in – yelling, singing the words which were, miracle of miracles, ringing out just as triumphant as anything these lot could have chanted during the actual football game . . . and yet Eddie Franks and his cronies were still there, no sign of leaving though it was clear now they weren't welcome. They were on their feet and bristling in fact, alert, eyes going everywhere as if somehow the eight of them might take on everyone in the pub. Charlie looked back across at Stan. He was still up on his chair, still chanting *you're a disgrace to Newford City* like all things depended on it. And Stan caught Charlie's eye then, and he raised his fist in the air. Charlie grinned, raised his fist back . . . and then he had a brilliant idea.

Eddie Franks and his mates may still not be budging, but they looked warier now, almost sheepish, the new guy with the signet ring positively terrified, clearly looking for a way out. All that was needed was one more push, one definitive move that would turn them on their tails. And with one last glance at Kate – and she was watching him now, looking at him, he couldn't help but notice, like she hadn't done in years, probably not since the early days, when they'd first met – he reached down and seized the neck of Eddie Franks's Newford City FC shirt. Eddie glanced up, shifted round, ready to fight him for it – but he'd been distracted, put too much on the back foot by all the commotion from the rest of the room, and in any case Charlie was too quick for him. With a tug and a pull and only a slight tearing sound as some of the stitching went underneath the armpits, he'd yanked Eddie Franks's shirt off, up and over his head. The pub was in uproar now, people cheering, people whistling, people laughing, James watching there with his eyes sparkling, and Eddie Franks with a bright blush spreading over his face to find himself like this, the jumped-up racist finally stripped of his armour, caught with his belly out on display in front of so many laughing people. His 'community', he'd called them. You almost had to feel sorry for him.

'Alright,' said Eddie then, at last. 'We're going. Are you happy now? We're leaving.'

This was met with jeers and cheers from the room at large.

'Come on, mate,' said one of the old England's Shield guys then, putting a hand on Eddie's sweating shoulder. 'Don't worry about it. They're all drunk. This kind of thing can happen to anybody. Let's go.'

Eddie shook him off though. 'Fuck you, don't you dare patronise me,' he said to the old guy. 'Don't think I haven't noticed it. You always think you know better.' And then he stalked off towards the door, people moving aside to let him and the rest of them pass, still chanting loud and clear.

*'You're a disgrace to Newford City,*
*You're a disgrace to Newford City,*
*You're a disgrace to Newford City,*
*And so are all your mates . . .'*

And, thought Charlie, watching the landlord – he'd gone back to his bar now, and was wiping down the taps, not even raising his eyes to all the cheering and applause sweeping his pub now as England's Shield finally filed out the front doors – it was amazing really. Just when you thought everything was irretrievable, people still had it in them to surprise you.

# 45

'Alright,' said Charlie, appearing now in front of Stan through the crowd of Newford City fans, all of whom were simmering down now that Eddie and his thugs had gone, splitting back off into their separate little groups, slapping Matthew the landlord on the back, sitting down at their tables. The thing was, he almost hadn't recognised Charlie at first, though it couldn't have been more than a few months since he'd last seen him. Back then he'd seemed a broken man – broken literally, even, after the fight. But he looked sharper now, younger. At once unfamiliar and yet somehow so much more like the boy Stan had first met all those years ago, who'd stopped to fix his bike on Goshawk Common.

'Alright,' said Stan back.

'That wasn't half bad, was it?'

Stan laughed. 'I suppose that's one way of putting it.'

'I wasn't sure you'd come.'

'Course I did.'

Charlie nodded, for a moment looking fully serious. 'I'm glad you did.' Then, 'Drink?' Charlie said, nodding over at the bar.

'Thought you'd given up?'

'There's always ginger beer.'

'You hate ginger beer.'

'Ah for old times' sake.'

The mood in the pub was still buzzy as they made their way over, people grinning and nodding to them as they passed.

'Pint of Amstel please,' said Stan to Matthew. 'And a ginger beer.'

'And thank you, mate,' Charlie jumped in, offering a hand to Matthew over the taps. 'Sorry I was a bit of a prick to you, earlier on. That really was brilliant, what you did back there.'

Matthew shrugged. 'Not really,' he said, though he shook Charlie's hand all the same. 'Just common decency. Didn't know they were drinking in my pub.'

'They meet at a different place each time,' Charlie said. 'That's what my brother says, anyway.'

'Right,' said Matthew as he poured Stan's pint. 'So some other poor bastard will get them next time. Someone who doesn't know who to look for yet.'

'That's it I suppose,' said Charlie.

'I don't like it, you know,' said Matthew, setting Stan's pint down on the bar. 'You see it on the news, in the streets. All sorts of things getting said nowadays you wouldn't believe. This hostile environment policy, all of that. It's a disgrace really, the way this country's going.' He shook his head, then turned to the fridge to get Charlie's ginger beer.

They headed back to the table after that with their drinks, to join James and Kate.

'Cheerful sort, that,' Stan said as they went.

'Yeah but he's kind of right though, isn't he?' said Charlie.

'I don't know,' Stan said. 'You saw what just happened. I think people tend to be alright, still, on the whole.'

Charlie shrugged. 'Maybe. Really I think they mostly just enjoy being led.'

Kate was looking better too, so much less strained and less worried than she had in London. She'd grown her hair out long and it suited her. James seemed more or less as he had been – except maybe, Stan liked to think, looking at least slightly better pleased to see him than he had on previous occasions. The two of them exchanged a nod and even an *alright?*, almost as if they were friends.

'D'you know something?' Stan told them when they'd all settled down at the table. 'I was at school with that guy. The one in the football shirt. He was one of the kids who used to beat me up in the playground.'

Charlie almost choked on his ginger beer. 'Bloody hell, mate. I thought he looked at you a bit funny. He wasn't the guy with the house?'

'No,' said Stan. 'Not that guy. Mate of his though.'

'Christ,' said Charlie. 'Small towns. You end up knowing everybody, even the fascists.'

'That's it,' said Stan.

'That was pretty amazing though,' said James. 'I bet hardly anyone will even believe it when we tell them. I bet Martin won't believe it.'

'I got it on video,' said Kate.

They all turned to look at her.

'You what?' said Charlie.

'I filmed it,' she said. 'On my phone. Filmed the whole thing.'

'Bloody hell,' said James. 'Then we can actually show Martin. And after that – I don't know. We should put it online.'

'That's what I was thinking,' said Kate.

'Fuck,' said Charlie. 'That's brilliant you know. You're brilliant.' He reached for Kate's hand.

'Oh shut your face,' she said, but she was smiling.

'You should do that though,' said Stan. 'It's important people see stuff like this. Grassroots examples of how this country can be better.'

'Listen to you,' said Charlie. 'Mr University politics.'

'It's true though. I'm right.'

'I know you are,' said Charlie. 'It's just the way you said it.'

James laughed at that, and after a moment Stan did, too.

*

'I've got an idea,' Stan said to Charlie later on, when Kate and James were absorbed in a slightly drunken argument about who was the most promising contestant on this year's *Bake Off*.

'An idea?' said Charlie. 'That's a first.'

'Shut up,' said Stan. 'Seriously. See, I was talking to someone at the *Newford Echo* the other day about maybe doing some articles.'

'The *Newford Echo*? Bloody hell, d'you know I'd even forgotten it was called that? The one with all the headlines about church fêtes and rubbish collections?'

'They said they were looking for pitches,' Stan said. 'For pieces with a more strongly political slant. Things with a little more *oomph*, was how they put it to me when I called them up.'

Charlie snorted. 'Yeah but from what I can remember a little more *oomph* could mean anything. Could mean a profile on the most legendary local cat ladies or something.'

'Yeah but it might not though. They might really mean it, about getting more political.'

'What's your point?' Charlie's eyes were already narrowing.

Stan gestured round at the pub, at all the people still laughing and chatting around them. 'What about this? What about what just happened? That's political, isn't it?'

'Jesus, Stan,' said Charlie. 'Seriously don't start this again, with your pieces for the paper.'

'But I really think this could work,' said Stan. 'Listen to me, Charlie. I think they would take it.'

'No, they wouldn't. And anyway I don't even know if I'd want them to take it. The way things always end up getting twisted around. Something would happen with it so that James came out looking – I don't know. Like a victim, I suppose. So that I looked like a victim too, at that.'

Stan took a sip of his pint. 'What if you wrote it?' he said then.

'What?'

'I'm serious. What if you wrote the piece? I think you should write it.'

Charlie stared at him for a long moment before looking away, laughing slightly, brushing the idea aside as if it were a joke that hadn't quite hit the mark but that he was polite enough to try and smile at, anyway.

'I'm serious, Charlie.'

'No you're not.'

'Why not?'

'Because they'd never run it. Gypsies don't sell papers, remember?'

'No but this . . . Of course it would sell papers, with all these lot involved.' Stan swept a hand around the pub at all the people there still, dressed in the local team's colours. 'And then if the video goes viral too, which it really might,' he said, speaking over Charlie, who was already beginning to voice his scepticism, 'and there's also the fact that if you wrote it, it would be something properly different from the usual stuff in the *Echo*. A different perspective. Think about it. Please do.'

Charlie opened his mouth as if to dismiss the whole idea with some retort – but then he took a sip of ginger beer instead, and set the glass down very neatly and decisively on the table in front of him before wiping his mouth on his sleeve.

'Okay,' he said. 'Alright. I will. I'll think about it.'

# 46

'*Singing Newford City fans throw race hate group out of local pub – by Charlie Wells.*'

'A thing of beauty,' Stan said, as they stared down at that day's paper, spread out between them where they were sitting cross-legged in the grass.

'You can say that again,' said Charlie, stretching out, adjusting his sunglasses. 'It's bloody unbelievable.'

'It's not though,' said Stan. 'Unbelievable. Or it shouldn't be. When you think about it.'

Charlie looked at him as if to argue, then said, 'Yeah, actually. You've got a point there, mate.'

It was a true autumn day, perfectly September, and the common was alive with crispness and colour. Low golden sunlight slanted through turning leaves, while the grass was still frazzled from summer.

'I don't know. I'm still surprised they printed it,' said Charlie.

'They did ask for more *oomph* I suppose.'

'Yeah,' Charlie said, eyeing Stan over his sunglasses, 'but I maintain that could have meant anything. Have you read the rest of this thing?' He picked up the paper, started flipping through. '*Planned Halloween decorations will be public eyesore, says local teashop owner?* And *Farmer's joy at unexpected turnip win?* How come that gets the front page?'

'I thought you loved all that stuff.'

'Oh I do,' Charlie said. 'Or at least . . . the relationship I have with it is complicated.' He sat back in the grass, leaning on his elbows, looking out.

'You shown it to the others yet?' Stan asked him.

Charlie nodded. 'This morning, yeah. Even showed it to Martin.'

'Right,' said Stan. 'And how's he?'

'Out of hospital,' said Charlie. 'And as much of a bastard as ever.'

'Why? What did he say?'

'*Never thought you had it in you but I suppose it isn't bad.*'

'Bloody hell,' said Stan. 'What's that meant to mean?'

'I think he liked it actually,' said Charlie. 'Probably just doesn't want me walking around thinking I'm really the shit now or something.'

'God,' said Stan. 'He never lets up, does he?'

Charlie laughed. 'I dunno. I think he's just looking out for me, really.'

'Looking out for you?'

Charlie shrugged. 'Yeah, well. Doing what he thinks is best for me and all. I realised that, you know. Properly, when he was back in hospital. I'd been angry at him my whole life, and then I just saw it differently, somehow. That it wasn't as simple as that.'

And something caught in Stan's thoughts, then. 'I went to see my mum again, you know,' he told Charlie.

'Really?' said Charlie. 'I was going to ask if you'd seen her, being down here a bit more again and all.'

'I meant earlier in the summer.'

'Right. And you haven't been back?'

'No,' Stan said. 'It's just . . . she's my mum, Charlie. I care about her, of course I do. I can't help caring about her. And it's like what you said with Martin, too. I think in some twisted way she's still just trying to do what she thinks is best.'

'What happened?'

Stan looked at him, then looked away. 'Honestly? You probably don't want to know.'

'Why?' Charlie sat up a little straighter in the grass. 'Was it about me?'

Stan didn't answer.

'Fuck. It was, wasn't it?'

'You did come up, somehow.'

'Jesus. I'm almost flattered she remembers me. What did she say?'

Stan only shrugged.

'Right,' Charlie said. 'Now I get it.'

'I walked out, Charlie. I didn't listen to her.'

Charlie nodded, looked down at the patch of grass next to him, started picking at it, pulling up weeds as he talked. 'I did meet her once, you know. Properly. It was when you were in hospital, still out cold from that fall off the roof.'

'She never said.'

'Yeah, well.'

'What happened? What did you talk about?'

'Mainly, she just told me I couldn't be friends with you any more. And – well. I was sixteen. I just sort of ran off, after that.'

'Charlie. I had no idea.'

'But yeah, like you said, mate. I suppose she did seem . . . she seemed like she was trying, kind of. Just like something had gone very wrong with her somewhere a while back, down the line.'

'That's generous of you,' Stan said.

Charlie half laughed at that. 'I try.'

'Except,' Stan carried on, 'what can I do with that, though? So she's trying her best in some kind of messed-up way, but does that make what she says and what she thinks any better? I'm not even sure that it doesn't just make it worse.'

'Honestly, mate? I don't know. I suppose that's just how it goes with family, sometimes.'

They sat for a moment in silence then, looking out over the sweep of the grass, to the trees.

'Will you see her again though, do you think, while you're here?' asked Charlie eventually.

'Honestly? I don't think I'll go back for a while.'

Charlie nodded. 'Sorry, mate.'

Stan shrugged. 'You know,' he said. 'I still stand by that whole idea, that family can be more than just the people you're born with. That it can be who you choose to have around you, more than anything to do with bloodlines, or anything like that.'

Charlie snorted. 'Was that a hint?' he said. 'Are you trying to rope me in to being your family now, is that it?'

Stan chucked a bit of grass at him for that, and Charlie threw a twig back. Then Stan retaliated with a whole handful of grass, before Charlie ripped a page out of the paper, balled it up and bounced it off Stan's forehead. They both watched as it began to roll away, through the dandelions, down the gentle slope of the hill. Then Stan reached out, grabbed it, and flattened it out again.

'*Crowdfund victory for garden centre hero,*' he read.

Charlie laughed at that at first, but then his laughter faded as his eyes drifted back to the remainder of the paper, still on the ground in front of him.

'I hope this actually does something about them,' he said.

'About what? Garden centre heroes?'

'No. About England's Shield. I hope it actually changes something. I hope it does something real.'

'Yeah,' Stan shrugged. 'Well. I suppose we'll have to wait and see.'

Charlie rolled up the paper then, tucked it under his arm, and jumped to his feet. 'You heading back into town?' he asked Stan.

'Thought I'd stay out here a bit longer,' Stan told him. 'My train's not for another hour.'

'Alright,' Charlie said, checking his watch. 'I'd best be off though. Don't like to leave Kate on her own with the van for too long.'

'Why? Is she alright?'

'Oh yeah, she's great. It's just that the police keep coming by, trying to move us on. Seems the council have some new powers now or something. Or maybe the police are just feeling a bit more enthusiastic these days, who knows. I mean, Kate can handle it fine, but still. I don't like to leave her to deal with it by herself.'

Stan got up then too, dusting off his jeans. 'Anything I can do?' he said. 'To help you out?'

'I'll let you know,' Charlie said. 'Just – you're not going to disappear on me again, are you?'

Stan couldn't help but wince slightly at that. 'No, course I'm not.'

'Good man.'

And Stan watched, squinting into the afternoon sun as his friend headed back over the grass, towards the path – until suddenly he found himself struck by an inexplicable sense that he couldn't let Charlie leave quite yet, that for some indefinable reason he had to stop him walking away, even if just for a moment, before the light and the distance between them had turned him completely into a silhouette.

'Nae pasaran,' he called after Charlie, and it came out sounding almost like a question.

At the sound of his voice Charlie stopped, and he turned, and he called back to Stan over the grass. 'For christssake, mate. You're so fucking cheesy, you know that?' He was smiling though. And, 'Nae pasaran,' he said then. 'If it'll make you happy.'

And Charlie held up his fist, and Stan mirrored it, and just for a moment the whole world around them – stretching out from where the two of them were standing, out on Goshawk Common, in the afternoon sun – felt like a better place, a brighter place, felt kinder.

# Acknowledgements

Thank you so much to my agent Peter Straus, to Eliza Plowden, Stephen Edwards, Laurence Laluyaux, and all the brilliant people at Rogers, Coleridge and White, and also to Molly Atlas at ICM. Huge thanks are obviously due to my brilliant editor Mary-Anne Harrington, to Amy Perkins, to Yeti Lambregts for the beautiful cover, and to everyone at Tinder Press. Thank you so much Harriet Avery for the invaluable feedback exactly when it was needed, and thank you Neil Ansell for all the suggestions, insights and support. Thank you to Ivy Manning for the hugely helpful advice, and for making the time to chat to me about this. Thank you also to Damian Le Bas for making the time to have a conversation. In general, everyone part of or connected to the Romany and Traveller communities who I mentioned *Common Ground* to was hugely kind and helpful – thank you so much, I really hope you enjoy this book, and I'm so sorry if I've got anything wrong, or misjudged anything. Thank you so much to my brilliant friends in London, in Norwich, in Bath, and everywhere else in the world. Thank you to Nic and Juliette at Mr B's Emporium for all the support and positive energy, and a huge thank you of course to the whole Mr B's gang – with a special mention to Ed Scotland for first telling me the story of Nae Pasaran and East Kilbride. A massive thank you to Niamh, Aoife, Terry and Erina MacSweeney for all the support and microadventure inspiration. Thank you so much to Megan Davis, Emily Ford, Sophie Kirkwood, Campaspe Lloyd-Jacob, Philly Malicka, Elizabeth Macneal, Gemma Reeves, and Tom Watson. Thank you so much to all of my UEA tutors and friends, and thanks to Rebecca Stott for letting me live in your beautiful house while I began on this project. Thank you so much to all the amazing English and Drama teachers I had while growing up. Thank you so much to the whole extended Noble family – and of course my hugest thank yous and absolutely all my love to Ben Noble, and to my parents, Lorna and Kazuo Ishiguro.